# The Cricket
# Beneath the Waterfall

*AND OTHER STORIES*

# The Cricket
# Beneath the Waterfall

*AND OTHER STORIES*

## by *Miroslav Krleža*

AUTHOR OF "THE RETURN OF
PHILIP LATINOVICZ,"
"THE GLEMBAYS," ETC.

*Edited by Branko Lenski*

The Vanguard Press, Inc.

New York

Library of Congress Catalogue Card Number: 72–83354
SBN 8149–0699–0
Designer: Ernst Reichl
Manufactured in the United States of America

# Contents

# A Key to Pronunciation
# of Croatian* Proper Names

With few exceptions, the original spelling of Croatian proper names has been retained throughout this volume. The following key will help the reader in pronouncing them:

c = ts   as in lots
č and ć = ch   as in change
š = sh   as in marsh
ž = s   as in pleasure
j = y   as in yes
lj = li   as in stallion
i = ee   as in feet
e = e   as in net
u = oo   as in soon
a = a   as in father

* Croatian is one of four Yugoslav *literary languages*, the other three being Serbian, Slovenian, and Macedonian. Krleža is a Croatian writer and, as he put it in an interview in the Sarajevo magazine *Svijet*, "Like all Croatian writers, I write in Croatian just as all Serbian writers write in Serbian."

# Introduction

*by Branko Lenski*

Miroslav Krleža is a titanic writer who comes from a small historically underprivileged country, Croatia—today one of the six republics of the Federative Peoples' Republic of Yugoslavia. An independent kingdom in the Middle Ages, Croatia was subsequently dominated by Hungary, the Hapsburg Empire, the Turks, Napoleon, and the Austro-Hungarian Empire before becoming part of the Kingdom of Serbs, Croats, and Slovenes in 1918, a name officially changed to the Kingdom of Yugoslavia in 1929. Between 1941 and 1945 Croatia was nominally an independent state headed by a Quisling; then it once again became part of Yugoslavia.

Born in 1893, Krleža spent his youth in Austria-Hungary, at a time his native city of Zagreb was called Agram in German. He interrupted his studies at the Budapest Military Academy Ludoviceum in 1912, when, in an outburst of militant nationalism, he volunteered in the Serbian army. He placed high hopes in Serbia for the future of the southern Slavs, but the Serbs, believing him to be an Austro-Hungarian spy, sent him back to the Austria he loathed. During World War I, he served in the Austro-Hungarian army as a private. Between that world war and the next, he was strongly opposed to King Alexander, and in 1929, when King Alexander established his royal dictatorship, Krleža became the regime's most virulent social critic, with whom the liberal-minded intelligentsia strongly identified.

Krleža's sway over the minds of several generations of young and not-so-young Yugoslav literati between the two world wars was as overwhelming as was Gide's influence on the French during the same period. Unlike Gide, however, Krleža was not only the mentor of the young, but also their black angel: the *bure-vjesnik*, the enunciator of political, social, and historical upheavals to come. He foretold them with the fervor and conviction of a prophet and a Marxist. Between 1929 and 1941, the opening night of a play by Krleža was a major cultural and often political event; the police were likely to close it down at the last minute. During the fascist occupation of Croatia, Krleža stayed in hiding. In Tito's Yugoslavia he became vice-president of the Yugoslav Academy of Arts and Sciences and editor in chief of the Yugoslav Encyclopedia.

The volume and scope of Krleža's writings is vast and impressive. He has written more than fifty volumes of prose and poetry. Among his plays, the best known are *The Glembays, In Agony,* and *Leda,* all published in 1929. These plays constitute an organic entity, along with the short stories of the *Glembay* prose cycle. Here we meet the Glembays and the Fabriczys, two patrician families who marry, give birth, and die on the soil of Austria, Hungary, and Croatia between the days of Empress Maria Theresa (1717–1780) and those of the Auschwitz, Buchenwald, and Jasenovac concentration camps (1941–1945).

Besides works of fiction—poems, novels, short stories, and plays—Krleža has written numerous essays, polemics, articles, speeches, and dissertations on art, literature, philosophy, music, medicine, and politics.* In trying to convey the variety of Krleža's literary endeavors, one must also mention his journals, in particular the four volumes of his *Diary for the Year 1942–1943;* his autobiographical notes for the years 1914–1921, published under the title *The Old Days;* his book of childhood reminiscences, *A Childhood in Agram;* his *Fragments from the Journal* for 1967 and 1968; his travelogues, among which his *Journey to Russia,* published in 1925, is a classic; his film scenario based on the short story in our collection, *The Cricket Beneath the Waterfall;* and, finally, his writings and annotations as editor in chief of the Yugoslav Encyclopedia, a work he has successfully brought to completion.

Krleža's first novel, *The Return of Philip Latinovicz,* was published in 1932 (American edition published by the Vanguard Press, Inc., 1969). His second novel, *On the Edge of Reason* (to be published by the Vanguard Press), originally appeared in 1938. The first part of his third novel, *Banquet in Blithuania,* came out in 1938, the second part in 1939, and the third in 1962. By 1972, Krleža published all six volumes of his historical roman-fleuve, *The Banners,* and at present he has almost completed his eagerly awaited novel, *The Devils Among Us.*

The short stories of Miroslav Krleža have appeared under various titles. Among these are, in chronological order, the collection of short stories *The Croatian God Mars,* published in 1920; the novella *Devil's Island,* 1924 and included here; The *Glembay* prose cycle, 1932, from which we have chosen three stories for this volume: *Dr. Gregor and the Evil One, The Love of Marcel Faber-Fabriczy for Miss Laura Warronigg,* and *A Funeral in Teresienburg.* In 1933 Krleža published a collection of short stories under the title *One Thousand and One Deaths,*

* Krleža's comments on various subjects, mostly concerning twentieth-century European literature, art, philosophy, and politics, gathered from numerous essays, speeches, and articles, have been published in Austria as dictionaries of ideas: *The European Alphabet* and *The Political Alphabet.*

from which we have chosen *Hodorlahomor the Great* and *The Cricket Beneath the Waterfall*. The present volume is the first collection of his stories to be published in English.

Since 1950 Krleža's works have been translated throughout the Eastern European countries including the Soviet Union, as well as in the West, notably in Austria, Germany, France, England, Sweden, Norway, and Holland. In the broader spectrum of European literature, Krleža's *The Return of Philip Latinovicz* can be said to have prefigured such classics as Sartre's *Nausea*, Camus's *The Stranger*, and in a general way the novels of Beckett. In 1961, Krleža, along with another remarkable Yugoslav writer, Ivo Andrić, was among the prime contenders for the Nobel Prize. Ivo Andrić won the prize while Krleža continues to be a nominee.

The geographical setting of almost all of Krleža's fiction is Pannonia, once a Roman province, today a territory encompassing western Hungary, eastern Austria, and northern Yugoslavia, bordered on the north and east by the Danube. The fact that Krleža refers to a modern region by its ancient name must be seen as both an attempt at universalization and as an ironical device: we are confronted with a part of the world that has been stagnating for many centuries. It is a real and at the same time mythical region, like Faulkner's Yoknapatawpha County, obeying the specific laws of the author's imagination. Nothing changes in Pannonia's utter desolation, where pigs eternally grunt, horses neigh, and somber women creep about in muddy hovels. As Philip, the hero of *The Return of Philip Latinovicz*, travels home after twenty-three years of wanderings throughout Europe, he sees the same old monotonous cottage roofs, the mares and cows in the pastures, the plowfields, the pigs. Just as on the day he left, red peppers hang from the windows, cheese is drying in nets hung on stakes, cocks are crowing, and hens are scurrying panic-stricken across the road just in front of cart wheels. Yet, not knowing better, the peasants seem happy. They are superstitious, most of them illiterate, blessedly ignorant. The

Bolteks, Yagas, and Rezikas of Pannonia, the laborers, coachmen, maidservants, soldiers, and vagrants, thrive in Pannonia's mud by unknowingly becoming a part of it. The small towns are hornets' nests of gossip.

Krleža presents us with various middle-class characters, from those who stand low on the ladder of importance, such as the father in *Devil's Island*, to important industrialists like Domaćinski in *On the Edge of Reason*. On the intermediate levels of the social hierarchy, busy with social climbing, pursuing their own interests, are eminent doctors, lawyers, magistrates, counselors, prosecutors, politicians, members of the government, sophisticated ladies and gentlemen, the Pannonian Bobbys and Robbys, Mukis and Kukis, Babys and Ladys.

With Voltairian irony, Rabelaisian laughter, and Orwellian satire, Krleža ridicules the degraded Pannonian intellectual and moral climate. He bombards bourgeois respectability and every kind of oppression of the free expression of man's thoughts. He analyzes the origins of wealth among the Pannonian rich and somewhere on each genealogical tree he finds a murderer or a swindler. The first accumulation of capital reeks with the stench of blood.

Beside the peasantry and the bourgeoisie, there move, heavily plumed like peacocks, decorated and titled, the nobility: numerous counts, dukes, barons, generals, eminences and excellencies, titleholders like Count Uexhuell-Gyllenband Cranensteeg, the Countess Orcyval, née de la Fontaine of Kissasszony-Fabarany, and the Baroness Inkey, born Ludmila Theodora Maria Gabriella. Krleža caricatures the Pannonian nobility's liking for everything foreign. He pokes fun at the shallow pretense and self-importance of those who parade in Pannonia like demigods and demigoddesses flaunting their titles. The upper middle class, following the example of the aristocracy, likes to embellish its names: Baloćanski signs himself von Ballocsanszki; Domaćinski, Domatchinski.

A *Funeral in Teresienburg* is a long procession of impressive names and titles—Krleža's funeral oration over the dead body of a condemned system. What is being buried in *A Funeral in Teresienburg* is not only the body of a young first lieutenant but, more generally, everyone who walks behind the coffin: the dignitaries with heads devoid of a single intelligent thought, dentured and coifed waxlike figures in cloaks, helmets, straps, chains, bronze lions' heads, two-headed golden eagles—all the pomp and ceremony of a crumbling empire.

When Krleža published *A Funeral in Teresienburg* in the *Glembay* prose cycle in 1932, Austria-Hungary had been dead and buried for fourteen years. Was Krleža only whipping a corpse? Was he only spitting on a tomb? Austria-Hungary was dead, but "Pannonianism" had survived and Krleža continued to fight against it. Fascism was on the move. From the ashes of a fallen empire ghosts would soon arise. New forms of Prussianism and Teutonism were to emerge. The extermination camps of the early forties were not far ahead. After *The Return of Philip Latinovicz*, in *On the Edge of Reason*, and most clearly in *Banquet in Blithuania*, Pannonianism goes beyond Austria-Hungary to become a European phenomenon.

Krleža portrays the peasants, the bourgeoisie, and the nobility who live in and around those small Pannonian towns with poplars along the roads, the blacksmith shops and taverns, the steeples in the distance, and the brickyards on the edge of town where, when the bus returns at a monotonous pace from the hotel on the main square, everybody already knows who arrived that afternoon: a new officer or a traveling tie salesman. . . . But there is a fourth group in his fiction; the Pannonian Don Quixotes—the seekers, the dreamers, the prodigal sons, the neurotic artists and vagabonds who refuse to succumb to the Pannonian mentality, fighting to the very last to escape it. These heroes are Krleža's fallen angels who seem to have retained the memory of a former paradise they seek to recapture. Through them Krleža castigates and brilliantly illuminates the Pannonian mode of existence while at the same time criticizing the heroes' lofty dreams and attitudes. Some of these dreams glorify a particular woman, others an escape to a foreign country, still others the return home after futile wanderings abroad. Philip struggles with his faltering capacity to give his ideas visual expression; Baloćanski discovers only when close to old age the possibilities of a freer life; Kyriales revels in wisdom and preaches it as he travels. All are defeated and end in suicide or abandon or are completely shattered and full of remorse for their initial folly.

Philip hopes to find new creative energies in his return, only gradually to discover that he will never fulfill his artist's dream: to express on canvas that barbaric, Pannonian instinct for dynamic movement coupled with the typically Pannonian impulse toward self-destruction. He will never be able to paint the smell of roasting pork, the noise of the fair, the horses' neighing, the cracking of the whip, because he lacks the brute force, the thick skin, the solid nerves, and the cunning required for survival and success in Pannonia. To paint pigs one has to be a talented "pig" oneself. Philip meets Kyriales, the extravagant Greek from the Caucasus who knows that in the Pannonias of this world one is better off selling pots and pans than trying to paint. This doctor of both philosophy and dermatology, who seems to have been everywhere and know everything, shatters Philip's remaining faith in his artist's calling and in the human race in general. According to Kyriales, man is a shameless, false, stupid, malicious, apelike beast, a beast greedier than the hyena, which at least, when gorged with carrion, falls asleep next to it; whereas man, stuffed, goes on eating and, seeing other hungry animals of his species, licks his lips with satisfaction. Kyriales has the appetite of a pig and gives the impression of being strong, but in the end he too succumbs. His body is found near the railroad. Tired of having deceived himself for so long with hypothetical truths about his clear-sightedness and superior outlook, he commits suicide.

The protagonist of *On the Edge of Reason*, the lawyer, for fifty-two years has lived a most respectable life from the viewpoint of his neighbors and fellow men: never a scandal in his life to feed the town gossip, professionally successful, faithful to his wife, the very prototype of a model citizen. Then, one night at a party, listening to the all-important Domatchinski bragging about how he once shot down four thieves who were trying to rob his wine cellar, he hears himself saying: "What you did was criminal, bloody, and depraved." This moment marks the lawyer's fall from society's grace. He is persecuted, tried, abandoned by friends and family alike, jailed, exiled, put into an insane asylum. . . . At the novel's end he sits alone in a hotel room trying station after station on the radio. But Europe has no solace to give. Quite the contrary: All he gets is a cacophony of sounds reflecting the chaos in the European mind—among them military marches, a premonition of the gathering storms.

In *Banquet in Blithuania* the liberal politician Niels Nielsen confronts the dictator Barutanski. The battle may appear at times to be futile; the ideal may seem weak compared to the political reality of the day. But Nielsen will continue to fight because—and this aptly illustrates one of Krleža's fundamental beliefs—against stupidity, violence, and arbitrariness the printed word still remains the most prestigious and effective weapon.

There are many more rebels, protesters, fantasts, and dropouts in Krleža's fiction. Leone, for instance, in the play *The Glembays*, is the prototype of Krleža's oversensitive, critical intellectual who denies his patrician family and the social order of his time. Krleža is fascinated, too, by Juraj Križanić, a seventeenth-century Croat who one day, laughed at by all his neighbors, set out from his village for Moscow in a horse-driven carriage full of books and documents, intent on alerting Russia's rulers to the historical obligation of Russia toward their Slavic brethren—only to be scorned and thrown into Siberian captivity where he remained for seventeen years—time enough to ponder his sin of idealism and imagine what his life could have been instead. In this volume we encounter various idolizers of women, like Ramong in *A Funeral in Teresienburg* and Marcel in *The Love of Marcel Faber-Fabriczy for Miss Laura Warronigg*; of escape to another country, like Orlić in *Hodorlahomor the Great*; and of the return home after a long absence, like young Gabriel Kavran in *Devil's Island*, a novella that can be viewed as a seed of Krleža's major novel, *The Return of Philip Latinovicz*.

Krleža is attracted by tortured men whose lives are manuals of self-destruction. The same holds true for Krleža's women. If there be some general truth in the saying that women of twenty are crude, like Africa; women of thirty full of hope, like Asia; women of forty generous, like America; and women of fifty wise, like Europe, then it can be advanced that Krleža shows a predilection for portraying women in their forties, former beauties full of autumnal charm, rich in experience, open, hurt by life, with nothing to hide.

Only with these women can his equally tortured heroes find a few moments of deep understanding and meaningful respite. In describing such relationships Krleža has written some of his most beautiful pages, as, for instance, when Philip and Xenia Raday console themselves by attributing their sufferings, the deep wounds and beatings they have taken from life, to some ancestral, primeval force, feeling as if someone else's life is streaming through their hands, revealing itself in chance touches. Xenia Raday in *The Return of Philip Latinovicz*, Yadwiga Yesenska and Wanda in *On the Edge of Reason*, are all women whose very names evoke something languorous, and strangely attractive. And Laura Warronigg, the silly "twenty-year-old goose" in *The Love of Marcel Faber-Fabriczy for Miss Laura Warronigg*, becomes interesting only twenty years later when, as the tired, disappointed, and anxious heroine Baroness Lenbach in the play *In Agony*, she slowly but inevitably slips into suicide, struggling in vain to retain her last lover, Dr. Križovec. Time is dealing out poetic justice; the old wounds have been cauterized;

life goes on. The rich texture of Krleža's prose integrates the swelling of memory, the nostalgia for childhood dreams and for a time of life and an epoch that are no longer:

> Twenty years later, when all that was to happen had happened, when Laura and Marcel stood in life like two shipwrecked persons, there emerged in their conversations the old recollections of their Bukovec adventures, distant and faded as old English rubbings in half-darkened rooms. Marcel, who had just returned from Russia, was lingering for a while in Zagreb, anchorless in the mist of his Croatian homeland. He and Laura would meet in the front room of Laura's fashion shop, Mercure Galant. At that time Laura was already doomed to commit suicide, but the somber and sad conversations about all their past involvements were infused with the silent, golden light of the bygone days of Bukovec.
>
> Their conversations about the Bukovec drawing room! Its enormous old-fashioned sofa in the corner with the Oriental rugs, the sofa piled high with too many red, black, pale blue, and yellow cushions, and above, on the golden console, the gilded baroque saint with outstretched arms. The embroidered designs on the silk cushions, the vases and the jars in the Viennese glass cabinet, the clocks on alabaster pillars, and the tabouret where the old butler set the silver tea tray: all this stood before Marcel like the silent replica of an afternoon with sun shining through the green crests of the linden trees under the balcony. . . .

In such passages we are close to the foundations of Krleža's fictional edifice upon which the author sheds much light in his remarkable book of reminiscences, *A Childhood in Agram*. As a child Krleža slept under a baroque ceiling, gazing at it intently before closing his eyes. Later, when he began to write and throughout his career, he was to translate into literature that rich ceiling with its fallen and not-yet-fallen angels, devils, saints, warriors, trumpets, flutes, cymbals, drums, bows, arrows, candles, banners, horses, eagles, prayer books, and wreaths. He was in love with the baroque architecture of his childhood and later, wherever he traveled in Central Europe, he would visit houses that followed the basic design of his own home, knowing where to locate, with eyes practically closed, a ceiling similar to the one in Zagreb.

In a broad sense, Central Europe is Krleža's literary territory, and Pannonia is part of Central Europe. He has peopled it with extravagant characters, corrupt and refined. He has ferociously attacked the Central European, Austro-Hungarian Pannonian bourgeois culture, but cannot help also admitting that this culture was able to produce a material civilization that on the whole compared favorably with that of the French. To understand Krleža one must bear in mind his own ambivalence. Along with his violent negation there exists a strong affirmation. He is in love with what he denigrates, just as he cannot help tearing apart the ideals of his dreamers for which, in the same breath, he voices profound nostalgia and admiration. When asked whether his Glembays and Fabriczys ever existed, he retorted: "Of course not. Had they existed, Zagreb would today be another Florence." They grew out of the baroque ceiling of his childhood and he made them live.

In *A Childhood in Agram*, Krleža recalls how, forty years later, the odor of old church books would bring back long-passed sensations of his earliest youth. Even today, while walking in places cherished in his youth, he inhales the perfumes of earlier years, his heart swelling with remembrance for things past, all the old sweetness and warmth preserved in memory. Krleža recalls the stillness of a room, the deep perspective formed in the shadow of a burning candle, the distant echo of thunder, the muffled roar of guns, the outpost with the young soldier who must kill for the first time, the penumbra of a church where one hears the twittering of swallows outside. All of these scents, noises, colors, perspectives Krleža weaves into the rich texture of his fiction.

One thing Krleža sensed from the very outset, deeply and intuitively—the existence of two different realities: One, a brute reality, used, abused, fragmentary, and diminished by the rational ideas of the man to whom the tree he observes hides the forest; the other, a pure, fantastic, virginally untouched reality that is fresh, childlike, and immediate, more real than the reality divided by reason. Consequently there are two kinds of people: First, men who have completely lost the link with their childhood, members of a molded and deformed humanity, actors reconciled to their parts, men turned gray and inert, fodder for statistics and consumer reports; the other, the poets, all those referred to by average talentless man as dreamers and schizoids, individuals who want to live life with the intensity of their childhood, for whom reality remains the prickly warm ball of a porcupine slowly moving in the dust under moonlight. The poet, the artist, the creator, the seeker is the man who remains, in the innermost core of himself, a child. And from the outset of his career Krleža has sided with that child against all the forces intent on annihilating him. As can be seen from *Conversations with Krleža* by Predrag Matvejević, published in Zagreb in 1969 and quickly sold out, Krleža is in sympathy with the often naïve student rebellions in both East and West in so far as they are an expression of the vital force of youth, of the child's voice inside the growing man, a manifestation of the Luciferian biological substance against the tyranny of suppressive forces, a new version of the old struggle between tradition and adventure.

But Krleža has lived through a succession of isms—fascism, communism, and socialism, among others, and knows both sides of the coin only too well. He is equally suspicious of the right and the left. He expresses as does no one else in today's letters the wisdom of a third world that has demystified many consecrated historical, political, and artistic cults. "Those rebellious leftist youngsters," he said in 1969, "who are being heard today in the cities of Western Europe believe that reality can be stepped over and that, as in a beautiful dream, they can free themselves overnight of their earthly shadow. They think they are more intelligent than we are, as if we too have not been persuaded in our dreams that centuries can be leaped over. The difference between us and them consists only in that we have been what they are today and the same thing will happen to them that happened to us—they will live to see their ideals come true."

Krleža has rebelled during his long career against the military and social establishment of the Austro-Hungarian Empire, against the despotism of the old Yugoslav monarchy, against fascism, against the communist bureaucracy of the Stalinist era, and in particular against Zhdanovism, the most odious and perverse interference of state-legislated mediocrity in the domain of artistic expression. After Yugoslavia's famous breach with the Cominform in 1948, Krleža saw a number of the ideals for which he had fought as a young man become realities under socialism. But Pannonianism remained, and with it the continuous need for the battle against human stupidity, under whatever label it performs at any given time its seemingly eternal functions. Paraphrasing Maupassant, who once wrote, "How beautiful was the Republic under the Empire," Krleža exclaimed in 1969, "How beautiful was socialism under capitalism . . . !" reminding us how easy and comfortable it is to be a socialist under capitalism when all the blame can be laid conveniently on the capitalistic system. But who is to be blamed under socialism where men also suffer from toothaches, illegitimate children are born, husbands and wives cheat each other, and where people can also be petty, nervous, mean, ailing, and poorly paid, trying to knife one another in every walk of life? Commenting on some petty feuds among Yugoslav intellectuals, Krleža appeals to his socialistic fellow men to transcend their futile disputes and open themselves to the light of intelligence and the possibilities of broader understanding. For "what matters most is intellectual and moral integrity."

In the meantime, whether as editor in chief of the Yugoslav encyclopedias* or writing about the cultural treasures of Dalmatia in *The Gold and Silver of Zadar*, or about the tombs of the Bogomils, or about the role of literature in socialism in his significant speech at the Writers' Congress in Ljubljana in 1952, Krleža fights unceasingly. "Let us emphasize and be proud of what we have and what is ours alone rather than bemoan what we lack," he seems to be suggesting to his countrymen who, in the course of centuries of historical adversity, have mastered to perfection the art of complaint. Inevitably he has moments of doubt, expressed so eloquently by Niels Nielsen in the first volume of the novel *Banquet in Blithuania:*

> To write? What? Empty sentences? Stupid, bombastic, empty sentences? To speak? To whom? For ten thousand years mankind does nothing but talk. From Socrates to the Vatican endless lecterns and pulpits . . . To print? For whom? To prove something? . . . Pointless. What's left? To lie? Where are the bridges that lead to salvation? The truth? What is truth? Truth is everything you feel that should be better kept to yourself, better not pronounced; it may harm us, because, spoken out, it certainly disagrees with our petty, egotistical momentary interest. That's what truth is. The truth is when you feel something should be said, but what in your own best interest it is wiser and more polite to hush. Is there any benefit in expressing truths? No, there isn't. Because for centuries prison warrants have been issued against truth.

* In addition to the eight-volume *Yugoslav Encyclopedia*, there appeared under Krleža's directorship, among others, a seven-volume *General Encyclopedia*, a six-volume *Medical Encyclopedia*, and a four-volume *Art Encyclopedia*.

Nevertheless, Krleža continues to express his truth. Writing may not lead to salvation, but words are his only weapon.

Krleža's denials of certain ways of living rest on a deep personal faith from which they derive their strength and conviction. "To refuse the world is a way of accepting it," says Krleža in a statement that permits us better to understand the negative universe he creates in order to transform it through the very power of negation into its opposite.

There is something insufferable about a hot Sunday afternoon in August in one of the many Pannonian small towns with "gray, dusty, unwashed windowpanes, bare curtain rods, mothballed rugs, paper lanterns in the windows of stationery stores." It is on such a Sunday afternoon that the narrator in *The Cricket Beneath the Waterfall* runs into his old acquaintance Dr. Siroček and in a tavern tells him about the unusual things that have been happening to him recently—of how, for instance, he has been hearing voices of people who are no longer. Dr. Siroček listens with interest and sympathy. He invites the narrator into the latrine where once, beneath the waterfall, he heard the voice of a cricket. Ever since, Dr. Siroček carries bread crumbs in his pocket in case the cricket is heard again. The mere possibility of hearing its voice from out of the heart of the Pannonian wasteland transforms the loneliness of two people into a shared experience of human understanding.

Since the early part of the century when he began writing, wherever he has gone—in classrooms and in military barracks, in hospitals and prisons, behind coffins and on devil's islands, on trains and in hiding—Krleža has been following that voice into the darkest recesses of the night and of the heart of man.

# The Cricket
# Beneath the Waterfall

*AND OTHER STORIES*

# Dr. Gregor and the Evil One

*That night Dr. Kamilo Gregor smoked sixty cigarettes and spoke in a low voice. He drank a lot, but it could not be affirmed that he was drunk. In the Glembay complex Dr. Gregor was a very important and interesting personage. In Moscow, about 1925, he told us of his first meeting with the Evil One.*

I met him one July night on board the Greek ship *Angeliki*, between Piraeus and Salonika, somewhere in the channel near Chalcis. That was twelve years ago. I was still wet behind the ears and thought within the framework of certain ideas. For example, I believed in Hegel along with Garibaldi and Mazzini, and I thought that the Idea of War could elevate human sorrow and grief to a higher, magnetic level and could transform all our human pettiness into one incredible supramundane ecstasy, so sublime that it would justify the shedding of human blood.

It was with this system of thought that I found myself on board the Greek ship *Angeliki*, bound for Salonika. I had just witnessed much bloodshed and suffering, but Hegel's and Garibaldi's ideas somehow remained in my head. It was a warm, starry night. The south wind rocked the *Angeliki* gently and monotonously, but was rising dangerously. On the third-class deck, among the chains and ropes, a little Egyptian Jewess lay dying. The women were wailing and said that she had had a sunstroke. Everything smelled of pitch and tar. He—that is, the Evil One—appeared in the semidarkness. He said that he was a doctor from Smyrna and that the crisis had passed. "The little girl will live."

Thus we became acquainted through the sunstroke of the little Egyptian Jewess. He took me for a Serbian soldier, came up, and began the most ordinary of conversations: he had been born in Epirus, was now employed in Smyrna, had fought as a Greek *komita* around Ioannina during the nineties; Serbian-Greek interests were parallel; Salonika would probably pass into the Serbian sphere of interest (but only if the Bulgarians had their megalomaniac necks broken)—the talk of newly met acquaintances aboard ship during wartime.

At that time my thoughts were something like this: when the masses are inspired by the National Idea, when they fall into a high, clear-sighted ecstasy, when they are carried away by the idea of the Vardar, of the Aegean Sea, of the White Eagles, that will be the great moment. In such a state one makes sacrifices with tears in one's eyes. Throats become dry. At that moment, matter is spiritualized. Matter, organized into a single racial, national state, becomes spiritual, and from the heavy material of earth a star is born.

The smoke from his pipe smelled of honey and figs. He offered me his tobacco, which was of the best English quality, and it was like drinking aromatic tea. He had the nervous hands of a gentleman, and on his left ring finger wore an antique, dark, blood-colored cameo that emitted green phosphorescent rays.

When he learned that I was not a Serb but had been born in Vienna, that I was a Croat studying comparative literature and the history of culture, his conversation became warmer, deeper, and more intimate. We darted and danced over the surface of the conversation like two dolphins darting over the conventional shoals, the conversational shoals of chance co-travelers, but then, suddenly, it seemed that he dived deeply and pulled me with him into the darkness, like a huge lead-colored dolphin, like a black cloud in the windy night.

At first his talk was of the modern, cheap, cosmopolitan humanism of the coffeehouse type, as silly as any Social Democrat editorial. "Science, art, religion—these three are the basis for a higher cosmopolitan civilization. The slaughter of war [this was in 1913] is completely unworthy of the human species. There neither is nor can be any Hegelian Idea that can justify slaughter."

I opposed his higher, literary, decadent skepticism, which was that of a former Parisian student (he had mentioned the fact that he had studied in Paris for five years) with the argument of the National Idea as such.

"How could there be no Idea? Was it not the Kosovo Idea that inspired that old, humpbacked, illiterate woman to appear before the military command with five gold ducats to outfit a son who was not her own, because she had none of her own to give, and that inspired the son to light a candle at Kosovo for the salvation of her soul? What was it that inspired that wretched, barren old woman, if not the Idea, in the metaphysical sense of the word? To serve the Idea as an impersonal unit! The university professor who shoulders a duffle bag on mobilization day, all the young national terrorists who sacrifice themselves completely, all of us who renounce our own ego for the sake of a collective Idea—are we not living proof that Ideas as such actually exist? These are moments of idealistic self-sacrifice. This is the Hegelian Logos in the process of events. These are the ethnic collectives taking part in historical reality, coming out of chaos. The Hegelian Idea makes its appearance through state organisms, and that is what is now happening to our race. We are!"

"Let me ask you, have you ever killed a man?"

"Why, what do you mean? What a bizarre question! Have I ever killed a man? I myself?"

"Exactly. You yourself. I ask you, have you yourself ever killed a man because of any of your great Hegelian Ideas?"

"No, I haven't."

"Really? You haven't?"

There was a pause. The stars disappeared behind the dark clouds. The *Angeliki* trembled violently and her sides creaked. One after the other, the passengers left the deck in the face of the storm. The wind moaned theatrically among the hawsers. In the glow of his pipe this unknown Greek doctor leaned toward me confidentially and touched me with his hand. To this very day, twelve years later, after all I've experienced, I can still feel the touch of his fingers on my flesh.

"So you have never killed a man! How about that young Albanian at Lookout Point nine fifty-three?"

"Excuse me, it was not I who killed him!"

"No, it was not you who killed him. It was the Hegelian Idea, Mazzini, Garibaldi, that killed him!"

Through the suggestive power of this unknown Greek, drunk with the fumes of his tobacco, I saw at that moment, as though in a delirium, the face of that young Albanian at Lookout Point 953. On guard duty on the Macedonian border, where we naïve students were practicing to become conspirators because we had sworn to the Idea that we would kill for it, a vast panorama opened out before us to the south. Standing on guard, I could count up to twenty-three mountain ranges, as in a Japanese woodcut. From below came the roar of dark waters, and in the distant villages in the valley fires twinkled. Down below, Abdul Hamid's counterrevolutionary Albanians had cut up and burned everything that was Christian. One evening our patrol captured a young Albanian who had killed an old shepherd and raped a girl, and it fell to my lot to shoot him. There had been shootings of this kind before, but as a student I had always been able to extricate myself. Now the eldest in command ordered me to see what it was like to take aim at living flesh.

I refused.

"You won't?"

"No."

"You must!"

"I won't!"

"Won't you?"

It was a dangerous situation. It was the Albanian or me. But it seemed to me that I would get it in the end anyway, and even if I were to shoot the Albanian, it would be too late. Some sense of delay kept me from shooting. Suddenly a revolver shot broke the silence. The shot was fired by a young fellow who had fought with us and to whom I had once given some bacon and cigarettes. Thus I escaped from the situation, and the same night left the guard. I ran from horror.

"Well, who killed that boy? Mazzini, Garibaldi, the Idea, who?"

This question from the unknown Greek upset me terribly. I became nauseated—from the sea, from the wind, from the night, from the oppressive heat, and from his unusually sweet tobacco. I suddenly found myself face to face with a terrible, criminal, dark reality, and it seemed to me that this Greek was a detective who was probing my most hidden secrets. With my hysterical hand, my quiet, trembling voice, my Rilke's *Stundenbuch*, how could I kill a man? I did not know.

Lost in my thoughts, I remained speechless. I could not even find the presence of mind to ask how he knew of this, my most intimate experience at Lookout Point 953, although it was certain that I had never, anywhere, told anyone of it. True, he had said that he had been in Tibet, that he had studied hypnotism, and one of his first remarks was that I was of the subjective, feminine type and as such would make an excellent medium, but the very fact that he knew all the details of my horrible experience at Lookout Point 953 overwhelmed me. He went on talking for a long time of how it is not the same thing to sit in the second window of the Beethoven Café in Vienna's Alserstrasse and read Rilke as it is to lie on Lookout Point 953, but then the clouds broke, lightning flashed, our ship lurched unbelievably, and I vomited all night.

In Salonika everything reeked of pandemonium, and for seven days there were earthquakes. The earthquake struck daily seven times, and the sea threw up potsherds and dead fish at the foot of an old laurel. Many died of cholera. We drank tea and ate French biscuits—our only food because of the fear of cholera. The south wind blew for nine days and nine nights without interruption. Lice, bedbugs, and ordinary mosquitoes; then the *Traviata* waltz from a restaurant on the quay, all the blessed night. In panic, people slept under the open sky, and a hundred and fifty battalions of Greek infantry, ten batteries, and a whole fleet of six torpedo boats and a man-of-war with 18-centimeter guns protected Salonika from two very weak battalions of Bulgarian infantry. Everything was so completely stupid that we almost perished from boredom beneath a sun of 120 degrees, without the shade of a single green tree, from typhus and cholera, in stench and nausea.

At the eastern end of the city there was a little cemetery, and my only evening walk was to this poor little graveyard where huge, fat jackdaws chirped and polluted the cypress trees above the markers. Greek priests in brocade vestments chanted here every evening over the corpses and loaded them on a barge for Kara Burun.

That day, around nine in the morning, the Greek gentlemen opened fire from their battleships and guns and batteries and torpedoes, and a hundred and fifty thousand Greeks swooped down upon the Bulgarian battalion. For one whole day a hundred and fifty thousand Greeks massacred a thousand Bulgarians, and even this, the cannonade and slaughter, was comparatively boring. As usual, I had gone to my little cemetery and listened to the fat jackdaws talk in the semidarkness and stared into space. Because a waiter had promised me a cheese pastry that he guaranteed to be disinfected, this pastry took on a much greater importance to me than all those bloody heads put together. I sat in the twilight, thought of the beautiful cheese pastry, and watched the moon as it rose in the east like a green lantern.

Then this happened: a shadow jumped over the stone wall and hid behind a marble tombstone. I could hear a stone slide and fall. The shadow near the tombstone seemed to move unusually fast. Two or three seconds later, four people jumped over the wall. First two, then one, then another Greek. This all happened in complete silence, gently. Knives were drawn, and they began to strike the bent shadow. This probably happened very rapidly, but it seemed to me that they continued to strike for a long time, perhaps for seven thousand years, and I remained speechless, motionless, like a statue.

The murmur of voices disturbed the jackdaws in the cypresses above our heads. There was a flutter of feathers, then peace again. For a long time I remained speechless and motionless, rigid. Perhaps for seven thousand years or more. I don't know where the four disappeared to, and I cannot recall what time it was. The moon was high, and from a café on the beach came the sound of a phonograph. Like a thief I arose and stole away as though in a dream. I recall that between the wall and the tombstone there lay a dark, bloody mass, but I did not have the strength to look at it. I dragged my feet as though I had walked sixty kilometers. An old woman was driving donkeys, and I could hear the water splashing in the barrels.

I lay in a fever for three nights, and later they told me that for three days and three nights I talked constantly with a Greek from Smyrna. About Hegel, about Ideas, about criminality, about death, and about murder as such. One thing is certain—that my belief in him dates from that night in Salonika. And a person who believes in him, they say, is a Satanist.

*Translated by Stanley Frye*

# The Cricket
# Beneath the Waterfall

Of late I've been living with the dead, holding long conversations with them, sometimes throughout the night. And I'll let you in on my secret: my conversations with the deceased are infinitely more alive than all the contacts and exchange of words with those around me who are allegedly alive. The doctor who treats me and who, in practicing his profession, takes care of my nerves, stolidly maintains that this is the result of "deterioration." He assures me there is nothing more to it than that. Just a kind of physical exhaustion that will "eventually disappear."

Actually, I don't eat properly nor am I able to sleep; I am irritatable and feel physically exhausted. It is quite obvious to me, even without any professional opinion, that my case is truly a case of "deteriorating nerves." But what I cannot understand is how in the world this exhaustion is going to "eventually disappear." On the contrary, it seems to be growing every day—my insomnia and headaches are only getting worse. Everything appears to me more dismal than ever, with no end in sight.

I practically live in doctors' waiting rooms. In these dark, uninviting, unventilated cubbyholes I scan various advertising brochures from travel agencies or sometimes leaf through the dated, tattered magazines that never seem to contain anything of real interest. All you find there are some tedious, uninspired poems or literary quibbles debating whether "literature is supposed to be politically committed or not." As far as I am concerned (dressed in rags with torn pockets I've been wearing lately; helpless in my destitute state, since I squander all I have on treatment), what do these literary debates have to do with me? Why in the world should I care whether "there is such a thing as literature without political commitment"? The travel agencies, on the other hand, with their colorful brochures, are addressing themselves to me, inviting me most hospitably to spend Easter in Florence or Christmas in Egypt. Here, however, in this stuffy waiting room, where one can hear from behind the wall a broken water tank of an adjoining toilet, like some distant waterfall, here there is nothing but the stench of wet rubbers and melted snow. The magazines that write about commitment in artistic creations are piled up on the table together with medical magazines. In them are more than twenty thousand ads, each product highly recommended to bring sufferers good health and total recovery. To spend Christmas in Aswan does not seem so bad, nor would Easter in Florence be something to despise, especially if it doesn't rain. And the twenty thousand drugs, wrapped in their silvery foil and cellophane, as tempting as the most expensive candies, the Egyptian moonlights, Florence Easter bells, cruise ships, women, halcyon skies, holy wafers, pills—they all prefigure a relief from insomnia, from bad digestion, headaches, and depression. In a word, they all imply well-being and recovery. A recovery, supernaturally miraculous for us miserable creatures who are now listening to the noise of a broken toilet from afar, crumpled up, gray, exhausted, sitting in the ashy light of a waiting room resembling hell itself. The waiting room is reeking of moldy, disintegrating bits of newspaper and wet umbrellas. An old woman is groaning as she massages her lips with the index finger and thumb of her left hand from one corner of her mouth to the other, pinching her mucous membranes as if squeezing an old prune, until the puffed-up skin of her lips between her bony fingers comes to resemble a hole of raw flesh, gaping like an open dark wound.

The mysterious padded door leading into the doctor's office opens, and in the doorframe appears a nearsighted man in a white coat. He is the magical performer in this enchanted theater, illuminated by a glaringly white shaft of light. With a cold, slightly moist touch of his palm on my cheek, he seems to carry me into a distant realm, across to the other shore somewhere behind those padded doors. He transports me, together with all my nervous entanglements, with all my aching teeth and intestines, with my muddled pre-existence, with all the diseased chaos within me (which all add up to simple diagnostic details, as far as he is concerned). He seems to have simply floated across, with me in tow, from the waiting room to his office. And without really knowing how I got up, how we shook hands, I find myself sitting here facing him again. All I remember is that I suddenly floated weightlessly, finding myself in front of him, a body, an object of diagnosis, a thing held in some alien hands.

"Well, my friend, did anything new happen since our last session?"

"Nothing new has happened, doctor, but my dead people are still talking to me. And they are doing it just as clearly and intensively as ever. I spoke with one of them last night. The summer moonlight was magnificent and he was eating cherries, speaking all the while about the Immaculate Conception of our Blessed Virgin. This religious mystery was clear to him to the end, and he never, for a single moment, had any doubts about it. I can't quote you his every word, but some details are still clear in my mind. His left front incisor was gray, as if made of lead. Besides that gray tooth, I remember that his hands were coated with cold sweat; the cherries he ate were wrapped in a bit of newspaper still damp from the dew of the June night. These are just the bare essentials that got stuck in my mind. I think I also recall the timbre of his voice. It was just a bit consumptive, a gnawed sound, impure and worn out. His lips were slightly discolored by the big black cherries. He spoke about the Blessed Virgin, whose devoted bridegroom he had been since childhood. Even in those years long ago, when we used to fish together in the muddy waters and play games underneath the old walnut tree, he wore a bright-blue congregational bow around his neck as a sign of this devotion."

"Did you, by any chance, steal anything from this dead childhood companion? No matter what! Some worthless trifle, perhaps? An eraser, a pen?"

"Me, steal from him? No, doctor. As far as I remember, I never stole anything from him. Just the opposite. He stole one of my water colors. It was a picture of the rising moon: an orange, deep-yellow disc of the moon rises out of the grayish, ashen mists above the plowed fields; in the left foreground I sketched in a tree, a somber, dark-green, almost black, solemn fir. And he stole that water color from me. He took it home and nailed it on the wall next to his schedule of classes, just as if it were 'his own work.' At least that's how he boasted about 'his' water color to his father. And I never exposed him. You are the first one to whom I am divulging this secret.

"His father was a shoemaker; he wore a bright-green cobbler's apron and had a thick, silky mustache. I still recall how the shiny cutting edge in his hands used to slide silently, with an uncanny sharpness, over the odorous and smooth kidskin. As a shoemaker, he specialized in orthopedic shoes. The window of his shop used to show several plaster casts of feet. They were deformed, crippled, painted bright-pink, and covered all over with bloody abscesses and wounds. And now these sore, disfigured, crippled orthopedic plaster models of feet, the silent movements of the fatherly hand with the keen edge over the surface of the kidskin, the moonlight and the consumptive voice, are about all that remain of him. And this too is gradually getting dimmer, and soon everything will recede into total grayness. Yes, total grayness will envelop everything, even the laughter of my friend in the moonlight, his eating of the cherries, and the huge archway you had to go through to reach their place. Over it were two plaster angels. Between them they held the oval surface of a blind gypsum mirror; and this mirror was decorated with pears, grapes, melons, and all the other usual symbols of fruitfulness and abundance spilling over it. The driveway continuously resounded with the hollow thumping of horses' hoofs, since in the courtyard of the same house lived a cabdriver with his horse carriage.

"You see, doctor, that's the way it is with me today. My whole life appears to me like a view into a room the doors of which are slowly and silently closing. One can see less and less, and the voices are heard more and more faintly. And there was so much laughter, so much commotion and sound behind those doors. And now they are inexorably closing. In the resulting semidarkness I am eating myself up with restlessness, trying to hear the voices of those who have departed still believing in the Immaculate Conception of the Blessed Virgin and are no longer with us. Yet I still hear them because their voices continue to echo within me, and this is precisely what I cannot understand. Please explain it to me, doctor! What am I to do with this countless accumulation of dead people inside me? Many of them have died in the insane asylum, and almost all of them wrote poetry and got drunk in wine pubs. Unwashed, they walked around like scarecrows in their crumpled suits, worndown heels, and greasy hatbands. Some freethinkers among them, though, did confess before their deaths and even took the last sacraments.

"I remember one who had a forehead hardly two inches wide, with thick hair, hard and bristly, that curled like the hair of a faun. When you talked to him, you half expected to see two horns protruding from that dark, impenetrable, wiry mane—that was the impression his head gave. And yet he was a weakling, a jellyfish. He tried to convince me that life was dirty, dirty in its very existential essence, and that all of life's phenomena should be handled exclusively with gloves. Aristocratically! He was a gray, starved-out bum, with torn shoes and a foul-smelling shirt, soiled like the shirt collars of travelers who spend a sleepless night on a train. This hatless fantast, this famished hobo, wore gray cloth gloves, and on his left hand, over the glove, a silver bracelet decorated with a scarab of hollow tin. The hollow tin bug, with its puffed-up belly perched on top of his bracelet, shimmered green, like a frog with bulging goggle eyes. During the burial, the sky darkened with heavy rain clouds and the frogs actually croaked in the young juicy grass. I was sure it was the little frog on the top of his glove that was croaking. Someone spoke a few words at the freshly dug grave, or rather read off a funeral speech, but everything somehow seemed so stupid—as is usually the case in such ceremonies. The funeral speaker wore a black top hat, had good digestion, and a good prospect for comfortable retirement. He didn't seem to be especially intelligent; otherwise how could he have spoken before an open grave? And then there was the one who played the flute. . . ."

"Please, excuse my interruption, but I don't understand what you mean by the 'one who played the flute.' "

"Oh, yes, of course, he was another one of my dead people, doctor, one of the departed we've been speaking about all this time. He played the flute, but he had a rather limited I.Q. I recall that the cookies baked in his house always tasted of pork lard, which has an unpleasant smell of animal urine. In his home even the raspberry juice had an insipid taste. And there, stuck in various vases, were peacock feathers that emitted some kind of foreboding of things to come. In fact, the flutist was later found shot in a cornfield. The man who found him covered with blood told me how it all happened. It was a sunny, quiet afternoon of a warm Indian-summer day. The air was perfectly still. Suddenly there was a single shot. The blast resounded across the wooded glens. It hovered for a long, long time, echoing over the entire landscape. Then it slowly floated down to the ground as if equipped with a small parachute."

"You mean to say he was shot in the war?"

"I mean that he was shot. In what way, and where, is absolutely unimportant to me."

"I see. For you the peacock feathers are more important than this death?"

"No, doctor. It's just the reverse. His death is far more important to me than all the peacock feathers. I'll try to explain. This particular dead person, this flute player who was shot, was married to a certain Zosia D, a woman with extraordinary blond hair. She had the complexion of an anemic new-born babe; and, incidentally, she is as dead today as the husband who was shot in a cornfield like a wild rabbit. She is dead now, Zosia D.

"She had herself photographed in her wedding gown with her husband on the steps of the church. He was pale, and the knees of his black parade pants—part of a reserve officer's uniform he had ordered especially for the occasion—showed two gray circles formed when he had knelt before the altar. While we stood in the church with our heads bowed, we were overcome by a distinct premonition that this war marriage couldn't be a happy one. For it had been arranged in haste, in a single night, like some improvised maneuver. And yet, in spite of our dark forebodings, the marriage *was* happy. It didn't last long, of course, because they shot him. Something quite natural, you see, if you just think a little, since those engaged in war business don't pay special attention to newlyweds.

"I was sitting in a restaurant with Zosia D and the flute player on the eve of their honeymoon trip into death. I didn't know any Polish and Zosia D didn't know any other language. I was there as a sort of best man. I was confused, absent-minded, deeply convinced that we were playing an extremely dangerous, deadly game. The deceased man, too, hardly knew a word of Zosia's mother tongue, but they were, nevertheless, happy with their stammering and their attempts to communicate by means of fingers and gestures, happy in their deaf-mute melancholy. I sat with them in the same restaurant in which I had been sitting for years with various sufferers, travelers, newlyweds, and adventurers; people who complain about their narrow existence and curse their destinies, preparing themselves all the while for the long trip. If all those dead with whom I sat at this restaurant table where we celebrated Zosia's wedding with two portions of ham and eggs and lemonades—if all those dead were to reappear in your office together, they would fill it to overflowing. This whole unsympathetic building, this entire city block, would swarm with an endless procession of the dead. The columns of the dead would march from all sides. There would be a sudden burst of their voices, and everybody would be frightened by their countless numbers. They would carry us along with them like a powerful deluge. They are marching, streaming, drumming all around us, doctor. Don't you hear them? They are rattling with their arms, they are whistling, doctor!"

And, in fact, a company of soldiers was thunderously marching at this very moment on the street below, accompanied by the rattling of windows. The company paraded stiffly and vigorously, wearing their helmets and carrying flags. The doctor glanced at me sympathetically from behind his glasses with a friendly and pitying look. He then commented with a condescending smile that these were not dead people, but an ordinary group of soldiers marching by.

"Yes, doctor, I know, these are just soldiers. But they are soldiers returning from a funeral. They served there as the honor guard. For the time being, only one of them is dead, doctor."

"You are not exactly an unintelligent person, you know, and you can readily understand that there is always dying going on in life. That's only natural. Life is a sort of pendulum swinging between two beats: one we call life, the other death."

"Yes, I know. But one of them, you see, suffered from angina pectoris. Whenever he ate an orange he had to take a deep breath. He used to tell me that his breathing difficulty came from angina pectoris. As I see it, that's approximately the same thing you wanted to explain to me with your pendulum. We die because that is the law of nature. But tell me, how is it possible that the very night there was guitar playing and singing going on in my room, a man living in the room next to mine poisoned himself? Never, neither before nor after this particular event, had anyone ever sung at my place. And yet that very night my guests were singing and a girl strummed on a guitar. And then we heard a din and uproar in the next room. When we got there, everything was over with; all that we saw in the semidark room was a yellow bedspread, the flickering light of a candle, and the lower jaw of the dead man properly bound with a napkin. We could also hear sobbing.

"I remember one fellow with a face covered with pockmarks. He was repellently ugly, a drunkard, strange and somber. No one knows why he died so young. On the other hand, another one was so old—old as a cawing crow. I don't know why, but whenever I recall him I always see a picture of a meadow on a quiet summer afternoon. This meadow is bathed in crystal-clear light, and from the distant vineyard one can hear the twitter of birds and the song of crickets in the tall uncut grass. And I've never been with this man on a sun-drenched meadow. In his apartment there were fruit preserves in his cupboards, and the smell of a cat. He personified for me all that is unpleasant in life, all that smacks of senile decrepitude. And yet, whenever I remember him, there surges in me a veritable flood of summer sounds and summer joys, accompanied by little light clouds and the twitter of birds.

"I took leave of several men in a field of mud. We were all

solemn and gloomy, afraid of the cannons; we were covered with dirt and full of bitterness. As we retreated through the mire, there was in the air that feeling that departure would be difficult and ominous, like a retreat into total oblivion. Night after night I spent with companions at tables covered with tablecloths soiled with ashes and spilled wine. We sat in the smoky, damp basement rooms, the walls of which were decorated with stuffed birds that seemed to flutter on their perches; next to these were gold-framed pictures depicting a Moor telling a white lady stories of his adventures. If one were to collect all that we babbled in wine and smoke and in the turmoil of disturbed digestions, one would accumulate clouds of thoughts—projects and dreams that issued from us like sweat and were, to be sure, nothing but vapor and fume rising from our intoxicated heads.

"What's at the bottom of all this, doctor? I am tired, I've had enough of the war, I've also boozed quite a bit and I am weary of working in offices for meager salaries. Besides that, there is one basic thought that gnaws in me incessantly: in the end we'll all die, and we'll die before our own and final death. So many have died before us, and their rooms, their childhood birthday celebrations with cakes and new toys, their books and words, the glimmer of candles on the ceilings of their rooms, and the ringing of their doorbells—all this continues to stir and live within me. Their memory of my voice and movements dies with them; the memory of them continues to live in my visions. But that which in me belongs to them, and the part that has belonged to me but is now with them, can hardly be separated. All this seems to be woven together in a way that is strangely alive; it surges and flows interchangeably; it becomes part of my circulatory system and part of my heartbeat. And then, when one of these days this froglike gland I call my heart stops puffing, all these shadows will finally become faint, they will grow dimmer, and fade away at the end like an unpleasant odor exuding from a casket that's been kept closed too long. But as long as I am breathing and moving, I remain irresistibly chained to my dead. And in that enormous procession in which I too am ordained to march, these countless shapes of the deceased are basically only my forerunners. They have just departed according to another train schedule.

"I recall, for instance, that dear, pale, lithe, fatally wounded ensign who slept in the Red Cross train in the berth above me. It was October, nineteen sixteen, and the train was going from Galicia to Vienna. The ensign tore me from my sleep, asking me to hand him the urine bottle. I was still drowsy and confused, trying to orient myself; and when I finally managed to get up and hand him the bottle, he filled it to the brim with a liquid as clear as distilled water. Then, bowing his head, he automatically fell asleep again. Only judging by the monotonous and lifeless up-and-down swaying of his boyish hand that followed in a regular rhythm the forward movement of the train could one discern that he had fallen into that final slumber from which he was no longer to wake. He died filled with pictures of my childhood that I had painted for him a few minutes before his death without ever suspecting I was confiding in a dying man. And thus the death of this unknown young man was simultaneously the death of my childhood. I now seriously doubt whether all those memories of my childhood will ever again be filled with such intensive life as they were that night when I sat vigil at the deathbed of an unknown boy. I poured out my heart to him, as if I somehow knew my voice would penetrate through the lobe of this dying ear way down to the depths of those realms that are not one iota more mysterious than our daily reality, but are just as unknown to us.

"Many of my dead disappeared even before we had a chance to talk to one another. Now we are forever separated by strange, unspoken words that often appear to us—at night—like questions to which there are no answers. An almost total darkness separates them from me, just as the rows of trees beneath a clouded darkened sky separate a train engine from one's view though one hears its whistling from the distance. But many others we still remember from long ago with the same hatred we had for those conditional clauses in our Latin lessons that seemed to have been put together with such fiendish confoundedness that, much as we tried, we were absolutely unable to grasp them.

"When someone from our circle of acquaintances leaves us and we find out he is no longer alive, we cold-bloodedly tear him from the list of the living the way we tear off the leaves of a calendar. We simply bow our heads in helpless resignation before the inevitable. There are also fresh dead in our consciousness, fresh as the impressions received from the surprises in the morning paper. There are those, on the other hand, who appear as wilted as old bills we are not sure we have paid. I once ate doughnuts with one such dead man. It was a carnival night. We drank brandy; the war was on. A south wind brought about a sudden change in the weather and suddenly he was gone. All I can recall today is a small indistinct detail: he was lying in bed with an inflamed throat; a wet blanket was stretched above his head so that he wouldn't catch pneumonia, but he was already dead. His room was on the street level and the steps of passersby could be heard. I had to think about his favorite food: roast turkey with dumplings and sour cream."

"This is all very nice, my friend, all these details are quite interesting and very informative, but so far we've been unable to establish from our conversations when it was, exactly, that this interesting idea first appeared to you. The idea, namely, that the dead live with us, and that they live in such a way that their lives become more important to us than our own?"

"That was in Paris, more than three years ago, sometime in the beginning of autumn. If you are really interested, doctor, I can tell you about it. I remember every single detail distinctly, even the most unimportant—at least unimportant at first sight.

"Autumn in Paris is usually mild and quiet, but that particular fall the air was full of the smell of dead game, accompanied by the scent of wet forests and far-off places. In the ancient narrow streets in the shadow of the tower of Saint-Germain suddenly appeared an unusually large quantity of skinned hares and shot pheasants. The sickly color of their transparently blue, mother-of-pearl eyes was an unpleasant reminder of gray death. The masses of dark-violet skinned tendons and bloody necks were everywhere. The necks seemed stuffed with comic rabbit faces that looked like the faces of good-natured, slightly idiotic *bon vivants* framed with fur collars—the only thing missing was a monocle and, of course, the posthumous honors due to respectable citizens of high rank. Tell me, what else could a neurotic wanderer think of at the sight of this bloody slaughter steaming in those sooty streets like a symbol of an early city autumn, but the empty irrationality of a rabbit's life? And beyond this, reflect about that strange animal called man, who, believing in God, slaughters thousands of rabbits, and in honor of Saint Catherine of Sienna sells carloads of asters? Anyway, All Saints' Day was coming closer, and you could smell the frying of pancakes in the French households. Cold showers were approaching, and that morning the iron steam-heating pipes started hissing and coughing in the wall of my hotel room. Only the night before, a dog's whining had echoed across the Seine so mournfully, with such deep melancholy—as if life really did have a deeper and more mysterious meaning than that bloody trafficking with dead birds and rabbits.

"In the midst of this mass of bloody eyes of rabbits and pheasants, I sensed someone's glance from the other side of the street. The glance was so penetrating and intense that within the sphere of its mystery lay vistas and horizons of distant unfocused pictures. There, on the sidewalk in front of a coffeehouse, underneath an orange-blue striped awning, sat a gentleman in a rattan chair in the company of a lady. He was drinking through a straw. The lady looked toward me with the greatest interest.

"Misty vapors; distances; autumn in one of those greasy, dirty, narrow streets on the Left Bank, eternally dark gray, like the tarred walls of public pissoirs; somewhere a female voice, accompanied by a harmonica, is singing: *Parlez-moi d'amour!*; the sound of the horse's hoofs on the cobbled streets. Pause.

"When did I meet that man? Ten, twenty years ago? Twenty bloody years? Twenty bloody and desperate years, years of wars, shipwrecks, revolutions, entire processions of dead, an unsurveyable horde of living and dead acquaintances. . . . And here, out of that mass of blood-covered rabbits' heads, emerges someone's eye, and it touches me with magnetic brilliance. Could all this be just the by-product of my bad nerves or the figment of my neurotic imagination? Probably only a tourist with his date. He has visited the room in which Oscar Wilde died, or Delacroix's atelier. They are now taking a breather like thousands of other tourists. It is just a play of fate, a perfectly accidental meeting of glances, a moment of self-deception. Really, nothing at all!

"In the shop window at which I stood during this occurrence stood a large aquarium. Brown-striped flatfishes glided and circled soundlessly through the dark-green water, excited by the spraying grapes of oxygen bubbles. Immediately adjoining the fish shop was the window of an antique shop; it resembled a miniature, brightly lit stage. The reflection of a dark-yellow silk lampshade luminously flooded the lavish surface of a golden-threaded gobelin. The tapestry depicted a scene of a wild-boar hunt: a copper-colored twilight of a dusky beech forest; a deep-green turf of the forest clearing forming the background. The clouds, the twilight, the bloody rabbit corpses, the flatfishes in the emerald-green water, the dirge of the harmonica, and above all this, a flash of a single unknown glance. It was like a flare in the darkness, something that lights up for a moment and immediately goes out. Pause. Discreetly, I turned away my glance from the window of the fish shop. Timidly, unnoticeably, without trying to attract attention, I looked across once more to the coffeehouse. Underneath its orange-blue sail the tourist sat there with the lady, immobile, watching me. I still stood in front of the startled fishes that continued to slide noiselessly in their aquarium back and forth under the foaming cascades of air, between the moss and shells, as if swimming beneath the crystal-clear treetops of a sunken avenue. The stranger, bearded, gray-haired, looking elegant in his basket chair, continued to suck on his straw cold-bloodedly. The young lady with him, a light blond, dressed simply in the English manner, with a cigarette between her lips, was obviously interested in my appearance. In all probability her escort had called me to her attention. She looked with a steady glance toward my side of the street, where the crossing was piled up with baskets of artichokes, oysters, and snails.

"Where and when could I have met this man? I must have met thousands of people in the course of my wanderings, and in that countless row of forgotten eyes, what was this single unknown glance supposed to mean? He may have been a steward on a South-American ship. Was it the ship from which an insane man jumped into the midst of some alligators, and the water around the ship's propeller turned red from blood while the ship continued on its journey as if nothing had happened? Or was this the glance of the Italian soldier who was sipping black coffee from his Thermos bottle on the southwestern front when we surprised him in his machine-gun nest? There is no sense, by the way, in stopping in the middle of the street just because the glance of someone unknown suddenly appears—a glance that may have just as little importance as the look of the dark-metallic flatfish swimming under the cascade of bubbling water. One fish, incidentally, floating in oxygen foam, kept swallowing its own diseased intestine, imagining it to be a worm; it fluttered in its mouth like a rotted mustache.

"Disturbed and restless, I stopped again in front of the antique shop and looked absent-mindedly between the silver baroque candlesticks at a whole series of colored lithographs framed in red mahogany. They had been made in honor of the French imperial visit to the Queen of England. The pictures showed Her Highness, Victoria, the Queen of Great Britain,

standing on marble steps beneath a purple canopy, ready to receive His Majesty, the Emperor Napoleon III. I was just about
to turn away and leave when the man from across the street got
up and walked toward me. I noticed that his walk was unusually
elastic, his trousers perfectly pressed; his decisive, muscular,
strong movements were those of an experienced fencer. I looked
helplessly toward the blond lady, sitting there beneath the
coffeehouse umbrella on the other side of the street.

"Suddenly I felt the man's warm, soft lips pressing against
mine. Embraced by this slender man, almost lifted in the air by
his bright and noble smile, I suddenly recognized that it was
Christian K. Among all of us restless spirits, he was the most
flaming, the first professed follower of the philosopher Stirner.
He was a star-intoxicated young man, an enthusiast of Christo-
pher Columbus, the fiery eddy of our student days at the Sor-
bonne. Christian, my old friend, whom I had not seen for
twenty years, the witness of my only duel in the forest of Vin-
cennes, my love messenger, my dearest friend! How often had I
shared with him a can of sardines in my attic room in the rue
Bonaparte, right around the corner of rue Jacob, just a few steps
from here. My God, it was Christian, the man from the dark,
remote East where strange peoples intermix: Slaves, Gypsies,
Mongols, and Bohemians. My intimate friend from Poland,
where there have always been shootings and unrest, just as in
Ireland. He, who always somehow managed to fraternize in
closed, mysterious Russian and Mongolian circles. I remember
that he once hid at my place a lady's hatbox containing a few
kilograms of explosives covered with moss, and in that moss he
placed a live turtle. All night long I listened, filled with fright at
the scratching of the turtle in the box. I was convinced we
would all be blown into the air—the turtle, rue Jacob, and the
old tower at the corner of rue Bonaparte. Dear old K, who was
always ready to claim that 'at this particular moment' he had
no time, who was always mixed up with at least three women.
He also—'just now,' after twenty years—was 'at the moment'

not free, being embroiled in something 'not exactly pleasant.' He told me several times, however, how happy indeed he was to have seen me, that he would be so overjoyed if I could give him the pleasure of coming to a soiree being given that very night at the Polish Embassy.

"I suggested to him that we meet after the soiree, if he did not already have a previous engagement, but he firmly insisted on his original suggestion.

"To be sure, he didn't exactly know whether it would be possible—in spite of his best intentions—to free himself from the scheduled meetings that were supposed to take place during the boring soiree. But he was immeasurably happy that we had met, since this meeting had for him a special surprise—he had, after all, heard I had been killed. He had been convinced I was dead. So when he saw me a few minutes before standing in front of those fishes, he thought he was dreaming, and was unable to recognize me immediately. Time, unfortunately, passes so quickly, we had started loosing our teeth, our beards were getting gray—first unmistakable signs of death. Nevertheless, this shouldn't have meant so much since we could still walk straight. Was I still able to remember his words spoken in the moonlight at the foot of the Lion of Belfort? Did I remember how he bet me a bottle of champagne that Europe, the old whore, had already been sentenced to death? That was on the eve of the European debacle, and I still owed him the bottle of champagne— for I had always been congenitally naïve and had no actual sense of reality.

"Now, that night, there would be an occasion for me to pay this old debt. Ah, did I remember those beautiful moonlights when we used to play the guitar in the cemetery of Montparnasse, and the time when we stole a whole basket of warm madeleines—sadly enough, no longer baked in public—from the fat, niggardly baker in Passy who had breathing difficulties. And could I still remember how once we spent a whole rainy night under the chestnut trees of le boulevard Aragon, just to witness a guillotine execution of some criminal, but were unable to see anything, hearing only the loud beating of the drums? In a word: he had absolutely no time 'at the moment,' since he was busy with a 'trifling stupidity,' but he positively counted— counted with an absolute certainty—on my not refusing him this small request to meet him tonight. Without regard to any other possibilities, we had to see each other again tonight, even if it were for only a few minutes. For me, after all, it should not be so difficult, since I was free anyway, and as far as he was concerned, he hoped he could somehow manage to extricate himself for at least a few minutes. If it should turn out that he just couldn't get free, we could at least meet tonight and arrange for a meeting at some other time. We could drive out and spend a day in Chantilly at the lake, where we used to shoot at Bonaparte's fat old carps with our revolvers.

"Besides, for him it would not matter if we went to Chantilly or St. Germain, since there was not a corner of those woods not full of memories from our boyhood days. And if I were not personally bound by some kind of business, we could even go to London for three or four days, where he was to purchase some submarines. I would, of course, be his guest. He was here heading a trade mission. The important thing about tonight was that we could arrange all this at the embassy, and it was not at all impossible that he could extricate himself in spite of everything.

"During this flood of words, recollections, handclasps, and enthusiasm—which seemed quite genuine—he pulled his calling card out of his wallet—just in case . . . embassy personnel could be such imbeciles. He wrote a few words on the card, and with joyous gestures, smiling all over, waved it a few times in the air to dry the wet ink. His cordial spontaneity enveloped me, like a storm seizing me completely. Before I was able to ask him a most logical question—what I was supposed to be doing at the soiree—he was already back with his blond lady beneath the coffeehouse awning. He then disappeared into the bustle of the city street with her and her lap dog, in a cloud of gas fumes emanating from a huge and elegant car.

"Fishes, flat and repulsive, were circling in the light green box in the fish shop window, and all around were those bloody hares and dead birds. I continued to stare in bewilderment at the strange calling card that was supposed to open doors for me tonight at the embassy on rue Yokohama."

"Well, did you go to the soiree at the embassy?"

"Of course I went there, doctor."

"And you met your friend there? You identified yourself with his calling card?"

"No, I did not meet him, because he did not appear. They told me that Colonel Christian Kavaljerski had fallen before Warsaw in July, nineteen-twenty. It appeared very strange to them that someone should be looking for him in the Parisian embassy thirteen years after his heroic and legendary death—a death now described in every Polish grammar-school reader."

"And what happened to his calling card? That was a sort of invitation, wasn't it? What did they tell you, when you tried to enter with an invitation from a dead man?"

· "I did not show it to anyone. I immediately assumed that no one would believe a word I said and that they could lock me up for a madman."

"Like a simpleton, I'd rather say—someone who fell for a bad joke. Do you have the calling card with you?"

"No, doctor, but I can bring it to you whenever you wish."

In that moment our glances met, and I knew at once that the doctor did not believe a word I said. Being experienced in dealing with people like me, the whole thing seemed to bore him. I could see, though, that he considered me a harmless fool who should be gotten rid of as painlessly and quickly as possible. At this moment I also understood how stupid it is to seek understanding from these gentlemen in white smocks, to seek warm sympathy for what to them are the lies, delusions, and

shadows of our troubled brains. It seemed as if both of us were
relieved when we turned to the objective part of our session.

. How was it going with my disturbed digestion since our last
meeting; was I still constipated; what about my excitability, restlessness, insomnia, apathy, the sudden heart palpitations, headaches, pains in the heel, chronic depression, bad taste in my
mouth, feelings of exhaustion caused by smoking, the general
absence of appetite, etc., etc.? . . . He wrote a new prescription
and, after clipping me for seventy-five dinars for the day's visit,
parted from me in a most amiable way at the padded door: good-
by, see you soon, I look forward to seeing you again.

Outside, on the street, it was raining. I roamed in the rain in
the gloomy light of the gas lanterns, eying the panes of curiously
strange curtained windows, and I let myself gradually be filled to
the brim, like some cursed vessel, with sighs and tired gestures.
To sleep under the arched ceilings of dark sublet rooms, to
wander through the muddy, nocturnal, and distant streets, getting more and more tired, listening to the sobbing of the rain,
buying medicine, waiting in the pharmacy—that is essentially
how the life of a small-town man exhausts itself.

Old tree trunks—black at first sight and incomprehensible,
like all revolting, demoniacally deformed phenomena of our
reality—these deaf-and-dumb tree trunks stood along the rainy
avenues, repulsive and horrible, like diseased prostates or old
smoked, puffed-up pigs' intestines hanging in the windows of
the butcher's store. And the rain splashes on those swollen,
horny elephant legs made of sticky threads of tar, and in the
rain, all around the inky trunks of this tree-lined avenue, appears
a soggy catastrophe. Rotting pieces of fruit, soaked newspapers
blaring a picture of a girl run over by a train, dog tracks, sodden
cigarette butts, they all float on the watery surface of the sidewalk as on a sooty mirror where everything exists only for the
moment. This moment seems to be as brief as the echo of a
distant, unknown sound welling up into innumerable circles and
disappearing, the way a drop of rain arrives simply and naturally

from inconceivable heights and circles restlessly around a squashed orange, then slides across the smutted asphalt, to surge again into the underworld where dirty waters rush and gurgle deep beneath our feet.

Beer houses have a smell of decay even on sunny days, and human habitations are filled with the stench of urinals and old unventilated closets. And yet nothing in the world seems to be as sad as the sight of a white satin shoe in the glass case of a shoe store in the rain. That maidenly white forlorn object, pointed and old-fashioned, with high heels, the dream of all brides—along with the white dress in the picture of the first communion —stands in its glass box in the rain, lit up like the glass coffin of Snow White. It stands there in the rain abandoned, cut off from the restless bustle around it, and as hopelessly isolated, as inexpressibly unreal as is thrown-away and forgotten reality. It is raining harder and harder, and everything around is sad and sodden: the horses, the sparrows in the treetops, and even the lonely monument standing in the damp shadow of the fir trees.

The grimy windowpanes look so gray that all those rooms appear like drowned realms, unfathomably sunk to the bottom where time has stopped and nothing moves. The submerged rooms stand there, glass-framed in the rain, resembling empty, illuminated boxes.

Among them one stands out, plain and unsightly, a woman's white shoe made of silk. The rain is falling on the old roofs of the incredibly idiotic-looking houses. It cascades down the roof tiles, along the gutters, on the ancient attics and deserted balconies. A waterdrop, like a tear, is running down the plaster cheek of the blind girl's head right over the main entrance to the staircase. The tiny drop snakes along the plaster hairdo and slides along the cold, classically proportioned cheek of this masklike female face decorated with a laurel wreath, standing upright and lofty, above all this terrestrial activity. Crouched tightly against the tragic female form, a soaked pigeon with its head protectively covered by its wing endures the rain. Who has built these little towns, now deserted, with all their symmetrical promenades, their ridiculous balconies and unlit dwellings, their autumn rains and unbearable boredoms? The small town stands in the rain—extinct, with no one around, absolutely no one. Only the rain is heard rustling through the dark veil of the dusk.

A man passes by along the empty row of trees. He carries a package and he moans. His cigarette leaves behind it a trail of warm smoke that disappears in the twilight like a horizontal line. A smell of tired feet trails after the passer-by, an odor of an unwashed body, of rain-soaked rags and stale smoke. He passes by with his packages and vanishes along the row of trees toward the waiting room of the railroad station. The station's high windows are bathed in orange light, and the whole building, heated, steamy, full of moldy vapor, looks like a huge hothouse in which exotic fleshy plants bloom. The tired passer-by, his head bowed, departs, huge and dark, as if carrying his own tombstone. And the stone's inscription reads: "He lived; he traveled; he moved around carrying packages through insignificant, unknown towns, departing one day to a place of no return." And all this time he was occupied with his last unhealthy thought that he could have washed his feet but had not done so, though he intended to and had thought about how good and necessary that would have been. And yet he took leave from this earth dirty and unwashed, just the way he had lived in dirt and the way it had been written in the books from the beginning of time. No trace was left of this tired anonymous man except, perhaps, a melancholy shadow in our brains.

He, however, departed for some distant place into an azure, pastel-green sunlit realm where a kind of radiant city stands bathed in the crystal glow of an eternal summer day. There, ants crawl among their hills, cats dream in warm shadows, sparrows twitter, and from a balcony flutters a dark-blue silk flag, decorated with the Swedish cross, transparent as a woman's blouse, its diminutive, ever tinier pleats creating in the quiet summer blaze a coolness as refreshing as the plashing of a fountain.

"And what in the world are you doing in this rain?"

"Nothing, really. I am indulging in fancies about a dead summer. I am mourning for a summer that will, unfortunately, never return. Besides, I am waiting for the medicine that's getting made up in the pharmacy. I am on a cure, you know. And I am bored."

"Good evening, anyway. I am always happy to see you. And as to your mourning for a lost summer, that's not so unintelligent after all. It's been years since I enjoyed a really decent summer, one worthy of a human being. Generally speaking, such a summer doesn't exist at all. Summer is an illusion—an illusion that is already dead by the tenth or eleventh grade. From a single plaintive buzz of a fly around a coffeehouse window you can experience in the midst of winter all the forest meadows, distant blue views, cowbells, mountains, and sheep much more keenly than you can during that early summer of silly boyhood when one goes through one's first gonorrhea. On the whole, what does 'summer' really mean to us big-city neurotics? Unwashed windowpanes, bare curtain rods, moth-balled rugs, paper lanterns in the windows of stationery stores, perhaps two or three drinks with other drifters. Tell me, can anything in this entire cosmos be less meaningful and more miserable than a summer Sunday afternoon in our little town? Indeed, is there anybody alive who could fathom—in a higher cosmic sense—a deeper meaning in one of our summer Sunday afternoons? And especially when the streets are literally flooded with such hellish creatures—such as the picture of housemaids in their black frame?"

"And I, you see, was reflecting only a minute ago on how sad a woman's lonely white shoe is in the shoemaker's window in the rain. It seemed to me as if that shoe was the saddest thing in the world."

"You are right. Your shoe is sadder than my photographs. That's true. Even this bronze statue of a monk on its granite pedestal doesn't feel comfortable in this rain. But just imagine this monk, bareheaded as he is, with a book in his hand, ninety-eight degrees in the shade, completely exposed to the broiling sun. And right around him petite secretaries are licking their ice-cream cones. That's even more unpleasant. And you, you said you were waiting to get your medicine concocted. Did you go to L.W.? I just visited him myself. He told me about your case. You know we are colleagues at the clinic. Now he is my benefactor. He supports me, so to speak—he does quite a few things for me. He is a total idiot as far as medicine is concerned. Let the medicine he prescribed go to hell. Come on, let's get a pint of good red wine, which is, I bet, far more effective."

The person speaking was Dr. Siroček, who is a case in himself. Dr. Siroček is an acquaintance of mine. Our relationship is—how should I say?—rather delicate. Truly speaking, we got acquainted by meeting in the men's rooms of our abominable drinking dives. Yes, we met in the depressing, coarse, inevitably alcoholic dinginess of our local boozing dens in which one gets drunk just to deaden one's sense of reasoning and poison the heart. From an urge for self-destruction, a man laps up his poison in order to die like a dog as soon as possible. And in this way we get rid of all our depressions, all our stupidities, our nihilism. In a word, our existence as such. For years I've been meeting Dr. Siroček in those nauseating places where there is an eternal stench of tar and pitch, and where across the blackened walls the curtain of water splashes and falls in this human life. Indeed, sometimes it seems as if the whole universe is made of a huge, water-swelled bladder, and that through us all this flows from the clouds into rivers and brooks and city sewers. If one really thinks about it, it begins to seem as if our earthly existence has no purpose other than to become a net of fleshy, bladdery arteries, a kind of heavenly plumbing system through which the water that poured from above flows into porcelain bowls. And we, on the other hand, drift on the bottom of the cloudy mess like so many water bubbles. We bloom there like pale under-water flowers, damp and blind; drunk or sober, completely confused; drowning in greater and greater pain in our own puddles of tears or in the puddles created by our loose bladders.

There we met for years, the unfortunate Dr. Siroček and I, with a mathematical precision, always on the same spot. During such all too-human situations we would exchange, like two exhausted mermen, a couple of empty, drab, insignificant, almost totally conventional phrases. Then we would return to our wine and smoke, back to the tavern and the fumes of our tables.

In the beginning I had a certain feeling that Dr. Siroček was one of those well-meaning, kind, and harmless people who are destined—mathematically calculated—to be run down. Through this pale, talented, poetical, but unstable personality, who was often somewhat confused as well as inconsistent in his views and opinions—through this drunken individual the belly spoke more often than the brain. And the voices of this invisible ventriloquist would speak from the depths of Dr. Siroček's digestive system, sounding more gruntlike than human. And yet, in spite of his glassy stare and trembling hand, in spite of the burning cigarette that seemed eternally glued to his lower lip, and in spite of those voices from his intestines and drunken belly, this Dionysiac would mumble a mixture of reason and nonsense about himself and his higher calling. Enveloped by alcoholic fumes, he would mutter in the midst of our puddle with such enthusiasm and self-assurance that his drunken monologues echoed in my head like some unforgettable musical theme. Once, for instance, standing erect in that glorious Adam posture, helpless as a newborn baby, he told me a story that he had written about a naked woman. According to his own testimony, he rewrote the story, word by word, seventeen times and he was still dissatisfied with it. He was dissatisfied, he said, because he was not able to hit on the right description of the naked woman's movements while she was squatting before a wash basin, rinsing her belly with a sponge. When the story appeared in one of our magazines, Dr. Siroček attracted considerable notice. The unanimous judgment seemed to have been that he was crazy, and that his writing—under various pseudonyms—was typical of the literature of lunacy.

In his civilian profession Dr. Siroček was a physician, a man for whom "a most brilliant academic career" was predicted. At twenty-six, he had already achieved a fine reputation as assistant to an international celebrity in Paris, by publishing in various scientific magazines. There was even a scientific-medical method of some specialized nerve cut honored with his name. Then, suddenly, this famous bearer of a scientific predicate got lost in his glorious ascent. He became involved with some shady women and turned into a thoroughgoing alcoholic. One day he "beat the hell out of his Herr Professor" from Berlin and had to spend a few years in various sanatoria. He returned to our provincial nest a total wreck. Here, too, he was unable to get a solid footing as a general practitioner because somehow he always got entangled with dubious patients. In addition, he quarreled through newspapers, continuously exalting the high calling of medicine while he physically insulted one of our best-known doctors, a medical professor and a local celebrity. Because of this, he went to the insane asylum for observation. And now he gets drunk in dingy pubs, drinking cheap local wine, starving himself occasionally in order to publish fragments of his unorthodox and confused prose.

Dr. Siroček is a sort of street poet now, living from the handouts of his ex-colleagues. They, for their part, treat him the same way parents treat their lost children who prefer eating out of pigs' troughs to eating from the richly set tables of their orderly, middle-class patriarchal homes.

He let me know that Dr. L.W.—who has been treating me for more than a year now—did indeed tell him all about "my case." Dr. Siroček had paid him a visit just a few minutes after I had left because he wanted to borrow a few dinars. Now he would be interested to hear how I interpreted "my case" since, after all, Dr. L.W. was a simple idiot, a fact about which there should be no doubt, and about which any debate would be entirely superfluous. Sitting now among the kegs and barrels in the wine cellar that looked like some underground pirate den, Dr. Siroček and I had already polished off the second quart of red wine after my return from the pharmacy with the medicine Dr. L.W. had prescribed anew for me. After that, "my case" was not only "mine" but also "his"; they became two "identical cases." The identity of "our" cases was important not only for us as "patients," but also in respect to the total surrounding in which we happened to live, and which could be characterized as still belonging to the troglodyte, cannibalistic Stone Age.

"Let's see now, you are bothered by your dead people like some old governesses, and on account of that those idiots are massaging your prostate! There you see the perfect example of our 'science.' Your basic idea—that we die before our death in the conscience of those who died before us—is the most normal, most fundamental, and most logical idea of every reflection about death, even the most primitive. A pilgrimage should be made from grave to grave, and above the mounds of the immense misery of those snuffed-out lives a candle of perception and experience should be lit. All those deceased—t.b. cases, widows, beggars, and all those murdered on operating tables—had something to say to us, to enlighten us with one or two honest words. And every light, even the smallest, emanating from the wisdom of the deceased could illuminate our darkness. Then this darkness in us, our incapacity to communicate with strangers, would appear less alien and less unintelligible, since it would turn out that our experiences are not so dissimilar after all, even though at first sight they may seem so. They have already passed their final test, and by learning from their experience, we could conclude that the examination we have to face may not be as difficult as it seems to us, coming as we do with not entirely clean conscience before this final and stupid examining board. As far as doctors are concerned, this is, of course, an unhealthy way to think, and the neurologists brand it as downright crazy. Everything that shows even a shade of lofty inspiration is considered by our great specialists, like Dr. L.W., a 'pathological case.'

· "Incidentally, everything here is a huge heap of garbage and junk. Our so-called 'science,' too, is just ordinary garbage. I don't know whether you noticed the fact—a very obvious one by the way—that we generally build on the mound of garbage and junk. Truck drivers come with their trucks full, and they raise our urban level by bringing in more and more garbage: old tin washbowls, torn sacks, pulp, rusty spoons, disintegrating hatboxes, and smelly rags that reek of burned cotton. Then pavilions of our autonomous home-grown culture are built upon these rusty washbowls, foot lockers, and all kinds of refuse and bales of rotten newspapers. And our civilization lives in these tents built from old sacks and decayed toothbrushes, in these gypsy pads made of plaster and tattered rags, in these huts and mudholes. And here too is located, among other things, our medical science. Here also live in a mandarin-like stance all our authorities. And though I don't want to be a prophet of evil tidings, pay sharp attention to what I am telling you now: All this stands like a theater backdrop made out of paper that waits only for the first blow of a strong wind and the whistling of a bomb. Then everything will be as it was before—old perforated washbowls, holed-out rusty cash registers, beaten-up piss pots, and empty tin cans. All our fortresses built on newspaper will be gone with the wind, and no one will know that once any of this existed. Our citizens wipe their behinds with newspaper and thus consume their own glory.

"You know that I wrote all this to the gentleman in charge and that is why they committed me. How can I fight against the mechanical blare of our science when my name is entered on the list of patients in the insane asylum? I declared to them publicly, under my full signature as a doctor, that if a single superficial glance is thrown at our surgery, our laryngology, or neurology, it would immediately be seen that taken together, from a scientific point of view, we have nothing but lowly clerks trying to fill the boots of generals. And as far as the international forum is concerned, we just do not count; in the eyes of European science we are still considered to be nothing but a most backward province. Our experimental researches, our original discoveries, our scientific initiative are equal to a great big zero. I am not, you see, impressed by small provincial practitioners wrapped in their academic gowns; I am not impressed by plagiarists, who are far more occupied with playing politics than with science. And I wrote to them all that they have become a bunch of commercial agents of big drug manufacturers, big European cartels. By the way, let me please see for a second what your genius prescribed for you."

I handed Dr. Siroček the prescription given to me by Dr. L.W. He scanned it with ironic contempt, like a stern professor taking into his hands the written work of a notoriously bad student. "Well now, let's see!

> "℞. Infusi Sennae   30.0
> Natrii Sennae   30.0
> Natrii chlorati ana   30.0
>      5–3 x daily
>      2–1 spoonfuls
> Gardenal pills
>      ½ 3 x daily
> Probilin p.
>      3–4 2 x daily
>   a. Evenings before bed
>   b. Mornings, 1 hour before breakfast
>      Natrii chlorati   15.0
>      Natrii sulfurici   40.0

Natrii bicarbonici   50.0
Kalii sulfurici   5.0
  M.F.p.   110.0
D.S.   ½ tsp. in ½ cup boiled water
       with pills A.M. and P.M.
Coffeini natriosalicylici   0.15
Ergotini Bonjouani   0.2
Acidi acetylosalycylici   0.4
in capsulisanylaceis
  D.D.   No. 15
  D.S. after each meal."

Dr. Siroček again scanned the rather detailed prescription, for which I had paid the pharmacy 176 dinars and 70 paras. He then touched my hand with his long spiderlike fingers discolored by tobacco—their tips were as cold as cocaine.

"How much did you pay that quack?"

"Seventy-five dinars."

"Which means that altogether you paid 251 dinars for this quack prescription. A famous doctor once said that the only difference between a physician and a veterinarian is in his patients. Do you know what he prescribed for you? Nothing but laxatives. Senna, you see, is an extract that has an effect on the smooth musculature of the intestines and promotes bowel movement. He has prescribed for you such a sacramental diarrhea that you'll lose your mind if you try to swallow this Egyptian nonsense. Trachoma is treated with it in Senegal and Egypt. Folia sennae are pale green leaves that feel woolly and cotton-soft when you touch them. They come from a tropical plant with yellow flowers, the odor of which can be rather penetrating. It has chubby fruit as sticky as hawthorn berry and is called manna—heavenly, Biblical manna. Once at the Parisian flea market I heard a Senegalese recommending it as the best remedy against gonorrhea. As you see, there is divided opinion about the healing power of this asinine remedy even among the scientists. And you probably don't suffer from constipation at all."

"Not really. I rather suffer from a chronic diarrhea."

"Just unbelievable. Simply unbelievable. Gardenal pills are, by the way, ordinary junk—a strictly commercial sell of the aspirin line. Probilin, on the other hand, is a preparation that promotes gall secretion. Natrium and kalium are headache cures. And what do you take when you have a headache?"

"Veramon."

"Of course. What the hell do you need a 'half teaspoon in a half cup of boiled water—together with probilin pills evening and morning'? You don't suffer from headaches but from nervous melancholy depressions. Probably because of an irregular sex life. When was the last time you slept with a woman?"

"About six months ago."

"You see. What you need, my friend, is a woman, and not that 'half teaspoonful' stuff. He is totally mad, that Dr. L.W. He's the one who should be locked up in the asylum—and as soon as possible. But I don't want to get too excited. I told these gentlemen once and for all, and I wrote them with my full signature, so why am I getting excited? Anyone who gets excited on account of those idiots doesn't deserve anything better than to be put in a strait jacket.

"Just take a look at this: Natrium sulphate promotes the functioning of the liver, and if you stuff yourself with so much sulphur paste, you'll ruin your disgestion so thoroughly that even the best wine won't be able to cure you any more. If you were to follow this prescription you'd spend the next three weeks doing nothing but running five or six times to the toilet and gulping three large teaspoonsful of that junk daily. All that is prescribed there, to be taken five times a day, mornings and nights, before and after meals, you could take in a form of simple aspirin or some harmless medicated candy that children take against worms. What did you say you paid that nincompoop? Seventy five dinars? I touched him for a hundred, which means it was your money he gave me, and now we'll drink it away. Waiter, another quart of red wine."

Like a purebred dog with taut nerves, Dr. Siroček jumped with a single leap toward a small iron stove that was steaming, all aglow, in the corner of the pub. With an elegant gesture he threw into the oven the package containing the medicine that was lying in front of him on an upturned barrel. Then he returned and tapped me on the shoulder with a triumphant gesture of a staunch old confidant.

"Well, that stupidity is done with. And now, my friend, you owe it to your health to find yourself a woman. Here comes the other bottle of wine. To your health!"

We now proceeded to get drunk, while Dr. Siroček talked all night long about women. He explained to me that women are like overripe decaying figs, and that all of us get stuck in this female fruit, digging into its moldering flesh. And not a single one of us has the courage to admit we are just strewn caterpillars that know only how to cling to these tainted figs like excited worms. And so our time passes in this worm-eaten rot while the cannons continue to thunder all around us, and we go on for centuries slaughtering one another. In this bloody pathos of cannon-thunder and trumpet-blaring, he, Dr. Siroček, is clearly conscious of only one thing: He senses fear, and he feels how comforting it would be to crawl into the chaos of the female uterus, just as in the remote past, in some distant place, he had flowed out of it. It was a long time ago, on some feathery cushions, in darkness, accompanied by the creaking of the bed and the whistling of the wind; snow was falling, wet and muddy, sticky and misty, enveloping him in an infinite emptiness.

His personal life is wretchedly stupid and miserable. It consists, on the one hand, of the infinitely cold and empty ringing of churchbells—which chime in honor of some turgid, hundred-headed doctrine that seems strangely difficult to interpret—and, on the other, of women who lately circle around him. One of these women has tubercular glands and wears black stockings;

her name is Musja. She works as a waitress somewhere on the edge of town where the military barracks are situated and where the lower military ranks come daily for their stew. No one else in the entire female cosmos but this tubercular Musja seems to possess the mysterious uterus toward which Dr. Siroček crawls like a snail. He inches into her interior, which opens to him like some gigantic, superterrestrial, Dante-esque underground.

"It is warm in those women's bellies. A man could let himself drown in those dusks, disintegrate as a human being, cease being, transform himself into something that, measured by his dignity, is tinier and more babbling than a newborn baby wrapped in diapers. One should crawl back into primeval matter and transmute oneself into a kind of cosmic, slippery slime that exists just on the level of the blissful sense of the warmth of the uterus. And then he should finally shrink to something without reason, without logic, without memory. What is left is a deaf-mute state of the warm flesh, without even the slightest thought of death, of transitoriness, of the dead among us and the entire artificially constructed reality around us. For what, indeed, is real in our daily lives? Streets? Are the streets actually a phenomenon of reality? Telephones? Wine pubs? The whole bureaucratic net enmeshing all this? The motion of my inflamed lungs? I move through the streets completely unrecognized, as unnoticed as if I were totally invisible. In actuality I am transparent and I flash with green sparks like the retort of an electric transformer, and I converse with stars, singing like my cricket down there in the pissoir.

"Yes, I discovered a cricket in the men's room, my dear fellow; down there in the men's room I discovered a cricket. Underneath the waterfall that splashes over the putrid black-tarred wall, where the citron slices float and the smell of ammonia bites our nostrils as in some laboratory, right down there at the very dregs of the human stench, one night I heard the voice of the cricket. There wasn't even a dog in the pub, the wind roared like a wild beast, and in the stench of the men's room was a voice of the ripe summer, the redolence of August, the breath of meadows surging like green velvet: the voice of the cricket out of the urine and feces, the voice of nature that transforms even stinking city toilets into starry sunsets, when the mills are softly humming in the russet horizon, and first crickets announce themselves as the harbingers of an early autumn. Here, you see, I've brought him some bread crumbs. Come, let's pay him a visit."

Helpless as a child, Dr. Siroček pulled out of his pocket a handful of bread crumbs and stood there motionless, the palm of his hand outstretched in a poignant gesture; he stood rather a long time, as if in a trance, his eyes sparkling with tears.

In the men's room the cricket did not appear. The silence was interrupted only by the plashing of the water draining like a trembling curtain over the surface of the tarred wall.

With pricked-up ears, with a look that seemed to be lost beyond all that we in this world designate as reality, Dr. Siroček endured for a while in that hell of acid. He stood there with his head bowed, and then, with a gesture of his hand, he flipped the burning cigarette butt, which crackled loudly and extinguished itself in the water.

"We are all butts in the urine," he uttered sentimentally, dispersing the crumbs by turning his left pocket inside out. Then he brushed off the remaining crumbs with his left hand, like a dog scratching behind its ear.

*Translated by Frank S. Lambasa*

# Devil's Island

For three years Gabriel Kavran had not been home. When he did return one night, his very own father, old Kavran, couldn't believe it was his son. It was carnival season and it seemed to the old man that this must be someone in costume who had shown up to frighten him! This pale corpse with deep, inflamed eye sockets; this bald, gray-haired, snaggle-toothed head, this ragged skeleton, this beggar whose bare flesh showed through tattered trousers—was this his only son, Gabriel? That strong, full-blooded bull, that hard-headed jackass who had fought with him at knife-point and broken a chair over his head? It's a thief, a ghost, some tramp who has made his way in in order to kill him! And the eyes aren't Gabriel's! This face is a painted mask!

"What kind of stupid joke is this? Wipe that chalk off your snout! I recognize you!" The old man walked toward Gabriel, who was sitting hunched over on the couch. At that moment it seemed natural to the old man that it was someone in disguise, and so it seemed to him that he even recognized the masked figure—'It's Zajčika's servant, Pišta, smeared with chalk!' "Pišta! Hey! Pišta!"

The old man's laugh resounded dry and empty in the room. In the silence he stopped, his laugh died on his lips, and from the eyes of the masked man on the couch, from those deeply tormented holes, flowed ice. A panicked pause set in, full of wordless danger and silence.

This is how it really started. Indeed, the first moment Gabriel had appeared before his father, the old man had recognized him by his voice and had no doubts. He had been in a tavern and was coming back about midnight; his cigar had been doused with wine and wouldn't light. He plodded along through wet patches of snow; the first roosters were piping up from the cellars; the old man stopped after every other step, cursed his cigar, lit one match after another, and so rolled along, bloated full of wine like a wineskin. The poplars rustled before the house and the water could be heard rumbling, powerful and black, beneath the bridge, while a freight train wailed in a willow thicket far on the other bank. In front of the single-storied river station, on the threshold, where by way of three cement stairs one enters the office, sat a crumpled figure. The old man thought it was the devil sitting on the stairs waiting for him. And so, with the instinct of a healthy animal in terror before something supernatural, he screwed up all the strength in his body and clenched his knotty stick to fight if need be.

. "Good evening!" the old man spat out. He threw away the dead cigar so it wouldn't get in the way of the fight.

"Good evening!" As Gabriel returned the greeting it seemed to the old man that he had heard that voice somewhere before.

"My God! Gabriel! By the merciful God! Is that you?"

"It's me!"

"Gabriel! You?"

Drunk, dazed, the old man wanted to throw himself on his son's neck and kiss him, but the latter jerked back with a rough, cruel movement. The physical nearness of the man had at first attracted him, and, hearing his father's voice after so long a time, a wave of intimate warmth flowed out of him. He felt as though he were sinking into a morass of emotion, as though diving into something blind, pleasant, familial and good. But having felt the touch of his father's greasy, sweaty body, wrapped in the vapors of alcohol, he jerked back; strange depths yawned in him. All the battles, the cursings and beatings, all that was dirty and sick, which for years had grown up between this drunk and himself, all of it, like some great weight, tipped the scales against the flicker of sympathy within him, and so he was unable to lift his arms to embrace his father.

"I've been waiting a long time! It's past midnight! Where have you been this time?"

In that "this time" was a deep revulsion. It was expressed so coldly, as if there had not been three years between father and son—as if only last night, here, in front of this house, they had quarreled about that same "this time"! The old man, his arms outspread, stood as if petrified in mid-air, and this drove him to keep talking—about how today the commissioner had been at the river station all afternoon, how the water was rising, how they had laid out the line for a new levee, and how he had stopped off at the Golden Fish, naturally, for a glass of wine. Talking thus, aimlessly and excitedly, the old man searched for his keys but didn't seem to be able to find the right one. He pulled out his wallet, worn and patched, and his change purse, and his handkerchief. His hands trembled as if he had a fever, and his jowls shook so much that he swallowed individual words and kept mumbling something—but it was impossible to make out what.

The station's office was unaired; it stank of dry spittle sprinkled with sawdust. One caught immediately the repulsively thick stench that in our country twists its way like a fog through offices in which stand worn-out couches covered with black sticky oilcloth; where, for days on end, iron stoves glow and gas valves whistle. Passing through the office into the living quarters, consisting of a single room, the old man, after feeling about for some time, finally lit the lamp and placed it on the table, on → the red felt tablecloth. Gabriel's glance fell on the lamp's scarlet reflection pouring out over the felt tablecloth, and on the kerosene lamp with its white milk-glass globe and copper Cupids on the lamp base, near which he had spent so many long, sleepless nights, and on the chairs and cabinets, the veneers of which had long since been stripped away. Then, having drunk in, in a single moment, all the familiar things, he lowered himself onto the couch. Only then did the full light of the lamp pour over his face, and the old man, seeing here before him the yellow death-mask of some alien, never-before-seen person, was terrified and wrung his hands.

"By the all-holy Jesus! Blessings of God! Is it really you?"

"Who else would it be? It's me!"

Old Kavran, still up to his ears in wine, again forgot his son's voice, forgot everything; it seemed to him this face must be a painted mask, and then again as if it weren't, and so he stopped, shaken to his foundations. In the rolling waves of his thoughts, in the complete chaos aroused by wine and fear, by nerves and hope, there remained intact one idea, massive and firm as a rock precipice: that in any case his own son had returned. His only son; no one else! As if a rockslide had rushed down over him and someone had sunk his nails into his throat and ripped out all the bloody veins and muscles, the old man began to whimper like a dog. He collapsed across the table and, clutching at the tablecloth and feeling his way along, like someone mortally wounded, he pulled himself toward the couch and fell at Gabriel's feet.

"My son! My son! Is it really you?"

Gabriel, hungry and exhausted, stared at his father. Everything seemed to him both natural and repulsive.

'This is so stupid! The old man's drunk! He reeks of wine! What does all this mean? What sort of comedy is this?'

The old man, from alcohol and the exhaustion of a tiring day (he had run about endlessly for the commissioner and they had done some hard rowing), couldn't control himself and sobbed ceaselessly, helplessly, like an old, old man, as if he had been beaten, and almost idiotically kept repeating, "Is it really you, my son? Is it really you?"

"Naturally it's me! Here, look! Here's the scar! Where you got me on the head with a bottle!"

⋅'That's right! There it is! There's the slash mark from the bottle! That's the truth!' (Father and son had fought in a tavern; then the police had broken the fight up. The slash mark had been covered by hair, but now it was completely visible on the bare skull.) 'Yes, yes! Oh, one and almighty God!'

"What the hell are you doing?" Gabriel leaped to his feet, feeling on his fingers and hands his father's warm tears; then he shoved his father away so that the old man tottered and almost fell to the floor. "Are you drunk? Why are you wailing over me! I'm not laid out in my coffin yet! Idiot!"

"It's nothing, nothing! Everything is fine! Don't get angry! The tears just come out! You see? They just come out by themselves! They'll stop; there, you see, they'll stop! Just don't get all upset!"

The old man became terrified that Gabriel might leave. 'He's capable of it! Just go out and not come back for another three years! That's how it had been the last time. And now he's barely gotten here and he's already going to leave so soon? Can this be? But everything's not lost yet! Everything can still be set right! Everything is going to be fine! Mustn't cry now! No, no! No tears now!'

"Are you tired? Eh? Are you hungry? Can I fix you something hot? But there's nothing in the house! Eggs! Let me hunt up at least two or three eggs! And there should be some tea somewhere! I'm living completely alone now! Frantz's Fanika died, so now Frantz takes care of everything himself! And he's already old! You know Frantz! Oh, dear God! And you need water to wash yourself! And a towel! But where are my towels?"

. And so the old man rose heavily and, brushing the tears away with the palms of his hands, went to a cabinet and began rummaging about in a confusion of sheets and pillowcases and pulling out some tattered, dirty rags. Muttering asthmatically, he bent over an open drawer of the cabinet, pulled out of somewhere a hot plate, poured in alcohol and lit it, placed a small pan on it, whereupon bluish flames began licking the bottom. Gabriel stared into the flickering tongues of fire and listened to his father as he whispered that he, Gabriel Kavran, three-year draft evader, was being sought by the police. That's right! Everything would be fine if it weren't for that damned army service. Gabriel listened to his drunken father idiotically mumbling all sorts of things, and stared at the room with its dilapidated furnishings—the entire extent of his birthplace, back into which he had fallen after three difficult years. Everything was alien to him.

'So this is that room? These cabinets, these holy pictures, this milk-glass lamp? That Christ framed in gold, in a scarlet robe with a staff in his hand, that Madonna with a halo in a blue robe, in whose eye a thick, glistening tear is frozen like a pea! And the old man there with the sheets and pillowcases! And he says they're still looking for him because of military service! After three years they are still after him! The police are still looking for him as a draft evader? How is all this going to turn out, all this business about military service and the police, this strange life? The old man asks him how he is going to straighten everything out now. Is he going to take his doctoral examinations? How will he resolve these questions? How is it going to turn out? And he listens to his father, sits on the couch, and doesn't know a thing! Hasn't the least idea how it's going to turn out! Knows absolutely nothing! Absolutely nothing!'

The old man fixes the bed, and asks him this and that, pulls the covers over the feather quilts, buttons the cases on the pillows, and talks about how some classmate and acquaintance of Gabriel's has gone out of his mind and all the doctors unanimously affirm there is no longer any hope or help for him. Still another said his first pastoral mass and was happy somewhere in the countryside, and a third hung himself, though he had already passed his doctoral examinations.

How strange all those names were to Gabriel! Where were the faces behind those masks? Where had they gone? Hung himself? And he had already passed his doctoral examinations?

"Yes, they found him in a hayloft on a rafter, hanging there. And no one ever found out why it happened! He didn't leave any sort of note!"

Gabriel listened to the water gurgling and bubbling in the pan on the hot plate. Inside him boiled the powerful complex of a life of three long years, while outside, beneath the bridge, the water flowed and one could hear its rumble. The old man talked of three persons, his comrades, who had lived through those three years just as he had, in these same dimensions and planes; one had hung himself, a second had gone mad, and the third was already a pastor and, in his own way, happy. But he personally had roamed for three years like a wolf, and now he sits here mute and, contemplating life, stares exhaustedly at the milk-white lamp glowing dimly. So this is life! Once there had been certain persons here, objects, relationships; but now everything has grown into other relationships. Life had pulled everything apart, erased it, shattered it, dragged it from tavern to tavern, from far-off land to far-off land.

The mute, exhausted silence lasted several days. It was a sunny February, full of warm breezes, and everything looked as if it would bud forth in twenty-four hours. The clothes in which Gabriel had returned were so ragged—all patches on patches—that he had put on an old discarded coat of his father's. It reeked of stuffy closets and aromatic herbs, and was far too long for him, so that Gabriel looked funny in it even to himself. He did not feel any need to go into the city. He would stare from a distance at the factories and churches and army barracks, and everything looked bright and white in the sun, as if life in the city were easy and pleasant. But he didn't feel like going there. He would lie on the rocks, listen to the water flow, sun himself in the February sun, and flounder about in a dismal interior monologue. Everything seemed to him senseless and pointless. There began to arise in him a deep exhaustion as a reaction to all his recent hardships, and he could feel how his thoughts were so scattered that there was no system to them, only a neurotic flickering of forms and figures wavering on the brain's screen like shadows.

⸢ He thought about spring and about how one ought to live freely, elementally, to become like the air and water. 'How wonderful the water sounds! It's rising again! What human brain can take in the massiveness of water in its entirety? Rain, clouds, rain, clouds, the watery veins, the sea, flood tide, ebb tide, what is it that makes water exist and live in an element? That's the way one should breathe! Deeply! Powerfully! That would be life! A great, an immediate life! A life that is not looked at through fictions and false prisms. Ultimately, what are those so-called "false" prisms? Does there exist any sort of life that is not seen through false prisms? This great, heavy, massive globe that turns, can it be perceived as a rotating globe if it isn't seen through some particular false prism? Really! This whole globe revolves! And this bridge and water, this river station, this personal life wrapped in time—like insignificant motes—all revolve precisely in mammoth revolutions from twenty-four-hour period to twenty-four-hour period. But that rotation doesn't exist as an immediate experience! Four hundred years earlier, the globe did not revolve! And what is four hundred years, taken properly? What are four hundred earthly revolutions in relation to the size of the earth's globe? It is relatively much less than four hundred revolutions of a propeller! And what do four hundred revolutions mean in the functioning of a motor? So too, today the globe revolves, but yesterday no one yet knew that obvious truth. From this it follows that in life there exist billions and billions of new permutations and possibilities. There exist possibilities that are obvious truths, about which today no one has the least notion, but in another four hundred years children will learn them in elementary school. And compared to all this, what is the meaning of one wasted life?'

Thus Gabriel sunned himself and thought about life and stared at the city in the sun. There there were cafés, people, newspapers, banks, all being ground up as in a mill. There lived his friends, acquaintances, and a woman who three years before had stabbed him in the back and abandoned him at the most crucial moment. He recalled that life of three years before and it revolted him. As if, from some hellish pot beneath him poisonous vapors were steaming, he had an urge to kick it all away. Stretching out on the rocks, he sighed deeply, like a wounded man whose every joint was shattered. 'Those nauseating provincial taverns! Those newspapers, books, sick people! He had left it far behind, but now, after three years, here he was, once more inhaling that same atmosphere. New crises were arising and everything was a closed circle—everything. There were many dark and tangled questions one needed to think over intently. First of all, the problem of the barracks, of the three-year draft evasion that hung over him like a paragraph of the law. Then the problem of health: lungs, nerves, teeth, digestion, everything broken down like a bad machine. And the question of money—the problem of food, shelter, clothing! And the social question of an occupation, of some income, of studies and examinations. And, of course, the main question, the most important: Her! What had happened to her? Was she alive? Where was there a solution? A closed circle!' And so, because of those thousands and thousands of questions, he didn't want to think about anything. From day to day he put off taking any concrete steps and would lie in bed, for the entire time not talking to his father about anything.

Old Kavran was frightened by all this.

Who in the devil ever saw a person sleep all day, get up at midnight, and go out to the water like a vampire? What was this son of his thinking? This was no joke! This boy was already a gray-haired man—balder than he was—getting along in years, and, by God, no one lived by sleeping all day. And then, what's going to happen about that damned army service? The old river-station supervisor, as a royal public servant, was especially frightened of the police and thought a great deal about what would happen if his son were arrested as a draft evader! Even back when he had been in that damned London or Paris or wherever it was, even then the police had come to the river station every third month. A warrant had been issued for his son, and he had made a statement that he didn't know where his son was living, and he had signed it, black on white. But if they came now and caught this draft evader under his roof, he might also suffer and even lose his pension. So old Kavran, since the first fire of joy had faded, hung about his son like a shadow and endlessly enumerated to Gabriel all those dark and difficult questions about which the latter did not want to think and before which he would hide his head beneath the pillows.

What about the army? What about his examinations? How does he expect to live?

The son, to calm his father, promised he would write a petition to the military authorities and in it explain that he had not been able to respond to his draft notice because he had been out of the country. To the petition he would add a doctor's certificate, and so everything would be satisfactorily straightened out. And he would take his doctoral examinations in the fall—just let the old man not get upset and leave him in peace, because his head ached and he didn't feel well. He had to get back on his feet, to get well, to catch up on his sleep, to rest!

· Sitting at the table in the evening, the old man wanted to talk with his son. He wanted to find out how people lived in far-off Europe: whether the police functioned there as they do here;

whether there were pensions, river stations, offices—what all that was like in those European countries.

"So what's it like in London! Is London such a large city? Is the fog and smoke so thick one can't see his finger in front of his nose and the street lights burn by day?"

"Yes! Not even your finger in front of your nose!"

In the "yes" and the "not even your finger in front of your nose" there was something so hard and resistant that for the old man, who had softened somewhat of late, these conversations became unbearably awkward, as if he were sitting before a superior; and so out of discomfort the old man would become silent for a while.

"And in London, you say, the trolley runs underground in the sewers? Then I ask you, don't they have a lot of rats in the trolley?"

Silence. A long pause. Silence.

"Have you got a headache, son? What's with you? Are you sick?"

"Yes! My head aches!"

Thus the evening would pass and the old man constantly thought about what was wrong with this son of his. In the light of the yellow lamp he peered secretively at him; he looked so pale, waxen as a corpse, God forgive us! And in the deep of night, after the lamp had long since been extinguished, murky thoughts rose up before the old man. Singly and together, they were shattering and distressing but still seemed likely. 'Could this son of his who for three years had roamed the world, could this man perhaps be abnormal? It could easily be so! There was something wrong with this man! Perhaps he had killed someone somewhere and it was weighing on his conscience like lead. Had something somewhere given way inside him? He's mad! He ought to be looked at by a doctor!' Such thoughts flickered in the brain of old Kavran like tiny flames beneath the ashes, and he rolled over and listened to his son quietly breathing beside him.

'He's breathing so quietly you can't hear him. Is he out of the room again? He's gotten up again and gone out to the water and is sitting under the bridge and listening to the sound of the water, like last night. So weak, miserable, so thin! The wind will blow right through him! Anyhow, he already has one foot in the grave! Where is he?'

So he leaned toward Gabriel to touch him, to see if he was in the room and what was wrong with him. 'He'll have to light the lamp again and go outside looking for him in the dark, in the wind.'

"What is it? Can't you leave me in peace?" His son started in surprise at the touch of his father's hand.

"Aren't you asleep? I thought you were gone!"

"And where would I be?"

"How would I know where? Somewhere out by the water! The devil knows, you're such a weird one!"

A pause. Silence. Deep sighing.

"My son! Does your head ache? Can't you sleep?"

A pause. For a long time.

Gabriel listened to the water under the bridge and smelled the cheap pipe-smoke with which every object in the room reeked heavily and harshly. The smoke-drenched room, rotted ticking, the creaky bed left over from the days of Malčika.

This Malčika, she had been old Kavran's first wife, and Gabriel knew her from the tattered family photograph album. A fat, goitrous little woman with a mole and a prayer book, in crinoline.

Then there was his departed mother, the "nun," and her holy pictures that were hanging on all the walls of the river station! After the "nun" came unhappy Eva, whom they pulled out of a swampy backwater on the fifth day, and there she had lain in the office, green, wet, rotting, her lips eaten away. The smoke-drenched room, the water rumbling under the bridge, the dead women and his father, old Kavran, who had pecked out the hearts and eyes of all these women, and now lay on his back and snored. The water rumbled beneath the bridge. Last night he had gone out to the water and for a long time stared at the light of the kerosene lamps trembling on the waves, and life seemed to him so hellishly jam-packed, something nailed together like a coffin.

'And here alongside him lies his father, a lump of peasant flesh with a huge head full of highway orders, rules, and regulations, snoring like an animal. All this is loathsome, unbearable.'

· The imperial river station was a single-storied building painted yellow, massively built of stone, like a fortress on the levee. With its thick vaulted walls and its iron window gratings, the station had a repellent and miserable appearance, the way all prisons and fortresses are repellent and miserable. A long levee, as straight as a ruler, connected it to a colony of taverns and butchershops at the bridge; when the water rose, all the surrounding fields and pastures and willow thickets would sink in the flood, and only the stone levee would stand out like a walled harbor jetty. Those were the high-water days—days of endless gray muddy water from which here and there an occasional rafter or beam jutted or a stray stalk of corn or willow branch wavered: they would not surrender to the water.

The water spreads, green and treacherous, where willow thickets rot and men drift along in dark boats and, with long poles, plumb the muddy bottom seeking the drowned. An oar keeps falling into the water; drops run down the oar's wooden blade and drip into the green sea as if someone were beating on porcelain with a slender knitting needle. The oar grabs heavily at the water, *shlop, shlop;* the boat glides quietly and secretively; the poles feel about the mud, and the boatman's voice can be heard out of the semidarkness, "Hoy-hoy! Hoy-hoy!" And over everything looms the gray sky of twilight as boatmen seek the drowned and the water flows relentlessly. Gulls cry out, streams of stagnant and muddy water flow together into the current beneath the bridge in powerful eddies that roar ceaselessly the whole night long.

. Across the water, in the distance, the towering crowns of white poplars are covered with the ruddy reflections of gypsy fires, and in the water flicker red fiery splotches. The beams and iron structures of the bridge shudder beneath the thunder of locomotives and railcars; red fire belches forth, and sparks leap from the black mass of the freight rumbling and howling over the bridge. Then, after a moment, everything has disappeared and one can hear only the distant roar of the train. The bloody Cyclopean splotches glow on; the water rumbles; dogs howl. Darkness.

Here, beneath the bridge, where lay story-high piles of planks and beams still smelling of the resin of the sap-filled pine, material for controlling the water: poles, bundles of sticks, crisscrossed piles of sacks of cement; where loomed the black figures of storage sheds with tar-smeared boats, anchors and pickaxes, tools and measuring equipment—here stood the river station, off to itself like a devil's island. On this devil's island, where one could hear the mournful, sad song of the horse bells of endless black wagons as they slowly dragged along the road from the bridge like a funeral procession, here, where poplars murmured and plane trees whined like wounded dogs; here, alongside the gray melancholy water, Gabriel Kavran, son of the river-station supervisor, was born.

His father was a solid, well-built man. As a young Pioneer corporal he had been decorated at the attack on Jajce with the silver medal for bravery by His Imperial and Royal Highness, the Archduke Charles. Besides the medal for bravery, he was also decorated with the Occupation Cross of '78 on a black and yellow ribbon and a bronze jubilee medal with a Latin inscription and, in relief, the laurel-crowned, imperial head of His Highness the Rex Imperator. Besides these military decorations, he also held the Silver Cross for civilian bravery and a certificate from the Society for the Protection of Animals for extraordinary merit, which he received in connection with saving things from a flood—cattle, pigs, and people. This, then, is old Kavran, who, no matter what happened, would calmly sigh: "There's a reason for everything in the end!" And so, with his peasant awareness of causality, he peacefully and naturally bore everything, as do all our peasants, both those who still plow as well as those who have cast aside the plow and harrow and put on uniforms and liveries as episcopal coachmen, provincial guardsmen, supervisors of tax offices, highway stations, and river stations.

 Old Kavran became the supervisor of the river station and so, in accordance with his civil duty, he filled out the logbooks as to whether the water level was normal or below normal, and, if it rose, how many centimeters it rose above normal. When the water rose and carried along material it had borne off from the impoverished villages of the hinterlands—those planks, sheds, pens, and dead cows with bloody, bulging eyes— old Kavran gazed on the catastrophe calmly. 'It's a natural thing for the water to rise. First, because the water rises twice a year anyhow, and second, in his logbook he had noted that the water had already been above normal for two or three days. If someone drowned (an "unidentified citizen"), that too seemed natural. The regulations clearly stated that swimming in open places and in the backwaters was strictly forbidden, and they were not written because someone had nothing better to do, but because "there's a reason for everything"! Clearly, not a single citizen would disobey the regulations since, in doing so, he invites punishment, and only harms himself. Everything has its place and its authority in the world. A dog without a license goes to the skinner.'

When the water was above normal, a red lamp was lit at the river station as a warning. If the people from Trnja, Rukavac, and Rugovica, in spite of the red lamp—which, in accordance with regulations, burns bright and clean—don't pull their pigs and calves back to high ground for a whole night, and put more faith in the water than in the red lamp as a regulatory organ— well then, that's their business! Everything that happens is classified somewhere in some office, on some list, at some magistrate's, in some registry or construction department. If someone drives his horses across the bridge at a gallop, that's a violation of highway regulations and he's fined two florins. For a violation of public safety one is arrested, but that doesn't come within the river station's jurisdiction. If someone is drowning, it is necessary to revive him by artificial respiration, as prescribed on the health department charts that, with a handbook, hang in the river-station office. If it works. But if it doesn't, one telephones the appropriate listing. Everything in life has its reason and appropriate listing. So, too, does death. A dead man is entered in the death register. The register is lithographed in the *Registry Bulletin* and then is reprinted in the *National News* in a column under the title: "Deaths in the Capital City" from such and such a date to such and such a date.

And so it happened that old Kavran buried his three spouses and was not upset at all. 'Anyhow, everything has its reason! You die and you live, it's all the same! His father died; his mother and grandfathers and grandmothers, they all died. You pour wine on the corpse, turn the mirror to the wall, stop the clocks, and that's that. A man is born and he dies. The dead man is entered in the death register. For the deceased, funerals are bought at the undertaker's. The price of third-class funerals changes; it falls and rises. Thus, for the departed Maria, Gabriel's mother, he paid seventeen florins and twenty-two kraicers, seven florins more than for Malčika, his first wife. Then again, when that miserable creature Eva drowned herself, then, by God, the price of a third-class funeral had risen to a full twenty-three florins!'

Gabriel had heard a great deal about his father's first wife. She was born in Fiume, and was nine or thirteen years older than the old man. (Just how much older she was, the old man was never able to find out. She burned her baptismal certificate just before her death.) This dearly departed Malčika had been the cook for some retired government magnifico and their relationship went back to the days when old Kavran wore the Imperial Pioneers uniform. The old man actually started his career as river-station supervisor through the connections of Malčika's magnifico, and their love would surely have collapsed if the magnifico hadn't died and old Kavran married Malčika out of sly, peasant selfishness.

The marriage involved various matters of old gold and furnishings, and an evil sales contract was worked out on the basis of which old Kavran sold his thirty-two years to Malčika and she to him her old closets, rotted teeth, and rheumatism. For four years old Kavran repented that he had been so shortsighted as to buy a "cat in a bag," and then the Lord God himself had mercy on him and within twenty-four hours killed off Malčika, thanks and praise be to Him. The old woman died of some unidentified convulsion and everything evaporated like an ugly dream.

Old Kavran awoke from it all and sighed deeply; as he returned from the funeral, black-haired, his step elastic, still slender with strong muscular shoulders, he felt like a flower when, with the strength of its roots, it bursts asunder its bud wrappings. It was just before spring and the streams in the ravines gurgled their xylophonic choruses: tock-tock-tock-tack, tack-tack-tack-tock. Just as once before, in the provincial Maria-Theresa garrison where he served as a young corporal (when he would carefully dust his jacket lest a speck be left on his sleeve and tightened his belt by another two notches), so too, now, he pulled himself in and with the same soldierly gesture tightened his belt. Then, lighting a cigarette, he stepped out as if he were going to circle all the continents.

'Women! Young women! Masses of young women! Masses of soft female thighs and calves! I should live now, just live! So many years vainly wasted! But it's not all over yet! Live! From the beginning!'

In his deep yearning for vast, endless life, old Kavran found Maria—Gabriel's mother—and took her like some beautiful lost object that belonged to no one; he once more cooked up a new sales contract that he made with Maria's brother, a drunkard and social democrat. Maria, who had been left alone in life, a weak-blooded and transparent young girl, had prepared to enter the novitiate with the nuns in the Monastery of St. Vincent de Paul and she was . . . "divine, as if made of wax!" Whereupon this divine little wax girl was bought by old Kavran from her brother for fifteen florins, and within two days he married her and experienced with her one of the greatest disillusionments of his life. This woman was not of flesh: in place of the kind of supernatural, divine eroticism that ought to be locked in the body of such a divine girl, in place of a glorious illusion such as is born in the opium of a special creation, under the veil of the young nun there lay no secret. Nothing. A lie. An unbelievable, nunnish, wax lie! In the wrestlings of old Kavran with this wax lie there began to take shape the foundation on which Gabriel began to build his life. From then on, the lives of father and son flowed in a parallel, like two poisonous snakes dreaming of getting each other's head. And so all this rolled along for long, long years—in fear, suspicion, and wanton destructiveness.

The father, convinced that the newborn child had ruined his wife, started off hating the son. As a matter of fact, after the birth his wife had bled profusely and thereafter remained dismal, hunched-over, abandoned, in semidarkness, in tears. This was when old Kavran began running about from tavern to tavern and started drinking heavily. He would sit with the waitresses in a tavern, over hot wine, and he could clearly sense what was going on back there under the bridge. That damned house! There, in place of a young, soft woman, a tubercular nun wept as a black spider gnawed in her belly. He could feel the spider in Maria's belly. A hard back that spider had, massive, like a turtle shell; the creature would plunge deep into the womb and gnaw and gnaw! The woman would quietly weep, "Oh, it hurts so!" And her murderer, the hairy thief born black-haired as the devil, would raise a commotion in his crib. The house was full of him! "It's all damned! Damned! So what? To hell with it! Let's drink!"

· That's how it began. Later, Maria reached the point where she wanted to drown herself, along with the child. But the first time they pulled her out in time, and for Gabriel, this remained one of the strongest impressions of his childhood.

In the boy were many great and beautiful potentialities. To the rich and overrefined imagination of his deceased mother had been joined the powerful and barbaric passion of his father, who knew how to live right down to the last ounce of flesh. If life had not thrown the child into the open, gangrenous wound at the river station beneath the bridge, the little fellow would probably have lived a joyful and positive life. But as it was, everything turned into streams of tears, and the powerful melancholia of events began to undermine him the way water undermines a river bank—invisibly, slowly, from day to day.

Such was the life of the child at the river station whither they brought the drowning victims for identification and entry into the logbook. Green corpses in wet, rotted clothing lay mute on the floor of the office. Heads alongside the spittoon, mouths open, and in their hands rotted moss, weeds, algae, twigs. So too, one day, they carried in his mother; he was seven years old. He bore the secret of the catastrophe deep within him and, in that lonely house by the water, lived with it for long, long years.

Around the river station bundles of telephone wires hummed in the wind; signal lights on the railroad tracks shone and the great water flowed by. Every fall it would rise and carry off wooden building materials, hewn beams, and broken-off rafts of planks and rafters. One day the flood rose, overflowing the levee. The river station stood like an island in the roaring water, rolling along with mattresses, cattle, chicken coops, and sties in which pigs grunted and squealed as before their slaughter. Everything was knocked down and sinking; the water ground up and swallowed everything without mercy. Raftsmen, soldiers, and firemen drifted in their boats and shouted helplessly.

The flood rose. The raftsmen were wet and cursed despairingly; fear and panic were everywhere, for the water had already carried off the planks in the lumber yards, undermined the cellars, and destroyed the winter supplies of potatoes and pickled cabbage. The gypsies folded their tents in the willow groves and moved before the flood; gypsy dances throbbed, dogs howled, terrified field mice and rats scurried about, and the river station was filled with people; everyone was shouting, everyone had lost his head, and the telephone kept ringing.

· The water had undermined the levee and was still rising. It roiled about the control dams, lifted stakes and layers of stone, foamed like a rapid, overflowed and roared. Everything in the storage sheds of the river station—resin, tar, cement and matting, everything—was flooded, picked up and flung against the wooden walls of the sheds so one could hear the iron bands, clamps, and nails in the sheds groaning and squealing, as if everything were floating on rafts.

By now everything around the river station was afloat. A child drowned and as the raftsmen pulled it out of the torrent, they tore open its chest with their barbed hook. A little girl, wet hair plastered flat. A dead yellow cat and someone's worn-out black hat with a bedraggled parrot's feather were caught on the fence. Now every blade of grass in the meadows, every brace of the control dam, every lath of the fence was a musical instrument playing to the flood. Beaklike, the boats cut and plowed the vast expanse. The rains poured down and in the willow thickets the tops of the trees floated like black rings. The water overflowed the roadway, reached the threshold of the river station, and now needed only a finger to overrun the top and begin spilling into the room. In the panicky rushing, telephoning, vain shouting, Gabriel alone remained calm and collected. He kept releasing boats he made from an old, greasy opposition newspaper into the lively current that poured by the left and right sides of the threshold and burbled like a brook, and kept measuring with his finger whether the water had reached its peak. Within him was a deep and indescribable fear that the flood would stop and thus kill his one shining hope—that the water would pick up the river station and everything would float off downstream, like his paper boats. That hope looked so probable to him this afternoon, he so warmly yearned for his world to float away.

'And why shouldn't it float away? The water has picked up so many buildings and carried them away. Why doesn't it carry off the river station?'

It was dusk and they had already lit the red lamp when someone noticed that the supervisor's wife was missing. They searched for her all night, and the next morning she was found not far from the river station. She was tightly clasping a bundle of stakes, but her face was peaceful and shining, as if she were dreaming.

After the death of Gabriel's mother Maria, old Aunt Veronika, one of Gabriel's many great-aunts, came to live at the river station. The old woman was one of thirteen sisters of his long dead grandmother on his mother's side, and since most of these women had had seven daughters, there were in the family about a hundred aunts, twelve of them great-aunts. These women, in dirty flannel blouses, their heads wrapped in black woolen kerchiefs, all deeply scarred by life—knotted veins, infected wombs, hysteria, chronic toothache, madness—swirled like banshees through those sad days of Gabriel's life. On the gnarled tree of the family's founders, Maria's branch had dried up miserably, and of her seven brothers not one had left living fruit. Six of the brothers died young: four had raised their hands against themselves, one after the other in the course of three years. One was disemboweled by a machine in a factory, and one—the most talented; he had even invented a patented acetylene lamp—perished in Australia. The seventh brother, a childless degenerate with strong signs of tuberculosis, was the one who sold his sister, the "nun," to the river-station supervisor for fifteen florins.

Maria also had two sisters. One died of typhus; the other had married in the country and there had given birth to a basketful of children with fused skulls who, over two decades, died off as if from the plague. That branch, therefore, had given in all: four male suicides, one patented acetylene lamp, one corpse disemboweled by a factory machine, and one alcoholic bum. Besides that: one drowned woman, one brood hen with a basketful of children, a case of typhus, and, finally, Gabriel Kavran, a man who in his lifetime had battled with his father, broken off his studies, and become a draft evader.

Old Aunt Veronika smoked a pipe and had a deep and thoughtful temperament. She had buried three husbands, had her house burned to the ground twice, and not saved so much as a distaff. Her livestock had died of plague, and at the weddings and funerals of her children and relations she had gotten drunk so many times that she couldn't even remember how many she had. Her hair, in spite of the fact that she had long since passed seventy, was coal black and, when combed out, reached clear to her knees and smelled richly. She could recall a life when wine was poured by the bucket at fairs and whole oxen were roasted on spits; living thus upright and powerful amid these drowned women, suicides, madmen, and sick people, she walked the river station like the heroine of some ancient drama, smoked her pipe, and beat little Gabriel till his ribs were bursting. She beat the child to drive out of him the demon that had led his mother astray; then, when the whole river station rang with the child's crying, she would continue smoking her pipe, spitting to the left and right, and would explain to the drunken Kavran how it was good for a child to be beaten from time to time. It was healthy. It made the lungs and mind grow.

Aunt Veronika's spartan rule had not lasted even a year when old Kavran brought to the river station his third wife, the waitress Eva. Everyone came squawking down on Eva as though she were a white raven. Veronika had a life-and-death battle with her and then, defeated, threw the keys at old Kavran's feet and left, never to return.

Eva was a waitress whom the old man had been seeing even during the lifetime of the dead Maria. Maria had found out about his having a waitress somewhere in the city for whom he bought silk blouses, and out of this marital triangle were born scenes after which Maria, weeping quietly, would threaten the old man that she would drown herself.

"I couldn't care less! Have a good trip! I've buried a few already and I'll do the same for you!"

This Eva, in her own way, meant a great deal to old Kavran; because of her he broke with all his acquaintances, relatives, and friends. The old man had always talked freely, but about his intentions regarding Eva he had never said a word to anyone. The publishing of the banns and the wedding itself took place in secret, so that the newlyweds descended on the river station like a rocket.

The philistines and idiots in the butchershops and taverns at the bridge, all those supervisors, plasterers, tavern-keepers, "uncles" and "aunties," all of them were dumfounded over this horrible and unheard-of scandal. They just could not get the idea into their heads that old Kavran could risk taking under his roof such a "fallen woman," a waitress and woman-for-hire. And so there began to rise over the bridge a scandal black as a cloud. Of the dirty rumors swirling about the river station, an occasional word made its way to old Kavran and, like a poisonous earwig, gnawed into his brain.

It was said in the taverns that Eva was to be seen in the city with some cavalry sergeants. And it was said too that Eva was riding about the city in carriages.

'That Eva goes into the city is certainly no wonder! She's young and lonely; it's boring for her here! She goes for walks! She's her own boss! I have no right to lock up such a wonderful young wife in the river station like a bird in a cage. But about her riding around in carriages? Hmm!'

And so, when they lay in bed in semidarkness, old Kavran, feeling Eva's warm neck in his hand and smelling her loosened hair, strewn over the sheet like some blessed aromatic herb, like a miracle, did not have the heart to be firm and severe with this soft creature. He would have liked to question her cuttingly and sharply—severely, the way patrolmen question ordinary citizens when they write them up for some infraction—as to why she was running around in carriages with cavalrymen. But he could not talk to Eva like a policeman. Rather, he suppressed such desires within himself and quietly, in a muffled voice, as if begging her for a favor revealed to her in a fearful and trembling tone his distrust of everything he had heard in the tavern and of his "uncle's" complaints about seeing her in a carriage.

Eva flared up in anger; then she laughed weakly, and said that all this talk was stuff and lies, that his "uncles" envied him because she was a real lady and he, old Kavran, an administrator! They weren't of administrative rank—they were only butchers and tavern-keepers! That's what it was all about! Common envy and nothing more. And it hurt her that he trusted those people in the tavern more than he trusted her. That insulted her.

And so there began to yawn between old Kavran and the "uncles" on the bridge a deeper and deeper chasm, and the boycott the colony began to carry out systematically against madam station-supervisor actually fell on the head of old Kavran, embittering him even more in his difficult life.

And as Eva would on occasion go to the theater—'she just died for the theater'—old Kavran would sit as he customarily did at the Golden Fish and, by the second drink, an argument with the "uncles" would break out.

'They ask him where his wife is? Yes, he knows very well what it means when they ask him where his wife is. She's at the theater! Whether anyone likes it or not, she's at the theater! Yes, that's how it is! And she is his wife, whether anyone likes it or not! And if he has nothing against that theater of hers, what business is it of anyone else? Let them leave her alone. She's young, she wants to live!'

Roused by the liquor, he saw much more clearly than when sober the entire situation into which his relationship with these people had developed. 'He lives eternally alone, and there never has been anyone who was able to understand him, before whom he could lay bare his heart. Only evil, treacherous people! Insincere animals! First the old witch who had drunk his blood for years! Then that nunnish sick thing, and now these poisonous spiders. They envy him because his wife is young! Poor thing! Doesn't even dare go to the theater!' All these people seemed to old Kavran repugnant, distant, unbearable, so that he would have preferred to leave them on the spot and have himself transferred to some other river station. 'These people have poisoned his life! Adder snakes—not "uncles." '

The "uncles" pleaded with old Kavran, trying to convince him of their love and respect and to show him that the matter was such that one day he would come over to their side.

'But he won't come over to their side! There! He swears by everything holiest in the world he will never come over to their side! Never!'

• And so, without a parting word, old Kavran went out into the night, left his friends, and headed toward Eva, who was at the theater! Somewhere at the railroad crossing, he sat on a pile of rusty rails and newly hewn ties and stared down the long line of chestnut trees, watching how, between the intensely green treetops, lamps flickered and went out. Thus he waited for Eva. The night freight trains passed one after the other, lamps glowed red, and locomotives wailed, thundering across the bridge in the night. 'That means rain.' His pipe went out; it was late. Eva didn't come and didn't come. 'She can't get along without the coffeehouse, without the orchestra! Yes! She can't get along without wine! Oh, it's late! There's the train whistle again and she's still not here.'

Gabriel began to realize that matters between his father and stepmother were serious only when complications began to take on dramatic form. There appeared at the river station a mysterious "uncle," an artillery cannoneer wearing a helmet with a red horse's tail, a heavy cavalry sword, and spurs that rang like the spurs of a medieval knight. At that time Gabriel still comprehended life in decorative, incoherent patches that whirled in his brain like unfurled banners, and this knightly "uncle" impressed him as something warrior-like and terrifying. A heroic and grand sight it was when "uncle's" battery would rumble by the river station in a powerful din of cannon and dust, harnesses, chains, bronze, and trumpets clanking; when "uncle" cannoneer would come riding right up to the window of the single-storied house and stop like a giant on his white horse. The horse would snort wildly; well-fed, nostrils flecked with bloody foam, he would grind the golden bit in his jaws, pawing the earth daintily and ostentatiously with his hoof. "Uncle" would bend over, caress Gabriel, and all the while be whispering some secrets to Eva; then he would take off at a gallop after the battery while far below the bridge the trumpets could be heard.

But how frightening were the late-afternoon meetings of Eva and uncle when old Kavran was away from the river station and there was no fear that he would return because he had rowed far off into the backwaters with the surveying commission. In the room on the red couch uncle and Eva would kiss while Gabriel would sit on the woodpile in the kitchen and gnaw his chocolate, look at his reader, and pretend to be studying his lesson; actually, he didn't read a word but listened tensely to everything going on in the room behind the glass door curtained with a red drapery. On the railroad near the river station sooty steam engines beat along in white clouds of smoke, their lanterns red, while the foundations of the station shook, the window glass rattled as if from an earthquake, and all the plaster saints on the cabinets, the cups and platters, the kitchen, the room, the glass door, the threshold—everything thundered, trembled, and creaked, and plaster dropped from the ceiling in flakes and black holes gaped.

One day his father returned unexpectedly and everything burst into flame—a common coachman's brawl, with chairs broken, plates, glasses, and dishes shattered. Uncle split open Kavran's head so that he bled profusely, tore his coat under the armpit and at the elbow, and threw him to the ground and trampled him. That evening Kavran, wrapped completely in bloody bandages, beat Eva until she bled. Thus hell began at the river station.

From that day on, every blessed evening old Kavran would carry out an inquisition as to whether uncle had been there or not.

"Where did the little one get this candy wrapper?"

"I don't know! How would I know how he got a candy wrapper?"

"I'm asking you, where did he get the *candy wrapper?*"

"I don't know! What do I know?"

"So that's how it is? You don't know? You don't really know?"

Then a rough, cruel slap. Eva wept.

"You damned roughneck! Disgusting old man! How do I know about his papers? He brought the paper from school!"

The father grabbed his son brutally, bloodthirstily. "Listen here, you little bastard! Pay close attention to what I ask you! Was anyone here at the river station this afternoon?"

The boy was frightened. His father held him in a vise and his murky, bloody eyes bored right through him. If he admitted that "that man" had been here, there would be trouble. A terrible beating, blood, wet compresses and towels, weeping and sobbing all night long. Then in the morning Eva would beat him. But if he didn't admit it, his father would beat him. What to do?

"I don't know! I didn't do anything, let me go!" The child wept under the inquisition and was terrified by this testifying and interrogation, this police-like collecting of information.

"Get out, you disgusting, revolting, lying brat!" The father shoved his son away so that he struck his head against a cabinet. "Get out! You're all lying to me, all of you ought to be murdered! To have your throats cut!" howled old Kavran, tossing a chair so that it shattered to pieces and pacing the room up and down, threatening and wild.

Or the scene with the celluloid soldier's star: "Where did the brat get this celluloid star?"

"I don't know! How would I know how he got it?"

"I'm asking you, where did he get this celluloid star?"

"I don't know!"

"So that's it? You don't know?"

Slap!

On another occasion, hunting for the kitchen knife to kill Eva, old Kavran found in the table drawer a toy nun. The little wax figure, wrapped in black cloth, had been bought by Eva for Gabriel two years before as a plaything, but the old man in his excitement almost went mad over the black rag.

"So this is it? In place of my hard-earned bread you stick a toy nun in here? Do you think I'm so stupid I don't know what this means?"

"God Almighty!"

"Not another word, do you understand? You're not fit to kiss the foot of that poor woman! Do you understand me? She was a saint!"

"Ha!"

"What are you leering about, you grinning garbage? Yes! She's on your conscience! Here, kiss her, because you're not going to live another minute. You destroyed her, you damned bitch!"

Eva kissed the rag-nun in deathly terror and wept. Gabriel joined her.

"What are you yowling about, you jackass? What? Where were you this afternoon—running around again with the dogs? Come over here and I'll give you your dogs!"

And so it went constantly. Deathly terror and beatings. Beatings today, beatings yesterday, eternally nothing but beatings and weeping in the corner. And the next day once more would appear uncle's costumed figure, and Gabriel would sit on the wood in the kitchen and listen through the glass door to the muffled whispers and wouldn't understand a thing. Once more in deathly panic he would suspect that every step on the gravel in front of the river station might be his father. 'And what if it is? Again those two wild men will beat each other bloody and bite each other and roll in the mud in an insane bundle out of which Father will get up with blood on his lips and everything will be red. Arms and lips—everything one single red smear.'

. This suppressed horror reached an unbearably high pitch on those wild drunken nights when the old man came home stirred up by wine, powerful and wild as a rockslide.

Oh, the terrifying depths of those fathomlessly dark nights when, in the room soaked in pipe smoke and stuffed with furniture, his father and Eva argued. In that jam-packed space voices mingled in muffled groans and the two animals in bed were constantly talking half aloud, as if trying to whisper so the child wouldn't wake up. But the child was awake—actually, more awake than that drunk and the poison-filled madwoman who laughed and cried at the same time.

Old Kavran, inflamed with alcohol, realized the horror of his life and how everything was in ruins. 'Everything is ruined. And this animal, this tigress, this pig, this creature who had ruined him, won't even confess! If she would only confess, then it would be possible to start over again! But to live like this, in mud, lies, filth, and shame!'

To Eva it was laughable, incomprehensible, and stupid that she should have to confess and that by doing so anything would be essentially changed. She pondered whether it would not be best to save herself from this drunk immediately, the very next day, and so, in an hysterical fever, she laughed and cried. She felt how Kavran's iron fingers clenched her limbs tighter and tighter, hurting her cruelly. She wouldn't let herself be tormented like this, she jerked away and wanted to jump up, but the old man stopped her and knocked her back with a strong blow on the breast.

"You're staying here! Where are you going? Don't whine! Did you hear me? Don't whine!"

Gabriel would listen to the muffled blows and Eva's voice as she whimpered under his father's hand; then he would cover his ears and press his head into the warm darkness under his pillow, as if to prevent the blows from falling on him. He would close his eyes tightly and be afraid to open them, and there above the pillow, in the room, the voices would rise. Eva wouldn't let him; Eva shrieked; Eva jerked away and ran, but the old man caught her and sent her reeling onto the bed and beat her head against the headboard. Eva would moan, whimper, wouldn't surrender herself, scratched, bit, and foamed at the mouth. Then all would be lost in whispers, tears, and hysterical laughter.

And so it went, on and on. Gasping, wrestling, spitting, then once more voices, a whisper, a laugh, a sob, and, from time to time, a wild beating of legs against the bed so that it seemed as if the bedboards would break; then again half-voices and whimpering and muffled blows in the belly. All the covers crumpled, all the pillows scattered, the mattresses torn. Such was the night. Into the room on such a night would fall a feeble ray from the red lamp outside that wavered in the wind and signaled high water, which since the night before had been rising again. The crimson light poured into the room. In the berry-red, ruddy, bloody semidarkness Gabriel watched two bodies biting and flaying each other alive, until everything would sink and drown into a leaden exhaustion. Gabriel would still be lying wide awake when nothing was to be heard any longer except his father's deep snoring and Eva's wheezy, painfully fast breathing.

Gabriel lay wide awake and thought about the cricket that piped up from the kitchen and about the bird that chirped far off somewhere above the water. Outside, the water rumbled black and powerful, the way it had rumbled the night his mother had been carried off into space and darkness. The wind had blown and beaten his mother's linen blouse, and, wet, it had glued itself to her flesh and he had sensed the icy black stench of the high waters into which his mother strode deeper and deeper.

The love plot of this tale of the river station wasn't exactly interesting, and it ended up stupidly and somewhat comically. Gabriel Kavran had fallen in love three years before with Miss Sorge, a philosophy student; he violated the young girl's innocence and madly tormented her in accordance with all the principles of so-called pure, sacred-springtime eroticism, and then abandoned everything and disappeared like the wind.

Miss Sorge was the only child of an industrialist who worked in the forests with several thousand slaves, operated many hundreds of miles of his own railroad line, and thundered in the leading banks of northern industrial centers. All the young lady had really experienced until then had been the realism of Russian novellas. She had studied abroad—more out of some coquettish capriciousness than from necessity—and thus she became acquainted with Gabriel Kavran at the time of most dangerous ferment, when the charges of spiritual mines explode and blast all bridges into the air, and when one wades into extremities with the same ease with which one floats on a midday sea, convinced that with two or three strokes a man can reach the horizon. To Miss Sorge, Gabriel seemed to be a hero who wasn't just thought up in a Russian book, but actually existed; the struggle of this hero did not seem to the young lady to be false, but noble and ideal: for whole nights he would engage in bloody battle with metaphysical specters, with the stars, with Bakunin, Pan-Slavism, Europe, God, and Marxism. The romanticism of this intense experience seemed to Miss Sorge gigantic; she threw herself into a floodtide of books, manuscripts, theses, and syntheses, and began to drift with the flood of youth in the warm ecstasy that is always born when the primrose and the pussy willow bloom. It was beautiful to keep vigil for long nights, to argue about the Middle Ages, which, behold, are just coming to an end in our own time, to fight till blood ran, to weep, to kiss until the morning bells rang, and to listen to the chirping of the birds at dawn.

. Suddenly Gabriel was called for military service. 'He, a free citizen of Europe, drafted!' The woman tried to convince him to go through with this soldier's comedy, to give in out of love for her, but he would not listen. He had decided to defy force and to leave, and she had to make up her mind, let the chips fall where they may! If she was so cowardly and lacking in character, let her stay by herself! He was going! That was that!

. Miss Sorge was terribly frightened. What did it mean to go off to an unknown country? It meant eventually "to die of starvation" there.

"Then we'll 'die of starvation'! If you're not a tramp, a nothing, if you're a human being, you won't leave me at the first crisis! That would be disgraceful! And if you're afraid of starvation, the hell with you. What kind of person are you anyway?"

In the course of this insane struggle and debate, Gabriel wrote the young lady a letter telling her she was sabotaging his intentions, that he had no desire to drag a mummy around with him, that he despised her, and that he wished her much idyllic happiness—at this point his pen punctured the paper and everything was blotted with ink—and he left the country. This all happened in the same order and tempo as is recorded here. They met, had their death struggle, lost thirty pounds, argued about problems, about character, about the International, and finished off the novel in the very first chapter.

Gabriel then lived like a tempest, not giving much thought to the whole affair. First there were the struggles in high school, then the first political betrayals, then the first police encounters, the first times in jail, the first published articles, the editorial work. So who, in the midst of this, could think of the woman as well? Gabriel was then busy with the idea of starting an anarchist weekly, and he couldn't understand how it was possible that the girl whom he had crushed as a locomotive would a pedestrian could hesitate about anything. What was there to hesitate about? Here existed an organization that stripped a man bare and stuffed him as a recruit into a barracks, like a sack. But he wasn't going to be a recruit or a sack. One had to go away to the Swiss cantons, to the French Republic, across the ocean, any damned place where the air was clean, where there weren't Hungarian gendarmes or police, or the sleepy liberalism of this place that rots away in editorial offices! Yes! But she was a capitalistic brat! She had a greyhound with a collar and little bells, a coach, servants, an asthmatic father, Badgastein, Baden-Baden, she . . . it was understandable—she! Anyhow, to hell with her!

Afterward it turned out that the young lady hadn't gone to hell but remained buried deep inside the young man. Not only had she taken his heart but all three ribs below it, so that under Gabriel's left breast gaped a deep wound that he dragged about with him all over Europe. He wandered, suffered injury and pain, but that shining, naïve girl became for him a symbol of everything clean and sunny in his life. When he was convulsed in torment, he would recall how he had destroyed her with his own hands.

• Having returned after three years to his river-station home, Gabriel was drinking one night in the city at the Golden Locomotive with two old comrades from the editorial offices of the *Liberal Word*, and it was there that he found out Miss Sorge had married. Gabriel was somewhat intoxicated by the wine and he wanted to tell his comrades what those three years had been like for him and what he had gone through. He wanted to tell his story simply, to present everything just the way it had happened, but it all seemed so grim that he himself took fright at such grimness; he felt that behind each of his words lay much more about which he wasn't speaking, that there existed areas that he himself didn't want to examine too closely. Finally, as to the fact that he had once jumped from a bridge and that the police had pulled him unconscious from the water; that he had wound up in prison and there become acquainted with strange men—nameless figures from the underground world who stood on the borderline between madness and crime—that he had spent some time in that underground and nameless world (he touched upon all this with a bitter-sweet smile); bah, what about it, ultimately? It's all part of life! And life is strange! At first glance anything in it seems improbable, but then, when it happens, it seems perfectly natural and logical that it happened —as if it could not have happened otherwise!

"Yes! And everything that had been horrible, yes, literally horrible—now all of it, looking back at it, from here in a tavern, over a glass of wine . . . ah!—" 'A man can't say anything! He would like to express himself, to underline certain things, but when it comes to the point of saying it, of finding the right word, it disappears! Why? How? Fear rises up in a man lest he say too much! There is an openness that is out of place even over a glass of wine! And a man may talk too much!'

So they drank and the night was late; slowly, in the wine, the border was passed where people dig and dig down to the bottom of their own bloody gut, where they put their nerves and heart out on a dirty table in a tavern, when they seek the last and final confessional truth that corresponds to their sufferings and is as strong and palpable as the very suffering itself.

The conversation wove in and around various events and persons and became snagged finally on the personality of the editor in chief of the *Liberal Word*, Dr. Drahenberg-Drakulić. Gabriel's comrades told him terrible things about this man: shady transactions, thefts from the printinghouse, huge dishonest lawsuits, political infamies and scandals. Gabriel listened; to him it was all remote and stupid.

. 'What have the deep and filthy lies of Dr. Drahenberg-Drakulić and his ambitions and infamies to do with him? That he had ruined this man, undermined that one, by intrigue cut the throat of X or Y. That he had betrayed and besmirched the ideas of certain efforts and movements, or that one day he had sold out everybody just like Judas! And that he was stupid, shallow, and ignorant, and that there was so much infamy in his threatening and dangerous stupidity.'

All this had nothing to do with Gabriel. He knew his two comrades, Petrek and Sturm, very well, and he knew they were soft and corrupt men. He had always felt a certain sympathy for such men, incapable of living. Dr. Drahenberg-Drakulić, head of a well-known law firm, politician and editor in chief of the *Liberal Word*, had made slaves of these friends of his, had trampled over them and outgrown them, and although they had been classmates from the same high school, he today was a banker, a chief, a personality, a master, a politician, while these friends didn't even have enough money to fill a decayed molar. Finally, to Gabriel Kavran all this seemed so natural. 'That a man in an environment such as ours attains some social standing doesn't really require any particular ability. In fact, just the opposite. It is impossible for men who are really gifted to be able, under these circumstances, to affirm themselves!'

And now here was Petrek telling him this same Drahenberg had married.

"So he got married, eh? And who married the wretch?"

Sturm replied quietly that Miss Sorge was the one who had married the wretch! At first he had thought of saying: "Bet you'll never guess who Drahenberg's wife is!" But this had seemed stupid. He tossed out the fact itself much more easily than he had thought he could.

Then he fell silent. Gabriel thought he must be drunk and joking. But Sturm, leaning on the back of the chair, let out fat puffs of smoke, one after the other. Everything had stopped short, still as wax figures, and no one laughed as Gabriel expected. In the silence, after a pause, Gabriel rose and went toward the stove.

Halfway between the table and the stove he turned. "Sturm! Is that so? Goddamn you! It isn't true!"

Sturm looked at Gabriel with great sympathy.

For a moment Gabriel stood in the middle of the room under the lamp; then he went on to the stove as if hypnotized. There on the wall hung a well-known oleograph that people from

Kranje sell at fairs and celebrations for three tenners, called
. "Adam and Eve Sing on the Hill." Depicted in the oleograph
was a symbolic stairway of life up which Adam and Eve were
climbing, in the role of husband and wife, through life's various
pleasures and pains. Thus Adam and Eve kiss in the moonlight
while a nightingale sings above them. Next, framed in a heart,
Adam and Eve stand as newlyweds before an altar, the bride in
white silk with a wreath of myrtle, and as the priest binds them
with the stole and the holy sacrament, two naked cherubs can
be seen on the altar forging the wedding ring in the furnace of
love into an unbreakable link. Then Adam and Eve sit by a
lamp and a stove, a cat purrs, fire flickers in the grate, one sees
there is great happiness. And then again, a silver anniversary
with grandchildren, and a golden anniversary with great-
grandchildren and the grave. All these pictures, framed in ellip-
tical hearts, are arranged in a wreath around a central vision of
Eden, where, in an equatorially lush garden, Adam and Eve lie
naked, above them the tree of good and evil. Around the tree of
good and evil is wrapped the green snake of Lucifer with a flaming tongue.

Gabriel stared at Adam and Eve with the apple for a long
time. He recalled how, when still a snot-nosed child roaming the
taverns with his father, he had always contemplated with awe
this tropical Garden of Eden and the naked couple in it. Then
it hadn't been to him some bad provincial oleograph on which
the two printings overlapped (indeed, Eve's nude flesh came
out reddish-orange, like a bloodshot egg yolk), but an Eden of
an incomprehensible secret and mystery. This same picture, this
same "Adam," this same "Eve," and this same Golden Locomotive! The old man would buy him a dry bun for him to choke
over here in the corner, while there at the table the cards would
fall. Ace of clubs! Queen of hearts! Seven of spades! Ace of
hearts! Today it was all exactly the same: Life hadn't shifted by
as much as a hair. Clubs! Spades! Only black cards!' He stood
like that in the corner near the stove, staring at Adam and Eve,

and everything seemed to him idiotically stupid and sick and picayune. He shrugged temperamentally and returned to the table with a strong, heavy step. He wanted to strike the table with his fist so that all the glasses and bottles and rolls and plates would fall under it, so the boards would break in some barbaric crash. But this, too, seemed idiotic to him, so he sat down quietly and resignedly.

Gabriel smiled convulsively and tensely, irritatedly. Then he became serious, tightened his face into a sullen and hard expression, so tight that the wrinkles made furrows all the way to his lower jaw, poured out a glass of wine, and drank it down without offering any to anyone.

They were silent as they drank. After a while Petrek began to tell about Miss Sorge and what had happened to her after Gabriel left—how she had tried to poison herself, how she had broken with her father, how he had disinherited her, how she had been left out on the street, abandoned and alone. . . . That she had broken with her father cast the whole love affair into a completely new light. This was what their whole disagreement had revolved around, this so-called father of hers!

What does a father mean? Gabriel had broken with his father while still in the third grade, so he considered it illogical that she couldn't do so at the age of twenty. But she could not, and she had struggled fiercely for her father. When Gabriel had broken down all her arguments—the importance of a profession, of studies and a career; the need for comfort and conveniences and some financial security—when, after endless nights of argument he had convinced her that it was necessary to meet things head on and that meeting things head on was the only salvation, that it was necessary to be thrown out on the street, become a beggar, starve, sacrifice oneself, suffer but remain firm and not give up, only then did she realize that this was how it was and how it had to be! But she just could not conceive what her father would do if she went off with a draft evader. It would break his heart! He had already had heart trouble for so long.

She'd kill her father. And she just could not become a parricide. And so she broke with Gabriel and then, after all, she had broken with her father! The damned old man had died! Then she had poisoned herself, been left out on the streets, and become Mrs. Drahenberg!

Because of all the facts, all the romantic excitement, the wine and sleepless nights, because of something that caught painfully in his throat like a fishbone, Gabriel rose and wanted to rip open his shirt! To get a breath of air! But inside the tavern there was no air. The small low room reeked of greasy boiled goulash, spilled wine, dirty tablecloths. From his miserable masquerade costume—his father's vest and trousers—came alien odors, a peasant stench of sweat and another body, the stink of tobacco and old unaired closets. In the clouds of thick tavern smoke Gabriel felt a gripping ache piercing the center of his belly, tying it into knots, and slumped as if he were going to faint. Then he got up and ran out down the rickety wooden stairway into the darkness.

. Outside there was no breeze, no air. Everything was saturated in thick early-spring mists in which people steamed like samovars and rain dripped down, thick and heavy as oil. Somewhere a tied dog dragged his chain back and forth along a wire, and one could hear how the chain screeched along it. In front of the fence, on the street, passed masked figures in groups, strumming guitars and yodeling: it was carnival time. Gabriel stood in the rain, water dripping down his neck; he inhaled deeply to ease the pain in his stomach. Then he realized suddenly that he was in darkness, his hands raised over his head like some immaterial apparition. The first object he noticed was the milk-white lighted glass of a square window that wasn't completely closed, so that in the yellowish light one could see an iron toilet bowl with a handle and chain. The iron bowl, the handle with a chain, lifted him out of his state of darkness; in a single moment he sobered up, collected his wits, and went back inside. He had thrown himself down those stairs as if he were rushing off never to return, but he did return, wet and beaten. 'Toilets, guitars, dogs on chains! And up there in the tavern they are waiting! Where else is there to go?'

Once more there was a long silence; then Sturm leaned over and caressed Gabriel on the head.

Gabriel threw off Sturm's hand. "Let me alone! I'm not being sentimental! Only there is a time when a man has to think things over! It doesn't matter anymore! How stupid that everything in life turns out even more stupid than it has to be! After all, why shouldn't I tell the truth? Believe me, every word is the absolute truth! Here it's been three years since all that happened, and by God, in those three years not a single day passed, not a single night that . . ."

Gabriel's voice stopped and he swallowed his words; then, lowering his head to the table, he became silent. Sturm once more began to stroke his hair, from temple to neck, as if he were smoothing the nap of a dropped hat, and Gabriel, like a sick cat, surrendered to it, not protesting the caresses.

"God, how I loved that woman!"

"And she you," said Petrek decisively, recalling some scenes of how Miss Sorge for a whole year waited for a letter from Gabriel that never came.

"Yes! And she me!" laughed Gabriel bittersweetly. "And she me!"

"Don't blame her! She was reasonable and correct! Why didn't you send her one single word—just one? You were wrong!"

"Right or wrong, it doesn't matter! But it's the truth, so help me God! In those three years everything happened to me. I was in gambling dens and prisons, but I always thought of her as a lamp! Why should I lie? There's no reason to lie! If I haven't killed myself, it's only because of her! And because of her I came back. Yes! Only because of her I returned! She is the only reason I can come up with when I ask myself why I really returned. Yes! She! And that is the only truth in this whole affair! Here it is, three weeks that I've been dragging around town like a lame dog, and I haven't had the nerve to come to you because of just this eventual possibility! I was afraid, like some snot-nosed high-school kid, 'that my beloved had married'! And this afternoon I babbled nonsense with Petrek, we chewed over idiocies, but I didn't have the strength to ask about her directly, like a man. Grotesque! Stupid! Unworthy! Men! Believe me, to me it doesn't matter any more! I am totally indifferent to it all! I'm even ashamed that I could have been so terribly stupid, so weak —yes, I'm ashamed. . . ."

"It's not good to spit on one's illusions! Anyhow, it is a shame! Hey, girl! Give us another liter!"

ᐟ And so they downed another liter—their eighth—and then ordered a ninth. Gabriel waved his arms and his head filled with blood. "But it doesn't matter! Poisoned herself or not, it doesn't matter! Let's drink! To your health!"

And whereas he had been quiet the whole evening, now he felt the need to talk. To talk an infinite amount. To drown in words what in reality he was: inexpressibly powerful even to be still alive! "Almighty God! Tell me, what is death? Why is it so difficult to die? It's been three full years now that I've been kill-ing myself day and night, but I still haven't finished the job! And everything seemed so complicated, but in the end nothing was complicated—it was all clear as day. To me it's as clear as if I were looking through a magnifying glass!"

Thus he began to speak broadly about life and its relation-ships. It would first of all be necessary to straighten out the concept of subjectivity, the concept of the essential "I" that is buried in the center of ourselves like the point on a geometry compass, with the whole circle of our awareness revolving around that center. "I" means a system, an organization, a me-chanical apparatus that functions and operates according to a basic plan. But we weren't born as machines! We were born as lumps of anarchy, bloody lumps of fleshy anarchy, and it took a long time to develop and work out and reconstruct ourselves into machines with our own central "I", into this central something that now guzzles sour wine here at the Golden Locomotive, sentimentally, stupidly, because of some unattractive, lying, snobbish, soft, corrupt female.

"Wait! Where did I stop? Oh, yes! We were talking about our 'I.' What is this 'I'? This anatomical shape of mine, thirty-three vertebrae in a wavy, crooked spine, neck bones, a skull, and two hemispheres of brain in this skull like two hemispheres of pickled cabbage in a dish. Is that it? This? This damned Golden Locomotive, nine liters of wine, two gentlemen of the press: Mr. Sturm and Mr. Petrek! Very well! You, gentlemen, here at this table, turned upside down in the camera obscura of my eyes and then set right side up again as normal, on your feet! So then, everything is normal! Everything is as it should be! This is all that exists—this, plus Madame Drahenberg-Drakulić née Sorge! So that's what you're telling me, my dear fellows! That's good! Everything that exists is what exists here! But what then, when it's gone?"

"Nonsense!" Sturm replied. "When it's gone, there is nothing! Nothing is equal to nothing! Let's drink! I see that all this is nonsense! To your health!" He raised his glass, outraged and tired, feeling indeed that all this was nothing but sophism and stupidity.

· "What a bore!" declared Petrek. "First of all, we aren't called upon to resolve these questions! Secondly, they have already been resolved, in so far as there is any solution. And thirdly—and this is most important, my friends—what's necessary is to live! To live is what's necessary! And not to stand around like this, fruitlessly, up to our necks in sick inanities! One must live!" The tone of his voice expressed his longing for a life that would yield more than beaten straw.

"There is no necessity to live! Absolutely nothing is necessary! One ought to think intelligently, with crystal clarity—that's all that's necessary. Do you think that in me too there is not a primitive need for life? It is always rising up just when I want to think something is finished! This babbling of Petrek's about life is a dialogue between yes and no! I don't want a dialogue! I want to follow my own individual, original concept. I want to think exclusively about what is when it is not! Friends! Perhaps this seems to you stupid, old-fashioned babbling; in the end it all may be out-of-date, but believe me, I've been tormenting myself over it for three full years."

Into the room burst a mob of masked revelers—rowdy, costumed figures, muffled deep basses and shrieking drunken hysterics shouting, beating chairs, tambourines, and bottles. Song, laughter, and smoke.

· Through the clouds of greasy stench, under the low sooty rafters, everything seemed even more suffocating and close. In the shouting, shrieking, and smoke, Gabriel sensed clearly that he could not control the rudder of his thoughts and that everything was sliding off somewhere and slowly evaporating into emptiness, into a murky emptiness that he himself felt to be utterly shallow and meaningless. He wanted to say something fundamental, crystalline, clear, but it became lost in stupidities, and even he himself wasn't sure as to how to formulate it. It had to do with Miss Sorge; about his wanting to die! What? How? The Golden Locomotive! People in costume! The problems of personality, the subject, the object . . . "These damned barbarians! But Sturm, why are you looking at me that way? Your look bothers me! I don't want you to feel sorry for me!"

"You're drunk, my friend! You're drunk and I'm drunk! To your health!"

· "I'm not drunk at all! I know exactly what I want to say! I was talking about the self! About the ultimate meaning of Me. About the facts that make up Me. Who am I? What am I? I'm a disgrace! Even when I jumped from the bridge and the police dragged me like a dog from the water, even when I was torn by incomprehensible animalistic unbearable pain; and now and forever, always one and the same: a nothing!"

The drunks began singing, "Hey, hey, I'm not by myself!

There are six or seven of us on this shelf!" In the corner by the stove under the picture "Adam and Eve Sing on the Hill," Sturm, who began to sing with them, spilled a glass of wine and ordered three coffees. A hundred glowing alleluias to him!

But young Kavran frowned even more and, gathering the skin of his forehead between his brows into two vertical furrows, he stopped his ears with his fingers so as not to hear the shouts; thus he stared at the dirty, wine-stained tablecloth on which were embroidered blue and red leaves of ivy and liverwort. Firmly determined to stick as closely as possible to his line of thought, he continued to talk to himself about all the minuses of life that have to be subtracted in order to remain a zero. If everything were subtracted, then one would remain a zero! Women, illusions, lies, sick nerves, exhausted body, everything —then one would remain a zero. Because zero is a larger number than minus! The process is called subtraction! Minus three minus a minus three equals zero. One learns that as early as the sixth grade. But minus legs, minus arms, minus woman, minus head equals zero! The thought arose, off to the side, tiny, insignificant, that he was still young, that he could still begin all over again! Because it could also be true that to die doesn't mean the subtraction of minuses, but their addition, and that to die doesn't mean to get closer to zero, but precisely the opposite, and therefore to be even further removed from all positive life potentials: from women, from youth, from motion! Yes and no! Eternally that yes and no!

'How stupid all this is! Here he is, in love like a high-school kid, and he is a coward and doesn't know what he wants! Here he is! For two full years he's been carrying a revolver in his pocket—he paid twenty-one francs for it—and nothing! He suffered, shamed himself, demeaned himself, reduced himself to filth in taverns, got drunk. And nothing! It was a fact, he couldn't do anything!'

With an involuntary movement, young Kavran reached into his pocket and pulled out the revolver; only when he felt the cold steel in his hand and saw the sparkling barrel, only then did it occur to him that what he was doing was tasteless and comical and sickly exalted. 'What sense can it make in front of these people?' At the same moment, excited and ashamed, he wanted to conceal the revolver again in the worn rags of his clothing, but Sturm, laughing loudly, jerked the weapon from his hand, unexpectedly and with extraordinary roughness.

. "Funny! It's so funny!" Sturm laughed, as if from some capricious whimsy, from wine, from nervous irritation. 'Can it be that this pale, tubercular child is waving a revolver around in front of everyone? As a matter of fact, it doesn't seem too improbable!' So he jerked the revolver from Gabriel's hand and, out of a deep need to turn everything into laughter, into a farce, he fired three times into the wall over the heads of the masked group at the table in the corner near the stove. The detonation of the shots resounded sharply. Women began to shriek in panic, everyone jumped to his feet, chairs were overturned, several bottles broke, the tavern swarmed, and from the wall, with a loud crash, the glass of the picture "Adam and Eve Sing on the Hill" shattered.

Through the tavern, through the nervous dance pattern of sweaty, painted flesh, the feverish movement and shouting, through it all wove a bluish veil of smoke in thin horizontal lines. Everything reeked sharply of gunpowder. Someone had left open the glass doors of the outer room and from it the band could be heard still playing, for itself, "Evening on the Sava," always that selfsame "Evening on the Sava."

"Where do you think we are, goddamn you? This isn't Mexico! Someone call the police! A scandal! The police! Show your identification, who are you?"

A storm of excited voices rose and several moments passed in arguing and debate, as Sturm struggled with figures in costume ('He wouldn't surrender the revolver because he was an anarchist, and he would always continue to shoot where and when he pleased'), and as the police took the revolver away and some drunken patrolman came along and wrote down the names of everyone present in a rumpled, greasy notebook. Then the revelers paid and disappeared, and in the empty tavern the friends sat down again at the table and continued their conversation about women, love, and death.

Gabriel plunged deep into murky, unmoving resignation. He was exhausted, because in the course of the day an immeasurable mass of impressions had been heaped upon him, and each of them had driven a knife into bare flesh. First of all, the city and his uncertainty the whole afternoon as to what he would and would not find out in town. Then some crisis or other of Petrek's. Then this powerful wine and smoke, and the late night, all thickened into heavy, impenetrable mists.

It seemed to young Kavran that he heard thunder somewhere in the distance. When the conversation had gotten around to how Miss Sorge had become the wife of Dr. Drahenberg-Drakulić, he had tried to gather all the strength of his mind to direct himself toward saying something pregnant and clear. He wanted to explain to his friends how he hated and despised this woman, but at the same time, that red-haired female thread was the thread that still kept him alive. But he could not express himself. He felt how everything was too enormous; how it suffocated him so that he could not speak, simply did not know what to say.

'But nonetheless, it seemed that he bore part of the responsibility for everything that had happened. He was volatile, capricious—one could even say he was hysterical! He hadn't written a word to anyone! Why had he not written? Here she had waited a full year for word from him, but in vain. And not only that! She had even borrowed money, broken with her father, and gone looking for him through the cities of Europe like a madwoman!

'Comical! And how he had searched for her! There wasn't a city in whose streets he hadn't gone running after her! He would catch sight of her and go after her, but she would always evaporate! These men tell him she had been in London two years before! Perhaps it really was she! Oh, that night! That London night!'

That evening he had walked, bent and helpless, lost in the midst of desire and masses of stone. He was so dispirited that he felt like the sick, wired-up tree on the street, wrapped in rags and covered with posters, rotting away buried in asphalt—that miserable tree, draped in soot and yellow mist! He stood thus beneath the tree and was completely lost in desire and vague half-thoughts, when it seemed to him he heard her voice. Dazed and downcast, he raised his head and actually, there, in a fiacre, she sat. In a brown outfit, with a fur hat; copper-haired, pale!

He wanted to shout but his voice stuck in his throat. He wanted to run but could not make himself move. After the three seconds it took to recover from his vision and for it to be incontrovertibly clear that it was really she, he started to race after her, but it was already too late—the fiacre had disappeared in a maze of carriages and automobiles. Since, at that point, eight major streets intersected, he ran down the first, then returned, and then down the second, down the third, down the fifth, and finally, completely out of breath and sweating, collapsed onto a bench. Right next to the bench stood a small, unattractive woman, with plastered-down hair. She stared down the street into the purplish electric lights gleaming in the twilight. The tiny woman was sobbing loudly. She had one rotted, black front incisor and beautiful eyes; her tears fell in streams.

The woman told him how her husband had died, how she had been left pregnant, and how now everything was in ruins. She worked in a wholesale textile firm and constantly suffered, along with her child.

They went to have a drink of punch and afterwards to her place on the seventh floor. This was the first woman whose body young Kavran had touched after long deprivation. Late in the night he sat on her bed and listened to the small, unknown child as it breathed under the coverlet. The room was semidark, a clock ticked away, and an oil lamp flickered before a crucifix.

He had the feeling of a black space full of night's darkness, an enormous place made of black London stone; and here, within this stony mass, in a garret on the seventh floor, on the bed of a tiny, unknown snaggle-toothed woman, he was, a half-naked madman in a high fever, who today had run through the streets after an hallucination, a vision. It was night, the child breathed, and somewhere immeasurably far away a river was flowing, a bridge stood, dogs barked in a willow thicket, water rumbled. There, in a far-off river station under the bridge, had breathed just such a child, who now on this seventh floor stared into the darkness and was filled with pain. Perhaps that night there awakened in him the sick passions of his dead, drowned mother; or perhaps there was some other reason for everything. He rose, and a few minutes after that patrolmen dragged him from the water under a bridge.

'What hellish stupidity! That had been no vision! She had really been in London then—perhaps somewhere in the same quarter, not a hundred yards from that bridge, she had been weeping in some hotel room the same night! What hellish stupidity!'

. And so they drank and talked about political action, about psychology, socialism, the mankind that was to come but that was not to come; that, according to all principles of progress, absolutely must come, but that would by no means come because it could not. If mankind could come, could develop, then it already would have developed!

Sturm tearfully started lamenting that something definitely was wrong, that something simply had to be done somewhere else! Because the way people live here is a terrible, filthy, scandalous shame. As he lamented and drank, one could see his black rotten teeth, eaten up by nicotine and all sorts of things. He spoke in despair of how something had to be done within twenty-four hours. Some action could still save the world. "Action! Some enormous, gigantic action, like Bakunin's! That could pull everything out of this stagnation and rot. They ought to plant mines under the whole city! Yes, let the water swell, let everything be carried away—that would clean it out! That would bring in new forms and new relationships! A high-style catastrophe! They could hang a man! They could shoot a man! They could spit on him, nail him to a cross! But the man would keep saying 'Forward' to whole generations! A man could be a symbol, if today there were only men of backbone, will, daring! How wonderful it would be to die that way! But today's men have no backbone! Men are bums, cretins, thieves, nothings! And I'm a bum and a cretin—the world's biggest bum!"

Petrek, on principle, opposed the notion that action made any sense. Action made absolutely no sense! He said this from experience. In high school he still was not sure. True life does not consist of action—true life is hidden and invisible.

"That's not true! True life is not hidden! It is clear and loud! If we were to destroy everything around us that is stupid, we would live much more worthily!" howled Sturm, and it seemed as if it were not some after-midnight phrase shouting out of him from too much wine, but as if it were really so—that he really believed in a more radiant, more worthy life.

"No, Man is within us, not outside us! It's all a strictly psychological problem!"

"That's a lie!" raged Sturm. "What the hell kind of a psychological problem?"

"You're trying to tell me it isn't a psychological problem? Am I nothing? Does my experience in life mean nothing? Didn't I want to destroy? Am I not as destructive as you?"

The waitress, tired and sleepy, listened to the drunks as they argued, and begged them for the tenth time to pay, because it was late; but who would pay attention to a waitress in the fires of polemics about a psychological question?

"There are no psychologists here, my dear fellow! Let's put our cards on the table so we can see how things stand! You're a cheat! You lie when you say you're destructive! You're too cowardly for that! You have no backbone!"

"You're drunk! You don't know what you're saying!"

"I'm not the least bit drunk! On my word of honor! Right away, girl! Wait! We're going, right away! Just a little longer!"

"Gentlemen! Please! It's after two! If the police come we'll be fined again! Gentlemen, I have to close up!" The waitress became upset and blew out the lamp. In the room the semidarkness was broken by a reddish light coming from outside through the curtains on the glass doors.

"What's your hurry, girl? What's your hurry? Here we are, celebrating the return of a prodigal son! A prodigal son who wallowed in pig swill! God! What stupidities don't we have in this world? The legend of the prodigal son!"

. So they paid and bought another three bottles. Each took one with him out into the night. A north wind had risen and was ripping apart the fabric of clouds, so that the stars in the dark patches of clear sky flashed by at great speed, like sparks from the smokestacks of a steam engine.

Sturm raised his bottle to the heavens, to the stars, to the clouds and telephone wires, and toasted God, Idealism, the Golden Locomotive, everything! "My dear resplendent stars, we are phantoms! All phantoms! Comical scarecrows, fools, idiots, sick! But you, my dear ones, are powerful! With you the so-called Lord God plays as with little glass bottles! Long life! Long life! Your health!"

Sturm waved his bottle and spilled wine over his clothes, over his head, over the mud. Behind him staggered Petrek and Gabriel; a patrolman on the corner stopped and stared after the drunks: 'Where were these three wine-brothers going?'

Gabriel had drunk a great deal, but the alcohol had not taken hold of him. He heard every single word of his comrades accurately and precisely and he knew what they were arguing about, but he was so bitter and unyielding—the feeling of exalted bitterness ruled his whole being—that all this bickering seemed insignificant, petty and superfluous.

'I'm unyielding—men must be unyielding toward "everything

earthly," as though they were composed of higher matter! None
of this has anything to do with me! It's all pure romanticism!
It's best when a man is brutally unyielding. That's best!'

For a long time they searched for the keyhole at Petrek's
quarters, lighting wine-soaked matches; finally, along a winding,
rotted wooden stairway, with great noise and clatter, they
climbed up to his room.

"Shhh! Shhh! Don't let anyone hear us! There'll be another
scandal!"

· Meanwhile, the whole house did hear them and in every bed
tired people, lighting smelly candles, cursed them: who could
this be at this time of night, what kind of drunken pigs are they
to wake a man from his soundest sleep just before dawn!

· In front of Petrek's door, Sturm lost his grip on his bottle and
it fell and broke. The wine gurgled down the stairs like some
humorous orchestral motif, and they all roared with laughter.
Inside, Sturm immediately stretched out on the bed, fully
dressed in his winter coat, scarf, and hat, draping his legs over
the head of the bed; his hand, holding a burning cigarette, hung
down as if a corpse lay on the red and white striped bedcover.

In a surly mood of depression, Sturm recalled his mad, hysterical wife who, when he got home, would make a scene: "You,
like this! You, like that! You this, you that! You ought to sink
into the earth out of shame in front of your own children!"

'Why, yes! There's something to that! It isn't exactly respectable or manly for a father and family man to get drunk! Hell!
That damned room, everything reeking of piss and lying around,
torn apart, thrown about, filthy, disgusting. That so-called wife
of his, that ex-chorus girl who sleeps till noon and smokes one
Egyptian cigarette after another like a mummy! And the brats
playing balloonist on the chandelier! Oh, that damned circus
that's called his home! The fundamental social unit! Why
wouldn't a man become an anarchist? That gilded theatrical
rococo furniture! It's hell! And the editorial offices are hell! And

to lie here like this, fully dressed and drunk, is hell! It's a mad-
house!'

And so Sturm, out of a powerful need to remove the strait-
jacket of his real and imaginary bonds, threw his hat in the corner, then his scarf, then a shoe; but the second one wouldn't
give. Having relieved himself to a certain extent of his burden,
he began to wail for a cup of coffee, for just one single cup of
coffee!

Gabriel, huddled on the couch, listened to Sturm's lamenta-
tion over his failure of a life: how he had foreseen very well and
accurately who and what his wife was! But he hadn't been able
to do otherwise! Simply couldn't! A man is young and stupid!
And the woman had thick legs—they had bothered him from
the beginning! And she made eyes at every damned devil! So
what? A man gets drunk once and finds himself in the soup! . . .
"To your health, men! It will all pass! Let's drink! Bottoms up!
Oh, for a single cup of coffee!"

'Boards! Those long boards in the floor. Just to nail up the
whole problem in four such boards like the ones here in the
floor and everything would be over with!' Gabriel thought about
those boards and stared at the room in the shaded, dark-yellow
light. Black coverings, ugly colored flowers on the walls; it
seemed to him as if all of them were already nailed up somewhere inside four boards and as if everything here was dead and
in the grave. 'These are two dead men, and he knows the two of
them well! One complains about his wife and the other is a
fool! But what about himself? He had lifted one of the boards
and gone wandering off somewhere outside. But this evening he
had returned. To this wine, to these boring, futile conversations
lasting endlessly through the night, among dead men who take
off their shoes and smoke cigarettes. This evening he had returned to all that. He had wanted not to return! He had wanted
to get out of all this for good! But the London police had pulled
him back! And he had been soaked through and the water had

run from him in streams. His shoes and clothes, everything soaked! They had given him a glass of warm milk to sip! Yes! Miss Sorge! Dear Miss Sorge! Here, he's come back!'

Gabriel laughed out loud at himself. How strange it sounded for someone to laugh aloud in the gray room where just one single candle burned.

The drinking spree at the Golden Locomotive had been on Friday night. On Sunday morning, when Gabriel was not at the river station, Dr. Drahenberg's doorman brought a letter for the young gentleman. Old Kavran accepted the letter, but when he gave it to his son, Gabriel, without a word, tore it up and threw it away. That night, as father and son prepared for bed, he told his father that in the future he was not to accept any letters for him from anyone!

On Tuesday, Drahenberg's doorman brought another letter, early, around seven o'clock. Gabriel was still sleeping. The old man accepted it and opened it in the office—skillfully, clerk-wise, with a heated knife—and then sealed it again.

In the letter Drahenberg-Drakulić, in the name of his wife and himself (always referring to himself as "we"), repeated his invitation that Gabriel visit them. "We salute you and beg you to be so kind as to come to see us at our home. . . . We wonder that you have not answered our friendly invitation, and we hope this was only an oversight. . . ." When the old man, around noon, handed the letter to his son, Gabriel tore it up, unread like the first.

"Who brought it?"

"A doorman!"

"What kind of doorman?"

"What kind? You already know very well what kind!"

"Listen, old man! In the future, please do *not* accept any letters for me! Not from anyone! Do you understand? I've told you for the last time!"

"Yes! But the man wanted an answer! I couldn't wake you up!"

"Then, you could have written the answer yourself! Why should I do it?"

"What do you mean?"

"You know very well what I mean! It's quite logical: he who reads letters ought to answer them as well!"

"Has someone twisted your head! What's with you? That gentleman, the doctor, was always so good to you!"

"That has nothing to do with you! And it's a disgrace, opening other people's mail! I could take you to court for that!"

That was true! It was clear to old Kavran that by opening someone else's mail he had violated some law, some regulation. For that one could wind up in court! But then again, he was really curious about what it could be that the gentleman, Gabriel's former employer, was writing his son—a man who in the past three years had been to the river station several times and shown great interest as well as sympathy for the young man's fate.

And so two days passed. The third day—a day of rain mixed with thick heavy snow—a fiacre stopped around two-thirty in the afternoon in front of the river station. Gabriel, who had been drinking the whole previous night, had returned at dawn and was still lying in bed. He heard the wheels of the fiacre as they sank into the gravel and it crossed his mind that most likely the engineers and the commission had arrived. Commissions always ride in fiacres. He listened to his father's voice in the river-station office, and yet another voice, strange and unfamiliar to him. Then the door from the office opened and his father came into the room. With servile, river-station-supervisorish movements, full of peasant fear and awe, he approached Gabriel's bed and, excitedly waving his powerful, large arms, whispered to his son that the doctor had come and was waiting in the office.

"Tell him I'm sick. I can't see him! I'm in bed!"

"But I already told him you would get up! I beg you, son, be sensible!"

The situation disgusted Gabriel and he got up. He put on some old, worn slippers, pulled the collar of his coat around his bare neck, and, still sleepy and unwashed, opened the glass door to the office.

"My respects, my dear sir." Dr. Drahenberg-Drakulić smiled kindly at Gabriel, having, with a single trained glance, circled the whole room with its scattered bedclothes, worn quilts, dirty plates on the table, old bread, the lamp, coats, bad air: the poverty.

"My respects!" Gabriel shook hands sourly and coldly with this repulsive fool in his fur greatcoat and pointed toward the couch from which he had just thrown some blankets full of feathers and stench.

"Please, sit down! I didn't know—"

"Please, please! Just the opposite! I should be the one to apologize! But I really didn't know how to get in touch with you!

Everything stopped. Gabriel stared at the expensive fur coat, at its soft, brown, glistening hairs, at the jeweled tiepin. He didn't know what to say.

"What do you think! Should I open a window? It stinks here!"

"I don't think that's necessary!"

"Nevertheless, it stinks. The whole night is concentrated in this space."

And so Gabriel got up, went to the window, and opened it wide. Outside, the snow was falling thick, ravens were cawing in the poplars, and the carriage horses steamed. Everything was gray and muddy.

Dr. Drahenberg studied Gabriel's figure from the rear, lost in his father's flapping trousers, in the worn slippers—a ghost, a consumptive ghost, not a young man! The doctor felt a sort of loathing, then again a certain nuance of pity for this young life, and, tapping nervously on the arm of the old couch, he thought of lighting a cigarette, of saying something. He was nervous and distraught and it upset him and somewhat offended him that he should be so shaken. Gabriel stood at the window. A damp mist blew into the room and wrapped itself around him like a wraith.

"Cigarette?"

"Thanks, I don't feel like smoking! My tongue is swollen like a cow's tail from tobacco!"

"But you'll permit me?"

A pause.

"You'll catch cold like that, Mr. Kavran! It's chilly here!"

"Oh, please! 'In a hundred years all is forgotten!' It makes no difference if a man catches a cold or not!"

"My God, that sounds resigned! Of course! For your age that's too resigned. That's Buddhism!"

"Not Buddhism, doctor! That was said by a quite 'modern' writer, with whom your so-called 'modern' generation is especially taken!"

"So? 'In a hundred years all is forgotten!' I have no idea who it could be!"

"It doesn't matter anyhow! But it's the truth! In a hundred years there won't be this fur coat of yours, or your tie, or your jeweled stickpin! And if that is so, then what is left for a man to do if not simply to die? That's not Buddhism; it's a 'statement of fact.' "

" 'A statement of fact.' Not bad! But why are you so macabre? Why so gloomy? You're still young, my dear sir! There's a whole life ahead of you! What sort of resignation is this? Where is your 'Hymn to Man'?" (Gabriel had been in the last year of high school when he became acquainted with Dr. Drahenberg. The doctor himself had never written much—in all, a book of anticlerical verse the high schools read and religiously, unswervingly believed in: that the host was simply baked dough, that there was no God, and that there were popes who had had relations with women. Thus the doctor, in the eyes of the high-school community, became a literary authority, and Gabriel Kavran had brought to this literary authority his first writings so the doctor might tell him if they were worth publishing. One of these poems had been called "A Hymn to Man" and it spoke of China, of the Pacific, of steamships, of latitudes and longitudes, all based on Nietzsche's motto: "*Zu nahe ist mir Wolkensitz, ich warte auf den ersten Blitz.*" The doctor published the poem, paid Gabriel his first honorarium, and thus introduced him to Parnassus.)

· Gabriel stared with distaste at the green-eyed man with gray, slicked-down hair sitting before him on the couch, and didn't know what to say to him. From outside could be heard the ravens cawing and the carriage horses pawing the gravel with their hoofs; mists blew into the room so that the breath froze and words became stuck between the two men, like the axles of broken wheels. Then Gabriel coughed loudly and blood rushed to his head.

"Close the window! You'll catch cold like this!"

"It doesn't make any difference! This is t.b.! There's nothing left to catch cold!"

"Then allow me to close the window if you won't! Because with that cough of yours, it's all the worse like this!" Whereupon Dr. Drahenberg rose, shut the window, and then returned and sat down on the couch, falling into a heavy, motionless silence.

Gabriel felt his hands sweating and an icy sweat pouring down his spine; trembling with cold, he drummed on the table with his fingers, on the checked shiny cloth, so that the tips of his fingers stuck to the oilcloth as though smeared with glue. By passion and temperament spiritually stronger than the doctor, he had always been able to manage their treacherous relationship simply and easily, with a certain smiling superiority. Now he could barely keep himself from bursting out and destroying the whole comedy of this miserable silence. 'But this is too much! Let him say what he has to say!'

"Sir, please don't be surprised if I ask you something that has no connection with poetry and my 'Hymn to Man.' Tell me why, in this stinking room, we've been hashing over all sorts of nonsense for three quarters of an hour?"

Around the doctor's lips appeared the shallow, barely noticeable wrinkle of a smile, actually the shadow of an ironic smirk. He felt how much mockery there was in Gabriel's repetition of that foolish "Hymn to Man" and it became clear to him that all this roundaboutness was stupid and comical, and that it would be best if he proceeded directly to the real matter. He recoiled coldly and, becoming serious, said firmly: "If you please!"

"Tell me then, sir, why did you come here to the river station?"

"Why did I come? I came in reference to my wife! You no doubt know . . ."

"Yes! I know! And I feel that in this matter every word between us is superfluous!"

"Permit me, my dear sir, only two or three words! I, surely, would not like this to come to a quarrel between us, which, if we look at it objectively, is a capricious thing at best! Certainly not that! And secondly, the matter is not exclusively yours, or even mine. There is a third party involved."

"What has that got to do with me? This so-called third party has absolutely nothing to do with me! I simply won't discuss it!"

"Your position is insulting, my dear sir! I didn't come here out of some personal whim—I have never believed in explanations—what, after all, can be explained in life? But if you please! This mission was confided to me by a person very dear to me, who means a lot to me. . . ."

"Permit me to say that in this matter neither you nor all your 'very dear persons' mean absolutely anything to me!"

No matter how firmly Dr. Drahenberg-Drakulić had resolved that at all costs he would remain cool and not lose his temper, and that he would stick fast to his line of thought, he nonetheless was unable to control himself. The blood poured into his brain; he jumped up and wanted to bang on the table; but at the last moment he got hold of himself, went around the table, and swiftly walked toward the window. He drummed with his fingers on the window glass and stared at the water, yellow and swollen. Silence fell. In the river-station office, on the other side of the glass door, one could hear old Kavran cleaning his pipe, coughing, wheezing and spitting. The unseen presence of his father noticeably upset Gabriel.

'That old jackass is listening from the other side!'

After long minutes of silence, the doctor returned to the couch, stood face to face with Gabriel (so that Gabriel could see the fresh hairs already beginning to pop from beneath the freshly shaven skin) and said, more intimately and quietly: "Do you know that after your exalted, unclear-to-everyone flight, Madame took poison?"

"Yes, I know! And I poisoned myself, but I stayed alive! Millions have poisoned themselves and remained alive! So what?"

"Yes! But Madame's wasn't an operetta poisoning! For a long time her life hung by a thread!"

Gabriel felt a deep need to say something drastic to this man, to grab hold deep inside the doctor's intimate life-nakedness and all the simulated staidness and strength that held the fool upright, to break him and smear him with filth. 'Her's wasn't an "operetta" poisoning! What did he mean by that, that her's wasn't an "operetta" poisoning? What kind of shabby remark is that? Was his own, perhaps, an "operetta" poisoning? Is everything in his present appearance from an "operetta"? "Your exalted and unclear-to-everyone flight"! "Her life hanging by a thread"! To hell with it! Stupid remarks!' Gabriel felt there was so much bitterness in him that with it he could fry this man, the way you do a bedbug with acid. If only this conventional idiot would give up and go away. But nonetheless, he was as if paralyzed and could not speak a word. He stared at the flecks of light crawling about the glossily smooth and strikingly white starched collar of the gentleman doctor. He stared at the gold filling gleaming beneath the brush-trimmed mustache, the gray wrinkles under the eyes, and the furrowed skin around the Adam's apple in the throat that moved about in the triangular opening of the collar secretively, here and there, like some sort of under-the-skin creature.

'Here he is, a monstrosity of flesh, fur coat, diplomas, and civic honors, this fool here before him, his former so-called chief, to whom he owed a thousand crowns—patron, protector, he talks to him here at the river station about her having poisoned herself, about her life hanging by a single thread! And she, this same "she," is now his wife!'

To the doctor it seemed that the situation was changing, that the scales were tipping in his direction, so he sat down once more on the couch. Leaning forward, he propped his elbows on his knees, and, crooking the ends of the fingers of each hand so that the fingertips of the right and the left hand kept touching each other (in rhythm, as he slowly drummed with his fingers), he began to speak with a surer voice of how Madame had wanted to die, and how this was one more undeniable proof of the unforgiveable frivolity with which Gabriel had played with her life back then.

"Did you, my dear man, have the faintest conception of this woman? Did you give any thought to who she was, from what circles, environment, upbringing? Good God almighty! You brought catastrophe to a good, simple child who played Chopin and read the Russians and who didn't have the slightest idea of what life really was! A little girl with a governess and a greyhound! You wanted to make an anarchist out of an immature young gentlewoman!"

"That isn't true! But even if everything really were that way, so what? What business is it of yours?"

"I understand that all this has nothing to do with me! But it does have its social and legal aspects! Don't you know what it means in this society to be a dishonored girl cast into the streets?"

"What?"

"What? That! Precisely that! We're not living on Sirius, you know! We live within certain specific social relationships! That you personally, for yourself, have ridden roughshod over these social frameworks and relationships is, my dear fellow, certainly your own affair! But you had no right to drag with you anyone too young for such views! Nonetheless, once you did it, you should have remained consistent and gone further."

"And does the lady think that way?"

"We're not talking about this or that lady now! We're talking about the world we live in! We're talking about views and the manner of viewing certain social forms and obligations! However, why so much talk? Here, please read this letter!"

So nervous that one could see his hand tremble, Dr. Drahenberg pulled from his pocket a wallet in which were many slips of paper; rustling through them, with two fingers he pulled out a gray envelope and gave it to Gabriel. On it, above the telephone number and cable address was printed in red script: F. S. Sorge D.D., Lumber and Lumber Products.

Gabriel's hand ached, his thumb began to throb; shrugging his shoulders, he opened the letter:

"My dear Doctor:

"If at the outside I stress to you that this letter is being written by an unhappy father who has lost everything he has in the world, his only child, you will understand everything. It is in all likelihood known to you that my only daughter, Ljiljana Sorge, is maintaining a liaison with a certain person employed at your newspaper. Should I be right in my notion that you are acquainted with this person, then I beg you to inform me who this person really is, and whether it is true that he was sentenced to seven months in prison for forgery and theft. His name is Kavran, and as far as I have been able to ascertain, he comes from the very lowest social levels—his father a servant, his mother a waitress or some such."

The letter went on to describe in detail the whole love affair as seen through the eyes of the industrialist and businessman F. S. Sorge D.D., and, from it all, it turned out that Gabriel was some sort of moral degenerate, someone who had ruined the "unhappy only child" of industrialist F. S. Sorge D.D. with calculated premeditation. The father therefore wished to obtain from the most reliable and most authentic source proof that this was a case of a common confidence man who had consciously seduced a minor.

He would like the doctor—both privately, as head of the newspaper, and officially, as the head of a legal firm—to give him his opinion about the whole affair, because he intended to turn over everything to his attorney and bring the affair to court so that at least the stain could be formally erased from his daughter's name. The letter ended on the sentimental note that the doctor would surely understand the heart of "an unhappy and bereft father" in this last attempt to save himself from the despair and shame that had fallen upon his "gray and honorable head."

At first Gabriel was reading word by word, the way one reads letters; but then he began nervously to skip, and ran his eye all the way to the signature; then, wanting to go back, he could not find the place he had stopped and became lost in the sentences. He made out clearly the purplish-gray color of the paper and the knotty letters, but sank under the unexpected tangle of all the possibilities and combinations about which he had never given a thought.

'Why, these are phrases, common sentimental phrases; stupidity, comical, arrogant stupidity! Not even stupidity! It's a scandal—filthy, dirty lies! False assumptions from the very beginning! Ignorance of the real situation, senile, bourgeois feeblemindedness. It is true—he never had dealt with her as a social creature. What environment? What obligations? What society? What home? He personally had destroyed his own home! He had no home! Had fought with his father, been left out on the streets, fed himself by hack writing, so it seemed logical to him that the woman who wanted to be his wife go the same route. These middle-class provincial prejudices! If she wasn't in a state to break with even these middle-class trivialities, she was not mature enough for anything! It had been spring then, the earth had given off a perfume, and her voice had been so warm and soft. . . .'

Gabriel cast a sullen glance at the doctor.

"What does all this mean?"

"What should it mean? Does it mean nothing? It means that you're so blind and egocentric that you see only yourself in everything."

"This is all moronic! What does she say to this? I don't understand any of it! What do you want with this whole comedy? Or do you, too, want to deceive me?" Gabriel wanted to shout, to jump up, to bang on the table with his fist, but he was so weak that he had to lean on the table top lest he fall over backwards. Outside on the railroad tracks a train thundered past and the whole building shook like a mill.

"Why are you getting upset? I don't want to offend you! I personally respect you and have no reason to lie to you! I would like to establish certain facts. Only those facts can destroy the attitudes you entertain toward me, and also toward Madame! Why won't you believe that my intentions are sincere? I beg you! Please sit down! Only for a minute!"

Under the influence of those calm, assured words, Gabriel sat back down in his place, his only feeling being that his legs were as ice-cold as a corpse's.

"Well, then. Receiving this letter, I thought it would be in your interest to do something serious about the matter. I therefore answered the old man with this. Please! Take it!"

The doctor handed Gabriel a second letter he had already

been holding ready between his thumb and index finger, beating out with it a rhythm for each word he spoke. Some sentences of this letter were underlined with blue pencil and the margins were filled with notes, but in the letter itself there was nothing of special importance. The doctor had written the old man that Gabriel had never been sentenced to jail because of personal crimes but because of politics; that his father was not a servant but the supervisor of a river station; and that his mother had been dead for fifteen years and she had not been a waitress but a nun. The letter stated too that young Kavran had always been an outstanding student, was majoring in philosophy, and was a co-worker on one of the most respected newspapers in the country; that he was a talent in whom everyone placed the greatest hopes, and a reliable and firm character. On the basis of all of this, therefore, the old man's assumptions must fall apart, one after the other.

The dry, legalistic tone of the doctor's letter had a solid, calming effect on Gabriel. 'Actually, the doctor in his letter hasn't done anything more than enumerate certain facts under first, second, and third. By enumerating the facts and signing the letter, he refuted the whole filthy idiocy.'

. "If you please. After that letter, there developed a correspondence between me and the old man, and, if it interests you, I have brought those letters with me! Here you are!"

The doctor placed on the table before Gabriel several of his own letters, and again several in gray envelopes with the printed title of the wholesale firm of F. S. Sorge D.D. The young man couldn't restrain himself and, after a moment's hesitation, began to rummage through the letters, to pull them out of their envelopes and then put them back again the way they had been. Thus by chance he opened one in which the doctor had written the old man that he guaranteed Gabriel's character with the full conviction, too, that he considered the young man completely worthy of the trust Miss Sorge placed in him.

On reading this letter, it seemed to Gabriel that what was

written here was not only a courtesy, and that this man before him was good and upright. He had always had a low opinion of the doctor and practically despised him, but here he had nonetheless taken his side. Because of some softness in his nature, Gabriel wanted to say something to demonstrate his willingness to listen further and admit he had been wrong in protesting against a full discussion; he wanted to find within himself a confidential and warm tone. But he could not squeeze out a single sound.

And when the doctor began to speak about letters Madame had written him from an Austrian sanatorium, and when Gabriel caught sight of her handwriting—the round, slanted letters, the violet ink, the familiar strokes of the hand—the letters began crawling over his brain like scorpions, and everything grew dim. A cousin had informed Miss Sorge of the doctor's correspondence with her father and had sent her copies of several of the doctor's letters, whereupon the young lady had thanked the doctor for concerning himself about Gabriel and emphasized that she would be happy to be able to shake his hand—a man who, out of all her acquaintances, was the only one worthy of being called a "man." This was when she lay pregnant in a sanatorium, when she had almost bled to death and paid for everything with her life.

Deeply affected by the knowledge that this woman had become pregnant and had almost died, Gabriel felt as though everything were empty, as if he himself were a lump of flesh out-of which all the nerves and senses had been cut. He withdrew into some lifeless, hollow dimension in which, to be sure, he did note that the doctor's lips were moving and that the doctor was saying something. But compared to the fact that Miss Sorge had become pregnant, what he was saying seemed completely inconsequential.

'The poor child! She too had borne her cross! She too had found herself out on the street, humiliated, alone! She had had her fill of suffering! And who was to blame? Only he . . . he!

No one else, only he! What has happened? Where have I fallen to? Into a river station, by the water, under a bridge! See, over there on the cabinet tremble an earthen Our Lady of Bistrica and an Our Lady of Lourdes, the water rumbles beneath the bridge, a steam engine rushes by; everything is moving away, everything is infinitely distant, nothing can be reached any longer.'

. Dusk was falling. Outside on the railroad line the signal lights were going on, and in the river-station office old supervisor Kavran was walking about. Then Gabriel sat down again in the corner by the stove and everything became still. A long silence. The room was so icy that the men's breath hung in the air, but to Gabriel it seemed steaming hot.

'What does this man want of me? He wants to inflict new wounds. He speaks so humanely, so Christian-like, but in fact he has a hellishly dirty plan. Why is he sitting here? He's stripped me completely. He's made me what I am! He was the first to publish my idiocies and declare me a talent! He lent me a thousand crowns! He took in off the streets the woman I had ruined! He's staring at me here as if I were naked. He's staring right into my gut! He's picked off every scab from my body and I'm sitting here one big open wound, anatomically laid bare. And what green eyes this man has. He's grinning! His lips are red! He's planning to do something with me.'

Just so! The doctor lowered his voice by a whole octave and, lighting another cigarette, spoke slowly and surely, as if everything in him were in order and he now was only putting together the elements of his schemes according to a plan. He spoke of the real state of affairs, of how now nothing more could be done—that it would be best to accept things as they were and resign oneself to them. He spoke about how Gabriel could return to the editorial offices of the *Liberal Word* and he would count the past year as if Gabriel had in effect worked there, and that he would place him on leave for yet another year so he could go away somewhere to a sanatorium to cure himself and get well. Now he was too worn out to go back to work. His strength was sapped.

When Gabriel had finished reading the last of the doctor's letters to the old man in which the doctor, under first, second, and third, had enumerated certain facts, there had been a moment when it seemed possible that he would get up, offer the doctor his hand, and everything would be wiped out with a single handshake (it would of course, have been false and conventional, but still, a handshake is a handshake, and everything would have taken on a certain formality). But it didn't turn out that way. The pregnancy, the crises, the poisoning, the break with her father and the travel—this woman's sacrificial and senseless tearing herself to pieces was a world apart from this unsympathetic and shallow fool in his fur coat.

'Why, this man is an ox to think he can buy him off with two years' pay! If only she had married anyone else but this very proper barrister! This jurist! Because that's what he is—a crafty jurist! He's a man who writes his letters in duplicate—one copy to send, and the other to present in court! A common provincial lawyer's trick! It is true, he did write that letter, but the question is, with what intention did he write it? He had given the woman money, he had planned well on getting the money back with interest! And he got it! Now he even wants to buy *him* off with that interest!'

Gabriel laughed aloud, a laugh that rang out like a saber when it is drawn from its sheath.

"Why the laughter? What does it mean?"

"Nothing! It means nothing! To me this is all a bore. I think it would be best if you and your wife just went to hell! What does all this mean to me? Both you and your wife!"

The night before, when the doctor had analyzed all the possibilities, it had, it is true, occurred to him that matters might take this turn, but he hadn't taken this variant as worth considering; what is more, he hadn't even mentioned this eventuality to his wife. But now it appeared that this young criminal was looking for a fight, and he regretted that he had softened. 'He had wanted to be human with an animal, and the contemptible creature spits in a man's face.'

- "Excuse me, sir, but I simply don't understand any of this! All these letters of yours—it's very touching, of course!" Gabriel riffled with one finger through the letters scattered on the table near the stove, and once more laughed with the same challenging tone. Equally sharp and bitter.

"Sir, if you will permit me, it is not the least bit proper or gentlemanly of you to twist everything around like this! If you had even a single crumb of objectivity, you would realize you are wrong!"

"At the very outset, if I don't deceive myself, I said that I consider all of what is going on between us superfluous. But as far as the 'right' side is concerned, you are a doctor of law and a 'jurist,' and you surely know better than I what is 'gentlemanly' and what is not! I will grant you that I am not a 'gentleman,' and that I am wrong!"

"It isn't necessary for you to keep stressing the matter so much, my good man! We've met here to carry out certain formalities! It was my wife's particular wish that this formality be carried out, and I unconditionally accepted her opinion. And now, just one more thing, please. I am to extend to you my wife's greetings. She begged me to greet you and to request that you come to see her tomorrow afternoon at five. I think I have finished."

The doctor gathered up the letters and began to put on his gloves.

"Tell Madame I won't come!"

"Very well! Thank you! My respects!"

The doctor took his hat from the couch, bowed with conventional severity, and left with a quick and energetic step. Gabriel could hear him conversing with old Kavran outside in the office, the outer glass doors clanging, the horses' hoofs sinking into the gravel, and the fiacre pulling farther and farther away. He had not even responded to the doctor's farewell. He remained motionless at the table, keeping three fingers on the same spot of sticky oilcloth on which a moment before had rested the doctor's letters. He stood thus for some time. Then he went to the couch and sank down into it. It was quiet. One could only hear how, under the bridge, the high water rumbled.

All that night Gabriel drank. Just before dawn he came upon the old man at the Golden Fish. Between father and son there developed an argument in the tavern that nearly ended in a fight.

"Do you think I didn't hear how rudely you behaved? You ungrateful ass—instead of kissing the man's hand, you were rude! Nothing will ever come of you! You're a freak, not a man!"

"Shut up, old man! Drink, and to hell with you! You gave birth to me—you take the blame!"

Gabriel felt the deep hatred that radiated from his father's every word, and he had no desire to make things worse. 'It's all the same! To hell with everything! What good would it do to have it out now with the old man too?' And so they paid and left, and the whole way home, staggering from left to right, the father lectured his son about how it was already time he pulled himself together and came to his senses, because the years were passing. And it wasn't respectable of him to chew out the doctor —only dogs do that. And if he were respectable—as he wasn't— if he had eyes—as he hadn't—he would have to admit that the learned doctor was pretty smart, and that everything he had taken him to task about at the river station was true.

It was getting light and the water rumbled menacingly. Gabriel listened to its roar and to his drunken father as he told him he was a nobody and a nothing, a moral and material failure, and thought about how all this was small and insignificant compared to the inexorable spinning of the globe. 'See, a bluish light is spreading over the globe. The day grows with the mechanical precision of a machine, and compared to this, what is the meaning of these people who spit on one another and throw mud on each other and torment each other? Fathers like his, and such sons and wives! And the day comes up, the light grows brighter, clocks in bell towers ring out—three o'clock, five o'clock, nine, twelve, three, five. Exactly five o'clock in the afternoon, when she had sent for him to come. Well, she had sent for him, but he wouldn't go! Never! Never! Nothing ever again!'

And so it was. He slept until three in the afternoon and then went to the Golden Locomotive. He stayed there for two full days. Three liters of wine, five liters of wine, seven liters of wine, cigars, rum, coffee with plum brandy, cheese, rolls, chocolate, then again three liters of wine; and through this there penetrated only one strong awareness: that the globe turns like a wheel and ceaselessly moves away from that one single possibility, from that glorious five in the afternoon when he could have . . .

'Anyhow, where is it? It's fifty-seven hours back! Fifty-nine hours! It's all trampled, smashed. New possibilities are beginning; one needs to live!'

. And thus he once more drank for three nights and slept until afternoon because the old man didn't come to throw him out of bed—he wasn't at the river station. During the last twenty-four hours the water had risen above normal and the engineers feared it would undermine their levees on the upper backwaters; work was going on there full steam.

So he woke before dusk and had scarcely gotten up when someone knocked timidly on the door of the room. He had already, half asleep, heard the glass door of the office open, but he had thought it was someone who had come to the river station looking for the old man or to make a phone call, when the knock came.

This is how it went.

When Gabriel opened the door and saw that into the room

was coming a woman in fur and that that woman in fur was "she," he moved back three full paces before this apparition; feeling behind his back with his left hand for the table in order to get hold of something solid, he felt something firm between his fingers. He grasped this object with both hands and clenched it so convulsively that it broke, cutting the flesh on his little finger so that it bled.

There occur in life moments in which events condense into small dramas built on exactly the same principles as the great dramas in which kings play the heroes and blood flows. It is the same elemental life that rips open its own belly and then stiffens in the despairing panic of the emptiness of knowledge—the catharsis of nothingness. Thus Gabriel felt that here at the door, entering the room, was the incarnation of all his dreams, a figure through whom he could see right to the bottom of all things; and here a toothbrush breaks in his hand and everything is mockery.

· To Madame Sorge Drahenberg-Drakulić this man seemed pale, like an old religious painting she had seen somewhere long ago in some church; having caught sight of this greenish-pale, drained mask with deep, black eye sockets, of this man shouting incomprehensible words on his knees, she shuddered, through her veins began to flow fire, and, carried away by a momentary tide of high fever, she began to weep loudly and despairingly, as in hysteria, her nerves contorted.

Gabriel let the broken toothbrush fall; it did so pathetically, like a battered ensign falling before total defeat. At the same instant he wanted to recall Dante's passage about the great pain when, in misery, a man recalls happy times, but in Gabriel's brain everything was muddled and so there came to him only the last half of the first verse: "*nessun maggior dolore . . .*"—oh, hell! Then there was the moment when the crusader Godfrey of Bouillon saw for the first time the walls of Jerusalem. Jerusalem! Those were moments when one had to fall to one's knees! Here one must also fall and bow down! Jerusalem! Jerusalem!

And so he crawled on his knees to the lady, embraced her knees, thighs, hips; she lowered herself to him, and thus they remained, on the floor, leaning back against the couch. This lasted for some time. She had forgotten that she still hadn't asked Gabriel why he had not answered her invitation, that she was on the floor of a strange, terrible, disordered, filthy room, even that three years had passed, full of suffering and distress. To her it seemed that nothing had happened, that those three years had never existed; that the two of them were what they had been in the beginning—innocent children; and that life was just beginning and everything was one great, incomprehensible, triumphal secret.

In the river-station office the glass doors opened and one could hear old Kavran's heavy boots as they sluggishly and wearily thumped along the floor and headed this way toward Gabriel's door. Gabriel was so dazed that he didn't realize until the very last moment what was happening; his father was already turning the knob as he wrenched himself from the embrace and leaped up. The old man did not find him with the woman who had pinned herself against the red felt of the couch, but the situation was clear to him. Dusk had begun to fall and the room was half dark, so the old man could not make out precisely who or what sort of woman it was sitting on the couch. But by the fur and the fine perfume, it seemed to him he had seen this lady before and that it could be the gracious wife of the doctor herself.

Old Kavran stopped as if struck dead; then he proceeded, bent and heavy, to the table and began feeling about with his hands over the oilcloth, as if he were seeking something.

"Where are the matches?"

"I don't know!"

The old man continued to feel about the oilcloth disconcertedly; the room was so quiet one could hear the tips of his hard, calloused fingers as they slid over the slick surface. One could hear his wheezing, and he mumbled something unintelligible.

Thus it was for some time; then he turned and slowly left, slamming the door rudely and demonstratively.

The woman had wanted to jump up, to shake herself to her senses, to fly from the room, but she could not. Her knees were numb and her whole body had dissolved into helplessness, and so she remained on the couch, having constricted her breath and lowered a heavy veil over her face. She dared not breathe, her heart beat in her throat like a hammer, and she felt as though the heavy, clawlike, iron-nailed thumb of the old boor was scraping over her whole body, painfully, shamefully.

'Lord God! He's even going to light the lamp! Anything but that! Anything but that! Oh, Lord God, anything but the lamp!'

Then, when the old man had not lit the lamp and afterward disappeared beyond the door, she heaved a deep sigh, rose exhausted and crushed, went up to Gabriel, and grasped him feverishly by the hand.

"In the name of God, please, let's get out of here!"

· Gabriel stood next to the table, his head bowed, and stared at the white and blue squares of the oilcloth, at the hot plate, at the coffee cups to which were glued damp crumbs of bread; he stared fixedly at those crumbs and filthy objects like someone who really wasn't there.

"Gabriel! Please! Let's get out of here!"

And so they left, without a word. Old Kavran was sitting in the river-station office, his face turned toward the white Swedish stove. He did not even look around at them, spitting contemptuously into the coal bin in the corner.

The woman was trembling like a bird; thus they went down the road; the mud was deep and thick. Neither of them was able to speak the first word. They maintained a melancholy silence and shivered with cold, and when they had already drawn near the trolley and the monotonous tinkling of the bell on the horse's neck could be heard, she pulled herself together and, pressing his hand warmly, said that that evening she would be at the costume ball.

"My darling! Till we see each other again! Everything is at stake! Everything!"

She had pressed Gabriel's hand so warmly that it was clear as the sun to him that he would go to the costume ball and that everything would be resolved there.

When Gabriel returned to the river station, he found his father sitting at the big table, a candle lit before the mirror, his legs spread wide, his face smeared with soap; he was shaving.

Gabriel was tired; as though drained dry, he collapsed onto the couch to rest for a minute. But the old man rocked forward in the chair and then back to see himself better in the mirror, and so the chair, old and battered, creaked. The light of the candle flickered restlessly. The idiotic, apelike gestures of the man pulling on the skin under his chin and throat like a rubber eraser and scraping with the razor the bulging flesh, pushing out the flesh of his cheek from within with his tongue—all this upset Gabriel.

'The old ape! He still hasn't gotten enough out of life! He's shaving now so this evening at the Fish he can chase after some waitress.'

Gabriel's hatred of his father rose to such a pitch that he could not understand it. The entire time he had been in the city he had spoken with the old man very little, practically not at all. The tension between them had increased so much that it needed only a single spark to set off the mines of explosive piled up over the years. Gabriel did not want to look at his father— the bald, bare head, the glistening skull, the gray hair gathered in a wreath at the back of his neck, the grimaces in front of the mirror—shameless leering—and so he turned to the wall and pressed his eyelids shut. But the old man kept whistling, coughing, snuffling, cursing half aloud, getting up every moment and banging about with his heavy, water-soaked boots. He would pour water, rinse out the basin, mix up soap lather, slam the door. Several times he went out into the river-station office and could be heard banging drawers, looking for something; he kept going to the closet where, on the inside of the closet door, a nail had been driven for the razor strop; kept opening the worm-eaten, creaky closet door and closing it again; kept honing the razor, rummaging through boxes and looking for another blade. There was neither peace nor quiet for a single second. Once more the old man banged the table drawer, knocked over a chair, and again went to the closet, opened it, and began to hone his razor, mumbling half aloud in a deep bass.

Gabriel could control himself no longer.

"What kind of consideration is this? Do you have to bang around like that?"

As if no one had said anything, the old man continued swiping at the strop with his razor; then he kicked the closet door shut, returned to the table just as noisily and demonstratively.

"You old clod!"

"Wha-a-a-t?"

"Clod! Why are you banging around like that? Don't you have a crumb of consideration?"

"Shut up! I don't feel like wasting words with you now! You'd better keep a civil tongue in your head!"

To Gabriel it was clear that the only logical thing to do would be to get up, take the old gnarled stick from the corner, and wham his father over the head and beat him like a dog. Repelled by his own criminal urge, he turned and buried his head in the felt of the back of the couch, so that he might forget all this and go to sleep.

Father and son had fought many times before, like two hack drivers, and once, in the parlor of Hungarian whores, Gabriel had even shot at his father with a revolver. He had been standing in the doorway of the parlor, staring at the drunken soldiers as they rattled their sabers and at a certain clean-shaven actor whom he knew wore false teeth, when it seemed to him that in a gilt-framed rococo mirror, he saw his father. 'It is, it is! This is his own father! Drinking beer, pouring it from a bottle, smoking a cigar, and a woman in her slip sitting on his knee.' He could have withdrawn unnoticed then, but whether there awakened in him the passions of his dead mother, the unhappy nun who had wept night after night while she was carrying him beneath her heart, or whether it was the jealous hatred of a child who has never experienced parental warmth, he remained, instead, standing in the doorway, staring into space.

To young Kavran, high-school senior, Jacobin, and atheist, it was clear that the sex life of his father had absolutely nothing to do with him; one's so-called sex life was the private affair of every individual. But perhaps because, from earliest childhood, he had lived as a mute witness to all the love crises of his parent, and because in that flood of women he had begun to hate these creatures, he felt a deep need to cause a scandal in that golden salon. He recalled the half-dark tobacco shops with their colorful screens, the Sunday afternoons when the bells rang in all the churches and he sat in the tobacco shop and stared at the bluish gas tongue at which gentlemen lit their cigars flickering in the corner, while behind the screen could be heard the laughter of "auntie" tobacconist—the same laugh as Eva's. He recalled the dead Eva, and his hatred mounted. And so, in that bordello chaos, accompanied by the repulsive laughter of drunks and half-naked women carrying trays, he had fought with his father till blood ran, had grabbed a cavalry officer's revolver, and fired twice into the air, destroying the large mirror.

Exhausted by everything that had happened during the afternoon, he felt a half sleep settling on his nerves, thick and heavy as mud, and thought how it would be good for him to rest before this evening's costume ball. But meanwhile the old man was madly banging his boots and rattling papers and mumbling as if possessed.

'Why the hell is he rattling those papers? What's he up to?'

He raised himself up to see what was rattling and, with inflamed eyelids and a dry, tight, burning throat, half dead, in the yellow half-light caught sight of the old man crumpling pages of his manuscript he had left on the table, and on those pages wiping his razor, full of blood-tinged lather and shaved hair.

"Have you gone mad?" Gabriel leaped up, tore from his father's hand his tattered philosophy thesis entitled "*De Corporis Humani Destructione*," and began smoothing out the crumpled tatters, scraping from them with his fingernails the smears of scummy lather, sweat, and hairs.

The old man looked at his son sullenly and impassively, shrugged his shoulders, and once more began scraping away with his razor; one could hear the razor rasping over the hairs, sharply, bitingly.

"What the hell are you yelling about? All these damned papers of yours aren't worth anything anyway! Better if you did some honest work!"

"And it would be best if you didn't bother about me, do you hear? Leave me and my papers alone!"

"Of course! Drinking in the taverns the whole night, that suits you? Yes, swilling at someone else's expense—that pleases the young gentleman! Sleeping the whole day. But to work, to get down to your books, to take your examinations, to become someone, that stinks to you! I'm so ashamed I can't even look people in the eye any more! I avoid everyone like a sneak thief."

'It's always that one and the same voice, one and the same self-pity, one and the same lie! Five years ago, seven years ago, fifteen years ago, always one and the same! And the old jackass keeps lying! He's faking. He only pretends he is interested in my examinations. He pretends it all and lies! But this evening, at the Fish, he'll eat up fifteen stuffed rolls and drink five liters of Schiller! Even now he's drunk! Everything there next to the couch reeks of liquor! Phew! To hell with it all!' Gabriel turned his face to the back of the couch, but as the worn, stinking velvet tickled his lips, he shuddered and spat, full of deep revulsion.

، The old man actually had been drinking since early morning. They had worked hard on the damaged levee, and the water had risen madly and undermined the thick bulwarks so that it seemed it would break through this very night. They had worn themselves out and gotten soaked through like dogs, so who wouldn't toss down a few extra shots? 'To hell with it! And now this bum tries to start something! The shameless snotnose! He doesn't mind rolling around with other men's wives on his couch! And yet he tries to start something! As if he were simon-pure! As if the police weren't here yesterday!' (The day before, around noon, a detective had come to ask whether it was true that Gabriel had returned and what he was up to. He was an acquaintance of old Kavran's, this damned detective, and it became suddenly clear to the old man that it was no joke, by God, to conceal a draft evader in one's own home. First, because there existed a statute on the books, and second, it was a violation of the law that could cause him to lose his pension, and, by God, wind up in prison. So he, a loyal and sworn appointee of this triune kingdom, told the detective it was true his only son had returned from abroad. Although he added that Gabriel was mortally ill with tuberculosis, was going to report to the military hospital himself, submit a petition for release from military service, and take his doctoral examinations, he had betrayed his son. Since Gabriel had not been home for more than twenty-four hours, and this morning he had been sound asleep when the old man left early because of the rising water, father and son were together now for the first time since this betrayal. Nonetheless, the old man thought it would be a good idea to warn this crazy son of his not to fool around, because the police were looking for him. What he had said about not looking people in the eye had to do with his conversation with the detective, whom he dared not look in the eye out of fear and respect for the law and the severe legal consequences of violating military statutes.)

He had wanted to steer this conversation with his son to the detective's visit, to warrants, statutes, legal consequences, but he lacked composure and lost himself in half-heard mutterings about shame and laziness and this damned sort of life. All Gabriel's peers were doctors, professors, lawyers, well-prepared men out on their own; Gabriel alone was a nobody, a nothing who wandered about the world like a sleepwalker.

In his ill-tempered, nervous anger, the old man gave a jerk and unexpectedly cut into the flesh on his cheek with his razor; the blood gushed forth and he paced the room in his massive and clumsy boots to pour fresh water into the basin, to fix the splashed candle, which was sputtering, to look for a clean towel in the closet in order to stop the dark blood pouring forth onto his greasy, fat hog's jowls. The muffled thuds of his heavy, water-soaked boots fell on Gabriel's head like logs and he snarled harshly: "I've already told you a hundred times not to bang around so much! Can't you be quiet?"

"No, I can't! And I won't! Do you understand me? I won't! I'm in my own home! And you, if you don't like it—you know what you can do. And something else! That a man in his own home lets himself be tyrannized by such a no-good bum! Go get a decent job and don't stink up this place day and night! I'm not putting up with it much longer! Do you hear me? I won't! Say one more word and I'll throw you out!"

Gabriel wanted to say something, but he only waved his hand and once more turned his face to the back of the couch, sighing deeply.

"You've got a thick skin, that's the truth! You've got that! You know how to be hypocritically silent! But if you had only so much shame [the old man hooked the nail of his left thumb behind a tooth, then snapped it loudly], you would have begun to think about all this some time ago!"

"About what, if you please?" Gabriel straightened up on the couch, leaning on both arms, and turned his face toward his father. He felt an intense pain in his shoulder muscles and elbow joints.

"About what? About everything! Just look at how you look! If I hadn't given you that old coat, you'd be going around naked!"

"I don't need your coat! Leave me in peace!" Gabriel lay down, his face to the couch, and pulled up over himself the blanket that had become entangled under his feet.

"Yes! Naturally! Now you won't need my coat any more! Now you've got prospects of finer coats than mine! Naturally! Gentlemen's coats, doctors'—"

Gabriel gave a jerk and, with a wrench of his whole body, leaped in a flash to the table.

"What does that mean?"

"What are you shouting at me for? You'd better start thinking about all this! Where is it all leading? What will come of it all? Time is passing, my dear boy!"

Gabriel tunneled into the old man's eyes with a stare that would not let him shift his glance away.

"That's not what we're talking about! What was it you said about the coat? That's what we're talking about! What kind of coats do I have prospects of?"

"Well, you don't have a coat, do you? Is that by any chance your coat you have on? You don't think I'm going to feed and clothe you till Judgment Day, do you? What's past is past—you were young! An inexperienced child, shortsighted! I always told you you'd break your neck, but what's the use when the chick is wiser than the hen? Yes! You constantly preached to me that in our country there were only barracks, police, jail—that this wasn't life! Well, what then? You were out there in that great life of yours, but now it's fine for you to be back under the roof of the same jail you complained of!"

"We're not talking about jail now!"

"Then what are we talking about? So you're sick! You cough, you spit up blood! So is it smart to drink all night and not sleep? You're not a snot-nosed kid any more! You've gotten old— you're even bald! I can still bite right through this table, but you're as stump-toothed as an old granny! But still you joke and play with life!"

This Jesuitical, fatherlike, false fluency, at once shallow and deep, so dumfounded Gabriel that he sat down at the table and stared at the lying, sly old man as at a marvel: 'There! Now he's babbling about everything and anything, only not about what's on his mind!'

"Yes, that's how it is, my son! That's what I had in mind! All right—he won't listen to someone older and wiser than he is, so let it go! Let him find out for himself! There's nothing better in life than experience! He doesn't want it any other way except to knock his head against the wall. Well, so be it, let him crack that mad head of his! As God is my witness, I was overjoyed when you returned! My heart beat with joy! My only child came back! My only-born son came back and had gotten some sense! And tell me, if you can, did I say a single unpleasant word about everything that had happened? No, I didn't. Not a single word! I waited a day, two, three, a week, two weeks, I waited and kept quiet! And what is your Gabriel doing, my friends and neighbors ask, and what do I tell them? He's studying, I lie, studying! He's going to take his doctoral examinations! That's how I lie to the neighbors. But nothing! It's all a lie! If you had any sort of capital, any interest or income, I could understand you. I wouldn't say a single word! But surely you're not figuring on my fifty-three florins in pay and allowances?" At the thought of his fifty-three florins in pay and allowances, the old man's voice trembled with excitement and his eyes sparkled with tears.

"Why are you clowning around and lying about everything and anything? Instead, give me an answer, what did you have in mind, what kind of coat do I have in prospect? I know very well what you had in mind by that coat! But listen to what I tell you! You'd better be careful with your words!"

"What do I have to watch out about? You're an ungrateful thief!"

"To whom am I ungrateful? To you? What should I be grateful to you for?"

"Not to me! I don't need anything from you! If you started paying me back from now to Judgment Day, you couldn't pay me back for all the good I've done you! But is it honorable for you to steal men's wives—and from men who have been good to you at that?" He knew the whole story about Miss Sorge. After she had broken with her father and gone away, the old gentleman, her deceased father, had come to the city to see with his own eyes where that damned home-wrecker had lived, that scoundrel who had dishonored his name and poisoned his only child so she had abandoned herself to licentiousness and debauchery. Old Kavran had fallen before the expensive fur coat of Mr. Sorge D.D. in panic and had begun, like a true river-station supervisor, to curse his son as an anarchist and antichrist. And when here, this evening, he had found his son with this same woman, he had confirmed for himself that this son was a libertine and an incorrigible criminal. "Yes! And why are you staring at me so blankly? did I make all this up in my head? I ask you! Is it honorable to roll around on couches with other men's wives? Be so good as to go to a hotel! This isn't a hotel! I forbid you to behave like this in my honorable home! Do you understand me?"

On an old kitchen cabinet lay the bread, wrapped in a colorful striped napkin, and, next to it, a large kitchen knife. Gabriel cast a glance at the naked blade of the knife; he began to feel uncomfortable. Then he rose from the table, turned without a word, and went to the window. After a long silence he came back.

"Listen, I've thought carefully about every word I am about to say now. In the whole world there isn't a more swinish house than this one that is my home! Do you understand me?"

"Is that so? Someone who rolls around with rich women for money, a person like that is going to howl scandals in my face?

You bum! Do you know the police are looking for you? A degenerate like you, a nothing who would even spit in the face of his own father!"

"What did you say? The police are looking for me?"

"Yes! They were here and wrote down everything! You'll go to jail, I tell you."

"What did they write down?"

"How would I know what they wrote down? Everything!"

"And you, of course, dictated everything into their notebook!"

"What else should I do? Should I, by chance, risk my pension?"

"And naturally, you couldn't keep your policeman's blood to yourself!"

"What kind of blood?"

"Oh, how sickening this is! How disgusting!"

Outside, a train thundered by, shaking the scaffolding, beams and ceiling rafters of the house so that it creaked right down to its foundation.

"I couldn't very well lie to officials!"

"What kind of officials? There weren't any officials here! You yourself reported me to the police for fear they might catch me under your roof! And now your heart's at rest; now you don't have to worry about your pension!"

"How could I, your father, do such a thing?"

"What the hell kind of father? You've never been my father! Do you hear me? Never!"

Gabriel spat this out sullenly, ruthlessly. When he had first said this, long ago, many years before, he had still been a child and the statement had caught in his throat. He had sobbed deeply and bitterly, beating his head on the floor and weeping uncontrollably over the idea that this man was not his father. But now he said it coldly, unemotionally, as if standing over an ancient grave.

"No! You are *not* my father!"

Even this seemed too weak to him, in view of what he had just been hearing: old Kavran's perfidious insinuations and his betrayal. 'Something even more brutal is necessary! Something stronger!' "You're an animal!"

"Wha-a-at?"

"An animal!"

"Huh! Take this, you animal!" The old man, his face twisted in a wild grimace, his rage boiling over from somewhere deep within him, swung and threw his razor at his son. It was a moment taut with danger.

Gabriel instinctively ducked, so that the razor struck the door, bounced off the wood, and fell with a clatter. At the same moment the naked blade flew from his hand, the old man sensed in his public-servant brain that this bordered on some specific regulation, a border he had now stepped over, and if that miserable jackass hadn't ducked in time, there could have been legal consequences and complications. The razor had flown with such force that Gabriel had felt it whistling over his head, and this enraged him even more.

"You old murderer!" Gabriel leaped to the razor and threw the blade onto the table among the soapy dishes and the old man's various boxes and bandages and toilet articles.

"A fine thing! He even tries to kill me! And you tell me you're my father! My father! Hah!"

The old man, still perturbed at having crossed legal bounds, was terrified by this hostility; his son's voice seemed to him so dangerously merciless that something contracted in his chest.

"My dear father! What have I ever had from you? Haven't I lived like a dog at your river station? Here among your drowned wives—watching them drown! That was my childhood! Watching as you went chasing after waitresses—that's how my life began! And today you want to cut my throat with a razor, is that it? Today you spit in my face as a good-for-nothing! Why? Where do you get the right? I ask you, where do you get the right? What did you give me as a father, tell me that!"

"I gave you everything I had!"

"That's a lie! You didn't give me anything! You dragged me around the taverns; my eyes burned from sleeplessness and stink; I was barely able to stand up while I had to go carousing with you and your waitresses! In the tobacco shops I would listen to the bells as they struck the hour and stare at the dirty glass door, waiting for us to leave. But you didn't come! You were making love on the couch behind the curtains and tobacco cabinets. There, under glass, were gumdrops and chocolates and bonbons; you might have bought me at least one gumdrop or chocolate! No! Instead, always that damn stale roll! And now you want to dictate to me what I should and should not do? Is that it? You're going to accuse me of stealing other men's wives? You, you?"

Gabriel began to pound wildly with his fist on the table, so that all the soapy dishes and brushes and bottles jumped about over the tablecloth. The old man became frightened that their screaming at each other would be heard by the ancient lamplighter who had just leaned his ladder against the wall and begun to climb rung by rung to light the red lamp. (Since noon the great water had risen so fast that it was necessary, according to provincial regulations and the water-level regulation book, to signal that a flood was coming.)

"Shh! Have you gone mad? The lamplighter will hear you!"

"Let him hear! I don't give a damn! What business is it of yours if someone comes to visit me? It has nothing to do with you! The lady was here today as a *lady*, but you're a bum and a drunken criminal! A razor-swinger!"

"Why are you shouting? Don't you see him? He's staring into the room!"

"Let him stare! There's something for him to see, too! Show him the razor! And you want to puff yourself up as a judge and a moralist? Hah! You! If it comes to that—that one of us acts as a judge—then I'm the one to judge! Do you understand me?"

"How have I done you wrong? If you lived like a man ought

to live, no one would say a single word! But you're not a man—
you're a lunatic! You shout like a lunatic! Aren't you ashamed in
front of the lamplighter? Don't you see him staring in? You
should be ashamed!"

And the old man, abashed and shaken, wobbled in his heavy
boots to the window where, in the dark-blue twilight, the rungs
of the ladder leaning against the wall were clearly visible; and on
their black relief the old lamplighter, blind and deaf, who had
for fifty years been lighting the red lamp as an alarm and signal
of a flood.

Turning toward his father, the son stared at the old man's
figure in the square of the window, washed in the strong bloody
light of the red lamp hanging over the window on a lyre-shaped
iron rod. All the rotten black blood of anger that had boiled up
in him settled slowly, and, contemplating this gray-haired old
man bathed in red light, all lathery and pitiful as he talked with
the deaf lamplighter (out of some superstitious fear, lest perhaps the old man had heard what they were arguing about), he
sensed the chasm that separated him from this miserable person,
and it seemed ridiculous to him that he had gotten so upset and
argued with an old river-station supervisor.

But along with this sympathetic indulgence, there arose in
him a tiny, tenuous, malicious need for ice-cold objective analysis: it would feel good for once not to be the one who swallowed
the bitter pill; for once let the old man hear the truth! 'What's
the point of too much consideration? He ought to be plucked,
completely, feather by feather. I ought to shove his head into all
those thoughts and tears and years of suffering I had to swallow,
so he can see, so he can feel the pain, so he'll think of all this
when he's receiving the last rites.' And when the old man returned to the table Gabriel repeated in a calm, dry voice—the
sort seconds use before a duel—that all this disgusted him, that
it was stupid even to talk to him, because he wasn't a man but
only a phantom in a river station. A drunken razor-swinger with
liquor, medals, and a pipe!

"Yes! To be heartless as a rock, to lick the hand of everyone higher in rank, to bow at angles measured according to whether it is an official or a construction consultant, to show your gums like a full moon in front of your superiors, and then, when you come home, to trample, to murder, to kill!"

"Who murdered anyone?"

"You, my dear father! You, specifically! Didn't you murder my youth? Didn't you murder my mother?"

"I? Murdered your mother?"

"You, you, my good man! You! Who, then, did kill that young woman? Who? Good Lord! Eighteen years younger than such a monster! Eighteen years younger! But naturally, that wasn't enough for you! You still had to make the rounds of coffeehouses with waitresses!"

"I killed the poor soul? God be with you, child! Wasn't she carried here into the river station the next morning by the raftsmen? How did I kill her? What's wrong with you? What kind of nonsense are you talking?"

"Yes! I'm talking nonsense! I'm lying! I'm lying about all this!"

Outside, a carless locomotive rushed by, the house shook, the glasses rattled in the cabinets as if a strong gust of wind had blown through the steel girders of the bridge, and then silence set in. Gabriel knew he probably would have shut up and sat down on the couch or spat and left, as he had so many times before, if he hadn't heard a band outside.

It was the last day of carnival; the snow was melting and the gutters dripped melodically; the water rumbled and rose higher, yellow and ugly; and the traditional parade headed onto the bridge to throw into the water Prince Carnival, in dress uniform, complete with vermilion cape. A string of carriages rolled along in the parade. Cavaliers, knights, monks, and monkeys sang; tambours and guslas, bagpipes and reed pipes, and tubas with their deep, muffled du-du, du-du, moaned like a funeral dirge; trumpets and clarinets, Spanish senoritas and toreadors on

horses ('now comes the first quadrille'), gypsy men and gypsy
girls, baronesses, marquises, and nobles in wigs, all passed by the
river station onto the bridge, laughing and shaking with
giggles.

Gabriel left the old man, went to the window, and stared at
the muddy carriages and fiacres bedecked with paper flowers;
guitars thrummed, firecrackers sputtered, paper snakes and hun-
dred-colored serpents twisted; confetti, trumpets, flutes, torches
—the procession shouted wantonly, horses reared, pistols were
fired as at a wedding; "Prince Carnival, Prince Carnival," sang
women and children, monks and coachmen. In front of the funeral carriage of the condemned prince rode a cavalcade of
trumpeters; the prince sat on a golden throne, a top hat jammed
on his head. Behind the funeral carriage cavorted a huge clown,
as tall as the river station itself, his arm long enough to reach the
telephone wires; one half of him was green and the other yellow.
In passing the river station the yellow-green apparition bent toward it so low that the clown's huge, swollen head, with its
bloody gaping jaws, almost banged against the windowpane. Gabriel jerked back before those dreaded red jaws—it seemed to
him that something awful was about to happen. Galvanized
with panic, he was terrified by the procession, the clown, the
river station—by life itself; he moved back two or three paces
into the room to hide himself from the horror.

He stepped only two or three instinctive paces backward, and
it took perhaps not even a split second; but in that barely exist-
ent moment of fear there burst open inside him scenes of his
childhood—his dead mother, the dead Eva—and he trembled at
everything he had experienced at the river station.

He recalled how, as an eighth-grader, he had lain with Eva in
his father's marital bed, felt on himself Eva's burning lips, and,
painfully poisoned in a fever of flesh, had trembled lest the old
man come in.

"It's the wind!" Eva had said to him, and her voice trembled
and she glowed all over like a burning coal. "It's the wind!"

'And were those not the same boots that had entered this room only today? And is it not possible that this life of his has stood eternally on one and the same spot? Has reality in these fifteen or twenty years moved even a single inch? Had he not been caught here this very evening with another man's wife? And what does all this mean? Was he not wasting away a whole life here with a man who was a phantom—a phantom just like that clown? How unreal and vapid all this is!'

The procession had already arrived at the water and the glare of the torches shone red and shimmered on the yellow muddy horizontal of the water; a great drum struck up the death march and one could hear through the window the people shouting. Gabriel turned from the window and looked at his father.

'There! This drunken criminal had lain on him like a block of wood from the first day he could recall being alive. He had been unable in any way to push against that block to the light. He had lost half his life while he outgrew and conquered it all. This man had always clipped his hair to the scalp, like a recruit or a prisoner, and beaten him with a belt and a dog leash. And when he would beg him to tell him stories, he would talk about hangings and criminals sentenced to death. He would take him to "uncle" jailor's at the courthouse and there, where there wasn't a single tree and where chained prisoners walked in a circle, there in the ashen, asphalt courtyard, he was allowed to play as a reward for his distinctions and commendations in school. How he feared those gray cells; how he waited for the old man, who, with "auntie," was planting horns on "uncle" keeper. The old cynic! He ought to be told everything! And those long nights with Eva in the marriage bed! That too! that too!'

To Gabriel the old man seemed sickly green, like a dead man; since he had his mouth open in front of the mirror—in order to reach better with the little brush and not dirty his skin—his lower jaw sagged down and in it could be seen black and corroded teeth. If at that moment the old man hadn't been darkening his mustache with some artificial black coloring, perhaps Gabriel would not have gone to extremes. But at that moment this comic mustache-daubing so terribly affected him that his voice began to tremble as at the start of their quarrel, and he exasperatedly asked his father who he thought had actually told him the old man had killed his deceased mother.

"Well! What about it? Why don't you say something? Aren't you interested at all?"

The old man, jaws stretched tight, was just coloring the left side of his mustache and so he let out a single unarticulated sound that supposedly meant he was not interested in who might have informed Gabriel about his life with the deceased nun.

"Eva told me about it!"

"Eva?"

"Yes! Eva! She told me how my mother would cry all night long, but you were out hitting the taverns and slapping cards on the table. And my mother would cry all night long!"

"And Eva told you that? Eva?"

"Yes! Eva! And do you know where? Here in this marriage bed of yours, when I would be lying in it with Eva. I was your wife's lover—in the eighth grade! Your rival!"

The old man stopped for a moment with the brush in his hand, as if intensely interested. Then he waved his hand indifferently, as if it all bored him.

"Come, come, you're lying!"

"I'm not lying! That was my upbringing and my youth!"

As if hitting at a fly, the old man lowered his hand, feeling for the back of the other chair in order to pull it out from under the table—it was caught on the crossed supports so it wouldn't come out—he found it preferable to put the basin on a chair to wash the lather from his face.

"Come, come, I ask you! That's all nonsense!"

At the beginning, when Gabriel had first accused him of kill-

ing his mother, it had sounded to the old man somehow significant. He himself had had the same thought on occasion, so it
was unpleasant for him to hear it from the lips of another. 'Hell!
This could be a criminal matter! And such a criminal matter
brings with it certain legal consequences!' But when he heard
that Eva had been the informer, it all seemed to him "legally
without foundation." Where is Eva? Eva, drowned so many
years ago! It's all nonsense!'

And so he poured water from the pitcher into the basin and
began to wash himself and to splutter and splash.

Watching his father as he washed the lather from his face like
a clown his makeup after a performance, Gabriel felt the total
idiocy of the situation and of how in life absolutely nothing
could be made clear!

And so, without a word, he took his hat and coat and went
outside by the water.


The water rumbled ominously; for a long time Gabriel stared
into the semidarkness where restless lights flickered. He recalled
that he already ought to be on his way into the city, to get ready,
to bathe, to shave, to borrow a frock coat for the costume ball.
'The woman is waiting for him, there everything will be resolved! Everything that had happened was stupid and it all must
be cast aside and begin again somewhere else. Everything was
still at the beginning!'

Standing thus on a pile of hewn stone blocks, up to which the
water already reached, foaming and gurgling, he felt the water
carry something to his feet. It was black and heavy, like a
drowned man. He bent over and made out Prince Carnival. The
water had carried away his top hat, so one could see the straw,
rotted and soaked through; its right arm floated on the surface
and the simple white sleeve was inflated like a bubble.

A feeling of deep revulsion swept over Gabriel Kavran, as if
he were standing on a corpse. He shoved the deformed creature

into the stream with his foot so violently that the dummy bounced off the rocks and floated away into the darkness. Then he shuddered and headed into the city with a strong, energetic step.

*Translated by Bob Whyte*

# A Funeral in Teresienburg

The Seventeenth Royal Imperial Aspern-Essling Dragoon Regiment possessed two garrisons, one in Vienna and the other in the Hungarian town of Maria Teresienburg, beyond the Danube. Laura's father, Cavalry Colonel Mihajlo von Warronigg, the husband of Olga Warronigg (a Glembay-Bárbóczy by birth), commanded the headquarters of the Maria Teresienburg cadres in 1905 nd 1906.

The Seventeenth Royal Imperial Aspern-Essling Dragoon Regiment had been formed as a cuirassier unit in 1628 by the famous quartermaster, Robert St. Quentin d'Espagne et de la Porte, who served under the Wallensteins; in 1632 that armored regiment, with the imperial patent bestowed upon it, played a very important role in the battle of Friedland. Its charge near the windmills of Lützen was immortalized on an imperial tapestry in the Museum of Military History in Vienna—in that glorious action seven hundred Croatian horsemen left behind their seven hundred nameless peasant hides. A first lieutenant of the empire and kingdom, Emil Sztatocsny, had copied the tapestry for the regimental honor hall of the Maria Teresienburg regiment; the reproduction hung there among the regimental trophies like some precious cardboard plaque.

The eminent spouse of Empress Maria Theresa, the great Tuscan general Franz von Lothringen, converted the heroic armored regiment into his own personal guard, the Chevaux-Légers Regiment; but during the Napoleonic Wars, under the guiding hand of Prince Montenuovo, the Aspern-Essling regiment was incorporated into the ranks of the dragoons and remained there up until the days of the Glembays. In 1878, the Seventeenth Royal Imperial Regiment pompously celebrated its two hundred and fiftieth anniversary, and its commandant at the time, the great Russian prince Aleksandr Aleksandrovich, gave fifty-three thousand florins to the treasury of the regimental endowment fund for the military instruction of officers' sons; and on that occasion His Highness the Emperor and King, Franz Joseph I, presented the regiment with a gold plaque bearing his very own Exalted Citation and Signature.

· In 1748, when Empress Maria Theresa yielded Her Inherited Right to Parma and Piacenza to the Bourbons according to the principle of secundogeniture, the Seventeenth Regiment moved from Parma to Alsóvár in the Turkish border zone and remained there until the Napoleonic Wars. During the forties, in Verona and Milan, its reputation became tarnished in the game of Austro-Lombardian politics; the Seventeenth was used as a martial police force· against the *Risorgimento*, arresting the rebels in accordance with Metternich's political directives. While sacrificing Croatian flesh for centuries, it moved here and there about the garrisons of the monarchy like a circus and only returned to Alsóvár with its headquarters and cadres when it received its last reassignment of the seventies, while its second division remained in Vienna with an administrative detachment of auxiliary cadres located in Aspern in lower Austria.

.The Seventeenth Regiment (then the Chevaux-Légers No. 3) lost four hundred men in the battle of Malplaquet, and for that "brilliant gesture on the field of honor" the Tuscan commander presented it with a silk flag embossed with an emblem and insignia in gold. Losing seven hundred horses and horsemen in the battle of Hochkirch, the cavalry regiment distinguished itself so valiantly that the Empress herself presented it with a gilded silver honorary trumpet, accompanied by her Exalted Citation of October 28, 1764, "for service under the command of Count Imra Báthory." In an elliptoid on the gilt horn three stallions at full gallop were skillfully depicted in relief; on the other side a gold medal was engraved with the Empress's portrait. Beneath the image of the Empress, decorated with golden lilies and engraved in cursive, was this Exalted Dedication: "The Empress to Her Faithful Teresienburg Cavalry Regiment." The silk brocade banner of the court trumpeter was draped across the precious gold and silver horn. It bore the standard of the Imperial Herald, with two massive braids, double-headed eagles embroidered in gold, and the initials of Her Highness intertwined with a laurel wreath into a heraldic motif of the Emperor's Monogram. Its yellow silk had turned somewhat gray, but the gold on the wings of the eagles and the threads of the letters still glistened brightly. The precious imperial relic, that pathetic reminder of seven hundred skulls riddled with bullets and cut to bits, was preserved in the regimental honor hall in a glass case framed in bronze on a pillow of lavender velvet. The bronze box lay on a dais in a gold display case (in the style of the gaudy Viennese *mauvais-goût*); and on the velvet shelves of the gold case were many other trophies—of silver laurel wreaths and dark-yellow watered silk, photographs and plaques, victory goblets, decrees and seals—all the bloodiest of documents attesting to the immeasurable wretchedness of

Croatian military glory. Standing there was a gold-framed daguerreotype of the regimental commander, the great Russian prince Aleksandr Aleksandrovich, wearing the Byzantine brocade of a Russian noble with beaver skin, and with his own violet signature and the crown of a great prince.

There was also a silver-framed photograph of the Imperial Supreme Commander, Felix Immaculatus, who had served as a cadet with the Seventeenth Regiment in the nineties and who, ten years later, still told of his adventures over black coffee in the mess hall: how he once halted the express train to Budapest on a wager for his mare Belladonna, and how at his instigation the officers of the Seventeenth one night threw a piano from the second floor of the city casino.

. Three historical regimental standards hung in the honor hall of regimental glory and history: one, distinguished by the Knightly Order of Maria Theresa in the battle of Sadowa (nine hundred victims on the field of honor); the second, riddled with bullets in the victorious clash at Aspern and Essling, where the whole regiment was left dead on the battlefield along with its full complement of horses and riders; and the third, made of silk and not yet bloodstained, created so the Seventeenth might carry it as a standard through the death-dealing whirlwind that rests in all the desk drawers of regimental offices beneath the secret seal of the Supreme Order of Mobilization.

The draperies of the regimental honor hall were of heavy damask, thick folds of opaque fabric that gave the whole room the dingy lighting of a morgue. Twelve heavy chairs stood at a long crimson-covered table, all of carved oak in the old German style of the Thirty Years' War—*à la* Wallenstein.

The honor hall of the Seventeenth Regiment was on the second floor of the main building of an old Jesuit monastery; entry onto the second floor was gained by a monumental staircase reconstructed at the end of the eighteenth century for the presentation of church mystery plays. A portal with columns, giants, heads of angels, and crests rose above the marble steps, and in front of the columns, to the left and right, were three old eighteenth-century cannons with their throats stuck in the ground like the crossbars for the old-fashioned fiacres that the elite of Teresienburg once used when visiting its hospitable cavalry regiment. On ceremonial occasions and celebrations, when the civil authorities and ladies of Teresienburg society were present, a red carpet was spread from the vestibule up to the second floor, and at every turn in the stairway—on the landings, at the ground-floor glass doors, and at the entrance to the corridor of the second floor—two dragoons stood in parade dress and white gloves. Seen from the plebeian perspective of the ordinary, subordinate, administrative ranks of a civil servant, it all looked very noble, resplendent, a chivalric dream. And there was not a single civil servant in the Teresienburg district who did not regret his socially inferior status. And to think that beautiful women drop like sheaves before the pastel-blue-laced dragoons and their swords, who reap the rich harvest!

The tapestries on the walls of the honor hall were a worn-out dark brown; along the walls hung nine portraits of regimental commanders in gold frames.

1: The Tuscan commander, Franz von Lothringen, in the ermine and purple vestments of a Roman emperor.

2: Count Esterházy Béla, son of the Seventeenth's second colonel, who fell on the battlefield (1768–1803).

3: Baron Lieutenant Field Marshal Albert Gleisstäten, who commanded the Seventeenth at the time of Bonaparte's Lombardian campaign (1803–1824).

4: Count Keglevich (1824–1849), the only painting of one of the grand seigneurs in civilian dress, with a white silk collar and a hound.

5: Grand Prince Aleksandr Aleksandrovich (1849–1869), in the dress uniform of a dragoon colonel of the Seventeenth Regiment, with the insignia of the Golden Fleece as a gift of the Emperor and a sign of gratitude for the personal participation of the Grand Prince in the counter-Hungarian expedition.

6: The Grand Commander, Mecklenburg-Schwerin (1869–1878).

7: Prince Auersperg-Lipschitz.

8: The King of Bavaria.

9: The major-general, Count Ségur-Cabanac (1888–1899).

The position of Honorary Keeper of the Seventeenth Dragoon Regiment was not filled during the time Cavalry Colonel von Warronigg was commander. It was thought that the office of the Keeper would be assumed by the Spanish king Alfonso XIII, renowned all over Europe as quite a ladies' man and golf virtuoso; or by the supreme commander, Ferdinand Albrecht; or by that Bulgarian Coburg who shot snipe in the Teresienburg marshes every third year and was very popular in the chief district town as a witty ladies' man and as the grandson of Louis Philippe, also a witty ladies' man.

· In the first decade of the twentieth century the Seventeenth Dragoon Regiment was no longer counted among the regiments made up exclusively of gentry. But in spite of this, it enjoyed the completely respectable reputation of a fine and distinguished regiment in which, although it was no longer especially chic to serve, it was no disgrace. Three counts were serving in the Teresienburg Division: Hollós, L'Ours-Walderode, and Buttler (the direct descendant of Wallenstein's murderer). Also serving were one of the Dukes of Mantua (as a cadet), four barons, and nine petty-noble nobodies—those stanch adherents of Verböczy's legal code who possessed nothing except their pitiful, ennobling predicate, that cheap, blue-blooded title tacked on to one's name like some tin rattle. Anyway, the other half of the officer corps, which numbered some thirty-two men, was, unfortunately, of town stock. True, they were all of more or less solid and completely proper town origin, the children of high-placed civil servants, landlords, and other gentlemen of the district. There were even five or six millionaires among them: for example, Lieutenant Mayer-Kolozsvári, whose father owned eleven beer breweries known throughout the monarchy by huge advertising posters on which King Matija Korvin welcomed his feudal, princely, drunken guests with a foamy mug of "double-malted Kolozsvári beer." But there were also some disturbingly shady faces of truly obscure background, as, for example, the best horseman of the whole regiment, First Lieutenant Szalai, whose father lived somewhere in Kaposvár as a pensioned district scribe.

Teresienburg (Terés-Vár, in Hungarian) was the main town of the Danubian district of Alsóvár, the birthplace of cardinal, statesman, and preacher Thurzói Thuróczy Aladár, the histori-cally famous executioner who butchered thousands of Calvinists and witches during his ingenious career as instructor of ecclesias-tical rhetoric. Its avenues were lined with maples, and it boasted a main promenade named after the Supreme Commander, Maria Valeria, and a brothel in the Glass Lily hotel next to the town tollhouse. In the vestibule of the Teresienburg railway sta-tion hung an oversized figure twelve feet high of Emperor Na-poleon Bonaparte in his historical cloak and two-cornered hat, with a label in Hungarian proclaiming that the American type-writer "Underwood" had conquered the earth. In front of the station, in the center between the flower beds planted with tulips and pansies, stood a bronze statue of King Matija Korvin on horseback and three marble women. One of them was hold-ing a flag in her hand, another had a laurel wreath, and the third, a decree with the royal seal in which King Matija pro-claimed Alsóvár a free town in 1467. The work was of dubious artistic value, done by some imitation of the Budapest master, Štrobl; and two years before, swallows, traveling from Cairo, had nested under Matija Korvin's crown in deified peace.

Teresienburg also had three factory smokestacks (belonging to the flour mill, the paper factory, and the glass factory), a town meeting hall with a tower and an illuminated clock, a baroque Jesuit monastery converted into barracks, and a square in front of the cathedral. The plane trees on the Alsóvár Square were old and decrepit; each year the wind would knock one of them over. In front of the wooden band pavilion stood a huge steel cage with a live squirrel. On the square's eastern side, between the evergreens and oleanders, the white marble bust of Kossuth sparkled, and on the western side stood a bust of the late and blessed Empress Jelisava, who particularly cherished her title as Queen of Hungary. In the summertime, an old man, a wounded veteran of the fighting in 1848, sold fancy cakes, raspberry juice, and balloons in front of the Empress; and in front of Kossuth, between the ivy and laurel tree, a grotesque wooden hand jutted out discreetly, holding a tablet on which two symmetrical ovals had been drawn (pretentiously symbolizing the local Pannonian symbols W.C.).

, This was Teresienburg, a town with two candy shops and a gray rococco theater in Deak Street, with plane trees and a cathedral, sitting between huge stretches of oak forests in country that rolled monotonously, rich with timber, from the Danube to the border of Steuer Province and Lake Balaton. The poplars along the highways, the blacksmith shops and taverns, the steeples in the distance and the brickyards on the edge of town, the patches of forest and the vineyards with wooden summer cottages—the whole panorama around the town was like a dime-store vignette, and when the autumn rains came, the vignette turned foggy and humdrum. At about two-thirty in the morning and four o'clock in the afternoon two express trains from Budapest cut through Teresienburg. By the time the buses from the King Matija and Hungarian Regent hotels returned at their monotonous pace along Prince Rudolf Avenue and Maria Valeria Street, even Žofika, the cashier girl in the coffeehouse Freedom, knew who had arrived in town: a new officer or a traveling tie salesman. . . .

· In the first window recess of the Teresienburg hotel and coffeehouse, the Hungarian Regent, every day from five to seven, His Excellency Lieutenant Field Marshal von Schwartner, a division general and commander of the garrison, sits like a wax doll in his uniform, wearing the Cross of Leopold, with a cappucino and a day-old *Reichspost* that arrived by the afternoon train. In Lieutenant Field Marshal von Schwartner's company, Brigadier Major General Draveczky reads the Hungarian paper from Budapest; and once in a while, usually on Saturdays after five, Von Warronigg joins the general's table politely, keeping a subordinate's proper distance. The cavalry officers play billiards in the narrow little street next to the cathedral; and the infantry officers of the 107th Infantry Regiment crowd the civilian coffeehouse Freedom. After eleven no one moves on the streets of Teresienburg. The night watchman stands in the main square next to the fountain, and in the dark behind the last oil lamp at the bottom of the avenue a black dog turns the corner. A woman in a kerchief crosses the street, probably on her way to the druggist. An organ echoes from the cathedral district. The dragoons carouse and smash glasses. A fiacre trots across the asphalt of Deak Street, heading toward the Glass Lily. A steam engine shrieks at the train station. It is late. Past midnight. . . .

Each year, on the twenty-second of May, the Aspern-Essling Regiment celebrated the victory of Aspern and Essling as its regimental victory, for the Seventeenth Regiment was the heroic flesh that, under the command of the Supreme Commander, Karl, threw back the attack of Marshal Masséna at the Danube Channel and pushed Napoleon back to Lobau. In that slaughter, in which seventeen generals perished, the Seventeenth was up to its knees in blood but did not retreat one step: it was "for generations an example of high morale" (three thousand dead). For the Seventeenth, the twenty-second of May was a day of triumph and on that day, in 1906, on the ninety-seventh anniversary of the battle of Aspern and Essling, that triumph was distinguished by an exceptional honor: a visit of His Excellency, the Lieutenant General of the Imperial Japanese Navy. The chief of the operations division in the office of the general headquarters of Lieutenant General Baron Kodama informed the victorious Seventeenth of this esteemed visit. Count Fudshi-

Hasegawa was the general who had defeated General Zaharov and Generals Kuropatkin and Blagovješčenski to the last man and who, by his ingenious operations at Liaoyang, captured the division generals, Barons Stackelberg, Papengut, Webelj, Tizengausen, Bilderljing, and Freiger von Geršeljman, together with their divisions, division convoys, and reserves (twenty thousand horses and soldiers lost their lives in that butchery). Count Fudshi-Hasegawa personally conducted operations with a hundred and sixteen battalions, thirty-three squadrons, and a hundred and twenty batteries; and now the operations chief of the victorious Marquis Oyama, who had won the battles of Wafangkou, Fenghwangcheng, Vindshu, and Mukden, was coming to congratulate the Seventeenth personally for its victory over Napoleon at Aspern and Essling. As long as forty-eight hours before this extraordinary event, tension was so high that it seemed that even the horses' equipage jangled more excitedly through the stables than on ordinary days. The hectic pace of the orderlies, the slamming of doors, the crowded regimental barbershop, the commotion in tailorshops all over Teresienburg, the feverish activity in the pawnshop—even Žofika, the cashier girl at the Freedom—everything reflected the excitement over Count Fudshi-Hasegawa, who was to arrive at 5:00 P.M. by the Budapest Express. The program was planned for only a twenty-four-hour period, since, according to his schedule, Count Fudshi had to depart the following day at 2:00 P.M. on the Fiume Express to attend an international shipping conference in Venice. The Count was to stay as a guest of the Seventeenth in a suite in the Hungarian Regent. At the last minute the arrival of the hero of Port Arthur, General Lin-tsi, and his retinue was announced and Cavalry Captain Count Hollós was to take them under his personal, most hospitable attention. A small program for the reception ceremony was hurriedly set up in the following way, according to instructions that arrived by telegraph from the War Ministry: At 5:00 P.M. the official reception at the railway station. Count Fudshi-Hasegawa to be escorted by the generals.

Snacks in the regimental mess hall. At 7:00 P.M. the officer corps of the Seventeenth awaits him *in corpore* in the honor hall. A welcoming speech from the regimental commander, Colonel von Warronigg. The reply of His Excellency Count Fudshi-Hasegawa. At 8:00 P.M. a lecture in the grand hall of the officers' club by First Lieutenant of the Seventeenth Regiment, Dr. Ramong Gejza of Örkényi and Magasfalva on the topic: "The Ninety-Seventh Anniversary of the Battle of Aspern and Essling, with lantern slides." At 9:15 a gala dinner in honor of the victor of Liaoyang and Mukden in the dining hall of the Seventeenth Regiment. After that, a "Venetian night" in the regimental park. The next day combined divisional maneuvers with infantry and artillery. Movement into positions at 2:00 A.M. Review of the Seventeenth on the terrain near Malomfalva at 9:30 A.M. At 11:30 a grand division luncheon in the field. The general returns to Teresienburg in a division four-in-hand. Departure by the express train to Fiume at 2:10 P.M.

• At exactly 5:33 the victor of Liaoyang, Count Fudshi-Hasegawa, entered the main doors of the regiment's honor hall, accompanied by the Japanese admiral, Baron Watanaba; the general of Port Arthur, Pei Lin-tsi; the commander of the Teresienburg infantry division, Lieutenant Field Marshal von Schwartner; the brigadier of the Seventy-Fourth Brigade, the Honorable Major General Draveczky-Draveczky Lajoš; and the commander of the Seventeenth, Colonel von Warronigg. At the head of the full suite of division adjutants, aides-de-camp, and orderly officers, in front of the complete officer corps of the Seventeenth Royal Imperial Dragoon Regiment, in the midst of that mass of dress uniforms, lacquer, nickel, and gold, Count Fudshi-Hasegawa wore a gray morning coat, white tie, a *démodé* top hat, and bright gloves. His glasses, thick as a finger for his nearsightedness, appeared old-fashioned, and his sharp incisors and eyeteeth made him look as if he were snarling.

Colonel von Warronigg threw the routine, director-like glance of an experienced commander at the officers of his Seventeenth Regiment. Standing there were the twenty-nine officers of the Teresienburg Dragoon Division, from Lieutenant Colonel von Redl to Cadet Fazekas Imra, all in full-dress uniform: spiked dragoon helmet under the right arm, light-blue surcoat with the Seventeenth's famous empire-yellow braid (the color of a canary, the reason they were called canaries or Alsóvár omeletteers), red trousers, shiny boots, and heavy cavalry sabers on their thighs; all regulation stiff, all in white gloves, shaven, mute, dignified as statues. At the moment Lieutenant General Fudshi-Hasegawa crossed the threshold of the massive oak door, twenty-nine pair of spurs clicked, their sharp report echoing unpleasantly through the hall like the sound of broken glass.

. The first to pass along the fourteen-and-a-half-meter red carpet in front of the rank of officers was General Count Fudshi-Hasegawa, the direct descendant of one of the most famous thunder gods of the yellow Mongolian Olympus and a fragile white elephant, so celebrated that she became the mother of demigods and demielephants in imperial vestments. After him came the admiral, Baron Watanaba, with General Pei Lin-tsi, and after the admiral, the dour, mute, extremely strict and formally reserved division commander, Lieutenant Field Marshal von Schwartner, in the modest glimmer of his title of nobility granted by His Highness, which he had held for exactly two years. Admiral Watanaba was in the full-dress uniform of a Japanese naval officer, with a two-cornered admiral's hat and white swan's plumage, richly bedecked with twenty-two of the highest international orders with stars, enameled insignia, silver decorations, and sashes; the hero of Port Arthur, Pei Lin-tsi, was in a simple khaki uniform with miniature ribbons of distinction in two lengthy, multicolored bands over the heart. Pei Lin-tsi, who had looked sure death in the eyes for nine months at Port Arthur, this superman, this *miles gloriosus*, had no sword: in his right hand he nervously tapped a forty-centimeter long bamboo reed sheathed in silver. The Japanese generals, escorted by the division general, the brigadier, and Colonel von Warronigg, passed to the back of the hall and stopped beneath the portrait of His Highness the Emperor and King, Franz Joseph I, mounted on a black Arab in the dress uniform of an Austrian field marshal—a monumental Italian composition from the time of Solferin and Magenta.

Approaching the podium, the Japanese gentlemen turned, while the suite of adjutants, escorts, and aides-de-camp discreetly remained to the left and right of the entrance. Warronigg, a tall, thin specter with a gray, untrimmed mustache, stood on the podium, almost half a head taller than the Japanese dignitaries, and, coming last in the suite of generals, he threw a restless glance over the faces of his officers, who were all lined up according to rank in the strictest of ceremonial postures waiting
· to hear the speech of their superior. There was a brief pause, which, according to regulations, was to be broken first by the division commandant, Lieutenant Field Marshal von Schwartner. Not very striking by nature and wheezing like an old man, the blue-blooded newcomer Von Schwartner dominated all those knightly dragoons with his general's outfit, red stripes, golden spurs, and high decorations. With the Order of Leopold, the Iron Cross of the Second Order, the Medal for Military Service on the banner of the Military Cross for Service, a silver collar ribbon for bravery, a war medal for the Bosnian occupation of 1878, the military service award of the third order for officers, a bronze jubilee commemorative ribbon, a jubilee military cross, an Italian service star—with all eleven orders on his chest and in a dress coat too tight for his asthma, Von Schwartner coughed loudly and dryly three times; then, with a hand sheathed in a newly cleaned doeskin glove of the cheapest possible grade that his wife had bought on the outskirts of Vienna from Jewish shopkeepers, he waved the officers to fall out of rank and join together to the left and right of the carpet facing the podium.

"Gentlemen, fall into ranks to the left and right!"

This action took place immediately, almost without a sound,

and after a momentary jangling of spurs it was quiet again. The officer corps of the Seventeenth Dragoon Regiment stood as still as if made of wax, without a single movement; barely blinking their eyelashes, they seemed like one individual looking at Lieutenant General Count Fudshi-Hasegawa. They were all there, the whole elite Seventeenth. The Counts Hollós, Walderode, and Buttler; the regiment's four barons, Swirsen, Lendway, Rimay, and Cziráky; the Duke of Mantua and nine nobles. Among them was First Lieutenant Ramong Gejza of Örkény and Magasfalva, the pride of the regiment, a doctor of mathematics at the University of Tübingen; and then eleven untitled officers, among them the best horsemen, Szalai, the son of a district scribe, and First Lieutenant Sztatocsny Emil, who possessed some small artistic talent and who copied the tapestry depicting the Circassians of St. Quentin attacking at the windmills of Lützen.

At that moment in the hall there were more than fifty pairs of spurs, fifty nickel escutcheons, fifty sabers, and more than two hundred precious orders: Japanese, Austro-Hungarian, and international ones made of silver and enamel, silk and blood. All the straps, all the little chains, bronze lions' heads, horses' tails on hussar shakos, hussar cloaks and dragoon dress uniforms, helmets and headgear, double-headed golden eagles, gloves, lions' paws and escutcheons, eyes, coiffures, dentures—all this looked dead and motionless, without a single intelligent thought. And beneath the fur of the hussars' cloaks and the pastel-blue cloth of the dragoons' coats, the tightly pressed human flesh breathed uniformly, hardly noticeable. The gloves were as white as if covered with chalk; the escutcheons shone as if made of some expensive metal; the handles of the heavy cavalry sabers, the fringe on the golden shoulder belts, the spurs, the eyebrows and mustaches—all was rigid, covered with polish, lacquer, and brilliantine, cleaned with solvent, ironed, put into order, trimmed and set out for show. Beneath the painting of His Imperial Majesty, beneath the old portraits of its deceased commanders, beneath its bloody banners, stood the Seventeenth Royal Imperial Dragoon Regiment in dress uniform, to honor the victor of Manchuria, Liaoyang, and Mukden, Count Fudshi-Hasegawa.

Lieutenant Field Marshal von Schwartner spoke in a boring and cliché-ridden fashion, as is usually the case on such occasions. He said that he considered it an exceptional honor to be able to greet one of the greatest of strategic geniuses in the name of one of the most elite imperial regiments, a man who must remain immortal in the Pantheon of international Glory and Honor, along with the immortal Von Clausewitz, Von Bleibtreu, and the Archduke Karl. Not that Count Fudshi is a man of only simple practical experience: he is a scientist who had already earned the right to the victor's laurels during the Sino-Japanese War of 1895 because of his heavy-mortar ballistics system, "Fudshi 306." America had already given him due recognition, Columbia University conferring upon him an honorary doctorate in 1897.

According to the program, Colonel von Warronigg next took the floor. He spoke of the skillful operations of Count Nodzu's and Baron Kuroki's armies, and he especially stressed the fact that the battle of Liaoyang was a masterpiece of military craft due to the amazing and harmonious cooperation of everyone, but especially due to the intuition and strategic perception of Count Fudshi. He was especially pleased to be speaking to the victor of the twenty-ninth of August on this very day, the twenty-second of May, the ninety-seventh anniversary of Bonaparte's first defeat. Having mentioned for the seventeenth time the word "especially," he loudly and pathetically cited General Kuroki's order of the day: "The Kuroki army, which has so often inflicted casualties on the enemy, must now carry out an attack at night with a larger number of troops than has ever before been the case. Let no one think he shall return alive. Therefore, let everyone put on a clean shirt." A command such as that from a general is no longer a matter of military style—it is pure epic!

Such heroes belong to the time of legends. But one of those legendary heroes is standing on the podium, and the Seventeenth Dragoon Regiment, especially thrilled, considers this twenty-second of May, 1906, its most glorious day after the twenty-second of May, 1809.

⁎ After a pause of forty seconds the legendary Japanese hero, clad in gray ceremonial coat with top hat in hand, shortsighted and humble as a professor at his lectern, began to speak, standing on the podium beneath the Lützen tapestry, the banners of Malplaquet, Kolin, Aspern and Essling, Magenta and Königgraetz, and the painting of His Imperial Majesty. He spoke in English. In subdued half tones, he asked the generals and officers of the Seventeenth to forgive him for not knowing German, but whatever he had not yet forgotten was so insignificant that he would be embarrassed to affront the high cultural level of this famous and victorious corps.

Count Fudshi-Hasegawa spoke slowly and at length, stressing certain words, but practically no one in the corps understood him other than Count Hollós, the Duke of Mantua, and First Lieutenant Ramong. One heard him mention Bonaparte's name, the battles of Aspern and Essling and Wagram, Moscow, Manchuria, Port Arthur, and Liaoyang; they could tell he was speaking with skill and knowledge; and standing there on the podium, Count Fudshi gave the impression of an empiricist "who, black from cannon powder, threw more than one hundred and fifty battalions into the jaws of death"—Field Marshal von Schwartner's words—thereby affecting the generals and dragoons and adjutants in a magical way. The yellow face, rough and hard as India rubber, the even incisors and eyeteeth beneath the red lips, the shaved Mongol mask with thick glasses, the text in English, imposing and enigmatic—they were all very effective and realistic. And for possibly a full minute following his final words, no one budged or spoke a word. The long silence was full of respect and the feeling of history. After the pause, His Excellency expressed the desire to meet each officer personally. At that, with one movement of his hand, Field Marshal von Schwartner divided the files of eight dragoons into ranks to the left and right of the red carpet, and, accompanied by Count Hollós and the Duke of Mantua as interpreters, Count Fudshi-Hasegawa made the prescribed rounds of all the officers present. He shook hands with each one, and Colonel Mihajlo von Warronigg pointed out to him the outstanding members of the Seventeenth. These included Baron Cziráky, a graduate of the War College, first in rank and future officer of the general staff; Count Buttler, the best shot; First Lieutenant Gejza Ramong, a doctor of mathematics at the University of Tübingen; First Lieutenant Emil Sztatocsny, a painter and student at the Budapest Academy of Art; and First Lieutenant Szalai, who had set an international world record by seven millimeters in the stadium jumping event at the international horse show in Copenhagen the previous fall. Escorted step by step by the general officers, Count Fudshi asked various questions and, bowing to the last dragoon, Cadet Fazekas, he grinned affably and left the hall, escorted by Lieutenant Field Marshal von Schwartner, Admiral Baron Watanaba, and the general of Port Arthur, Pei Lintsi. The trumpets could still be heard echoing their martial salute at the portal of the old Jesuit cloister; the gentlemen climbed into the four-in-hand, followed by five coaches with adjutants and orderly officers, and the procession set off at a trot for the Hungarian Regent on Cathedral Square.

First Lieutenant Ramong Gejza was out of sorts for several reasons. Two months earlier he had sent his dissertation on elliptoids to Tübingen, and in so doing had hoped to rid himself of both Maria Teresienburg and the Seventeenth Dragoons, with which he had now been serving for five years; he was rather bored by such a fate. However, he had received no answer from Tübingen and, according to his private sources of information, he learned that the matter of obtaining a faculty post at the University of Tübingen would not go as smoothly as had at first appeared. Unforeseen obstacles and complications arose everywhere. Besides Tübingen, he had reliable connections through a Budapest technical agency with the Department of Fortifications in the War Ministry of the Republic of Bolivia, which was seeking a highly qualified military engineer and mathematics specialist. Lieutenant Ramong was not really a military engineer, having only completed a one-year course in that field two years before; but now, since the Republic of Bolivia was asking for new documents, the whole business was even more complicated. His chances of earning a few thousand pounds a year had never become anything concrete, and those few thousand pounds seemed to him the only way out of the romantic predicament in which he found himself with the wife of his commander, Warronigg. Colonel von Warronigg was not satisfied for several reasons with having Ramong in the regiment, and he had, "on his own initiative," as they say, recommended him as an instructor of technology in the cadet school in Mährisch Weisskirchen in order to get rid of this unpleasant and haughty person about whom his wife had been dreaming since last New Year's Eve. Lieutenant Ramong was not accepted as a technical specialist at Mährisch Weisskirchen. And now, just when Olga was preparing to travel to Sicily, that stupid ninety-seventh anniversary of Aspern and Essling came around, those Japanese arrived, and Colonel von Warronigg began to harass him to give some impossible lecture with lantern slides in the casino.

"After all, what can be said about the 'victory' at Aspern when it wasn't a victory at all, but only an insignificant strategic intermezzo between Vienna and Wagram?—a series of debacles from Regensburg to Thaun, from Abensberg to Wagram, each bigger than the one before. And what good comes from lying about historical facts? Bonaparte sits in Schönbrunn, and they falsify the facts as victories! Unbelievable!"

Bent over the map somewhere between Regensburg and Vienna, where everything was covered with red arrows indicating the direction of the movements of Bonaparte's marshals, Masséna, Davout, Lannes, and Bessières, Lieutenant Ramong stared mechanically at the names on the map and thought about the colonel's wife, Olga. Last night at dusk her maid had come by his place and delivered a letter from her. He knew she was ready to go to Sicily, but that she would brush him off with an ordinary calling card with the three letters, p.p.c. (*pour prendre congé*)—that was a little too much, even from Olga Warronigg. That might be how a Pomeranian is brushed from one's lap, but not a doctor of mathematics and an officer of the Seventeenth. Is he some sack to be tossed overboard? Now, what was the deployment of forces between Aspern and Wagram? Bonaparte: Oudinot—three divisions; Davout—four divisions, cavalry reserves; Bessières—five mounted divisions; Bernadotte, Wrède, and Broussier in a concentric movement from Graz to Linz. But what happened to Archduke Karl's Major General Schoustek? Where is that idiot Schoustek? (How could anyone be called Schoustek? Ridiculous!) So, a calling card with p.p.c. . . . Does Olga think he will forget this challenge? It would not be worthy of a Ramong to let this pass in silence. And if she shows up tomorrow at the dinner for the Japanese, he will let her know what he thinks. He is going to clarify his relations with that woman at any cost! She's going to remember this!

Ramong Gejza had a rather complex personality. The only son of a retired hussar, Lieutenant Colonel Ramong Aurel, the young man had spent a very sad childhood with his father, who had been left a widower and had also, as a young officer, been thrown in a horse race thereby unhappily and silently wearing a wooden leg the rest of his life. According to family legend, the Ramongs were of Spanish descent; their crest of nobility, dating from 1694, bore the Spanish colors: a red eagle-lion on a yellow field. For his son's twenty-seventh birthday, in September of the previous year, Ramong's father sent him *The Letters to a Young Officer* bound in yellow-orange silk, along with the comment that he was, of course, pleased that his son had passed the doctoral examinations in mathematics, but that he considered his son's imperial officer's commission as a First Lieutenant a much more important distinction than his Tübingen elliptoids.

As a disabled veteran with one wooden leg, old Ramong became an accountant and, full of longing for life in the squadron, worked for twenty years as a clerk in military accounting offices, in the end only to find himself degraded and pensioned off. Sad and empty, he lived in one of those unclean and gloomy streets near Eastside Station in Budapest, where secondhand dealers sell broken furniture and music boxes echo from inside the taverns. Old Ramong occupied a three-room apartment on the second floor of a huge tenement house with a Renaissance balcony and an ugly northern façade washed by rain and wind, where plump, goitrous pigeons cooed all day long beneath the plaster caryatids. In 1899 he had the most up-to-date artificial limb, with rubber joints, made by a French health-aids company, and that same year he showed up at the Red Cross ball, looking dashing in the full-dress uniform of a hussar and in brand-new patent-leather shoes.

The very fact that his father wore a wooden leg had alienated the son to the point of reticent withdrawal. From the start, he thought of his father as of a third person, as of some strange man with a wooden leg. That gray street near Eastside Station, those three rooms on the second floor with a balcony, that cold unheated living room with the red velvet easy chairs and the stools in imitation French gilt, which looked as flimsy as the furniture in photography studios—all this seemed to Ramong very strange and distant. From earliest childhood he had an unpleasant feeling whenever he thought of his father's wooden leg, of how he went to stupid balls with that leg, of the furniture in the living room always in white linen slipcovers, of his father drinking brandy every morning and smoking stinking Puerto Rican cigars; and in that complex of unpleasant associations Ramong became so indifferent to his father's home that the house never had any real meaning for him.

After his eleventh year in military institutions, Ramong always thought of his home coldly, as of some unpleasant place one goes on leave, the fried chicken always done thinly and without fat, the noodles hard, the rooms unheated. Later, when he came to the regiment—first the Ninth and then the Seventeenth—Ramong lived at the same withdrawn distance, removed from actuality, always involved in his single passion: mathematics. From the first grade in the elementary military academy of Kiseg until Mährisch Weisskirchen, Ramong was exceptional in mathematics, possessing true mathematical insight in the highest sense of the word, and isolated from every reality of life. He had never shown any special knowledge of women, and in the eyes of such a young man, the charming Baroness Warronigg was an ideal of the most naïve, noble, post-Petrarchan type.

"A man, a cavalry officer, can go ahead and be a woman chaser, but then he gets ill, catches syphilis, smells of perfume from Budapest, makes wry faces dressed in his red trousers like a circus monkey, walks around in his patent-leather shoes, and has his so-called success with the ladies. He's a roué, stinks of filthy brilliantine, greases himself all over, has his own rakish logic, and lives according to it! He marries the landlord's daughter, lives in his own house as her dignified spouse, has a yearly income of thirty thousand crowns, collects rent at eight per cent, drinks beer on the promenade on Sunday mornings, nibbles pretzels, travels second class on night express trains, and dies as a cavalry major, a paralytic, and a cuckold."

Ramong Gejza could never understand the secret nature of such so-called success with the ladies. Even in puberty it seemed beneath his personal dignity to approach any lady at all (of middle-class stock) and address her as "dear young lady," dressed in his red trousers like a circus ape: pardon, if you have nothing better to do, I would like a waltz with you! Even to himself he seemed as ridiculous as some caricature from those old-fashioned albums bound in velvet: pardon, "my dear young lady," if you have no objection, allow me, young lady, to introduce myself. I am Ramong Gejza of Magasfalva and Örkény, a first lieutenant in the Seventeenth. I'm a syphilitic in red trousers and I smear my hair with brilliantine! Your father is a druggist, he owns a reputable and successful pharmacy in the main square, he sells worm tablets, digestive teas, and Franz Joseph Epsom salt; your venerable father owns a marvelous drugstore with dark violet vessels of potassium permanganate in the window, and I, my dear young lady, would be most honored to sire the grandchildren of a druggist, my future father-in-law, who will be so generous as to present to me and to deed over to my name as dowry a two-story house with a balcony on the corner of Maria Valeria and Matija Korvin! You, my kind lady, will openly cheat on me in Opatija, Vienna, and Roič, and we will become an ideal couple; dare I ask you to waltz "On the Beautiful Blue Danube"? There! That's how one so stupidly gets his women! But what kind of women? Silly young girls of Teresienburg who laugh raucously at the balls, while the old owls, the mothers, the wives of druggists, follow us with the look of the cursed Erinyes! Ridiculous! This always seemed beneath his dignity, and at such times he would think himself as stupid as a character from such an old-fashioned velvet album: pardon, if you have no objection, allow me to introduce myself. I am Ramong Gejza! Reprehensible! Stupid! Silly! But even if a fellow doesn't skate, dance, chase women, play cards, and isn't syphilitic, he still has to amount to something in this world of horses, champagne, women, and cards! But how?

Kállay Bandi, for example, was a real rake! First Lieutenant Kállay Bandi had experienced the most satisfying kind of love with no less than thirty women over the last fifteen years. Always elegant, wearing patent-leather slippers, bathed and fully manicured, pedicured, groomed, cleansed, massaged, exercised, free of gonorrhea, shaved, powdered—Kállay Bandi studied English by the Berlitz method, corresponded with seven ladies at the same time (but never any connected with his own regiment, in line with the famed regulations of old and experienced lovers), studied the most modern dances, the bon-ton and cake-walk, played "La Machicha" on the guitar, sang the newest couplet by Medgyaszay, "Little Lady, oh yes, oh yes," and was one of the most successful ladies' men in the whole Seventeenth. He was a dressy lover without fault or fear; he wore three golden bracelets on his left wrist, stayed in the Hungarian Regent, and had an inscribed picture album with a whole series of naked women.

· Or take the Duke of Mantua! He painted, wrote music, toyed with technical inventions, had subscriptions to English newspapers, took photographs, studied law, hunted with imperial princes, was the sensation of all the ladies, and had money. Yes, the Duke of Mantua was a profligate down to the blue-blooded, princely prestige of his blue stockings. Women fell for him without a second thought, happy that they could do so, for he raised them to the heights of his own princely brilliance and respectability. And he was the only one to be blamed socially for all his affairs in Maria Teresienburg. For instance, Dr. Ujhelyi, the district assessor and husband of the duke's latest flame, Mme. Ujhelyi, considered the prince's visits to his humble apartment in Petőfi Šandor Street a particular honor.

All the aristocrats of the Seventeenth were roués. It was said that Cavalry Captain L'Ours-Walderode was a progressive paralytic; even Captain Döbrentey, himself a progressive paralytic, proclaimed aloud, when drunk, that the Teresienburg Seventeenth was more like a *variété ensemble* than a regiment of true nobles. Captain Döbrentey was a well-defined Mongol type with strong, sharp cheekbones and horizontal slits for eyes; and as the commander of the regimental machine-gun detachment, he always spoke in a deep baritone, as if screaming from the bottom of a black barrel during heavy fire. "Gentlemen, I tell you, an officer is an officer when he is black from gunpowder, smoke, and explosives, when he is bloody and covered with mud. That's a real man's officer. But today there are only wax dolls, models wearing the latest fashionable cut, mannequins who fall from the display windows onto the sidewalk of Maria Valeria Street!"

First Lieutenant Ramong did not dance, play cards, chase women, or exhibit much interest in military science. His energetic, shaved face, thin chiseled lips, his high forehead and wavy hair, his persistent silence—all this betrayed a person who was considered a somewhat strange and unapproachable eccentric in the regiment. Just as Lieutenant Winterfeld was the regimental "aesthete" and published poems under the Hungarian pseudonym Téli Viktor (moreover, his collection of Venetian sonnets, *Torre del' orologio*, was mentioned by the provincial newspaper critic with considerable respect), and just as Lieutenant Sztatocsny painted, so, too, Ramong continued his interest in mathematics instead of chattering about waltzes with the pretty cashier girl Žofika, or babbling about horses and cards. At first this was due to boredom, but then mathematics became for Ramong a real substitute for cigars, horses, and cards: in time he turned into a passionate mathematician.

At night he read Euler, La Grange, and Descartes, and in the morning he was afraid of the bugle. The yellow lights in the stables, the smell of horses, the chewing of hay, the jangle of chains, the shouting of the night guards—this was all so gloomy and prisonlike in his monotonous life in the cavalry, so disgustingly filthy. The fog, the dark autumn mornings, the stench of wet sawdust on the riding track, the unpleasant touch of one's superiors were paled by the brighter glow of formulae whenever the latest copy of *The Cambridge Mathematical Journal* with its light-yellow cover would arrive. Ramong read his *Cambridge Mathematical Journal* with the pleasure of someone reading music scores. For Lieutenant Ramong the cover of light ocher, the lemon-yellow wrapper, represented a genuine, deep, simple joy, the joy one sees in the eyes of children when their fingers touch a yellow, rustling, silk-covered package full of dates or chocolate bonbons; and when the *Annual Report of German Mathematicians* published his work on Gauss's disquisitions, Ramong was like a sailor who has been waiting for a wind in the

lull of a sad and wretched harbor. The one picture that decorated his room was a four-color engraving of Géricault's work,
"The Raft of the Medusa," which he had cut from a Viennese
coffeehouse illustration a year before, right after his first physical
contact with Olga. Olga chased him to the edge of insanity with
that picture. For her the picture was a symbol of her life, the
picture of all her shipwrecks. But Ramong, a man with a live
and virginally pure imagination, fell in love with this ingenious
artist's shipwreck, although not without a strange foreboding of
his own drowning.

⸰ Following a transfer to a military engineering course at the
university in Vienna, Ramong attended lectures for almost a
year by Müller, the Jacobian enthusiast, who recommended him
to one of his students, Lichthofen, a professor at Tübingen and
a world figure of first rank; and so a mathematical correspondence developed between Ramong and Lichthofen that culmi-
nated with the honor of doctor of mathematics at Tübingen
being conferred upon Ramong. His doctoral degree made him
one of the Seventeenth's most interesting officers, and so, of
course, from New Year's Eve until May (exactly a year before),
the colonel's wife Olga demonstrated her extremely good-
natured interest in the young "professor of mathematics" with
the moist, dark, melancholy eyes of a young pointer.

It came about in very ordinary fashion, in accordance with the
rules of Olga's method. The adventure took definite shape the
past September in a sanatorium at Baden near Vienna, and
Ramong, for whom Olga was one of his first serious experiences,
lost control over himself completely. All his ideas about the assistantship at Tübingen, his hopes and dreams of those thousands of Bolivian pounds, became so drowned in his feelings for
Olga that, in his fevered state, Ramong forgot reality. For Olga
it was a completely ordinary affair ("My God, after all, it's all
the same, one experience more or less"), and the whole winter
she had been trying to dissolve this quite superficial, unpleasant,
and insignificant association with as little friction and conflict as

possible. The whole spring she had met Ramong only two or three times, the last time in the middle of April, during a morning ride along the oak-lined trail of the bishop's game preserve; and yesterday, before her departure for Sicily, she had sent him a calling card, *pour prendre congé.*

• Lieutenant Ramong's lecture on the "Ninety-Seventh Anniversary of the Battle of Aspern and Essling" in the officers' club before the distinguished Japanese guests could not have been more boring. The club's small hall was unbearably hot. There was such a mass of dignitaries from Teresienburg society jammed into the one hall with its six windows that the seven neighboring rooms, along with two anterooms and the corridors, were overflowing with guests. Ramong was totally lacking in spirit. He read his manuscript dryly and so quietly that his voice could not be heard beyond the first rows. The parquet floor creaked, the people stirred restlessly, and spurs jangled; in the corridors orderlies were constantly carrying chairs and lemonade back and forth, the lamp in the lantern-slide projector failed several times, and Lieutenant Ramong was completely unable to concentrate. Olga Warronigg sat beside two Teresienburg generals' wives in the brown semidarkness of the second row, carrying a cream-colored parasol and dressed in a white lace dress and long black gloves up to her elbows, which were white as alabaster. No matter how he strained to concentrate on the events between Regensburg and Wagram, Ramong constantly thought of Olga, of her three letters of farewell, of how her diaphanous beauty surpassed that of all the generals' wives (those wretched offspring of druggists); how her somber black gloves, dark as the darkest pansy, symbolized at this moment a wondrously pathetic collapse, the collapse of everything that made life seem worth living to him; how this pale, alabaster woman had slept in his arms in the full radiance of her beauty—how velvety and naked she was, how her long hair overflowed in a fragrant, dark, venomous, infernal cascade. And tomorrow she will no longer be on this planet, but will disappear like a shadow at dawn, just fade away noiselessly, and he will remain alone in his shameful and foolish predicament.

Undoubtedly, that woman had a hand in her husband's suggestion that he be transferred to Mährisch Weisskirchen! She is traveling to Sicily; afterwards she will spend the summer in Agram, and by autumn he will be far away in Weisskirchen! Fine treatment!

"And on the fifth of July the commander, Archduke Karl, had a hundred and thirty-five thousand rifles and more than four hundred cannon at his disposal. Major General von Klenau's Sixth Corps was at Floridsdorf, Wagram, Hirschstetten, Aspern, and Essling. The Seventeenth Regiment made up the left flank between Count Nordmann and Kolowrat in General Schoustek's brigade. The water level of the Danube was two point one seven above normal!"

She is nervous! She is constantly wiping her nose as if she has a cold! Her eyes are moist; she is biting her lips! And he had named her Galatea! What happened to those days? Galatea is chewing her lip nervously! Her gloves are as dark as the canvas on the drums at cavalry funeral processions!

They had read D'Annunzio together: *"Le vergine delle rocce"* —and Galatea's knees were silver, like that baroque crucifix in Mantua. Oh, those knees of Galatea when she bathed in his apartment in Vienna, triply resplendent in the crystal of the mirrors, illuminated with the seven colors of the prism, the light, alabaster knees and thick, silken hair, and with his warm palm he felt her kneecaps, cold as marble. Galatea had always been cold as stone, the rough, unfeeling marble of a gravestone; her ancestors were crude Balkan, Slavic peasants, barbarians, and everything about them was bare, mute, stony, rough. . . .

"And in the early morning of July the fifth, Napoleon threw bridges over the Danube channel during the worst of storms and extended his base line from Oudinot to Bernadotte, thus having one hundred seventy thousand rifles under his command. And so the bloody overture to the battle of Wagram began to unfold, one of the most fatal and horrible strategic catastrophes in all military history."

This enumeration of strategic facts in half tones lasted for something over thirty-five minutes. Then the chandelier in the hall burst forth with light and the din of the guests' voices filled the space. Ramong was warmly congratulated by Count Fudshi-Hasegawa, and the general of Port Arthur, Lin-tsi, spoke to him briefly, mixing his poor English so much with Japanese expressions that Ramong did not understand a word. Colonel von Warronigg came up after Lieutenant Field Marshal von Schwartner, who had shaken Ramong's hand coldly.

"I'm very dissatisfied with you, Ramong! You put the emphasis of your report on the events between Regensburg and Wagram, so that, according to your interpretation, it seemed that practically nothing happened at Aspern and Essling. This evening we are not celebrating Wagram, the greatest strategic catastrophe in world history, but Aspern and Essling, dear fellow. It's really quite inexplicable! And then, the role of Schoustek's brigade and our Seventeenth Regiment—what bungling! Besides, if you had shown the slightest tact toward our guests, you would have drawn a parallel. If nothing else, you could have used the number of cannon as an example: the ratio was approximately the same at both Wagram and Liaoyang! But we will discuss the matter in detail tomorrow at report!"

Without offering the lieutenant his hand, Colonel von Warronigg turned away with a slight nod of his head and walked toward the group surrounding Count Fudshi, who was being introduced to Countess Margita Hollós, by birth the Countess Hussarek-Walderode. Von Warronigg was hurt and furious. He had expected that Ramong would mention General Albert von Warronigg, his great-grandfather, who, as a first lieutenant of the Chevaux-Légers in General Schoustek's brigade at the battle of Aspern and Essling, had been cited by name in an Order of the Supreme Command and received his title of baron. This fact was known to all the officers of the regiment, and Lieuten-ant Colonel Redl, as master-of-ceremonies at last night's torch light ceremony, had especially stressed it. Ramong's omission of this seemed particularly neglectful to Colonel von Warronigg, since he felt it would have been proper to mention this before the Japanese guests out of a feeling of regimental camaraderie and a spirit of unity.

Ramong was standing at the table, tall, trim, nervous, sweaty, gathering his papers and maps and looking at the guests in the hall as if daydreaming. The chandelier shone with a yellowish light, the warm May evening cast a blue haze on the street out-side and on the windowpanes; out there the gentlemen, ladies, syphilitics, and druggists' daughters were moving about—all the high life of Teresienburg; Lieutenant Baron Rimay was smiling and carrying a wicker chair high over the heads of the ladies; and Galatea had disappeared mysteriously. Galatea was gone. Gone! No, Olga is here, she is smiling ever so charmingly at Admiral Watanaba; of course she is speaking English with him—Olga speaks English well!

"What's wrong with you this evening, Gejza?" Kállay Bandi said, coming up to Ramong. "You sounded so lifeless tonight that I thought you would faint! What's wrong? Are you ill? You're pale as a lemon!"

A horseshoe-shaped table with sixty-two places was laid in the grand hall of the Seventeenth Regiment's officers' mess. Hochnjetz, the maître d'hôtel of the Hungarian Regent, a skilled old bordello manager in the grand style with a fine repu-tation in all the establishments of the Empire, who had worked in first-class Swiss establishments where he was renowned for his fish, wine, and sweet ices of all kinds, succeeded in turning that ordinary horseshoe-shaped table for sixty-two persons into an event talked about in Teresienburg long afterward. Instead of a tablecloth, Hochnjetz laid the center of the table with a green carpet of soft moss and decorated it with tulips and lilies of the valley; in front of each place was a *cocarde à la mode anglaise*, draped in red and white Japanese and yellow and black Imperial colors. The silver candelabra only three meters above the table, the crystal bowls with roses, the garlands of fir branches, the decorative *cocardes*, all had the effect of some "Austro-Hungarian magic à la Hochnjetz." In addition to the heavy somogy bikavér that was served there was also a Tokay, thick and yellow as amber, called "Gray Friar" as early as the sixteenth century, a wine famed throughout Hungary for its honey bouquet—a gift of the Lord used by the Holy Father, Pope Leo XIII in all the ceremonial masses in the Basilica of St. Peter. There was also an imperial reserve Törley champagne and fish from Lake Balaton as well as quail from the Teresienburg district. This was all topped off with a heavy, dark Danubian wine from the district of Somogy, which, after the first toasts to the Mikado and the Emperor, Franz Joseph I, went to everybody's head.

Lieutenant General Count Fudshi-Hasegawa sat at the place of honor between two generals' wives: the Honorable Mizzi Schwartner, wife of the division commander, and the very Honorable Draveczky-Draveczka, wife of the brigade commander, the Baroness Lendvay by birth. It was said that Mizzi Schwartner had been a chambermaid, and that the conversation in her Louis XV salon touched on servants, laundry, and preserves, while the brigade commander's wife had been a famous equestrienne at the Spanish School, spending each morning on horseback along the lanes in the apple orchards on the eastern edge of town. So the victor of Liaoyang, Count Fudshi-Hasegawa, a truly fine psychologist and connoisseur of the female soul, for whom it was easy to lay bare all the secrets of these naïve Viennese women, proceeded to explain to the gracious Mizzi Schwartner that the question of good and faithful servants was not so important in Japan as in Teresienburg, where, according to the general's wife, "one is simply unable to find a good Hungarian chambermaid at any price."

"Your Excellency, you must know that we Japanese, the

happy people of our esteemed Mikado, are still living, to our great fortune, in the eighteenth century! Thanks to our tradition, your idea of Western European democracy is completely foreign to us. None of us has an inkling of what the odious and stupid word means! Thank God, we Japanese are a feudal people; the concept of revolution is unknown to us. With us, service is silent—deaf and dumb!"

"Well, of course you don't have revolution, thank God, but you also don't have any Hungarians, you don't speak Hungarian; every one of you speaks Japanese! You are all Japanese! But as for us!

"If a maid is from Vienna, she can't speak a word of Hungarian, and you can't send her to the store even for coffee, because nowadays Hungarian chauvinism is so extreme that no one gets service anywhere if he doesn't know Hungarian! The Japanese are lucky that they all speak Japanese and don't have to worry about their maids, at least as far as language goes!"

To the left and right, next to the generals' wives, sat the two Japanese heroes, Pei Lin-tsi and Admiral Watanaba. Olga Warronigg was next to Admiral Watanaba; Countess Hollós sat next to Pei Lin-tsi. Generals von Schwartner and von Draveczky and Colonels von Warronigg and Fuchs sat across from the Japanese, together with the countesses, baronesses, and ladies of Teresienburg, according to a bizarre, somewhat Asiatic protocol that Olga had fretted over for a full twenty-four hours. Everything came off according to plan, without incident: the Törley wine was good, the champagne opened without exploding, the orderlies served very politely and discreetly, the band of the 107th, under the personal leadership of Kapellmeister Czibulka, played quietly and sweetly. In a word: the Seventeenth Dragoon Regiment had no reason to be ashamed of its victory over Bonaparte on May 22, 1809.

By the time the English meat dish arrived it turned out that Count Fudshi-Hasegawa spoke German quite well; he was explaining the secrets of his victory over General Blagovješčenski to the generals on the other side of the table. So that the distances of his base of operations would be completely clear to them, Count Fudshi compared the distances of the far-off Manchurian battlefield with distances in Austria, and it turned out that Count Fudshi knew the Austro-Hungarian map with great precision: "The distance from Pula to Bruck on the Mura corresponds approximately to the distance between Port Arthur and Liaoyang, and that from Pula to Bečko Novo Mjesto, to the distance between Port Arthur and Mukden. Wafangkou is Ljubljana, Fenghwangcheng is Zalaegerszeg, and Vindshu is Kiskomárom."

This rather puzzling pyrotechnical display of masterfully handled material concerning local Austrian topography and distance, and the dazzling feat of memory of the Japanese general evoked a surprise among the humble provincial strategists bordering on dumfounded astonishment. The reputation of the Japanese generals began to skyrocket beyond belief. Like some kind of giants, these small yellow cats imposed themselves totally on the Teresienburg general staff. There was nothing but affirmative nodding in the officers' ranks at every other word from these heroes.

Admiral Watanaba, who had completely charmed Olga Warronigg with his perfect English manner, sipped the Törley and told of how, during the Port Arthur action, he had found the head of the Russian general, Count Rutkovski, in a trench. This was only one insignificant episode in a whole series of Kuropatkin's "rear-guard actions" at Wafangkou. Seven and a half kilometers behind the artillery line, General von Raaben, Prince Nitko, and Count Rutkovski had been sitting in a pagoda playing poker when, with one explosion of a Japanese shell, three generals were turned into three pieces of decapitated flesh. Eight hours afterward General Rutkovski's head still held a cigarette, the gold holder in his mouth. The head was identified later by the gold cigarette holder—now Admiral Watanaba's

most treasured souvenir of that gallant war. As if hypnotized by
the words of a mysterious magician, all the beaming faces
flashed snake-like in the direction of the shining object that
gleamed like an ominous token from some legendary battle between the thin, transparent, arachnoid fingers of this panther.

، Admiral Watanaba told his bloody tales with a kind of super-
cilious smile on his face, as if he could see much farther than all
these other military ignoramuses; and in his description of the
miserable Manchurian populace he did not spare even the most
revolting details. He told of individual cases of cannibalism in
Manchuria, where mothers cooked their own children, for the
war had trampled the pitiful province and then had abandoned
it to the mercy of the elements as an "international neutral
zone." Today Manchuria did not belong either to the Russian
or the Japanese sphere; not even a bird was left there, since the
people had eaten everything—birds, dogs, cats, horses, cows,
children, even beasts of burden! Nevertheless, the Japanese,
guided by the spirit of fellow love, had founded international
committees to aid provinces thus demolished by the catastrophe,
and, with American Quakers and the Salvation Army, were
founding charity committees in separate countries under international aegis. The American-Japanese activities had, to date,
shown very fine results.

Olga Warronigg showed great interest in the miserable plight
of the Manchurian widows and war orphans, but unfortunately
she was leaving for Sicily in a few days. But Mizzi Schwartner
promised the admiral that she, Draveczky-Draveczka, and
Countess Hollós would immediately set up a Danube commit-
tee corresponding to that of the American and Japanese and
would undertake the project for the whole Kingdom of Szent
István. This philanthropic gesture, coming from the generous
hearts of such charming ladies, reverberated sentimentally
throughout the whole drunken company, and Colonel Fuchs's
wife (a Sachs-Lohner by birth, of Jewish faith, and co-owner of

the Original Imperial Bitter Water) took off her diamond bracelet, as an example to all the millionairesses in the Empire of Saint Stephen.

Lieutenant Ramong sat with the non-commissioned and un-married officers on the left side of the horseshoe-shaped table; he was so inconveniently placed that his view of the generals, Admiral Watanaba, and Olga was blocked by a burning cande-labrum and the foliage. Through the sooty, warm flicker of the candles, the green of the boughs, the laurels and the roses, Ramong caught brief glimpses of the white splash of Olga's dé-colleté, and from time to time, amid the clinking of glasses and the soughing of the violins, he heard Olga laughing, happy, nervous, wonderful, distant.

Galatea was quoting Shelley—a dangerous thing! She quoted Shelley to him too, but it was all a lie! How insolently this re-pugnant, pretentious nymphomaniac lied, how she lied from the beginning as if according to some higher plan. And nothing was true! Everything about that woman is false! Why did she lie to him? Why had she told him, in tears, of her first morning of marriage with that Barnabas in a cavalry uniform? Why had she invented the whole romantic story of her suicide? She had been sleek and half naked under the silk Chinese shawl, soft as a butterfly under his fingers, and her rich, aromatic, thick hair steamed like incense in the small Viennese room; she spoke to him of the cursed, yellow, foggy morning in the Admiral Teget-thoff Hotel, when a seventeen-year-old girl's life-long Calvary began with an aristocratic gorilla—an unhappy, miserable girl in the hands of a vulgar, drunken syphilitic, a cavalryman, in idi-otic Vienna, where the twilight is so sad and where she, a pitiful orphan, had no one with whom she could exchange a human word! Galatea was alone, oh, God, alone, and when she threw herself into the muddy gray water it was her deeply human, noble, poetic way of finding salvation.

Ramong felt the sharp steel of a knife, cold as a guillotine, digging into his diaphragm, and it was she who had rammed that knife into his side, this smiling liar, grinning so properly at the drunken Japanese monkeys! She had taught him to like Géricault, his "Raft of the Medusa," the symbolic picture of her own shipwreck with Warronigg, that ingenious apology for every shipwreck in history; and now all of it—her suicide, her letters, her Shelley, her Géricault—it was all a common lie, an obvious trick to seduce the immature and weak-minded, cretins from the cavalry regiment just like him!

On his right, Captain Döbrentey was speaking enthusiastically about the Japanese.

"Those yellow-skinned heroes are true officers! An officer is really in his element in the middle of gunpowder and dust, smoke and blood, and not out parading on Maria Valeria! Did you hear Fudshi's command to the army: 'Let everyone put on a clean shirt as if dressing for death!' Colossal!"

And on the other side of the table Lieutenant Colonel Redl was explaining to the wife of the regimental staff physician, Mrs. Schredl (a Szamuelli by birth, of Jewish faith) how stupid it is to be a landlord in the provinces.

"In the provinces a house brings you four and a half per cent maximum, but in Budapest it's often eight to eleven per cent! In the provinces a person loses any chance for a really decent interest—and all due to his own personal inability."

The hum of voices on every side, the humdrum conversations about money and servants, about gunpowder and smoke, cards and horses, the burning candles, the band, the generals, the ladies in low-cut dresses—Ramong was looking and listening as if the whole scene consisted of multicolored blotches of sound and color with neither internal order nor logical foundation. But there was one thought Ramong could not shake and that absorbed all his thinking: Olga's attempt at suicide that foggy morning in Vienna! After all, she had thrown herself in the water! She did have some character! Why would she have lied to him? She had no reason to lie to him! She had told him the truth in the pure, ecstatic inspiration of sincere physical submission. In that small hotel she had been wet from warm tears, limp as a dying butterfly, as she told him the details of her suicide attempt, and just like that, in tears, had given herself to him completely. Why would she have done so if she had not felt genuine passion? Smoldering inside, she had told him about her suicide attempt and then, flaming like a torch, had surrendered to him when she had discovered in him a partner she could trust! She had jumped when she realized she could not go on with Warronigg any longer, and now, she had broken off with him just as abruptly—What fickleness! What does she want, how dare she act this way toward others?

· Ramong's head was full of agitated thoughts, a whole mass of ideas about Olga flitting around his glass of Törley, then his black coffee, and back again to the Törley. He drank glass after glass of cognac, and with each second it seemed clearer and clearer to him that he must speak with Olga this evening. It won't be possible here in the hall! But in the garden below, during the dance, he will ask her for a waltz and during the waltz he will have it out with her! About just who he is, about propriety, and about how one should act in a civilized society! During a waltz; that will be best!

The Venetian night in the regimental park came off according to plan. Everything was decorated with red and yellow lanterns; in addition to beer, a reserve Littke was served that smelled like the pomade maids use on Sunday afternoons; the infantry officers of the 107th danced the chardash on the tennis courts; the May night was warm and moonlit. And when the former artilleryman and accounting officer for the 107th, Janaček, set off his fireworks masterpiece—huge orange letters bursting in showers in a flaming cursive, 22-V-1809—22-V-1906, all framed by a burning dragoon helmet with a red 17—the wonderment flamed up into a rapture. The distinguished guests were served near the fountain between the flower beds and the spray of water. Some thickly woven wicker chairs and red damask and silver couches were there; long tables used by the dragoons stood near the tennis courts, covered with plain white tablecloths for the local guests, district officials and judges, the infantry and the infantry N.C.O.s. The orchestra of the 107th, under the direction of Kapellmeister Czibulka, played Strauss near the fountain: "On the Beautiful Blue Danube"; and on the playing field near the greenhouse the gypsies were fiddling mournfully, as at a farewell gathering.

At about midnight Kállay Bandi met Ramong near the fountain, beneath the plane trees. The fellow was wandering aimlessly among the couples.

"You're drunk, Gejza! What's wrong?"

"Have you seen her? Where is she?"

"Who?"

"Her! She's disappeared. I haven't seen her for fifteen minutes. They were in her apartment!"

"Who?"

"Who? Those Japanese creatures! Now she's at the fishpond with that admiral, that Japanese frog! I'm going to find her! I have to speak to her this evening!"

"You're crazy! Listen, Gejza, I'm warning you, old Warronigg has noticed how jittery you are! He's watching you! You're not normal! You're playing with fire! You're drunk! You're so drunk, you're swaying!"

"She is drunk! I saw her drinking a bottle of whiskey with those Japanese creatures! I have to speak with her, Bandi, I'm going to shoot myself if I don't speak to her! She invited those Japanese monkeys to her place for coffee! She's reciting Shelley! Inconceivable! Impossible!"

"You're crazy! Why, they're the Colonel's guests! She's only acting like a hostess! It's a question of form!"

"I'll spit on that Japanese frog, do you understand? I'll get him with my boot—then we'll see what's a question of form!"

"You're drunk! You don't know what you're saying!"

"Of course I'm drunk! I wouldn't dare not be drunk! I'm not going to allow myself to be thrown aside; I'm not a package in the post office. I won't be anybody's goat! I'm going to speak to her tonight, whatever happens!"

Kállay Bandi, who was very experienced in the craft of love and who had always stuck to his principle that it is never a good thing to have a mistress with any attachments to one's own regiment, saw how unwise all this was and thought it would be best to drag Ramong to the table, drink a bottle or so, and head home. What stupidity! What imbecilic, scandalous stupidity to have a mistress attached to one's own regiment! *Voilà!* He took his friend by the arm and with every good intention began to pull him along in order to shake him and put him in a good mood, when suddenly Ramong broke away violently and rushed toward the dancers near the fountain. It was too late to run after him and stop him.

All in white, noble and supple, Olga was coming from the playing field near the blooming lilac, a head taller than Admiral Watanaba. At the moment they were talking about how fortunate it was that she was traveling to Sicily, since Admiral Watanaba was on his way to Rome. An unusual concurrence of events: her trip to Sicily and his arrival in Teresienburg! He shall await her in Venice since, according to his schedule, he has to remain there a week.

Czibulka's orchestra was playing "Roses from the South," and inspired by such weak lemonade by Strauss and completely drunk, Ramong thought this would be the best time to ask Olga for a dance—the plan he had thought of during his lecture in the club. Running after Olga beside a clump of lilac bushes, he came up from behind on her right side, at the edge of the ring near the fountain, where dancing couples whirled about them.

"Pardon, madam, may I ask you for a waltz?"

"Ah, it's you, Ramong? Thank you, I don't feel like dancing any more! Thank you very much!"

"But, madam, I beg you, only one waltz!"

"What's wrong tonight, Ramong? No thank you, I don't feel like dancing!"

"Madam, I'm only asking for one waltz; I have a few words to say to you!"

"You see I'm with the Admiral! I'm not free! Excuse me, but . . ."

Olga turned toward Admiral Watanaba, who had retreated three paces and stood, quiet and motionless, without a word, watching Ramong attentively. Smiling nervously at the admiral, Olga asked him in English to be patient for a second. Admiral Watanaba bowed to her and, stretching his India-rubber face, retreated a few more steps. Watching the dancers, he stood discreetly turned away from Olga and Ramong.

"Galatea, I beg of you!"

"But, dear Ramong, what's wrong? What sort of queer ideas are in your head?"

"Galatea! Please, forget that cretin tonight! It's possible we won't ever see each other again!"

Ramong's voice quavered plaintively and he was ashamed of his whimpering appearance. This was the only feeling that dominated his drunken consciousness: the feeling of shame. He was ashamed that he was groveling for a waltz, that the Japanese toad was standing there, that he was drunk and choking, that he had received Olga's card with the three letters, and that she was going to Sicily. He was ashamed of himself, of her, of everything between them, and it all seemed disgraceful and inane. Slowly Ramong's shame grew into rage. In his drunken, furious look Olga sensed the possibility of an unpleasant and dangerous situation, and with a quiet and nervous voice, both warm and distant, she made an effort to get rid of him.

"Well, what is it? What do you want? You have no reason to be disagreeable this evening!"

"I forbid you to speak one more word to that yellow mask! That isn't a man, it's an ape!"

"For God's sake, Ramong, what's the matter with you? You're drunk! I resent your poor manners! What is wrong, for God's sake? You're a boor! What will he think?"

"Olga, this is too awful; Olga, please, it's a matter of life or death!"

She turned and went toward the Japanese admiral. It looked as though she really would leave, and that Ramong, completely resigned, would let her go and say nothing more. He bowed. It all seemed to have ended when suddenly he swerved around and jumped two steps after her, catching her by the arm.

"Galatea!"

The moment was dangerous and long. Olga turned and looked at Ramong. No one could have known what might have happened if Colonel von Warronigg had not appeared from behind the lilac bushes. He was excited and pale and held Olga's white Venetian shawl in his hand.

"Olga, child, it's cold! I've been looking for you; where have you been? You won't catch cold?"

Von Warronigg's appearance gave a new turn to the unpleasant situation. Olga pulled herself up and at that moment was in full command of both herself and Ramong.

"Thank you, dear, right away, only please look after His Excellency! The Admiral is alone! I'll be right with you, I'll just dance a round with Ramong!"

With complete ease, coldly and calculatedly, she went up to Ramong and danced the sweet "Roses from the South" with him. They did not say a word. On the last beat she bowed to Ramong and, taking his arm, let him escort her to her husband, moving so lightly that she seemed not to be there at all. She smiled sweetly with the smile of a commander's wife, extended her hand to be kissed, and enveloped herself in the white Venetian shawl.

After the departure of the Japanese general, events took an unexpected turn. The division commander, Lieutenant Field Marshal von Schwartner, notified the War Ministry by telegram (in accordance with War Ministry dispatch 2022, dated 21 May), that he had carried out the order of the Ministry's Department of Foreign Affairs concerning the reception of the high Japanese officials in orderly fashion and according to regulations covering a directive from the highest echelons; that General Count Fudshi-Hasegawa and his escort had been present at the celebrations of the Seventeenth Dragoon Regiment; that he had been at the garrison's field exercises; and that he had departed for Fiume at the appointed time, precisely according to schedule. The War Ministry answered the Lieutenant Field Marshal that it knew nothing about the stay of General Fudshi-Hasegawa in Teresienburg and requested a detailed report. In reply, the division sent by express telegram the order 2022 that had been dispatched by the War Ministry's external affairs section on May 21, and according to which the whole reception for the Japanese had been arranged. Two hours later an express dispatch arrived from the War Ministry in which it was claimed that the order of May 21 concerning the reception for the Japanese guests was a mystery. Half an hour later a new coded dispatch arrived, number 017, from the Ministry of Foreign Affairs, according to which the Ministry had issued no order about a reception for the Japanese guests to the Teresienburg division, and the Imperial Embassy of the exalted Japanese Mikado in Vienna had no information about the stay of Count Fudshi-Hasegawa in Europe. As far as the Imperial Embassy of the exalted Japanese Mikado knew through private sources, Count Fudshi-Hasegawa was the commandant of the Yokohama Corps and was living at the time on his estate near Yokohama.

On the basis of these dispatches panic spread among the military circles of Teresienburg. And twenty-four hours later, when the War Ministry sent information that the private sources of the Japanese embassy had been located and that Count Fudshi-Hasegawa had indeed never left his official duties as commander of the Yokohama Corps, this panic was fast becoming a gigantic scandal.

The shame, the grandiose deception of the high military circles of Teresienburg, the fantastic rumors among the whole populace of the Kingdom of Szent István, the extra editions of the entire Austro-Hungarian press exaggerating the comical side of this ridiculous adventure—all this grew into an avalanche that caused an inquiry to be instituted against the commander of the division, Lieutenant Field Marshal von Schwartner, as the person responsible for this improbable disgrace. On the heels of the new light thrown upon the festive reception for the Japanese and the celebration of the victory of Aspern and Essling, many details of the foreigners' stay in Teresienburg took on a new dimension and many insignificant facts were cleared up, such as the mystery of the gambling party at Count Hollós's place, where Lieutenant Kolozsvári-Mayer of the Seventeenth had lost 4,300 crowns, Count Hollós 7,200 crowns, Baron Rimay 17,000 crowns—all to Count Fudshi-Hasegawa. There was also an explanation for the fact that Admiral Watanaba, during the honorary dinner in the mess hall, had collected 6,300 crowns for the relief of the widows and war orphans in pitiful, crushed Manchuria, and that Division Commander von Schwartner had turned over to Admiral Watanaba 7,500 crowns in the name of the Teresienburg infantry division for the same cause. It also became clear—and this was the most fatal—that Kárdossy, the general director of the Teresienburg savings bank (Alsóvári Magyar Takarék Pénztár), had cashed a check on the Shanghai Banking Corporation for $4,700 from Count Fudshi-Hasegawa, and that it had not been necessary for Count Fudshi to wait for verification of his check from Budapest, which would surely have prolonged his stay in Teresienburg until the evening express—all this at the personal recommendation of Division Commander Lieutenant Field Marshal von Schwartner. In the meantime, as it was essential, according to the telegraphed command from the War Ministry, that Marshal von Schwartner adhere to the established schedule precisely, he personally carried out this financial transaction half an hour before the departure of the express train, making use of his own private business connections.

Naturally, an all-out alert was issued for the Japanese, but to no avail, as is often the case with such merry events. The investigation confirmed that the Japanese, escorted from the Budapest line by the division adjutant, Captain Bleich, had parted very cordially with their escort at Kaposvár Station, and from there on all trace of them disappeared and no one knew a thing of the Japanese generals along the whole route to Rijeka.

Count Fudshi-Hasegawa's visit did, of course, leave a much stronger impression upon the Seventeenth Dragoon Regiment. The day after returning from the field, Colonel von Warronigg held an officer's hearing for First Lieutenant Ramong and sentenced him to twenty days' house arrest for his irregular conduct at the reception for a high Japanese military official. This idiotic disciplinary measure was framed in imbecilic and stereotyped administrative language: "By his behavior before an Admiral of the victorious Japanese Navy, First Lieutenant Ramong has compromised the reputation of one of the most distinguished Imperial Regiments. In a thoroughly inebriated state he approached the distinguished guest of the Imperial Regiment and, depriving him of his escort, demonstrated a complete absence of tact and manner. By his cursory and insubstantial lecture he has belittled the fame of the Regiment; before the foreign representatives of a victorious army he displayed a complete lack of feeling for duty and attentiveness. This mild punishment of twenty days' confinement to quarters will be a serious warning that an officer is not to trifle with his noble calling. All duties, however insignificant, must be carried out with high conscience: all officers' functions are executed in the uniform and under the flag of the Empire."

When it had been confirmed, by the dispatch from the War Ministry, that the swindlers had not been high Japanese officials at all and that the presuppositions that had served as grounds for Lieutenant Ramong's punishment were unfounded, Ramong appeared at a regimental hearing and requested his exoneration by filing a complaint against the division. At this

second hearing there was a personal clash between him and
Warronigg, and the result of the second hearing was a further
twenty days' house arrest. On the fifth day of confinement, just
past midnight, Lieutenant Ramong shot himself. The next
morning an orderly found him on the floor with his face turned
down toward the rug. He was cold. The blood on his wound had
dried completely.

According to a regimental order, the funeral of First Lieutenant Ramong Gejza of Örkény and Magasfalva was to be at 11:00
A.M. In the regimental order giving the exact schedule of the
funeral procession, specifying the precise position of Colonel
von Warronigg's mare, Berenice, as well as of the dead officer's
grieved father, Lieutenant Colonel Ramong of the hussars, Von
Warronigg ordered the whole officer corps of the Seventeenth
to await him in full-dress uniform and in full complement in the
Ceremonial Hall at 9:30 A.M. the same day.

Twenty-eight pairs of spurs rang out at the very instant
Colonel von Warronigg entered the hall, precisely at 9:45 A.M.
The first to snap to was dragoon orderly Heinrich, who, wearing
white imperial gloves, helmet, sword, and a morning coat, was
playing the role of ceremonial doorman, for more than forty
minutes opening the heavy oak door for those arriving. After the
desperately sharp clang of Heinrich's spurs, as cutting as the
sound of the highest key on an untuned piano, the nickel steel
of twenty-eight cavalry sabers resounded as coldly as if butcher
knives were being whetted, and twenty-eight glowering officers
stood in mute grief. Gloomy and absorbed in thought, Colonel
von Warronigg passed along the fourteen-and-a-half-meter rug
to the podium, stopped next to the crimson tablecloth, and
carefully placed his helmet, gloves, pince-nez case, and a roll of
papers and letters on it. A mysterious silver dish lay on the crimson tablecloth; next to it was a bottle of spirits. All the men,
gathered in the hall more than ten minutes before the commander's arrival, had stared at the silver dish and bottle with

great interest, but no one understood what these rather comic objects were for. Colonel von Warronigg picked up the outline of his speech, lifted the lid of the silver dish, and, after a long, quiet pause, put it back in place. Making sure that the bottle of spirits was ready, he turned toward the whole officer corps. They were all there: Counts Hollós, L'Ours-Walderode, and Buttler; the regiment's four barons, the nine nobles, Lieutenant Colonel Redl, Captain Döbrentey, Kállay Bandi, Sztatocsny Emil, the Duke of Mantua—all twenty-eight were standing there, watching the ritual with the silver dish, and no one alive could comprehend the meaning of this mysterious performance. Only one member of the regiment was not there: Ramong Gejza of Örkény and Magasfalva, first lieutenant of the Seventeenth Royal Imperial Dragoon Regiment, doctor of mathematics at the University of Tübingen, was lying on a black catafalque in the regimental morgue, a bloody hole in his skull, stiff, pale, and cold.

With the prestige of a commander of the Seventeenth, his nine decorations and a heavy cavalry saber drawn in tight by a chain, Colonel von Warronigg stood for more than two minutes without a word, stiff as a suit of armor. It was a long silence; only the distant signal of a cavalry trumpet could be heard echoing through the walls. After this awkward and unnatural pause, Colonel von Warronigg opened the little case, put on his pince-nez, and, looking over his papers, threw a nervous glance over the glasses at his officers. They stood tense, expectant, quite surprised that the colonel still, after a full two minutes, had not ordered them to be at ease. Again, the fact that the whole corps had stood at attention for so long was an indication that this gathering in the honor hall just before the funeral of a dead comrade would not be some common, banal obituary.

Indeed! Immediately following the first words of their superior officer, after the first harsh, aggressive staccatos spoken with great power, they all knew that Colonel von Warronigg's necrology was to be his final duel with an enemy. Panic spread throughout the hall at that terrible and unpleasant speech. They all stood stiff and yellow, as if in some strange, poisonous hypnosis, sensing only enough to understand that all this tangled play of words was nothing but one man's excessive revenge against a poor, shamed wife-stealer.

"Gentlemen, the occasion that has brought us together for this sad epilogue is pitiful for two reasons! First, suicide itself is an act unworthy of every serious person, and the suicide of an officer on duty is completely unreconcilable with official duties listed in Regulations Manual III. Second—and this is even more pitiful—we have not gathered here to bury a comrade, but a man who was unworthy in every respect to wear the uniform that is the pride of our supreme commander, His Highness, the King and Emperor!"

They all remained stiff, at attention, only their faces showing terror. Numbed by this statement, the officers glanced at one another like small, well-trained terriers. No one knew what it meant.

"Yes, gentlemen, I am aware of the gravity of each of my words and I am asking you to pay undivided attention to me and to hear me out as your senior comrade and superior officer, one who has the honor to stand before you beneath the flag of the Seventeenth Regiment and who is convinced that the honor of our flag is the single, most sacred thing for which we have all, always—yes, always—been ready to sacrifice unhesitatingly everything that is ours, even the most precious thing we have: our own lives!

"Gentlemen, I can say only this much: if First Lieutenant Ramong were not the son of one of our comrades, and if a lieutenant colonel of the Royal Imperial Cavalry were not standing bent over him in the morgue in deep fatherly grief, then I give my word of honor, gentlemen, that our Royal Imperial Seventeenth Regiment would under no circumstances march behind the body of someone who, in any case, has been unworthy of our confidence, our flag, and our honor, which he bore as an officer on active duty, especially as an officer of our Seventeenth Regiment. Gentlemen, this pitiful suicide is the third in the annals of our regiment since the day it received its glorious flag from the hands of our patron, the glorious Franz von Lothringen, the German Emperor. This is the third suicide, but it is the most shameful! The first was Captain Harpner, commander of the second division, who shot himself at the battle of Malplaquet during the catastrophe that was the regiment's ruin. It was a desperate gesture, but a gesture worthy of a Roman centurion who prefers to die rather than see the humiliation of his flag! The second incident was that of Lieutenant Parniczay-Parneczki two years go, an incident well known to us. The reason was, as we all know, cards. Either honor or death! A knightly dilemma, and a knightly decision!

"But this deed of Lieutenant Ramong, gentlemen, this deed can be interpreted in no other way than what it is: the womanly act of a coward, the deceitful gesture of an insincere scoundrel!"

A stir of faces in the hall. Terror. A pause.

"Yes, gentlemen, an insincere scoundrel—those, gentlemen, are the right words in the right place! And I can tell you that if this officer had not put a bullet in his own head, we would have gathered together like this one morning to hear the trumpet of the Court Martial and to hear the Court Martial announce that First Lieutenant Ramong be stripped of his decorations, stars and escutcheons, his shoulder strap unfastened, and that he be dressed in the only clothing befitting him: the sackcloth of a convict!

"Gentlemen, I tell you this with the complete awareness that each of my words is heavier than the heaviest of cavalry sabers, but my bitterness is so deep and my disappointment so great that I can use no other words! Lieutenant Ramong has shot himself while in our regiment, and in half an hour we shall bury him with all due honors. I ask you as comrades and friends, gentlemen, to bury after the funeral each of my words in your hearts in the same way and after my speech to cover the memory of this man with a black veil, as if there had been nothing between us! I repeat: if I did not feel some respect and comradely solidarity with his father, the old lieutenant colonel, and if I did not have to act according to my sense of duty, I would turn over the memory of Lieutenant Ramong to the Court Martial so that the authorized steps might be taken to degrade him according to regulations and thereby erase any sign from the cross over his grave connecting him with our regiment, with our flags and sabers, with our untainted sense of duty, and with everything that raises us above ordinary civilian society and distinguishes us and makes us worthy of being on the highest steps of the Highest Throne.

"The fact that I gave the order for us to assemble here and made the decision for us to go to the funeral as a body rose out of a necessity to unburden my feeling of responsibility together with you! It is only in this way, gentlemen, together with you, shoulder to shoulder as stanch comrades, that I will be able to march behind the body of this man, this officer who was more lacking in morality than the worst of scoundrels. I ask you, gentlemen, to hear me out and judge whether I made the correct decision, and whether any of you, gentlemen, would have done otherwise in my place!

"Gentlemen, I must admit to you, in as much as you are all equally dear to me—in principle and in duty, both as subordinates and as comrades—I must admit to you that I have always felt some hidden feeling of cold mistrust toward our former comrade. His constant, truly maniacal obsession with mathematics, his success at the University of Tübingen, his unfortunate doctorate and pre-professional work, his whole view of the world, manner of speech, and unceasing and unpleasant reserve toward all of us—from me, the commander, down to the last unknown dragoon in the stalls—I must admit, gentlemen, that this was all strange and barely comprehensible to me. And today, when I look back, I see clearly that these were all vague forebodings that, unfortunately, came true to such a degree that one's mind is completely baffled by them. Gentlemen, I am a modern officer, a modern man; I can say without exaggeration that I have leafed through many books; I still have today—as I had from the very beginning—higher intellectual ambitions, and I understand fully that it is a good thing for modern officers to nurture such high ambitions. But, gentlemen, I am also an old and experienced empiricist, and I can tell you from experience that for officers sabers are of primary importance; horsemanship is of primary importance, as is the study of strategy and tactics. Not the university in Tübingen or Descartes! He who seeks success at the University of Tübingen, let him go to Tübingen with the mathematicians, let him become a professor at Tübingen and not serve with the Seventeenth Dragoons in Teresienburg!

· "So you see, gentlemen, these are deep, basic contradictions, the fundamental reasons that give rise to misunderstandings, and now you can realize the pitiful consequences, like this shameful suicide! Gentlemen, we don't need talent of any kind! We need no infinitesimals, no hyperboloids or doctorates; we need an iron sense of duty and nothing else! With a palette in our hands to paint banal roses on silk [here Colonel von Warronigg glanced significantly at Lieutenant Sztatocsny, the amateur painter who had filled all the boudoirs of Teresienburg with roses on silk pillowcases] we would not be able to stand up under the highest of struggles, the struggles that can be borne only by one who is conscious of his high sense of duty at a time when he must stand before the enemy eye to eye, chest to chest, when he must be as unflinchable as armor, and not like some lady from the promenade on Maria Valeria—contemplative and hyperintelligent! Roses on silk, a palette in one's hand, infinitesimals—they serve no purpose. Gentlemen, leave the painting of roses on silk pillowcases to the young ladies of the town, leave mathematical discussions to professors; we are officers, we are dragoons, and as such we should have a completely different sense of duty, a completely different view of things, and a completely different, more moral and higher awareness of our duty than all the journalists, civilians, professors, and scribblers, and whatever else they call those drunkards to be found in offices, cafés, and universities.

"I say now what I have always said: Gentlemen, an officer is not an officer when he is strolling along the promenade of Maria Valeria in a morning coat or a dress cape; an officer is not an officer when he is babbling about mathematics and waltzes; instead, gentlemen, we are officers when we are bloody, muddy, in the midst of fire and smoke, black from gunpowder, highly moral, and, with saber in hand, facing the enemy, one hundred per cent dedicated to our highest Ideal; it is then that we are officers, and that is the ultimate and most perfect performance of our high duty!"

"Exactly! Indeed! True!" blurted out the senile cavalry captain, Döbrentey, as if he had just heard his own words echoing back to him. The interruption was very annoying, and a long and unpleasant silence followed. The silence demoralized Von Warronigg. As a man long accustomed to routine, used to barking at troops for years, he had begun his monologue on the death of a lieutenant just as he had spoken of various things in and around the camp for years: about field locations, elevated positions, carbines, horses, women. And now, with his senseless interruption, this drunken pig, Döbrentey, had thrown him off cue and he was lost on the boards of the podium like a provincial actor with stage fright. He sensed he was acting poorly and losing rapport with his listeners.

Feeling that the elements were carrying him away and that all this was not as harmless an adventure as it had first seemed, he was aware of a wave of disagreeable associations splashing over the fragile shell of his mind. He was swimming, and it was still unbelievably far to the other shore! He had already been forcefully thundering out his indictment for fifteen minutes and still had not said a single important thing!

When they had awakened him two days earlier in the dark, repulsive dawn, and when he entered Ramong's room, he had been more shocked by the polychrome engraving of Géricault's "Raft of the Medusa" than by the dead body on the floor; the picture was fastened to the wall with four nails above the simple writing desk in the same crude way students tack their class schedules to the wall.

There was something student-like, boyish, pubescent in that shipwreck of Géricault, in that picture fastened to the wall with four nails! Von Warronigg felt the vast difference in age between himself and the dead man on the floor, and the idea was felt somehow in his bloodstream, inside, in the dark venous weight of blood deep in his body, and he inhaled to keep from being seized by a fit. Von Warronigg had known, of course—he had known for a full year—that Ramong's relationship with Olga was a sentimental one, but he was surprised that it had penetrated to the quick so much, that Olga had entrusted the secret of her Géricault reproduction to him! That meant Olga had told this feeble-minded boy everything. She had confessed to him, she had told him of her suicide attempt, she must also have told him of the details of the suicide and of how they had carried her into the hotel lobby, wet all over from the water of the Danube. Wet as a dead bird in the rain. That wet. And in reality, Olga's abortive suicide in Vienna symbolized the mysterious connection between Von Warronigg and his young wife: from the long-past morning in Vienna when he sobbed helplessly on his knees, holding her soft, childish body (from which muddy water was streaming as from a dead, wet bird), Von Warronigg had reduced his relationship with Olga to that of an animal, which had made of him the most ridiculous cuckold in the whole Austrian cavalry. In his relation with his frivolous and not too intelligent wife, Von Warronigg was not, in fact, a guileless cuckold—as was believed in the garrisons—but a stubborn and, it might even be said, a fanatic penitent wearing a hair shirt, a man on his knees who sincerely and devotedly thanked God that the death which might have come about through his personal guilt had not happened.

Olga considered Géricault's "Raft of the Medusa" a symbol of her own personal marital shipwreck, and the fact that she, proud and untameable by nature, had confided such a vital, intimate secret to Ramong could only mean that this newest of Olga's frivolous caprices (or so he thought) had not been one of those charming scandals he had been fated to bear passively for years: it was, it seemed, something deeper, more in the blood. And it bore in itself an element of some dark public scandal, of a danger that might show its head at any moment.

Socially restricted, burdened with a whole array of conventional, blue-blood prejudices because of his upbringing as a baron, Von Warronigg feared scandals as he feared nothing else, and of all scandals divorce was the most vulgar! Anything in the world, but not raising the bedroom curtains! Strangers in the half-dark alcove by the bed, as at a funeral—horrible!  . . .

Anything, only not the scandal of a public divorce in court! What he saw before him there that morning was without doubt, logically and inescapably, divorce. The young officer in front of him on the floor, his body bloody and seen by the light of the sooty oil lamp held in the nervous hand of the orderly, dumb as a lifeless animal—this stripling had wanted to take away his wife, the mother of his only daughter, Laura, and flee with her to Bolivia! The fact that he had found a whole series of letters to Ramong in his writing desk, written by Olga in purple ink, "Galatea," that he had found nude pictures of the divine Galatea in the Hellenic style (the marble torso of her still virginal bust)—these facts were undoubtedly the elements of an unavoidable, scandalous divorce, a trial, an inescapable duel, a moral disgrace *par excellence!*

Yes, this suicide was his wife's lover! She told him everything; she admitted everything to him. After the drama in Vienna, Von Warronigg had traveled with Olga to Paris, and one late

August afternoon, wandering through the Louvre, en passant, they stopped in front of Géricault's composition. Looking at the dramatic scene, Olga began to sob convulsively, clutching at him. They cried together and her warm tears flowed down along his arms; a scandal in the Louvre, a sensation for the visitors; and now, here, this stripling had become privy to the most intimate secret of their marriage. . . .

Warronigg could not rid himself of the impression of Géricault's shipwreck in Ramong's room. He was unable to take his eyes from those ominous waves on Géricault's vast expanse of green water: a dead man on the floor, and on the wall that damned shipwreck hanging by four nails!

Standing in the recess of the honor hall, he felt the huge, dark, stormy sea rolling over him; he felt the tide carrying him along, the green water pounding against him, the whole hall, with its old Jesuit cloister, rocking and creaking like a wooden ship, everything sinking under the gigantic moaning of a vast wind that hovered over the scene like the wing of some enormous black bird. His officers were standing on the deck; they were all drifting together. He was speaking to them from the rail of the captain's bridge, a ship that had not yet sunk. One of his second officers was lying dead, he had drowned; he was lying there before them in a white shroud, green, motionless, a very dead doctor of mathematics at Tübingen, a doctor of mathematics who had wanted to take Olga away, to run away with her.

He had seen to it that a silver dish was brought and placed on the crimson cloth like a helmet, and he had decided to burn all this business; to prove with words before God and history that none of this had happened, that it was all only dust and ashes. But now he had lost the thread of his thought in a labyrinth—the drunken Döbrentey had yelled something at him and everything was as still as a morgue. The bells in the town were tolling. Olga had left, she is rocking in a gondola somewhere on the Grand Canal, she is waiting for Admiral Watanaba, and the poor thing, the naïve child, she has no idea that there is no Admiral Watanaba, that Watanaba is a phantom, that Ramong has shot himself, that her secret about Galatea and Bolivia has been discovered, that the bells are tolling. . . .

With a nervous gesture, as if driving away these hallucinatory visions like bothersome gnats, Von Warronigg removed his pince-nez, wiped the glass with a deerskin glove, put it back on his nose, and began to speak with the crisp, metallic voice of a true commander, one sending his company right into the jaws of death.

"Gentlemen, it is a question of our condition under fire before the enemy, and not of some filthy amorous exploit. In Egypt, in Athens, in London, in Teresienburg—first of all we stand with our squadrons, and without us, without our discipline, without our squadrons there would be no mathematics, universities, Descartes, pictures by Géricault, roses on silk, color photographs, or anything else one usually talks about when drinking coffee. Without us and our morality there would be no civilization at all, and therefore, gentlemen, my viewpoint remains: the least possible talent and the greatest sense of duty!

"In a word, it is precisely because I have consistently looked at things from this point of view that I have always, I must admit, been skeptical and unsympathetic toward the stress on Lieutenant Ramong's exceptional talent. It was said that the University of Tübingen had accepted his qualifying thesis on parabolas and hyperboloids, and that he would receive an assistantship at Tübingen; to us this seemed like something supernatural, really superhuman. And it turned out that a whole year went by after his thesis was submitted and that nothing came of the assistantship that had been spoken of so often, and that hyperboloids are one thing, while the performance of the duty of a dragoon officer is quite another!

"It is true, gentlemen, that the dead man did not drink or play cards, but in spite of this he did receive from me this year four written reprimands, seven verbal ones, and three seven-day periods of confinement to quarters—all due to an unbelievable neglect of duty. He read and wrote his thesis during inspections; not once did he oversee the night guard; he was regularly late to duty; and it is a well-known fact in the second squadron that Ramong's troop was as unruly as a traveling circus!

"Gentlemen, I am not going to digress! As your commander, I think I have the right to sketch objectively a picture of a former comrade who was my subordinate, and I don't think I exaggerate if I say that Lieutenant Ramong was a living specimen of a neglectful officer, absent-minded in the performance of his duties, meek in service, nervous and whimsical, one who had far too much confidence in his own capabilities. In his example it is easy for us to see an ancient truth: it is impossible to kill two birds with one stone! Either a man jumps his horse in training school or he holds chalk in his hand as a professor of mathematics!

"But all this would not be so important and, standing before the flags of our regiment today, speaking of one of our dead comrades, I would not consider Lieutenant Ramong one of our worst officers if even more grave and shady circumstances had not come to light! Lieutenant Ramong was assigned to be a professor of technology at the cadet school in Mährisch Weisskirchen by order of the War Ministry. As a fine mathematician he would surely have thrown a bright light upon the fame of our Seventeenth in this field, so that in the face of such facts I would not have reason to speak of him so severely and so negatively, nor would I have the right to accuse him so vehemently, if I did not have documents in my hands that throw a new and completely different light upon this suicide.

"As you know, gentlemen, Lieutenant Ramong shot himself in his room, lying on a couch. As soon as I was awakened that early morning, I went to the dead man's apartment. As I found no farewell note, I took the liberty of putting his belongings in some order and—as far as I could—of trying to find some explanation for his unexpected act. I thought this was my duty as his superior, his most senior comrade, and the substitute for his father, a lieutenant colonel in the cavalry.

"Here, gentlemen, is what I found. I found on the table a copy of that day's paper, *Alsóvári Napló*, and among the society news about the town this item was underlined in red pencil."

Colonel von Warronigg spread out on the table the rolls of manuscripts and letters and the evening edition of the *Alsóvári Napló*. In the monotonous and tedious voice of a jury foreman, without emphasis or emotion, he began reading a domestic item from the evening paper in a hasty and casual manner: " *The Suicide of a Man Who Spoke Nine Languages*. Last night an unidentified man jumped from the third floor of the post-office building and was found dead on the spot. Prior to this, he had gone to the postmaster and applied for the position of a part-time letter carrier. He stressed his qualifications, the fact that he spoke nine languages. Since all the positions for letter carriers were filled, the postmaster explained to the unknown man that he could not give him a job at the moment. Having left the office, he jumped onto the paved yard and died immediately. It is impossible to establish his identity.'

"The dead officer had underlined this whole item in red pencil sharply and decisively, and here let me read to you what he wrote in the margin as his sarcastic commentary: 'Polyglots are completely superfluous to cannibals.' . . . Besides this, there lay on his table a registered letter from the rector of the University of Tübingen in which he had returned Ramong's thesis with the remark that the question of an assistantship was temporarily pointless for technical reasons. This letter was also marked with a red pencil and over the whole thing a large zero had been energetically scrawled. Gentlemen, other than this letter and the newspaper item I found nothing that might be construed as any indication, even the faintest, of suicide.

"My deepest conviction tells me that this suicide was not a thing of the moment, but had been smoldering inside Lieutenant Ramong all last year. It is necessary to lift the veil as much as possible from his intimate inner life in order to consider his invisible moral profile and to understand how impossible it is to exist without ideals, without a sense of duty, without the morality of an officer. For, gentlemen, besides these mathematical papers and manuscripts, I found this notebook, written in the dead officer's hand, in which he had recorded his emotions and thoughts during the last seven or eight months, beginning exactly at the time when the question of his assistantship at Tübingen became important.

"In these notes, which might be called the lieutenant's diary, I saw the dark picture of an inner moral crumbling, something I believe gives me the right to disqualify him in your eyes as a comrade and a man. Gentlemen, the man who wrote such impressions and thoughts—even while he was sharing life with us in our club, our mess, our training field, on exercises, under our flags, in our uniform—that lieutenant had such vile and repulsive thoughts about us that it seems he was our most distant and terrible enemy! I do not have the words to express my disgust and bitterness, so I believe it would be best for me to read to you a few lines from the diary of a comrade we sincerely loved and respected, never suspecting that a character with a masked face and a closed visor was walking among us. For example, one day he dubbed one of our older comrades a cretin because in the mess hall he had declared 'that the one thing that impressed him most about the French Revolution was the death of Lafayette's Swiss Guard.' Gentlemen, please be kind enough to turn your attention for a moment to the statement our 'free thinker' wrote about this declaration by our comrade: 'Socrates predicts that mankind will fight wars until people begin to think of the generals as mule drivers.'

"Gentlemen, he eavesdropped like a spy on our personal conversations, and when one of our comrades, Count Buttler, once declared that our younger generation no longer deserved asparagus and crab at the gentlemen's table, he remarked: 'There are criminal types who put a lot of stress on formalities, such as how asparagus is to be eaten!' Gentlemen, for Ramong we were all murderers, card cheats, syphilitics with holes in our brains, fighting in an indefensible manner with our sabers, all because we did not know about cosines and correct spelling!"

Colonel von Warronigg threw Ramong's blue notebook aside in disgust, stepped off the podium, strolled to the heavy damask curtain in the old-fashioned bay window, and stood there in thought for a full minute.

No one in the hall moved. Everyone stood stock-still. The stiff ceremonial pose was now turning into an arduous and tiresome apathy of the body. Under their escutcheons, restricted by chains and belts, with heavy helmets on their heads and sabers in their hands, immobile, the officers of the Seventeenth started to overcome the feeling of gravity with a heavy, deep breathing. Still absorbed in his thoughts, as if speaking to himself, Von Warronigg returned to the podium and, passing in front of the formation of officers, began to speak again, gloomy and brutal:

"All this might still be excusable and understandable! Such a young and inexperienced officer values his own capabilities and, carried away by his doctorate, dreams of how he will conquer the world! All this might still be considered a youthful conges- tion of blood in his head, a moral aberration that might explain these consequences. He was negligent in his duties, unconscien- tious and superficial. In his own moral turmoil he despised us like a megalomaniac, carrying the grimace of the devil in his heart. And in the turbulence and disorder of his own spiritual chaos he reached for a revolver and cleansed himself.

"Gentlemen, if we were standing over his dead body now, and if this were all I had to tell you concerning his legacy, believe me, I would not be uttering a single word against him. Gentle- men, you cannot imagine his incredible impertinence at his final hearing, when he asked me to reverse the first sentence of con- finement to quarters because he had been punished for insulting the honor of a swindler and not of a foreign admiral. He de- manded that a division-level report be filed against me. During the hearing he smirked at me challengingly with an unheard-of arrogance of both tone and gesture, declaring with special emphasis that he could not be held personally responsible for the simple-minded inefficiency of the entire Teresienburg officer corps and general command. . . .

"But fine, then, a hothead, fine; it was not so tragic, that house arrest! But, gentlemen, that is not the worst! Insult to our morality, weakness of personal character, and neglect of duty—a person could excuse all this out of pity for such a young and really sad death! But the one thing that cannot be understood at all in this case is the fact that Lieutenant Ramong was a traitor!"

A stirring of heads, unrest.

"Yes, gentlemen, this suicide is a disgrace for our regiment because it is the suicide of a common traitor. And if he had not shot himself, a court martial would have decreed death. Lieutenant Ramong, as an active officer of our Seventeenth Regiment, was carrying on negotiations for a job like some itinerant actor. The spirit of regimental honor, fidelity to the Royal House, the loyalty of a citizen and commissioned officer, a sense of duty and the skill of our calling—in the mind of this unfortunate fellow all these were only ideas to be marketed like any other piece of merchandise. I have found in his correspondence four letters from the technical department of the War Ministry of the Republic of Bolivia in which he is informed that he is asking too much."

When Ramong's letters from Bolivia appeared on the crimson tablecloth in front of the mysterious silver dish, Kállay Bandi's helmet almost rolled out of his hand from his indignant start. Kállay Bandi was quite familiar with Ramong's plans to be accepted as an engineer in the distant and fantastic land of Bolivia. Personally, he considered them stupid and naïve; to him it was very funny that such a romantically enamored dilettante as Ramong Gejza might take part in dangerous adventure, that Olga had swallowed him like a sponge cake absorbs wine, dissolved him and lapped him up, that she had hounded him like a fly, that he had gone so crazy as to think it necessary to travel to Bolivia in order to be able to live with this ordinary slut.

Listening for more than half an hour, to this senile, malicious old man ranting shamelessly in front of everyone and spitting on his friend, Kállay Bandi felt: "That good-for-nothing on the podium ought to be shot like a dog! The fool should have a bullet in his thick skull! You ought to smash your helmet against the floor hard enough for it to ring out like a protest and drop the curtain on this idiotic disgrace! You ought to strike out with your foot, your saber, your fist, you ought to challenge the old man to a duel, step up to the immoral swine and smack him on the snout with your glove, smash the huge pince-nez on his fleshy nose, speak a few brave words. And just why is Warronigg holding forth about some Spanish and Bolivian love adventures? As if everybody didn't know that Olga was Ramong's mistress. And not only Ramong's, but his, Bandi's, as well—yes, his too, everyone's mistress; from Sztatocsny to him, she liked her jockies, and Ramong, a simple mathematician, was a wonder of the world for her! Warronigg's telling about Bolivia concerns only an ordinary technical job overseas. And this is all the posthumous defamation of one of their dead comrades—moral murder of the lowest sort!"

Feeling that he should set off decisively along the red velvet rug toward the podium, take the path of knightly honor or else leave this cave with such a loud bang of the door that the ancient windows would fall out of their lead frames like rotten teeth from a skull, challenge the commander to a duel, be the cause of an unprecedented insubordination, Kállay Bandi knew in his whirling head that this would not be quite correct according to the regulations of Barbasetti, that there were rules of the duel and the Last Judgment, that all this could be decided more properly by written procedure, by a commission and seconds, that it would be a scandal without head or tail, and, finally, that the only one who would end up being defamed would be Olga.

After all, the commander's wife was not to blame for that

lofty gesture by Ramong Gejza! Ramong always was over-wrought, so why compromise a woman at the very moment when the comedy is over anyway and the most opportune time is no longer at hand—something we learn from the old truth: to be silent and keep on serving. . . .

"Gentlemen, I cannot go on about this any longer because I am afraid I will exceed the limits I decided to maintain. Gentle-men, I have decided, out of respect for our comrade, Ramong's father, not to make an issue of this entire incident. The dead officer wore a mask and is not worthy of the honor of our regi-ment. He was not a gentleman, but a fool, and I ask you, gentle-men, to help me in the execution of this difficult duty and to remain behind me. I have decided that we will attend the fu-neral as a body for reasons of formality—not out of pity, but out of sympathy for a lieutenant colonel of the Empire, a wounded veteran for whom in this case the truth would mean sure death. And now, here, together with you, I have decided to destroy by fire all the documents that have soiled the honor of our flag and have cast such a heavy responsibility upon us!"

At that, Colonel von Warronigg put the blue notebook and the four letters from Bolivia in the silver dish, poured alcohol into it, and lit it. At that moment he looked like the grand mas-ter of some mystical order, lighting a sacrifice to an invisible deity.

Lieutenant Kállay Bandi was in command of the funeral es-cort made up of half a squadron. As commander of the entire procession, he rode on the right flank of the first troop. Behind the first troop of dragoons, which was moving very slowly with drawn sabers, rode eight regimental trumpeters with trumpets at their sides, sullen and identical-looking on their fat Danubian mares. Behind the trumpeters and the band of the 101st Regi-ment, the orderly Heinrich was leading not the mare Berenice, but Warronigg's Dolores, wearing Flemish blinders and covered with black canvas. At the moment Berenice was to be masked with the black Flemish coverlet and the dark mourning cloth over her head, the mare, seeing the dragoon stable attendant appear before her holding the black costume in his hand like some specter, had split his head with a single blow of her hoof. Berenice had gone wild because of the black rag, and news of the tragic death of the attendant, a nineteen-year-old boy, spread through the post and to its outskirts like a gloomy, mysterious omen of the funeral. At that moment there was nothing to be done but deck out Dolores, Colonel von Warronigg's most docile mare, gentle as a cow at a salt lick, in as much as Colonel von Warronigg would be walking behind the body with the rest of the officers; and so it was to Colonel von Warronigg's mare, Dolores, dressed in Flemish mourning attire, that the rare honor fell of accompanying Ramong Gejza on his last ride.

The dragoons behind Dolores were carrying wreaths: six of them, at intervals of three meters. Then came the gravedigger with the cross, the prior of Saint Theresa with two assistants, a glass carriage bearing the dead officer's body covered with yellow and black canvas. On the body, across the yellow and black cloth, lay a heavy cavalry saber with the helmet of a dragoon and a solitary wreath: from Ramong's father. Behind the glass carriage came old Ramong with his wooden leg, in a hussar dress uniform of a blue waistcoat and red trousers, bareheaded and minuscule as a doll. Behind the withered old man, in step with the slow cadence of the drums swathed in black, at the head of the twenty-eight officers of the Teresienburg Seventeenth Dragoon Regiment, came Colonel von Warronigg, stooped and lost in thought. The conductor, Czibulka, was playing Chopin up front ahead of the four-in-hand, but Von Warronigg could not shake his grim thoughts. He had spoken to the men about Ramong's diary, about the Bolivian escapade, and about the letter from Tübingen. But about the fact that there had also been among Ramong's letters a few intimate letters from his wife Olga—about this he had said nothing. This rested with him, and he thought about Olga in Venice, on the Piazzetti, feeding the pigeons in her new lace dress from Brussels, and about the fact that he would not see her until September.

At the end of the procession rode another troop of dragoons commanded by Lieutenant Kolozsvári-Mayer, the son of the manufacturer of "double-malted Kolozsvári beer."

A small boy watching the funeral procession at the pavement's edge was frightened by Warronigg's Dolores in her black Flemish mantle, by her satanic black head, cocking her ears and neighing; and so in panic he threw his arms apart and let go of his red balloon, which tore away from his wet little fingers and flew straight up into the sky.

The red balloon made a sharp parabola and, carried along by the breeze from the phalanx of cavalry soldiers, flew as far as Kállay Bandi's squadron. Then it jumped away from the ground in a reckless vertical line right above the glass funeral hearse and disappeared above the rooftops, the maple trees, and the bell tower in the bright air of a sunny May afternoon.

*Translated by Ralph Bogart*

# Hodorlahomor the Great

Pero Orlić was already dreaming about Paris when he was in primary school. Down the corridor, next to the Orlić kitchen, there lived a certain Frau Mayer, a German from Düsseldorf or Berlin. Her son, "her God," who was an upholsterer, had left for Paris at the turn of the century. Pero was a boy of three or four at the time, but his memory of the evening of the upholsterer's departure was so clear that nothing that subsequently happened could shake it loose. Unquestionably it was on that evening, when Franz Mayer took leave of his mother and father in the kitchen, that Pero's longing for Paris first took form. Pero was sitting at the large kitchen table playing with blocks; it was raining. Franz Mayer stood in the yellow light of a kerosene lamp in a striped waistcoat, a medallion of St. George banging away against its buttons. It was this golden St. George killing the dragon that, together with the yellow light of the kerosene lamp and the rain, impressed Pero so indelibly.

So this stout red man is going to Paris! This German is going to Paris!

The magic of this unknown word enchanted Pero, and that very night he had many fantasies about Paris. Paris became for him a life-force, and his fanciful childish stories were a sensation both in the Orlić household and in the entire neighborhood. The family would assemble—the usual group of aunts, the Roses and Lenas and Antonias and Rezas and Minas and Finas—and little Pero would tell the story of how, long before he appeared in this house on Potok, No. 76, he had lived in Paris as a man of the world. And Pero would tell his aunts of his baroque visions of brass bands, fountains, and churches, mixing the visions and molding them in the process, while his aunts would listen, nodding their heads in astonishment.

"He will either end up on the gallows or become a government minister!" was the general verdict after one of these literary evenings in the Orlić kitchen, filled with smoke, the smell of onions, tomatoes, and jam. At the time Frau Mayer went away, Pero was in the third grade and going through that intense religious crisis that occurs when an altar boy has his first doubts about afterlife. Frau Mayer's son, the upholsterer—that same Franz who had gone off to Paris—had meanwhile married an umbrella maker, bought two houses in the suburb of Villemomble, and was doing extremely well. So the mother decided to join her son. True, she was old and the journey was long. And in thirty-two years she had grown accustomed to Zagreb. But her son wrote of his good fortune (drinking red wine instead of water), and of his wife's pregnancy, and Frau Mayer decided to go after all.

She entrusted the grave of her late husband to Pero's mother and set off, all by herself, for Paris via Basel. Pero went with his father to the travel agency to buy the ticket for her "to Paris, via Basel." He was fascinated by the trials and tribulations involved in the great preparations for a journey "to Paris, via Basel." He studied the route carefully and went to the trouble of marking it on a map with a red pencil. But his effort was discarded as superfluous. Then Pero and his father went to the South Station to see old Frau Mayer off. What's more, they drove in a fiacre, and Pero cried all night with longing for Paris.

From time to time postcards and letters came from Paris. The old lady wrote that Paris was a big city, but that the water was not good, and that she did not understand a word, and was sorry that she had ever left Zagreb. And Pero read those German letters carefully, studied the awkward Gothic script, and filed these authentic Paris documents, these stamps and postcards, away in his schoolbooks. At school he would open his books and study the postcards, projecting himself into that small painted Parisian square and losing himself in it. The confusion of Paris would spread through the book and through the school. And Pero would disappear into the Paris streets.

For example, he looked at the Hôtel des Invalides.

The blue spring skies spread over the golden cupola, the distant roofs were covered in a silver mist, unreal red chimneys appeared as dreams appear when one dreams about Paris from Potok, No. 76.

Strange red omnibuses and ladies with parasols, and an officer in red breeches riding in the shade of tree-lined sweet-smelling streets. And then the Champs-Élysées. There had just been a warm spring rain; the omnibuses, carriages, and bicycles were reflected in the asphalt pavement, and the shadow of a guard officer, in formal uniform with a long red tail flowing from his bright shiny helmet, burst over the gray puddles, lost its shape, and vanished. Cars were screeching, porters yelling, and white horses in the marble frieze soared in the azure sky that was adorned with an orange glow and sprinkled with the aqua light of a May evening. Trees quivered in the twilight, and in the distance, far far in the distance, the contours of the gigantic Arc de Triomphe sank in the gray veil of the dusk so that the Champs-Élysées, with its procession of cars and riders and carriages, seemed to flow in a triumphal path above the city like a heavenly bridge!

Or the Trocadéro. Pero placed "Trocadéro" in his notebook, and as he looked at the Moorish towers and galleries and the fountains that bubbled like fairy tale fountains, he trembled as if confronted by a thousand-eyed beast. And those gray sooty palaces and bridges and golden cupolas and children with sailboats in fishponds inflamed little Orlić's imagination and danced with a fiery rhythm in his feverish mind. "Orlić! You lazy nincompoop! What are you staring at this time? What have you got there? You watch out, young man, or you'll be in the corner again."

Pero stiffened and, still half dreaming, looked around the room, at the blackboard and the map and the classroom and the teacher, all of which seemed strange, incomprehensible, wooden, and stupid.

Thus, a sick illusion was beginning to undermine little Pero, and as time passed its dimensions grew.

In those days, book salesmen—agents for the large publishing houses of Berlin, Leipzig, and Vienna—used to go from house to house selling stupid books to stupid people on the installment plan. Once Pero's mother ordered a large illustrated novel about the French Revolution entitled *Graf Axel von Ferson*. This book was about a well-known Swedish counterrevolutionary, one of Marie Antoinette's lovers. The novel was very bad and the illustrations grotesque. But little Pero studied it in detail and pondered for many an evening over those black crude drawings that still stank of machine oil. Noble ladies with wigs; the Trianon; and the waterfalls and parks; and those tense episodes connected with the seizure of the royal family at Varennes, when someone slipped a lamp under the very nose of the fat king; and then the innumerable court intrigues and affairs and crowds of armed men—such were the materials with which little Pero nursed his passion for Paris.

As time went on, certain symbols crystallized out of this huge chaos that, like visions, hovered in his inflamed imagination. At first the severed heads on stakes, the storming of the Bastille, the guillotines, the huge celebrations of the Republic, with torches smoking over monumental catafalques; and then, out of this torrent there emerged Danton, Marat, and Robespierre, and finally Napoleon himself. And afterwards Napoleon's empire liquidated the Revolution and established the great religious cult for the Corsican that burned in Pero like a sanctuary light, replacing Caesar in the boy's subconscious hierarchy.

In high school Pero devoured the entire Napoleonic literature and began writing a long novel of his own: *Napoleon, The Imperial Star.* In time Pero's Napoleon cult became identified with the Paris cult, and Pero stormed like a comet across the Lombardy plains from victory to victory, and then rushed off from the Danube to Moscow, across the whole of Europe, intoxicated by banners, artillery, and imperial eagles.

In Pero's fourth year of high school, a new idol, the poet Kranjčević, defeated Napoleon; once more the guillotine, the barricades, and the Revolution were in the forefront—that same horrible Jacobean revolution that had destroyed the aristocratic reptiles in their golden overcoats and white powdered wigs. And Pero dreamed of Paris, seeing before his very eyes the ruined palaces and the crowds of bloody sans-culottes singing the "Marseillaise," carrying aloft the severed heads of the French aristocracy.

It was in those days that the late journalist Matoš was writing his articles from Paris. In his shallow journalistic style Matoš had converted this bloody vision into a sweet cultural dream, full of poetry and harmony and the scents of gentle tranquillity—not too clear but, at any rate, modern. Matoš turned Paris into a sonnet that scanned well. The nostalgia of the age penetrated Pero painfully and sharply. The good old days when one read Matoš's articles in school! "Oh, if only I didn't have to do my Greek lesson! If only I were in Paris! I'm sure they perform *Hamlet* magnificently in Paris, and not in the sleepy way they do here!

"If I were in Paris I would go for a walk in the Bois de Boulogne, and not in this damned Zrinjevac.

"Zagreb is a village! Just one street, the Ilica! And look at Paris!"

That was young Orlić in the fourth year of high school, the young Orlić who had bought a torn Baedeker and was skimming through the maps and walking through the Paris streets and cursing Zagreb and fighting constantly over his marks, and living more on the Seine than on the Potok.

Orlić knew Paris by heart: the neighborhoods, the galleries, the museums. He knew the location of all the stations, cemeteries, boulevards; he knew when each bridge was built, to whom each monument was dedicated, where new streets had been laid out, and where and when famous people were born. He knew it all, in every detail. As he sat over his Latin or Mathematics homework, he would take out the red Baedeker, like a prayer book, and with a deep sigh bow to the "city of cities, the Babylon of Babylons, most holy Paris."

. Later he got hold of Musset and Baudelaire. And in the Zagreb cafés he came upon the *Revue des Deux Mondes* and *Le Temps*, as well as other articles and reports, and it was no wonder that, at the first opportunity, when he found himself with a few extra crowns in his pocket, Pero Orlić rushed off to Paris.

It was a fever and a madness, this flight of his. Realizing that in a day or two he would see the city from a platform of the Gare de Lyon, Orlić trembled with a high fever and holy excitement.

"Babylon, Babylon," sang Orlić in his soul, and from the Swiss frontier onward he could not sit still. He trembled and shivered and shook and sniffed the air and flickered like a lamp.

"How good these French carriages smell!

"Even the seats are covered in lace and velvet, and not in worn old leather as at home.

"Everything smells of perfume! Even the third-class carriage smells of perfume!

"Look, look! These villages! How gentle they are! How warm! How pleasant! How sweet! And this famous ringing of bells! French bells! And these rivers, these French rivers!

"And these green canals and the glistening streams! What riches, what beauty! What solemn beauty!"

In his excitement, Orlić babbled and talked to himself. He placed his swollen feverish head on the cold glass of the windowpane, feeling the blood rushing into his eyes, thickening his veins.

"Babylon, Babylon," he exclaimed as the train cut across rich black fields, through long lines of poplars and mulberries, and the hamlets appeared one after another on the hills like distant ships on the green waves. The red bell towers, the park-enclosed mansions, the farms, and the wheels of the train, and the sweet-smelling earth that smoked after the spring rain, and the steeples in the small towns, and the tracks and railway crossings—together they thundered and sang, Babylon, Babylon!

It was a victorious, dashing flight across space, the flight of a happy, fiery soul that, like a burning spark, falls into a large hearth. And then it grew dark and night fell, and the train wound and rattled through the evening mist, thundering across iron tracks and bridges and rivers in which the last rays of the sun were reflected.

Orlić began to sense the nearness of the city, the City of Cities blossoming like a huge rose set in a plate bordered with blue. Houses sprang up in front of the window, first one isolated house, followed by two or three in a bunch, and then a café with a colorful sign out in front, and roads and viaducts and willow thickets and clearings filled with grunting pigs, and roads flowing parallel to the tracks, and carts laden with sacks and barrels crawling past in the mud.

The sad spring rain was dripping, and the drivers were covered with cheap blankets, and everything was sad and tearful.

The fat black horses steamed in the mist, and the small oil lamps along the way burned hopelessly as though they would go out at any minute.

· Wreaths of red bulbs illuminated the road, and now and then a reddish light exposed a factory with its burning throat, and through gray dirty windows human shadows could be seen contorting and vibrating in the yellow light, as giant wheels rattled fiercely and black belts wound and crawled, appearing and disappearing miraculously. A forest of black chimneys gaped wide open, some standing out like gigantic tree trunks, and others vomiting up fireworks of glowing soot. But above the flame and dirt glowed the holy aura of the city, like a white line of magnesium or a wondrous polar light.

"Paris, Paris," whispered Orlić devoutly, watching the infinite white fan of light that spread above the black contours of buildings which disappeared one after another in the darkness. Advertisements flashed on the crystal panes, fragmented into shiny points of light like sunflowers springing up along the tracks at home. Wooden cows licking chocolate, geese with paté, and Negroes, and brightly lit villas, and five-story buildings, and factories and bridges thundering, and the burning sparks falling, and the people down there in the underpass walking indifferently, lifting their heads from time to time to glance at the train speeding across the dike in the forest of pillars, switches, and red and green lights on tall semaphores.

Two or three times the train raced through arched damp tunnels or sped above the yellow river on which a ship was pulling barges that cut red and blue lines in the troubled waters. Then sooty naked walls and gray buildings and black warehouses, and here and there bursts of yellow lights, and again walls and walls, and then suddenly the train came to a stop.

On all sides were other trains, speeding backwards in unknown directions. In the lighted cars people could be seen going to sleep, and waiters in white jackets hurried back and forth, waving napkins. For a long time the train stood and puffed with difficulty, and then slowly and pompously it crawled into the crystal throat of the great terminal to spew out of its insides the nervous and pale Pero Orlić.

Orlić felt that he had entered a temple. He had had much the same feeling when, as an altar boy, he had rung the bells in the cathedral during a great pontifical mass officiated over by the bishop himself. He had had the same feeling once when he had gone to confession three times, lest he should receive his first communion in a state of impurity and sin.

He paused and looked out at the noisy confusion, and it reminded him of holy things. So! He, Pero Orlić, was there! After fifteen years of longing, he was there at last, in Paris, by God! In Paris!

In front of Orlić were the famous boulevards flowing with carriages, buses, men and women, boulevards as straight as if drawn with a ruler, cut away from the rock like a great ravine.

The crowd danced, whirled, thundered, whistled, cried, and laughed, and Orlić flung himself headlong into the tide, swimming proudly across the current, just as he would in the River Sava.

As he threw himself into this swelling, unknown mass, Orlić completely forgot the plan on which he had worked so carefully for years and about which he had dreamed so many nights. The plan had been to cross the Seine, and then, following the river, to find his lodgings. And now he had forgotten this plan and had rushed straight down the street, in any direction, so long as he was in the heart of things! In the very nucleus! In the light! In Paris!

He forgot the fatigue of the journey, his hunger and thirst, and it was not until morning that, defeated and as though wounded, he found refuge in a modest hotel on a remote and disreputable street.

The street is called de l'Harpe, and it runs parallel to Boulevard St. Michel, and it was there that Orlić found a dirty, miserable little room with a gas lamp and a balcony, where everything smelled of burned sauces and the children were forever crying behind the wallpaper, and on the spiral staircase rats chased one another in the twilight. Across the street was a restaurant run by Hungarian gypsies, and some distance away a fountain gurgled and sprinkled by day and by night, and in Orlić's building, on the floor above his, a woman took her own life the very night Orlić rented his room.

That was the first thing that happened: this woman, her throat cut, and the bloody blanket and the pool of blood on the floor, and the police.

And then Paris with its mad rush and passionate drinking, animal-like, with both hands clutching the glass, intoxicating and teasing the nerves with the melody of dull indolence. Mad rushing through streets and water, galleries and towers, steeples and palaces and cathedrals and museums and parks, rushing in circles, every day ending in surfeit and defeat. When Orlić climbed the spiral staircase to his room he found he had already fallen asleep; that was the last straw.

And operas and ballets and stock exchanges and cemeteries and Rembrandts and Renaissance Italians and Cubists and Futurists and sculptors and painters and gardens and streets and restaurants whirled in Orlić's mad head.

He tried to embrace everything and was left with nothing. He wanted to grasp everything, and understood nothing. The only thing he did find was fatigue, the fatigue of the miserable Balkan rabble lost in the whirlpool. A poor animal, persecuted and whipped to death, yet aspiring to fresh adventure. Pero Orlić was still a child, just barely twenty, and he believed that he might come upon new adventures in the streets of Paris, like finding a louis d'or or a diamond pin. But he found neither the louis d'or nor the diamond pin, and as he walked wearily home one night, crossing a bridge illuminated with red lights, he said to himself:

"All this is a lie and a vacuum. An ugly vacuum. Paris does not exist. There is no Paris, there is no Paris.

"What is Paris? What is it, after all? Is Paris the lame Sarah

Bernhardt whom I saw this evening for twenty francs and who is a screaming parrot and stupid to boot, may God have mercy on her? Or is Paris that Spanish king with the long nose who takes rides in his carriage with his enormous entourage, and is greeted everywhere with fireworks by the Republic and given receptions to which I am not invited? Is that Paris?

"Who says they are freethinkers? Just fat burghers, as odious as our Zagreb butchers. Where is Paris? To hell with it!

. "Is this Paris? This hunchbacked shoemaker, leaning over his work just as our shoemakers do on the Potok? He invents stupid patriotic phrases such as 'the great people,' 'the revolution,' just as our people talk about 'King Tomislav's fleet,' 'the Croatian Crown,' and 'Svačić.' It all amounts to the same thing, and it is all stupid. And someday these people will go to war for their 'great patriots,' those invisible gentlemen who live behind closed doors in their villas, feed monkeys and parrots and greyhounds, and sit on moneybags.

"Hey, Paris! Why don't you grab the moneybags from underneath those fat behinds? Why do they suck your blood and goad you like a horse? You blockheads of the Republic! Millions of blockheads in a heap! What do I care about kings and shoemakers and guillotines and skulls that do not exist? None of this exists! It is all dead! Buried! Paris is a cemetery!

"A phantom in a graveyard—this is what I believed in for so long! A dirty mass of stone, and my room full of cockroaches, and these shallow cretins who carry a woman in their hearts and on their lips, and those twenty people who commit suicide every day and die nameless and lie in greenish morgues and stare out at stupid black nothing! Is this the Paris about which I dreamed for so many black Balkan nights? There, in the mist, where Turkish fires still burn, where maidens are captured and revenge is celebrated! Where stakes are greasy with blood and women are silent and walk at a distance behind their men, where everything is rotten and cursed, and at the break of day the gendarmes' green roosters sing? Oh, there I had dreamed of Paris, and those dreams of mine were more Parisian than the whole of Paris. When I first listened to their songs, and felt the electrifying strength emanating from human words that have torn down prison walls, and saw the guns firing and the banners waving, my heart beat in my throat and I thought I had made a discovery! But I had discovered nothing. There is nothing to discover. It all amounts to the same thing! Budapest and Paris and Peking and Zagreb! Nothing but barracks and prisons and churches, barracks and prisons and churches—the eternal human stupidities —but there is no Paris. Paris is within us! Paris is in the poems of Kranjčević, that poor Sarajevo scholar who had more feeling for Paris than all of these fat cretins. Parisian, Parisian! You who know and feel Paris, where are you? Parisian, oh where are you?"

Thus, standing on a bridge over the Seine and waving his arms in the air, engulfed by a strange bloody emotion, Orlić cried out his sick fiery monologue, calling for a true Parisian to arise. He stared down at the yellow muddy water rolling past him, covered by layers of tar and slicks of oil. Lines of red lights trembled and vibrated on the water, and Paris murmured like an underground beast that has buried its snout in the darkness. Paris murmured and the vacuum was vast and black, and the Parisian did not respond.

"God only knows at what depths and in what pain the real Parisian now lives! If only I could see the flickering of his oil lamp, feel the avalanche of his thoughts, to know that there are Parisians in Paris!

"And so it goes! Nothing but the notorious 'red lights' burn in Paris! And black gendarmes and policemen and guard officers and detectives suspiciously watch everyone. And now they are watching me, those damned black dogs! Why is it? Isn't a man allowed to scream on a bridge?"

"My dear sir, it is forbidden to loiter on the bridge." The policeman seized Orlić.

"Leave me alone! I have no intention of drowning myself. I am only crying over Paris!"

"Forget the tears, sir, and show me your papers."

Orlić's papers were, of course, not in order, and he spent a night in the police station with a few drunkards.

The following morning Orlić was interviewed by a fool in white, well-pressed trousers. After his release Orlić took to drink, systematically, like a Croat, and soon became a drunkard himself.

He would get drunk in shady nightclubs, where soldiers played billiards in shirt sleeves and red trousers (perhaps they belonged to some colonial African regiment). Their sleeves rolled up, the soldiers drank and cursed, and Orlić drank too, some thick colored alcohol, squandering his money in holes and pigsties. And he gambled too, and won and lost. One night he won 520 francs, and then, in an instant, lost everything. He even gambled away the silver watch his grandfather had given him at confirmation. And with the loss of his silver watch he had nothing left. No money. No room. No illusions. Nothing. Not even those holy illusions that he had invented while still a boy in grade school. What was left of the city of the "Marseillaise," the barricades, and the guillotine? Of those café and Baedeker dreams, the articles of Matoš, oh, what was left?

What actually remained was Orlić's expulsion from his room and the confiscation of his raincoat. His revolver, which he had never used but which he put in his mouth two or three times every night (and then took out, of course), was not taken from him. The old woman laughed cynically and said that she spat on his Russian stupidity—that is, on the revolver. So she merely took his raincoat for the rent he owed her.

As a result the spring rains found Orlić in the street without so much as a raincoat.

And it rained and rained, and Orlić was hungry and roamed the streets like a bedraggled wolf, and that was Paris. He wandered through a cemetery arcade for days on end, and once spent two nights in a mortuary. He sat there, listening to the song of Paris, dully watching the corpse of a dead railway worker with a sharp nose on which the light of a candle danced. The man's name had been Victorien Hébrard. Just before dawn the mortuary was closed down and Orlić was locked out. He found a quiet spot near an imposing gate and there, for a short while, he was able to get away from his pointless and senseless wanderings. Unwashed and sooty, hungry, his shoes torn, Orlić walked whole mornings through museums. Oh, he cursed the classics, those endlessly stupid and superfluous lies. He came to hate them, and he scorned all of Europe from the bottom of his heart.

"God damn it! Why don't I tear into this Van Dyke with a knife? Those fat damned women of his! What do I care for Van Dyke? Or Van Gogh! Damn you, Van Gogh! So that's who you are? That's what you look like?"

With bloodshot eyes Orlić stared at the stretched canvas and flicked open the knife in his pocket, seized by the desire to rip everything to pieces. Then he watched children in the park as they ate biscuits and chocolate. He ingeniously stole a large box of candied fruit from a nurse, which lasted him for two days. One day Orlić remembered that he had intended to earn a living in Paris by writing articles. And he wanted to write, but each of his thoughts, and every line, turned into an ugly curse, directed not only at those who would read his articles and those who would print them, but at Paris, the world, everything. Only accusations, convulsions, curses, and protestations.

But nothing was as bad as those nightly walks in the streets. Exhausted from lack of sleep, heavy with hunger and fatigue, his knees would buckle and he would slump down on a bench, and the bitter and cruel struggle with sleep would begin. From one side sleep would approach with its warm, generous hand, caressing his brows and sprinkling them with a sweet balm; from the other side Orlić would be approached by the green squinting eyes of a demoniac policeman, who was everywhere at all times, crawling about like a beetle, leering at each new victim, grabbing him by the neck and tossing him into the hole of darkness. Into the police station, into filth, into Europe.

Yes, yes, an atrocity! A starving man! The streets! Night, rain, fatigue! And this is freedom, this is freedom, this is Paris!

And Orlić's heavy, too heavy, head swayed on his shoulders. Circles of divine sleep began to dance before his eyes and then, suddenly, the dance was interrupted by a jolt of fear, and the will was broken once again, and the wounded body tottered farther along, still farther, retreating to a more comfortable bench where the police might be forgotten.

As Orlić roamed the streets, everything seemed to be growling at him. He was pursued by black shadows, and bronze lions roared at him as he paused before a woman standing silently on a marble pedestal adorned with laurel.

"Oh, Mother Republic! All this is false and empty! I am hungry, I am hungry, Mother Republic, and you are made of stone and you are silent! These bastard sons of your Republic, they are terrible, and they do not understand you! And all this is false! And I am hungry, Republic! Republic, I am hungry!"

And so Orlić cried and yammered and wailed before the pedestal on which the huge marble Republic stood, and this must have been the eighth night of his wandering and hunger and suffering. The day before he had eaten two cakes and drunk a cup of coffee in a crowded bar, and then skillfully disappeared into the crowd. But since then he had had nothing. And now it was morning, and the hunger surged forth inexorably, wildly, powerfully.

His mouth was watering, his teeth grinding. A crowd of revelers walked past eating raisin-filled cakes, and when Orlić pleaded for a piece of cake they sneered at his barbaric pronunciation and kissed their scented women as though this hungry, fallen man were not even there. In his torment Orlić clenched his fists and buried his nails into the palms of his hands so as not to scream from pain and sorrow. And these drunkards were eating cake and kissing their women and laughing at him.

"Are there any people here? Is it only in Russian literature that people live? Is everyone a scoundrel, a villain in this cursed

Sodom?" And Orlić walked on, hoping to find someone, man or beast, from whom he could ask a crumb of bread. Only a crumb.

Nearby, at a construction site illuminated by a red flare, an old man was roasting bacon over a fire and sipping wine from a flask.

Orlić approached him gently, very gently. Inaudibly, like a slave. Orlić had withdrawn, reducing himself to the shape of a dog. He approached the old man as would a hungry dog wagging his tail, swaying his head obsequiously.

And the old man chased Orlić away, as though he were indeed a dog, telling him to go to the devil and waving a large stick.

As for Orlić, he wanted to bark, to jump at the old bastard, to bite the ugly monster's throat. And so, with the impulse of a healthy animal, Orlić threw himself on the old man, brought him to the ground, snatched the bacon and the rolls and the flask of wine, and started running.

Several men chased Orlić along the winding street and he barely got away. Orlić had a great deal to eat. Orlić had a lot of wine. Orlić was full. A comfortable lassitude spread through his body, and there, in front of him, stood a wall, a rampart, and some strange red barracks.

Dawn was approaching.

In the barracks the trumpets sounded and soldiers in rough blue uniforms scurried past, carrying cauldrons of hot coffee. A roll of drums was heard, officers mounted their horses, and a crude mustached sergeant slapped the face of a young boy. Strange shouts were heard and the earth resounded, as always when a battalion is on the move.

"Look at these men of the Republic!" thought Orlić as he peered through the grass and over the ramparts and into the large smelly barracks yard where soldiers were stamping the earth. And he, miserable, exhausted animal that he was, moving through the streets without bread or roof over his head, torn and tired, felt an indescribable sense of freedom. Stretching himself out in the damp grass, he fell asleep.

It was daylight when Orlić awoke, still on the ramparts of Paris. The skies were overcast and it was raining again. Wet through and exhausted, he walked along the gray dirty streets, back into the center of the city.

Quite by accident, Orlić found himself in front of the huge stone bulk of the sooty Louvre.

A thought struck him. He had spent a great deal of time at the Louvre of late, and knew all its corners, armchairs, and guards. He knew when each guard went outside for a smoke, and this enabled him to fall asleep in comfort, not fearing that his snores would be overheard and that he would be thrown out. You could snore to your heart's content, because the guard was smoking somewhere in the corridor, talking about his pension or God knows what. But today a particularly happy thought struck Orlić. Why shouldn't he sneak into the Egyptian or Babylonian gallery? Among the huge pile of rocks and sarcophagi, in some dark corner, there might be a spot where he could get some sleep. If only he could get some sleep! Then all should be well! He would beg for two or three sous, and that would give him a chance to put together his article at the café—a good article, by God! A sensational article about the Spanish king and the great maneuvers at which a hundred batteries fired and airplanes roared past. A long article of five hundred lines! Five hundred multiplied by four—five hundred times four—that will bring twenty crowns, by God! That will bring twenty crowns from the *Narodni List!* And then, quickly, another article! Three hundred lines. But what would he write about? The Russian ballet? Sarah Bernhardt? Expressionism? It doesn't matter! Three hundred lines in *Zagrebački Dnevnik.* They pay at the rate of seven filirs, and three hundred times seven is twenty-one crowns! And twenty plus twenty-one makes a total of forty-one crowns—a small fortune. And all this in no more than a week! By God, he must not allow himself to be ruined! He must have courage, he must survive. He must survive at any price, and again acquire a room. Then something will happen; something always does!

Thus refreshed with new speculations and encouraged by new illusions, Orlić stole into the Assyrian room of the Louvre. As a rule no one was there on rainy days. Who the devil cares for mummies anyway? The mob with red Baedekers lolled past on the floors above, and here it was nice and empty and quiet.

˻ In fact, there was not a soul around: mummies and sarcophagi and the ruins of old temples were slumbering wisely, gloriously, and dumbly. Orlić caught sight of a beautiful marble sarcophagus that resembled a comfortable bed. A minute later, without knowing what he was doing, he lifted the glass top and slipped into the sarcophagus, covered himself comfortably, and fell asleep.

Outside, the warm spring rain was falling proudly, intoning a gentle lullaby. The strain of the last few days, the sleepless nights, and the hunger were now, like wounds, being dressed by balmy sleep. The fine bluish fluid in which the marble lions and winged bulls and heroes were swimming trickled down into Orlić's soul, and a gentle peace infiltrated his limbs and muscles.

Shadows vibrated on the old colorful mosaics and green bronzes, and outside the city was humming like a distant organ. From time to time he could hear the tooting of horns from the Rue de Rivoli, or the sound of boats on the Seine. Orlić dreamed about Babylon. Along with his passion for modern Europe, Orlić was consumed by a great love for the world of antiquity and the Orient. One half of his heart bled for Europe and the other half for the East. His eagerness to see Paris did not for a moment mean that he ignored the existence of the East. Oh, he loved Japan and China and India, and believed that his voice would someday be heard at the equator.

And now, in his general depression, these feelings were projected into the stones, into the bas-reliefs in which bearded men massacred birds and lions with bows and arrows.

"Any one of these old stones is worth more than the whole of Paris!" So ran his thoughts, and he dreamed about Babylon.

He dreamed that he was drinking wine on a marble terrace

ringed by curtains of gold and portals stiffened with red agate. The night was green, and the boatmen on the Tigris were singing, and the bright metal of their oars gleamed like the colors of the rainbow. The song of the boatmen sounded pleasantly, and Orlić felt precious life in his veins. He was sipping wine from a glass mug and listening to the parrots screeching; black slaves were waving above the red-hot coals, and a bluish smoke was rising into the skies.

In this way Orlić fled from the dirty "city of cities" where people live in dark holes and scream about everything and never tell the truth, fled from the mud and dirt, from the hunger and shame, the barracks and police stations—and found salvation on this Eastern shore of stories and legends. Then suddenly someone jabbed him in the ribs, throwing him into complete confusion.

"Hey, young man, don't think you are so light."

Orlić jumped into the air, and at first could not grasp what was happening. But then he remembered the money he had gambled away; strangely enough, he remembered the last banknote that he had won and immediately afterward lost, and he remembered that they had thrown him into the streets, and that he was hungry and had no room, and that he had sneaked into the Louvre and had come into the Assyrian gallery, Room No. 16, and had fallen asleep there. And now he had been awakened.

At first he could not credit his senses. He thought it was an apparition. But the eyes of the man who stood before him burned with a greenish light, and Orlić believed in this green fire, and collected himself.

"I'll be damned! It's a live man! He has beautiful healthy teeth. It is no apparition."

In front of Orlić stood a mummy from the sarcophagus, an Assyrian apparition, a man from the times of the dead. The folds of his cloak fell harmoniously, and his long black curly beard smelled of strange spices. Orlić, our miserable shabby Bohemian, felt shame before the bold dignity of this unknown man. He realized that while tossing in his sleep he had awakened the corpse in the sarcophagus. He always tossed in his sleep.

"I am Hodorlahomor," said the man in a deep voice, and Orlić shook in fear and anxiety.

"I am Hodorlahomor the Great! I chased innumerable herds of wingéd bulls, and loved a thousand women. My priests caught the stars with their hands. I listened to the poets wailing under the palm trees. We nailed them to the cross, to wail the more beautifully! I am Hodorlahomor the Great, and who, pray, are you?"

"I am, if you please, Orlić! Pero Orlić, that is. I have no specific bourgeois occupation. I live from day to day. I am a journalist for Zagrebački Dnevnik."

"I defeated Lugašlagengur totally. And Lugašlagengur was a powerful king and had iron-plated cavalry. I defeated him totally and scratched out his eyes and pulled out his tongue, merely because he once had a bad dream about me. And you dare to touch me in my eternal peace! Speak up!"

"If you please, Your Majesty! I beg you humbly. It is not my fault. I did not know. I did not wish. . . ." Orlić became confused in his speech and was stammering nervously. "I have not slept in a long time! I am hungry! I live in the street! I never suspected that Your Majesty . . ."

"I defeated Lugašlagengur totally. I did! And I swear by all the lights of heaven that because of your sacrilege I will have you drawn and quartered. If only I felt better! And what are you, anyway? What is it you are talking about? Are you a beggar or a thief?"

"I am, if you please, a journalist for Zagrebački Dnevnik, seven filirs per line. I am from Zagreb. From the Balkans, if you please. And we are now in Paris, Your Majesty!"

"Zagreb? The Balkans? Paris? What on earth are you talking about? You must indeed be a madman. What is Paris?"

However, Orlić had already grasped the situation. It was not for nothing that he was a journalist for the Zagrebački Dnevnik, seven filirs per line. Instantly he perceived the proper angle by which he must approach His Majesty. My God! It was not His Majesty's fault that he is unacquainted with civilization's progress, as are we who have gotten good marks in school. His Majesty has been asleep for some time. Things must be explained to him. Nicely! Wittily! In the form of an article.

"The Balkans, if you please, are a peninsula of Europe. And Europe is, so to speak, an insignificant peninsula of Asia. A superfluous appendix, so to speak. Some sort of an appendix, if Your Majesty knows what that is. That appendix can be inflamed, and then you should see the trouble. You lived in the heart of the world, and not in its appendix where it is dark and smelly. You lived in the heart and we in this poor extremity. And you were right, Your Majesty! To concern oneself with Europe is not worth the effort. Since your day the earth has circled the sun nearly five thousand times. We discovered this only a few centuries ago. I mean, that the earth flies around the sun. It's like this: it turns, it turns like a bug on a needle. The poor headless thing turns and grows old, and we exist sadly. We haven't created anything, Your Majesty, during the past five thousand years. We still hog meat and butcher one another. At least you had an idea! You built a tower to bring God down to earth. You at Babylon! And we have done nothing! We are nervous, that's it! You played with the stars, and we perish in factories. You chased after wingéd bulls, and we wear boots and carry knapsacks and live in swarms. We build barracks, but still live off your wisdom. We are miserable, and our poets go hungry and homeless. I swear to God you would be better off in your sarcophagus. To tell the truth, this Babylon of ours is not worth a penny, Your Majesty, not a penny!"

But His Majesty, Hodorlahomor the Great, did not show the slightest inclination to return to his sarcophagus. On the contrary, his eyes brightened and he exhibited a dangerous greed for life.

"Listen, good man! I shall reward you royally if you show me this Babylon of yours. I should very much like to take a walk. Here! I have jewels and gold, I have everything! I shall reward you royally!"

Hodorlahomor's inlaid buttons glistened with jewels of yellow and red hues. And Orlić, who realized that he was being rescued in a moment of danger, could not resist the temptation.

Cautiously he walked into the hallway in which the guard, lulled by the warm spring rain, was dozing. Fighting to stay awake, the guard's head would fall against his chest as though severed, and he would bring it back up again with a jolt. As the guard was thus suffering, Orlić quietly removed a cloak from a closet, placed it on Hodorlahomor's shoulders, and the two of them sneaked out into the street and disappeared into the crowd.

Orlić sold one yellow jewel for next to nothing to a Jewish jeweler on Avenue de l'Opéra. He knew that he had sold it for a song, and the jeweler knew that he had bought it from a thief, so they were both pleased. Orlić had organized everything well. With those nine thousand francs he and Hodorlahomor acquired elegant luggage and wardrobe, as befitted Eastern princes. Dressed in this aristocratic clothing, Orlić boldly sold another two or three pieces of jewelry, assembling a small fortune, and the next day he and Hodorlahomor took possession of a nine-room apartment along with an entourage of uniformed servants. Hodorlahomor had his shiny, curly Assyrian beard shaved fashionably into an oval, Don Juan-like shape that appealed to women, and he looked quite dapper in his new black suit. His starched shirt front was as hard and as white as a breastplate, his tails like those of a penguin, and in his buttonhole there was a high international order in distinguished colors. These important trifles gave rise to the legend about which the whole of the Ritz was talking: the mystical Eastern prince who lived on the first floor.

"My God! Have you seen his alabaster teeth, Madame?"

"And those bronze muscles under his silk robe, Madame?"

"Not to say anything of that burning Eastern eye, Madame! Oh, my God! Oh, my God!"

This was the talk among titled ladies, marquises, baronesses, and whores in the dining hall, and when Hodorlahomor appeared in a sea of light between the draperies of yellow and purple silk, strutting like a tiger, he would hypnotize the whole hall with his monocle.

World renowned stars and the finest dancers supped with him, and golden cobwebs were being spun about this magnificent dark figure from whom money poured like rain. The evening newspapers printed photographs of the charming prince. His poor secretary, Orlić, was besieged by reporters and other flunkies of the great city seeking further information about His Asian Majesty. People melted like wax, their backbones bent like bows, when the prince and his secretary passed down the hall carpeted in red. White breasts of beautiful women burned with greed for the fantastic prince, in whose wake sequins dropped like beads. Paris overwhelmed Hodorlahomor. It overwhelmed him and defeated him. His face was burning passionately, and he sang a drunken hymn to Paris, as befits a barbarian charmed by its invisible splendor. And Orlić was just as disgusted by the pomp and splendor as he had been in the days when, still hungry, he peeped through the closed blinds of rich villas and watched countesses and marquises riding along shaded avenues. Now his stomach rose with disgust and he wanted to vomit. He scorned the Ritz, and the soirées, and the press, and the races, and the premiers, and the parades, and the women, and Hodorlahomor himself.

His contempt for Hodorlahomor grew each day. So this is the famous king of Babylon, the king of wingéd bulls and milky-skinned women! This ignorant barbarian, who is as primitive as a simple maid in the kitchen of a dirty village pub, and who, like a common soldier, takes pleasure in breastplates and armies and shows respect for bemedaled idiots and titled cavaliers. So this is the ideal that had acted as the antidote for Pero's disillusionment. And Orlić sang a dirge over the grave of this simpleton whose knowledge did not equal even that of a schoolgirl. Hodorlahomor knew nothing, nothing under the sun, and his greatest joy came in the evening when, after the rush of the day, he devoured chunks of raw meat in his room. He especially liked raw meat.

· Paris seduced and overcame Hodorlahomor. Like sweet Delilah, he cut off those locks of fear and resistance and gave himself over to the mercy of pleasure. He sang a hymn to Paris, but what was even more base and ignoble, he destroyed Orlić's last illusions in an ugly, brutal peasant manner. He destroyed everything for Orlić, and Orlić treated Hodorlahomor like an open wound that stank. Hodorlahomor became unbearable to Orlić, and Orlić was obsessed by the idea of leaving this despicable mummy. As the days went by, this thought ripened within him and took definite shape in occasional instinctive outbursts climaxed by tasteless scenes.

In the morning they would stand in front of the stock exchange, where thousands were milling up and down the steps in top hats. Brokers yelled and automobiles tooted, and the morning panic was on, wild and powerful. And Hodorlahomor admired it all, gaping at the spectacle like a peasant, his legs spread wide.

"Oh, by the bloody moon, I never possessed such battalions, not even when Lugašlagengur strode across the desert. By God, this Babylon is beautiful! Excellent Babylon, heavenly Babylon!"

"Some heaven! They are all swine, all thieves and scoundrels, not people at all! They are animals! They drink the blood of millions!"

"Ah! That's an excellent thing! Human blood." Hodorlahomor smacked his lips enthusiastically. "If I really loved a woman, truly loved her, I would drink her blood. My men would slit her throat and I would sip warm female blood from a silver goblet! Ah, yes! From a silver goblet!"

Or they would be standing in front of a church. Hodorlahomor, his mouth wide open, his legs spread apart, would look in admiration at the Gothic steeple and the ornate façade.

"Ah, the stakes surrounding our camps were never so finely pointed, and in our temples there was a stink of smoke that filled our eyes with tears. You are much wiser than we were, and it is splendid that I am able to see it all. I had a madman killed because he prophesied the approach of a world full of wisdom. But it turned out that he was right; you are a wise people. How beautiful is this stained glass! And these musical instruments play so well! Ah, lovely, lovely! Your God is beautiful and noble. He lives much more splendidly than our gods."

And so he admired the stained glass and he greeted the cavalrymen in the streets and Orlić ground his teeth and watched this poor nomad who had lost his head. Hodorlahomor was as afraid of airplanes as he was of Jewish cherubs, and he bowed to the locomotive at the station with religious awe, trembling as if before a black god. And at night, after carousing and drinking, genuinely tragic scenes would unfold. Orlić would be asleep, and Hodorlahomor would timidly knock on the door, enter the room, stand reverently beside Orlić's bed, waiting for Orlić to awaken. Paris is beautiful and noisy, of course, and there are musicians and drums and women; but one cannot live on perfumed beans and boiled leaves and badly prepared beef drenched in colored water. There must be blood! Red, juicy meat with its heavenly smell to make one's mouth water! Ah! Meat, bloody, fresh meat! That's what Hodorlahomor did not have. And Orlić was the only one who could get it for him. Hodorlahomor was too awkward and shy, like every other mummy of an Assyrian king who might be walking the streets of Paris. One morning he started to eat in a butcher shop. But the butchers quickly spotted him and tried to seize him; he only barely made his escape.

So His Majesty Hodorlahomor the Great stood at Orlić's feet and waited, and Orlić, having some nightmare or other, suddenly woke up.

"Ah, it's you again! What is it you want now? Let me sleep! Didn't you hog enough yesterday, you beast?"

"I am hungry, my friend, I cannot live this way any longer. I shall die! When was yesterday? That was such a long time ago!"

"Die if you must! Die this minute! What do I care? What's the use of your living, you damned animal!"

Hodorlahomor and Orlić would quarrel through the night, and the following morning Orlić would go to the butcher shop and bring home a whole calf's leg to feed the animal. And Hodorlahomor drank royally, too.

One night, as he and Orlić were staggering home drunk, they paused on a bridge across the Seine. The red lights burned prettily and underneath flowed the yellow water, dirty with tar and oil.

And Hodorlahomor, intoxicated with life and Asiatic enthusiasm, exclaimed, "Ah, how beautiful it is! Not even the wisest among us could have dreamed of such things! We could never have built such towers and such cities! Like greyhounds, you charge into the path of fiery lions! You swim like whales and you create fires on the waters! You are fishes and you wave your fins and you eat fires, oh, you great and powerful people! You play with flames like hawks, and your women are beautiful! In comparison to you we were nothing, nothing! I spit! I spit a thousand times on that dirty village rotting in the damned muck. Our houses were made of reeds thatched together with mud, and our cows stank under the same roofs with our people, and pus flowed in the streets, and grasshoppers nibbled at us. And God trod on us as if we were sawdust, and annihilated us with plague and leprosy. And you have defeated God himself, and now you stand alone and victorious. Oh, I spit, I spit a thousand times on that village of mine!"

Thus cried Hodorlahomor the Great in his Asiatic enthusiasm, falling drunkenly on his knees before Orlić, kissing the tips of Orlić's patent leather shoes. And Orlić was disgusted by this accursed idiot, and he wanted to grab him and hurl him into the river.

However, he did not hurl him into the river.

This nightmare reached its climax one afternoon at the Eiffel Tower. It was a warm, bluish day, the sun piercing the canopy of heaven with innumerable shafts, and the May greenery spreading across the whole of Paris. The city sailed in an ethereal mist, and the distant lights could only be dimly seen. The blue dome of the Pantheon and the bright white basilica of Montmartre and the white boats on the water and the masses of houses all swelled in the May warmth. And above, on the Eiffel Tower, from the topmost gallery, everything glistened in the spring fire.

The two of them climbed up the tower and, overwhelmed by summer happiness, Hodorlahomor resumed his hymn in praise of life while Orlić winced in pain.

"What sense does this damned city make? Can its life be reduced to a single value? No, all of us—Hodorlahomor, myself, the whole of Paris—are nothing but a sick illusion. We would be better off if nothing at all existed."

While such sad thoughts were tormenting Orlić's soul, Hodorlahomor was bursting with capricious life, moving about buoyantly, like a colt. That very morning he had consumed one entire bloody calf's leg.

"Oh, Paris, Paris! Supreme joy of the world! Discovery of my life! Paris!"

As the exuberant Hodorlahomor was waving and shouting and laughing, he came across someone selling those horoscopes so popular with Russian emigrés, revolutionaries, and anarchists. Hodorlahomor picked one, and on this bluish slip of paper was the sign of a sorcerer with a skull and certain mystical hieroglyphs that Orlić could not decipher. But Hodorlahomor was so disturbed by the signs that he turned pale and began to tremble. Suddenly he realized that he was in fact a mummy, lying eternally in the dark. His was but a momentary walk in the May warmth to hear women laughing at the Ritz and see them dancing at the Opéra. The military bands, and the cavalry, and the dancing, the performances and the races, the sun and joy and Paris—all this would vanish and he would return to the sarcophagus at the Louvre in the Assyrian gallery, No. 16, to the right on the ground floor. Hodorlahomor was shaken by an indescribable fear: the premonition of death. And since Orlić was the only positive thing in his life, Hodorlahomor clutched him passionately, fell before him, and cried loudly.

"Oh, my only friend, I feel I am near death! Death is already sneering at me. You resurrected me, you saved me; save me once more!"

Hodorlahomor cried bitterly, his arms around Orlić's legs, and the scene grew increasingly embarrassing. Those fat German women in tourist uniform, with canes and eyeglasses, and those icy stiff English misses, and those dark Italian women, and gentlemen in checked caps and fine socks—this whole world of globe-trotting idlers sunning themselves that May afternoon on the Eiffel Tower—nervously milled around Orlić and Hodorlahomor, producing a most unpleasant tumult.

Hodorlahomor took no notice. He screamed even more desperately, and it was in vain that Orlić battered him on the head with his feet. Hodolahomor cried out more loudly than ever.

"Oh! Oh! I, Hodorlahomor the Great, Assyrian conqueror, beg you to save me. I beg with you and plead with you. Save me!"

The commotion grew. Old women selling medallions were dashing this way and that. They are madmen! They must be Africans! They are Croats! This man speaks Russian! What is a Croat? I think they are cannibals from some God-forsaken place. Hungarians! shouted the crowd, and from somewhere the police appeared, which frightened Orlić terribly. He remembered instantly that his papers were not in order. He had been afraid of the police ever since the Khuen demonstrations, when he had broken some Zagreb shop windows. He was aware that a decisive step had to be taken at once. He grabbed Hodorlahomor and tossed him over the railing.

People screamed, and the Eiffel Tower came down in a great crash, and Orlić woke up.

It must have been late in the afternoon. Rested and desperate, Orlić rubbed his eyes, and one thing was immediately clear to him: he must leave Paris at once. For Paris was the most superfluous thing in this universe. In a provincial town he would get work, not die of hunger, and write articles for *Zagrebački Dnevnik*, seven *filirs* per line.

And he started courageously on his way. When he was quite a distance from the city, with only the dark contours of Babylon still visible, and as the evening lights went on in the valley, he removed his shoes and dusted them off.

And from his pocket he took out his revolver and, turning toward Paris, fired a round of six shots.

*Translated by Drenka Willen*

# The Love of
# Marcel Faber-Fabriczy
# for Miss Laura Warronigg

Twenty years later, when all that was to happen had happened, when Laura and Marcel stood in life like two shipwrecked persons, there emerged in their conversations the old recollections of their Bukovec adventures, distant and faded as old English rubbings in half-darkened rooms. Marcel, who had just returned from Russia, was lingering for a while in Zagreb, anchorless in the mist of his Croatian homeland. He and Laura would meet in the front room of Laura's fashion shop, Mercure Galant. At that time Laura was already doomed to commit suicide, but the somber and sad conversations about all their past involvements were infused with the silent, golden light of the bygone days of Bukovec.

Their conversations about the Bukovec drawing room! Its enormous old-fashioned sofa in the corner with the oriental rugs, the sofa piled high with too many red, black, pale blue, and yellow cushions, and above, on the golden console, the gilded baroque saint with outstretched arms. The embroidered designs on the silk cushions, the vases and the jars in the Viennese glass cabinet, the clocks on alabaster pillars, and the tabouret where the old butler set the silver tea tray: all this stood before Marcel like the silent replica of an afternoon with sun shining through the green crests of linden trees under the balcony. . . .

The door of the balcony is open. One can sense the soft, warm, palpitating blue distance of the Maksimir and Dubrava horizon. The half silent movement of the leaves on the faded linden trees and laughter in the vineyard! Below on the lawn, near the fountain, under the yellow and red sunshade, Laura's friends are laughing: the Ballochanska and the Wagner girl, Melita Szlougan, some naval ensign and Laura's escort, Lieutenant Fabiani. They play crazy games in the vineyard, and all are impressed by Lieutenant Fabiani's fine talk about his recent admission to the Vienna Military Academy, while upstairs, in the drawing room, Marcel lies on the sofa and like a tired dog strains to hear Laura's voice! The mere echo of Laura's voice! The slightest quiver of air exhaled through her lips that would enter by the open balcony door and circle in perfumed incense-like whiffs around the drawing room. Silence. In the distance, somewhere on the Remete path, a girl sings. On the road an oxcart creaks. A bird flies from the tree. Marcel is in love; yet not for the first time.

Before Laura there was a certain Darinka, a girl two years older than he, a girl who had so overwhelmingly taken hold of his life, his existence, and his fifteen-year-old destiny that Marcel's wound did not heal for two entire years. Only when his cousin Laura Warronigg arrived in Zagreb from Vienna did he use Laura as an antidote to Darinka, thus creating new complications that were to follow him for many more years, throughout the haze and daze of puberty.

Darinka was approximately the thirtieth woman in his life. Marcel was as conscious of this gallery of female figures then as he was to remain faithful to their memory ten or twenty years later. At the time of Darinka, Marcel was a shy but perfect lover in whose eye Woman loomed more portentously than she would later, after all his sad experiences. He then sought in Woman a supernatural, spiritual mission; he thought that Woman's role should consist in making life easier for us in a "higher sense," in transporting us away from the futility of Latin and Greek and mathematical complexities. Naturally, "inferior as only an eleventh grader can be," Darinka could not have had the faintest idea of what storms were raging in the ninth-grader Marcel Faber, who waited for her like a faithful dog day after day near the tramway station to trudge behind her down the street named after a famous Dubrovnik writer of comedies on which she lived. As he was to find out later through experience, everything had been then as it would be with all women: the woman had not understood, and the woman would never understand, for the simple reason that woman is incapable of understanding. But in the case of Darinka (as so many times later in life), Marcel believed that this was not so and that it was possible that woman might understand after all; indeed, Darinka was not Marcel's first love experience, but she was his first entirely conscious encounter with frustration.

Between Miss Darinka and the dark, uncertain totterings preceding her, many bleeding and sorrowful loves had faded away. Miss Darinka was, in fact, only the first conscious climax in the rich love instrumentation that orchestrally accompanies every Godsent childhood—from fighting and quarreling over Karlsbad omelets, variegated marbles, red balloons, and punch cakes to hide-and-seek games in wine cellars where in the darkness girls' tresses smell like linden blossoms to boys. In the love history of Marcel Faber there existed prior to Darinka girls of inferior social standing, who smelled of humid scrubbed floors and bread soaked in creamy coffee. While Marcel Faber-Fabriczy walked about in his fine Kiel-made sailor suit with a red silk anchor on the left sleeve, these girls (daughters of charwomen, servants, and janitors), dressed in ordinary homespun, envied Marcel's little brass bells, lacquered hoops, and tennis balls in woolen nets. In his benevolent attitude toward the lower social strata, there was always something perversely merciful about Marcel's tender feelings for these "poor little ones" while, at the same time, he was attracted to them by his certainty of success; among these girls of his who admired his clothes and toys, great respect for the "upper social bracket" was noticeable at all times. The noble Fabriczy child, often spotted at his mother's side in the Glembay carriage, the doctor's son, the little gentleman and rich boy, was sure of a lordship's victory over these "miserable creatures." In a superior Don Juan-like manner, he mistreated the ugly, myopic cross-eyed girls with their thick glasses and greasy braids; being the only one in the group who had ever been to the gold rococo theater where musical comedy stars sang with heavenly voices amid violet lights and brocaded costumes, only he could fascinate the girls with tales of what love adventures unfolded on the stage. In the days before Darinka Marcel had taken much interest in the limping, tubercular widow of a suicide (said to have been deaf) who, day after day, locked in her attic room, embroidered gigantic, blooming La France roses on wool cushions and made covers for pocket watches. Servant girls and chambermaids in the service of his mother's friends in the city struck Marcel as mysterious beings, naked under their skirts like Titian's Venuses framed in green plush in Aunt Agatha's drawing room. . . .

Like an Impressionistic aquatint, its colors spilled from a most audacious palette, the enormous space in the interior of the cathedral seems permeated with light, perfume, organ music, and incense. At the altar of St. Jerome with the Lion Marcel assists the priest and Genoveva Rochard-Flieder stands in the second row among the girls of her class. A golden light shines upon all things. In the right nave, in front of the altar of St. Jerome, the entire school is assembled for the Holy Sunday Mass—the old director with his white waistcoat and gray umbrella, the teacher in her bell skirt tightened at the waist, falling in rich folds like a train and looking like the tube of some poisonous flower. The teacher's hat is enormous, like the nest of some unknown tropical bird, and under that hat, under the rich, black, Empress Elizabeth hair-do, next to that bell skirt, in the second row stands Genoveva Rochard-Flieder, a pale, anemic girl with an ebony prayer book, a rich girl for whom a carriage and an old top-hatted coachman are sent to school every day. . . .

Marcel was struggling through his paper on the Subject. For more than half a year now he had worked on this treatise based on Schopenhauer's epigraph, "The Subject, the Comprehending, never Comprehended," and when his work had attained sufficient clarity so that he had dared show it to Laura, she had returned his manuscript because "such things don't interest me; indeed, they truly bore me!" He had appended to his treatise several charts drawn in different colors of ink. The Table of Quantity, Quality, Relation, and Modality, the Table of Receptivity of Impression, and the Table of Observation. From the little Toldt Anatomical Atlas (from the library of his late father), Marcel had skillfully enlarged the anatomical cross section of the eye, colored the small brain in yellow, the lines of the *nervus facialis*, the *nervus opticus*, and the *nervus oculomotorius* in red, whereas the eyeball and lids he outlined like a symmetrical globe, in blue. The Table of Observation, with the red line of optical stimulation (from the pupil to the point of association), drawn in three colors on a double sheet of the finest cardboard, was a particularly decorative addition to Marcel's treatise on the Subject, and yet Laura had returned it all with the superficial observation that none of it "interests me in the least!"

The question of the difference between pure and empirical apprehension, the problem of pure Reason, the problems concerning the analysis of notions, the problem of Existence and of the Thing in Itself, these are naturally boring questions for Laura, but flirting with Fabiani. naturally, does not bore her.

· With all the impassioned enthusiasm of his intelligence, Marcel defiantly skimmed through the leaves of his manuscript with a Copernican craving for beauty and with contempt for the unkind Laura who had no understanding whatsoever of all the pitfalls one stumbles across in reasoning and in the quest for truth. What is transcendentality of Space and Time to such a Viennese brat; what are all of Marcel's intellectual efforts when the only important questions for her are the Coronelli dance and the party at the Szlougans?

"The thinking of my Subject, the pure perception of my own inner consciousness and self-assertion, this transcendental inner power of mine, this heaven in me—this is what thinks in us. Our thinking must be like the finest yarn, covering everything that exists because it encompasses all that comes forth and appears to us, for otherwise, if something appeared to us of which we were unable to think, we would not be able to comprehend this unknown, and it would remain forever unimaginable and incomprehensible to us."

Marcel had copied his philosophical treatise for the ninth time and thought how unable we are to imagine a phenomenon without a category and how Schopenhauer approves of transcendentality in aesthetics but refuses to accept it in categories, how we encounter in notions something that is not a notion but something commonplace and sensual, how everything disintegrates into a mass of contradictions, how all thoughts evaporate like smoke, how nevertheless there remains beyond it all the terrible reality of Laura and the Idea of Laura. What are his tables and treatises when they don't interest Laura, why does he so persistently copy them when they lead nowhere and he should be working instead! Whenever he thought of his schoolwork, he was assailed with worries, feeling like the sleeping traveler who has no strength to awaken and to hasten despite the certainty that his ship is going to leave and that he will be late. This obsession with Laura was indeed a game played to the limits of endurance. Marcel knew how wise it would be to consult certain obscure chapters that he had ignored since the beginning of the semester, and yet, constantly torn between reality and illusion, he felt utterly powerless to resist his somber instincts and to confront facts. What did he care for the formula

$$\frac{x^2}{a^2} - \frac{y^2}{b^2} = 1,$$

when tomorrow in the concert hall some sort of Spanish virtuoso would perform and when in twenty hours he would see Laura. All right,

$$\cos x \, i = \frac{1}{2} \left( e^x + e^{-x} \right), \text{ or } \frac{x^2}{a^2} + \frac{y^2}{b^2} - \frac{z^2}{c^2} = 1.$$

To hell with all the hyperboloids and functions and written and oral work, when in twenty hours he will see her! Tomorrow Brenner, that disagreeable old man with fishy eyes and hairy hands, will stand at the back of the class and watch to see that nobody hides a book under the bench or copies from his neighbor. There he will stand, his back against the wall, drumming on the wall with his heavy butcher's hand. His fingernails are uncut, tough, black; his pockets reek with the stench of extinguished cigars. Then comes Latin. Cornelius Tacitus: "Whereas the worshipers of antiquity usually place the ones who were active before Cassius toward the end of the olden period and accuse Cassius of having abandoned the direct old style of expression, I claim that Cassius did not adopt such a style because of lack of talent or ignorance in matters of literature, but on purpose and in full cognizance of what he was doing . . ." (Tacitus, *Dialogus de oratoribus*, 19). And thirty-five other such idiocies; then physics with a dirty wet sponge, humid chalk breaking between one's fingers, superfluous formulas $\frac{h^1 - ho}{ho} = \frac{v^1 - vo}{vo}$. But all this is for tomorrow. It's all for tomorrow only, and until then there is plenty of time and it's all of no consequence when in twenty hours he will see Laura.

He last saw her on Sunday before Mass, in St. Catherine's Square. She was with her two intimate friends, Melita Szlougan and Blanka Balloczanska. They did not see him. He had shuddered and been unable to breathe. His throat and chest had tightened; a yellow mist blinded him. He was also with friends; then, noticing her hat (what redness, no young lady in town wears such a shade of red), his words stuck. He was talking with his friends of oil paints, of the Berlin blue tube and the shellac he had purchased for a good price at the stationer's in Duga Ulica, when he spotted her red hat and froze. He continued talking of yellow chrome and Berlin blue; he continued to walk erect; he moved forward mechanically, as one always continues to move, as if nothing has happened, when, in fact, the utmost of what can happen in life has happened: her red silk hat, with its ribbon and varnished cherries, was revealed to him. Tired, pale, exhausted, with trembling lips, listening to the voices of his friends as if they came from a distance, only seemingly present, Marcel Faber watched the red color of his cousin Laura Warronigg crossing St. Catherine's Square, and all those pigeons, telephone wires, closed blinds on the windows, and sunlight achieved a greater clarity, a tension deep as unconsciousness. This high-powered stimulation was surely bad for his health. Marcel spent an entire semester in desperate circumstances, with F's in Latin, Greek, and mathematics and two dubious D's in logic and physics. The unread material constantly grew in volume and there was no chance whatever that something could turn in his favor; in this already almost certainly lost game, in this compromised existence, in all this trouble, he sensed his slow sinking and ruination. But under the magic spell of a single thought of her, all that was black would change into a bewildering white light, and these thoughts of her would play over him like the vibrations of a bow on a fiddle. As Marcel thought of Laura, his gloomy moods brightened like a mirror in a darkened room suddenly hit by a ray of distant light. For more than half a year he was no more than a mirror of her as such. As he knew his

Handel by heart, so he knew by heart her walk in its every rhythm, the way her body was bent (in the hip, a little on the right), the tender pliability of her waist, the movement of her elbows, the scrubbed glow of the flesh on her bare arms, the curve of the nape of her neck, her Greek hair-do, and the nonchalant swaying of her hips from left to right, winding and restless. He knew her time schedule, the books she read, the expressions she used, and he knew Fabiani whom she adored, that goose, that eleventh-grader, that snob! On Sunday he had seen her for the last time in St. Catherine's Square, and on Monday he had waited for her for a whole hour in the rain in front of the house in which her piano teacher lived. On Monday from four to five; but she had not come. On Tuesday, Wednesday, and Thursday he had thought of her continuously, day and night, for twenty-four hours, of how on Friday at eight o'clock he would see her at the concert of the Spanish virtuoso. She would come in her new dress (of which Aunt Angelique Barboczy had talked last time at tea), in her splendid new dress and a Greek hair-do: clean, white, slender, with her oval face and dimples, her half profile (which Marcel was unable to draw). She, Laura, his cousin, accompanied by her mother and that chasseur Fabiani. He would stand in the concert hall, backed up against the wall so as not to collapse from fright, and for two and a half hours, as if hypnotized, he would watch her, her Person, among all those ladies, officers, chairs, and chandeliers, amid the warmth and scents of female bodies. He would watch Laura for two and a half hours—only her and no one else—with sweaty fingers, swallowing bitter lumps of terror, asking himself: would she perhaps after all turn around and honor him with a single look, kindly returning his greetings, openly, intimately, as is customary among relatives, the way eleventh-grade cousins are supposed to return greetings in concert halls when escorted by army officers facing promising careers? With this one single glance of hers he would go out into the midnight darkness, stroll through the streets and parks, and finally stand in front of old

Glembay's one-story house until the last light went out in that glorious room of hers next to the balcony. Her glance would be a sign that somewhere on earth one can begin living in different spheres, unlike the ones he has known thus far. From her Marcel, in fact, needs absolutely nothing—just to look at her, to contemplate in her the embodiment of some outer, more perfect world, some higher order that lies stretched out beyond his vain agonies and school entanglements. Her gaze suggests some sort of infinite possibility, a confident island that we are going to reach someday after all. Her gaze means the end of being hurt, and painful and difficult as this expectation is since last Sunday, it is nonetheless a grandiose event for Marcel, shining above, cold and green like a polar light.

Everything around Marcel is quite black. He is plunged into constant depression by the three F's, the clash with the religion teacher, the sixteen-hour detentions, the numerous warnings and unexplained absences; but above it all, like a glimmer of hope amid a dark shipwreck, are his thoughts of her. In them Marcel is totally immersed, lost in those fantastic regions as cold as a starlit night. It is bitter to dream about her and know that she does not understand. Her look, her conventional look, the look of a relative, of a Glembay, is vague and empty. In conversation and in touch with her beauty, in the too great nearness of real contact with her as a living person, in that passionate turmoil and hazard, Marcel suffered for nearly a year a hell of rapture and doubt. This is a vulnerable state, anatomically exposed to everyday, hairy, idiotic, logical school facts; yet compared with the heavy and repulsive smells of the classroom this state is a perfumed and other-worldly veil. At night Marcel would awaken, disturbed by a somewhat louder tick of the clock, and immediately his first thoughts would be: She, she, Laura, Laura, she is living together with him on the same planet, on the same continent, in the same city. She breathes the same air, she, Laura Warronigg. She exists, she is, she sleeps, great Lord, she is alive!

And side by side with this heavenly joy dimly bellows an entire complex of ruination and terror. In his nocturnal dialogues with her, Marcel has logically analyzed and discussed these things for hours. He is slipping downhill because of her, she does not understand him, he cannot concentrate on Greek or mathematics—she has totally hypnotized him. Yet when he meets her he blushes, sweats, panics, and with blood pounding in his brain, his heart in his throat, collapses in front of this cool, superior, rational eleventh-grade goose. He knows perfectly well that her horizon is compressed between the Szlougan party and the Coronelli dance, that her mother Olga Warronigg née Glembay is a lady who reads Kellermann, believing that Kellermann is a serious writer, that Laura seriously discusses Schopenhauer with Fabiani. But what? Where to? How? Pale, trembling, timidly sweating, Marcel knows and feels how truly unworthy of a man it is to sit silent, sad, and alone at parties, in a corner of the drawing room, while the pack of Glembay youth dances and rumbles through all the rooms of the apartment. But what is the use of all the reasoning power in him when he cannot stop dreaming of the slightest detail concerning her? They spent last summer in Rimske Toplice—his mother, Laura's grandmother, and Laura. Now, in the cold of winter, as he looks back on the sunny Rimske Toplice, Marcel comes close to choking with tears. The dawns and morning promenades. One can hear the first cocks and see the miners marching in the near darkness and the first light coming on in the mills. The icy morning air streams down from the brown chain of mountains, and poplars sway in the morning wind in the green and blue light of the forest. And Laura has come, still warm and transparent, in an orange-red sweater, in her hiking shoes, and has given him a bar of Suchard chocolate to store in the knapsack. The pine trees give off their scent, a superb silence reigns among the silver firs. And there, in the silver fir wood, Marcel first saw Laura's knee. In the company of boys and girls her age on excursion from Vienna (the children of generals and lawyers at court), she stopped to rest on an enormous tree that had been felled by lightning, and Marcel saw her knee.

He wakes up at night, sits up in bed, and thinks of that far-away afternoon, of Laura's knee, of her voice, of the colors in the wood, and of how strangely the flies buzzed in the stillness. As he remembers, his throat tightens and he sighs, sad and broken. Laura is a stupid Viennese general's daughter. She is limited; she reads stupid novels; she is more interested in the light cavalry officer Fabiani than in a student from Croatia who is flunking and who happens to be her cousin. She has no idea of what is going on within him, and even if she knew, she could not understand. She thoroughly enjoys Fabiani's jokes, and she does not know who Burckhardt is! He is tired of her; she bothers him; she is ruining his life, and it most certainly would be best for him if he could let it all drift away—let it evaporate and disappear!

In the course of his nocturnal meditations there come moments when he feels superior, proud and confident, strong enough to resist and to annihilate her in his thoughts, since it is only too clear to him that it makes no sense whatever to submit to her with such servility; after all, who is she and what has she given him? It's so simple! He should rid himself of this state of mind; it is all a phantasmagoria, and Laura knows nothing about it. In such moments of complete lucidity Marcel even senses hatred and scorn for that sweetly smiling Viennese doll; what a foolish and rotten way to suffer. But the next morning, when he would meet her, dewy, supple, and soft, her tan skin transparent in the sunlight, he would clearly understand that she is a shadow and that she does not really exist, but he knows also that should she order him to do so, he would unhesitatingly jump from the third floor.

Days went by in this debilitating fatigue and futile gloom.

As he thought about Laura, he became very frightened. He wished and desired to see her; yet he was somehow pleased when she was absent. Then he would spend two or three peaceful days in the negative delight of his ardent longing. In the passive lyricism of uninterrupted dreams there was more vivid happiness than in direct contemplation. This very afternoon he will ring the bell at the old Glembays, enter old Angelique Barboczy's open drawing room, and there, in the twilight, kiss his aunt's hand and learn that Laura is not at home, that "she is at the Szlougans." In the moments between his apprehension and the realization that he need not be afraid, since she is "not at home," he will fully perceive the vanity of his love. Then for a while it will seem as if his Laura had never existed, as if she were an optical illusion and no more. She would often vanish from his field of vision, and he would be unable to reconstruct her. Her dress yes, the knee too, also the left joint, the hair, the color of the cheeks, the movements, but not her. He saw her in the Glembay carriage, but was that really she? That was no more than her lingonberry red coat and peach-colored parasol. Frantically he tried to master her, to subdue her, to be the stronger, to overcome his obsession, but he could not. Instead, he found himself all the more entangled in these golden veils, and a merely superficial confrontation with the presence of her person sufficed to provoke a swelling throughout him that was like church bells ringing, and those bells would ring for days and nights. Indeed, Laura was not there. She was no more than his fancies! While she was absent, while she was only his Idea, while skyborne in his imagination, she was a glorious and unique feeling. As long as he feared that he might not see her, panicked that she might not be what he believed her to be, as long as he suspected her inferiority and thrilled over her existence, her incredibly beautiful eyes, the transparence of her hand, and the color of her voice, he floated upon the most sublime of waters. But when he saw her in the flesh at a party, all smiles for that idiotic Lieutenant Fabiani, talking in the clichés of a pseudo-fashionable education, a silk scarf from the Maison Chapeau d'Or more important to her than Schiller, then Marcel's sublime visions paled and only visions of death remained. She was inane and unintelligent, and there was really nothing beneath her Viennese veneer. On closer examination she really was rather short and her eyes were hazy, her voice weepy, and her spelling miserable, and there was no chance it would ever improve; so why should he lose time on such an eleventh-grader and such a goose? When she stood alive near him in the drawing room, under the lamp, surrounded by laughter, the clatter of plates, the click of spurs, and the piano, he looked at her and it struck him that Laura was a terrible carnivorous beast. Indeed, her teeth were strong, her incisors rapacious; she was unintelligent, unworthy of his sacrifice, too stupid and weak to understand and sustain the stream of yearning, dreams, desires, illusions, fever, and nightmares in which he reveled with increasing passion and lunacy. Laura was absent—the passionate, wild, sensual, grotesque, panicky feeling that Laura was absent!

Five days have passed since Sunday, since he last saw her, time enough to destroy himself on a number of counts. He has not worked at all; he has not read at all; he has thought of her the whole time. He has gone for walks in the streets, waited for her at street corners, looked at the passers-by as if they were a funeral procession; he has gone to the opera and visited the cemetery, and uninterruptedly, for five days and five nights, he has carried her in his every step and heartbeat, in mist and in rain. And finally, with her mother and Fabiani, she came to the recital of the Spanish virtuoso. During the entire concert Marcel stood in a solitary niche in the wall, deaf to all sounds. Laura did not turn once. Laura did not notice him. After the concert, the General's wife left first; Laura and Fabiani followed her. Fabiani bade good-by to the ladies in front of the carriage and was lost in the crowd. It was raining. Somehow Marcel managed to bring himself to the front of the one-story Glembay house, and there, tired and wet, he remained standing under the foliage of a tree like a dead man. In the quiet one could hear the rustle of rain drops among the leaves. At the end of the street a gas lamp gleamed, and there was Marcel looking into the apartment of old Glembay. His heart pounded as if it were jumping now to the left, now to the right. On the second floor of the house next Glembay's a woman in a nightgown moved the curtains aside and opened the window. In the green light of the room thus disclosed, Marcel saw a clock and a pendulum in a black frame and a potted palm on a chest of drawers. A bitter taste invaded his throat and tears came into his eyes. A frightful pain burned and hurt him all over; he felt like a dog on a heap of ashes. He was craving for her, but in fact she did not exist.

*Translated by Branko Lenski*